the
Last
Blue
Mile

Also by Kim Ponders

The Art of Uncontrolled Flight

the
Last
Blue
Mile

KIM PONDERS

To Annie,
So very wonderful
to meet you and
share the APOLLO
experience. Best
in love, life, and
poetry!

Kim Ponders

Ghost Ranch
June 2007

HarperCollins*Publishers*

HarperCollins books may be purchased for educational, business, or sales promotional use. For information, please write: Special Markets Department, Harper-Collins Publishers, 10 East 53rd Street, New York, NY 10022.

FIRST EDITION

Designed by Emily Cavett Taff

Library of Congress Cataloging-in-Publication Data is available upon request.

ISBN: 978-0-06-084706-7
ISBN-10: 0-06-084706-9

07 08 09 10 11 ID/RRD 10 9 8 7 6 5 4 3 2 1

*For the cadets of the United States
Air Force Academy, past, present, and future,
and for Bill*

KEY

Smack or Doolie = Cadet Fourth-Class before Recognition
Cadet Fourth-Class/Four-Degree = Freshman
Cadet Third-Class/Three-Degree = Sophomore
Cadet Second-Class/Two-Degree = Junior
Cadet First-Class/ Firstie = Senior

Brigadier General = One-star General
Major General = Two-star General
Lieutenant General = Three-star General
General = Four-star General
Chief of Staff of the Air Force (CSAF) =
    Senior Four-star General

PART I

Recognition

One

The cold crept through her soles and the sand spattered the sides of her shoes. Brook Searcy leaned forward, suspended on the balls of her feet, and facing the shorn scalp of the cadet standing thirty inches in front of her, waited for the command. Thumbs pressed downward, pinching the seams of her trousers, she sensed the training officer strolling among them with his head cocked, eyeing their shoes, their chins tucked like goose bills into the folds of their scarves, their zippers buried in the lips of their coats. The wind whipped a moistness into her eyes. She stood poised, listening for his words, ready to spring.

Horaard, harch!

At once, the flight moved forward in a single, fluid procession. Their pale, clenched knuckles swung in unison. Brook, fourth down in the right-hand column, looked over the shoulders of the cadets preceding her. It was late morning. The training officer, Bregs, was somewhere off to the side, no doubt watching them with his ritual surliness. She closed her fingers together and affected a natural swing to the arms. Despite the wind, it felt better to be marching than to be standing still.

Ahead lay a thick, high wall, a kind of bastion separating the main cadet area from the rest of the Air Force Academy. What they'd been doing out here all morning, marching around the perimeter, was anyone's guess. Perhaps Bregs considered it one of his last opportunities to offer them the bittersweet lessons of absolute command. This was the day before Recognition, the end of Hell Week, capping eight months of humiliation and struggle. Tomorrow, the remaining nine hundred and ninety-eight freshman smacks would be welcomed, finally, into the ranks of the upper classes, acknowledged as legitimate cadets and not *smacks* or *doolies* or *bitches* or *wops* or *faggots* or whatever other terms the upperclassmen had inflicted upon them daily, at random, and with malicious pleasure. Tomorrow. But at the moment, the smacks were still subject to the whims of their training officers. And twenty-one of them, including Brook, from the Thirty-second Squadron "Hogs" were marching toward a giant ramp tunneling upward, through the bastion, and leading to the broad terrace—The Terrazzo—at the center of campus. Now she knew. They were headed toward the grand midday assembly, the noon meal parade.

Mounted in burnished steel on the wall above the tunnel stood the words INTEGRITY FIRST. SERVICE BEFORE SELF. EXCELLENCE IN ALL WE DO. A recent sign, replacing the words BRING ME MEN…, which had greeted new classes of cadets for forty years until last spring, when a rape scandal had sent the Academy reeling. Brook, in her final months of high school, had watched the news in her father's woodsy den, a fear igniting in her belly—*what was she getting herself into?*—as the Academy leadership was sacked, and the relics of the old guard hastily dismantled. At the time, she'd been relieved. But now, she saw what could happen when too many changes were enforced too quickly. The Culture of Transformation, a sort of social desexing, a reprogramming of the old code, had been rammed down their throats. Resentment grew. A general sense of distrust hung over the female cadets. Brook had felt it immediately, as though the whole scandal had been her fault. Now, marching under the new slogan, she yearned to have the old words back. She didn't want to be held responsible.

Through the broad mouth of the tunnel, a gray light filtered down from the Terrazzo. The walls resounded with the echoes of their shoes, the admonishment of old heroes. Sun Tzu. Clausewitz. Machiavelli. Billy Mitchell. None of *those* men—paradigms quoted at length in their first-year primers—had bent under the political will of a civilian populace pressing a democratic equality even upon its most undemocratic institution. Was all this her fault? She didn't think so. She hadn't asked the military to bend to her level. Rather, she'd proposed to hoist herself up to its standards. She wanted favors from no one.

On the Terrazzo, the ice and crusted snow lay glimmering in pockets on the cement. Bregs led them to the southwest quadrant to stand in formation until the rest of the cadet wing arrived for the noon meal parade. He wore a thin line of silver etching on his epaulets, the lowest kind of rank bestowed at the Academy, and it was treated as such by the two-degrees and firsties, who bore superior markings. But the three-degrees' rank was new and the memory of their own subjugation fresh. The line of silver thread on Bregs's epaulets, so subtly setting him off from the smacks with their plain blue epaulets, meant the most severe kind of authority, one they feared more than the random humiliation of the more senior cadets.

Halt!

They stood shivering in rows of three, facing the chapel with its seventeen prickly spires fixed defensively at the sky. Above that, the mountains, supine and majestic, led the eye upward, to the promise of triumph.

Mac Cherry, a smack, had lost his glove.

Bregs had given them an option while they assembled in the alcove. They could all march without gloves or march, gloved, without Cherry, while Cherry waited in the warmth of the squadron, after which time, Cherry could march tours on the Terrazzo all afternoon as a reprimand for inattention to detail. The commandant had put out a notice that tours were not to be assigned on days when the wind chill exceeded zero, and the smacks thought about that while they removed their gloves and folded them in their pockets, but no one mentioned it or even spoke to Mac Cherry, who looked at the ground, loathing himself, as they assembled and marched out.

In the broad view, it didn't matter. They'd marched for months, in heat and cold, through rain and snow, across the mountains and in their sleep. Brook sometimes marched in her dreams. She awoke tired, thirsty. And then she rose and marched again, and the marching was like a continuation of the dream, where the destination was irrelevant and all that mattered was the procession itself.

"You're only as strong as your weakest member," Bregs told them, needlessly, as they stood hating and fearing him, and hating and fearing the cold. "You have to look out for each other. What will you do when I'm gone? You'll have to look out for yourselves. You'll die. You'll freeze."

"We're freezing now," whispered Billy Claymore, a smack on the left side of the third row, producing a murmur of snickers around him.

Bregs strode over to him and frowned.

"There, there. Would you like to go inside?"

A thread from Billy's scarf had unraveled and lay across his shoulder. Bregs reached up and pinched it between his gloved fingers. He flicked it away.

"Yes, sir."

"You can go right now. See the commandant's office over there? Just walk on over and call up your rich parents and tell them you don't like the cold."

Bregs was short, with thick shoulders and a round piggish face. Billy, tall and muscular, was a varsity soccer player who had already built himself a reputation as the starting center forward. Bregs hated him. Bregs hated that he was blond and talked easily with the instructors and that Bregs couldn't get to him. Billy's shoes were turned out from the heel forty-five degrees, his silver belt buckle shiny and centered above his fly, his shorn head topped with a wheel cap, elbows cocked and thumbs downward, his fingers curled against the seams of his blue trousers, blemished only by a single thread that Bregs had so courteously flicked away. Bregs briefly considered assigning a punishment, but it couldn't be severe enough to satisfy his sense of justice. He simply stared at Billy, hating him. He had to look up at Billy, and that made him hate him more.

"You think you're clever, don't you?"

"Yes, sir."

"I don't think you're clever. I think you're arrogant."

"Yes, sir. I'm that, too."

There was muffled laughter in the line, but Bregs ignored it. "You think you're funny, but all you're doing is keeping everyone else out here in the cold. You're prolonging the pain for everyone. On the other hand, I can stand out here all day." He paused, as if to consider where to go next. "Where'm I from? Tell me."

"Wyoming, sir."

"Where in Wyoming?"

"Beget, Wyoming, population twelve thousand, seven-hundred and fifty-two. Sir."

"I didn't ask you for the population, you sniveling rat."

"I was being proactive, sir."

> Smack = Soldiers Minus Aptitude, Coordination, and Knowledge. And the sound shit makes when it hits a wall.

Brook had written that in small print in the margin of her notebook in the first week of Beast—basic cadet training—so that she wouldn't forget. It made her laugh, later, to see those cramped words and believe she ever could.

"Do you see the Commandant's office over there?" Bregs said. "Turn your head and look. Maybe he's watching us right now. Maybe he's going to come down here and stick your proactive attitude right up your frigging ass."

Brook took a cleansing breath and settled into her core. Bregs was on a roll, and once he started, he could go on and on. Better to forget the tightness in her shoulders, her tingling fingers, and the faint, alarming burn in her knuckles. The clouds were drifting across the ridgeline, obscuring the sun and then abruptly revealing it. Waves of brightness traveled across the frozen Terrazzo and washed over the cadets, igniting the chapel in a blinding glare. Its spires shot skyward, enmeshed in a sort of skirmish with heaven.

Brook swayed in a metronomic rhythm between grayness and light, coldness and heat. Between Bregs's husky, unrelenting voice and the voices of the masters, low and insistent, that promised the kind of enlightenment that came only with suffering.

She thought: What is the nature of war?

Seventeen folders carrying seventeen letters of merit, primly paper-clipped to each back flap, sat on Brigadier General John Waller's desk awaiting his signature. The front flap of each folder was adorned with a staff summary sheet, also paper-clipped and bearing the name of each recipient, what s/he had done to justify the letter, and the chain of supervisors through which the folders had traveled and been initialed and couriered to the next level, until reaching the rarified office of the Commandant of Cadets, where it now sat *ensemble* awaiting his attention. Each letter was typed on Waller's heavy bond stationery, adorned with a small blue flag and single star that indicated Waller's rank, and required only his cramped, scrubby endorsement before doubling back through the complex circuitry of academy officialdom to reach the intended person(s), who were often startled, initially, to receive personal correspondence from the commandant and, secondly, to read in two brief paragraphs praise for certain actions they themselves had long forgotten. Waller squared the folders against the muted blue lines of his desk calendar. He didn't open the top folder. Nor did he pick up his pen.

Instead, he swiveled his chair around to the window. Below his office in Fairchild Hall lay the green, crusted in snow and rising in one corner to Spirit Hill. On either side of the green, against the dormitories, lay the twin drill pads. Etched into the cement were strips of white marble, forming a grid of perfect squares where the new four-degree cadets had to run, squaring their corners, from one building to another for the first seven months of their academic careers. On the side of the green nearest his office stood the Air Garden with its perfect rows of honey locust trees, barren in late winter, and the rectangular pool with its dormant fountain. Past the green, the chapel spires jutted toward the mountains, which were green and clay-colored, the edges clotted with snow and the canyon thick with bluish-white drifts winding deep into the crevice like a glacier.

On the Terrazzo, three rows of smacks stood stiffly against the cold. In a corner of his mind, Waller wondered, without exactly forming the words, why the cadets were standing alone like a flock of lost geese and why none of them, except the one in charge, was wearing gloves. But the principal part of his mind was needling a much bigger problem. As he gazed at the Terrazzo, it was not so much the cadets, but the Air Force itself, the whole institution, that he pondered with uncomprehending concern. He saw it as degenerating, deteriorating, eating itself from the inside, and he saw himself as helpless to stop it.

To his staff, these bouts of brooding appeared to be structured, at least in part, for show. Waller was a tall man with peppered hair thinning elegantly at the temples, an ex–fighter pilot who in temperate months played golf with the academy superintendent, Lieutenant General Susan Long, and whose wife of twenty-two years had sacrificed her law career to follow him through countless moves, raising their two teenage daughters, while he climbed through a succession of challenging positions to achieve a rank that few officers ever reached. His staff endured these episodes with stoic tolerance, raised their eyes at each other and tiptoed, as necessary, into his office. Otherwise, they left him in monkish silence.

Waller ignored them, went on with his brooding. A cheating ring in the behavioral sciences department had been uncovered the previous week by the local press. Waller's first whiff of the scandal had come from his secretary, Mrs. Purvel, who put the *Gazette* on hold to shout in her nasally, allergenic voice, "Betty Wise wants to talk about the cheating ring in psych. Do you want to comment?"

The incident had led to an orgy of finger pointing, a display of cowardice and irresponsibility by both students and staff. The students accused the instructors of manipulating them and encouraging them to cheat, a charge the instructors shrugged off.

"Human behavior is so predictable, Balls," Colonel Coyle, the department chair and former strategist from the Air Force Special Operations Command, psychological operations division, had explained to him in his office in Vandenberg Hall when Waller had found him perched like a troll in the clutter of his office, two Escher lithographs tacked on the wall over his desk. "*Of course* we were trying to manipulate the students. That was the whole point."

Waller had always respected Colonel Coyle, with his pickled skin and burgeoning ear hair, in the same way that he respected the civilian scientists who came and went from the Bio-physics Operational Research Group (BORG) laboratory on the far side of the parking lot under Fairchild Hall. He respected them without wanting to get too close, and he hoped, in his negligence, that nothing ever exploded or escaped or went indescribably wrong in one of the experiments they conducted behind the doors with the proximity lock that he declined to have programmed into his area badge. During the Gulf War, while Waller flew nighttime bombing sorties in his F-117, Colonel Coyle had dropped anti-Baathist party leaflets from Special Forces C-130s and "done some other stuff" which he often summarized with raised eyebrows, indicating that he could not elaborate in the un-secure hallways of the Air Force Academy.

Waller liked the straightforward idea of dropping bombs on the enemy. He slightly feared *psyops* the way other people slightly feared spiders. It was a fear that disgusted him, and try as he might to look Coyle in the eye when he spoke, he found himself drumming his fingers or poking peevishly at pens, forks, coffee mugs, whatever loose items were at hand, like some distracted child. He was certain Coyle noticed his anxiety and did his best to aggravate it.

"My problem," Waller explained, "is that somehow the press found out about it, and I don't think it would be such a great thing to go on the record saying that we were encouraging the cadets to cheat."

Slouched in the armchair opposite Coyle's desk, he'd been idly fingering the carpet and come across a pen that had rolled under a leg of the chair. He picked up the pen and began weaving it around his fingers in a way that he'd always suspected showed off his impressive dexterity. When Coyle didn't respond but sat watching Waller perform his pen trick the way a coyote watches a grazing rabbit, Waller slid the pen across Coyle's desk and sat back with his hands tucked casually but firmly into his armpits. The wait game was something he knew how to play.

"All right," Coyle said at last. "We'll handle them. Give me back the students, take them off probation, everything. I've got it. Tell the press whatever you want. You'll never have a problem again."

Waller had gone warily into the agreement with this particular devil in the same way that he'd had access to the BORG lab removed from his proximity badge. He knew the problem would be handled, but he did not want to know exactly how the handling would be done. He'd left Coyle's office feeling only mildly guilty.

From Vandenberg Hall, Waller had gone straight to Susan Long's office. He explained the situation to her, but Long distrusted Colonel Coyle more than Waller did. During the meetings with department heads that Coyle occasionally deigned to attend, he stared down the length of the conference table at her with open contempt—either because she was a woman, or because she was not a pilot, or because she outranked him, or a combination of those things. Whenever Coyle suggested a course of action, her instinct was to oppose it. And anyway, as she told Waller now with a dramatic flaring arm gesture, she hated to "sit by and watch academy laundry billowing in the open air."

If the press already knew about the problem, something had to be done. Something had to be *seen* to be done. The twenty-four cadets involved were too many to expel—the Pentagon would howl over lost dollars and the need for manpower and, "blah, blah, blah," Long said, standing from her Louis XIV–style desk to gain height over him.

She walked to the window overlooking the Terrazzo. Her office almost directly opposed Waller's. She was short, and all of her movements had a theatrical air as though to compensate for that one defect.

"Find the ringleaders," she said. "Expel them."

"It won't work," he told her. "They'll put up a plausible fight, and then they'll accuse each other."

"Why would they do that?"

"Because they learn it from us."

But she'd sent him away. Waller didn't believe in rationing punishment. What kind of message did it send to the cadets, that it was okay to cheat as long as you weren't the instigator? He'd rather have kept the leaders and expelled the followers, who were not only cheaters but cowards, too. It made no sense, and it taught the cadets nothing more than to cover their own asses.

He was now waiting in his office for a two-degree, Cadet Paula Snowe, who'd at last been fingered by the honor department as the single ringleader. She was late. That ticked him off. Tardiness was a sloppy habit. In the fighter squadrons, you might break your fingers in a bar fight or get a ticket for speeding or throw up, hungover, in the parking lot on your way to fly the morning mission, but you were never late. He might start off with a reprimand, or then he might take a softer approach. He might invite her to sit down, to open up. What did obedience matter now? He wanted to know why she'd thrown her Air Force career away over a single test. He wanted to know if it was worth it.

In the doorway, Captain Kord, his executive officer, appeared. "Cadet Snowe is here to see you, sir."

"Send her in."

Paula Snowe, a pert, thin-hipped girl with a short ponytail, strode toward his desk and saluted.

"Sir, Cadet Paula Snowe reporting as ordered."

She looked like they all did, too young to cut their own meat, let alone drive, drink, vote, handle weapons, give orders, and the other things he tried very hard not to imagine, to keep from locking his own daughters in their rooms until he could find them suitable husbands. She was smaller than most, a cadet in miniature. She wore a doll's uniform, a parody of a soldier. She made the whole enterprise of military training look cute.

He returned her salute, and she took the proper stance, feet at shoulder width and hands clasped behind her back.

"At ease, Cadet Snowe." He leaned back in his chair. Her eyes were blue and clear and they regarded him with a kind of curiosity, devoid of fear. He would not ask her to sit just yet.

"Have trouble getting here?"

"No, sir."

"Any particular reason you're late?"

She glanced at his desk and at the wall behind him, again with curiosity, as if to determine just how late she was. There were no clocks. He wore a kinetic Breitling watch on his wrist, set daily against the master clock at the naval observatory. It was an old habit, born from the days before GPS, and one he was loath to give up. Her eyes stopped momentarily at something on the wall above him—the rubber chicken, its beak turned in howling protest at the ceiling, pressed inside a gilded frame with the words "Fowl of the Year" engraved on a brass plate. Her eyes flickered for a moment, reading the words, and she said, "No, sir."

"You can always tell when someone's ready to leave the academy by how they get sloppy with the little things."

Her eyes dropped to his. "Have I been sloppy, sir?"

"You're not exactly showing a desire to stay."

She said nothing. She was looking, now, at the model of the F-117 on his desk. It was mounted on a stand, poised in a gentle, rolling climb. He'd built it with his younger daughter, Toni, when she was ten.

"You understand your situation, don't you? Let's start there. You understand the honor department has recommended you be expelled."

"Yes, sir."

"And that I'm going to do it."

"Do what, sir?"

"Expel you."

She looked at him as though the idea hadn't occurred to her. She put a hand out for the chair in front of his desk.

"Sir, may I—"

"You may not."

Her hand jolted back. She was wary, now, and to Waller's surprise, this pleased him. It was, perhaps, what he'd been seeking all along. To be heard. To be respected. They don't have to like me, he thought. Devotion might come down the road, long after the discipline had replaced the marrow in their bones, but from the first moment they would have to listen.

"It wasn't my fault," she blurted out.

"That's the wrong way to start. Let me tell you right now. With me, that's the wrong way to go."

The best form of defense is attack.

Dark, brutal Machiavelli. Brook loved him. Everyone did. She'd read *The Prince* in high school, pulling it from the clutter of her father's bookshelves one afternoon and absorbing the passages, adding them to her social arsenal. Her father, a well-regarded trial lawyer who was taken to deep silences, dramatic lapses, roused himself enough to notice what she'd gotten into.

"Be careful with that stuff," he warned. "It's corrosive. You're better off with the *Discourses*."

But the *Discourses* were long and cautious. She read a few weary pages and abandoned them for *The Prince*. *If injury must be done, it should be so severe that vengeance need not be feared.* Who wouldn't be seduced by the infantile fury of war, the dark continent of human rage? She felt drawn to it. At eight years old, during the Gulf War, she had watched, on television, the crosshairs of a monochrome screen puff up in silent annihilation. What she craved now was sound advice—how did you master the secrets of war, legally speaking?

That she might learn those secrets at the Air Force Academy was a romantic idea. That had become clear enough. The Academy was less about war, more about posture. Less about soul struggle and more about insignia. There was an entire page in the *Contrails* study guide on how to administer the proper salute. It was like a boarding school for the analytically obsessed. Instructions on how to carry a rifle (the first step was always to make sure it wasn't loaded), how to respond to a superior, fold clothes, appear in public (with the right arm free, prepared to salute). *When in public,* a captain had lectured, *an officer should always appear unencumbered, always ready to respond.*

She squeezed her numbing toes inside the thin shield of leather sole, the numbness traveling upward into her heels and ankles. Bregs's tirade had reached fanatic levels. How long could he keep it up? Long enough for the cold to climb up her calves, into her knees and hips, all the way to her heart? She imagined them all freezing here, monuments to Bregs's insanity. It would serve him right, serve them all right, the academy and their passion for discipline. The way socks had to be rolled tight as softballs with a smile coaxed into the seam; panties to be folded in thirds; tampons stacked like Lincoln Logs in the back of her drawers. Beds made tight as tennis rackets. Every inch of their lives was examined, prodded, put in order. What if they all froze here at eternal attention? What if they gave up their last and greatest needs, for breath, for movement, a symbolic gesture to the extremity of academy life?

Pointless. That's what it would be. There was no room for irony at the academy. Yesterday, Bregs charged her five tours, marching with her rifle across the icy Terrazzo, because her hair was flirting with the bottom of her collar. She marched the tours but she didn't go to the beauty shop as he'd commanded. She'd meant to go, but the minutes had slipped by while she stood at the window in Sijan Hall and watched the gliders soaring along the ridgeline. She couldn't help it. There was something about the gliders—the way they flaunted the odds, they seemed to flout decree, to will themselves through the air. Before she knew it, the beauty shop was closed.

Standing in front of her, Mac Cherry trembled at the shoulders. A glossy sheen of stubble tapered at the base of his neck, the neck itself folded evenly, like vellum, at the base of his collar, as if by regulation. Brook knew the back of his neck better than he did, surely, better than any other person in the world. In the summer, it broke out in red blotches, and in the winter, a thick blue vein ran diagonally along his neck, branching upward into the scalp. What would it feel like to wear her own head so clean to the bone, to feel every shift of wind upon a tender skull?

"Will you accept the call?" Bregs was yelling. "Are you the chosen one?" He was insane. There was no other possibility. He paced among them, delivering his diatribe, perhaps the greatest of his life. Beyond the wall and rising thirteen feet above the Terrazzo stood the court of honor, where on temperate days, the tourists sometimes stood for a peek at the noon meal formation. Tourists. Congressmen. Distinguished visitors. Chambers of commerce. Cadets called the academy *The Zoo*. In fact, today, there were no tourists to witness this display. The cold had driven them back to their houses, their RVs, their ski lodges. We're the only ones left, Brook thought. The eternal soldiers. The mighty few.

A mass of clouds swelled over the ridgeline. No gliders in this weather. Perhaps this was where the soldier's life began, at the point where civilians turned back. And if she were to give her life, as they say, for her country where there would be no witnesses—was that the ultimate test of faith?

Brook's gaze snapped back into place. Bregs had begun the inspection. She couldn't see him, but she tried, the way a horse will roll its eyes, to conjure up some sense of where he was. She didn't want him stepping abruptly in front of her, startling her, reading the dreaminess in her face.

———

She was sitting now. He'd allowed that, finally.

"The honor code is difficult. It's contradictory. It's like we're set up to fail."

"How so?"

"We're not allowed to lie, or cheat, or steal. That's pretty clear. But that other part. We're not allowed to tolerate those among us who do.

Meaning we're supposed to rat on our classmates. But how can we work together that way? We're supposed to trust each other and work together as teams, but then if someone screws up, we're supposed to rat them out. How are we supposed to work that way?"

"But if, say, you've lied, cheated, or stolen, you've already abused the trust of your team members. They shouldn't have any regrets about turning you in."

"See, that's the thing. For some reason, those three things, lying, cheating, stealing, don't seem as bad a crime as turning someone in for doing them. Do you understand? That's the way they see things."

"Who?'

"Everyone. The cadets. The staff, even."

"What staff?"

She shrugged, lifting her mini-shoulders, and looked away.

"Any team," he said, "is organized for a higher good. Your dedication to duty is your most important commonality."

Too didactic, he thought. He tried again. "Imagine yourself at war. You have to trust your team with everything. And to trust that each of you will carry out the mission. The mission. That's everything."

She seemed to consider his words. But how could she understand the importance of the mission? How could she imagine, for example, an aircraft loitering over a handful of SEALs, trying to pick off the guerrillas ducking between the rocks like so many hyenas sensing blood? How could she feel, as he could, how the body will fight pain and heat, willing the jet to stay airborne even as the fuel dwindles to fumes?

"Listen," he said. "Why not speak frankly?"

"Do you mean it?"

"Say what's on your mind."

"All right, sir." She leaned forward now. "What's our mission here? There's so much bullshit. Excuse me, but our mission is bullshit. Have you ever had a mission that was bullshit? That's what it's like here every day."

"You want what? You want to go out and fly fighters this afternoon? You think you just get that kind of privilege? You don't. You have to earn it."

"I don't want to fly fighters," she said. She paused, watching him. Waller had never heard anyone say he didn't want to fly fighters. "I really love the idea of flying fighters, but I don't think that's the best choice, ultimately."

"Why not?" It was true that not everyone wanted to fly fighters. Some secretly wanted to be engineers or scientists or lawyers, but they never admitted it. They simply went through flight training and quietly washed out and went on with their lives. But nobody flat out announced it, and not to Academy leadership.

"It's so *yesterday*," she said. She was slumped in the chair now. "It's not fair, really. I wish I'd been born ten years ago. I wish I'd been Martha McSally, the first female fighter squadron commander, one of the first fighter pilots. How lucky she was! I could have been that. You know? I could have been the first."

"And what if you were?"

She gnawed briefly on the side of her thumbnail and frowned at him. "All the records have been broken. First woman fighter pilot. First woman in combat. First woman commander. It's all been done. I missed my chance."

"Your chance at what?"

"At fame. Immortality. I want to be in the history books. I'm *that* good. It sounds terribly conceited, I know, but I really am that good."

"You cheated on a test. You broke the honor code."

"Oh, that." She sat back. "They wanted us to cheat. Didn't they tell you? It was so obvious to everyone. Nobody would do it. I felt bad for them. Day after day, nobody stole the test answers. This big label, 'Psych 305 Midterm Answers,' on the folder and they kept leaving it on the top of the secretary's desk. We figured it was some kind of BORG experiment. I thought I'd do them a favor."

"How did the press find out about it?" Waller found himself asking, half expecting Paula to know.

"Beats me. They're always sniffing around for dirt. Maybe Colonel Coyle called them."

"You think Colonel Coyle called the *Gazette?*" The idea wasn't completely implausible.

"Why not?" She shrugged a childish shrug. "Maybe it *was* a BORG experiment."

Waller squared the Stealth Fighter model against a dark line of grain running across his mahogany desk. He tried to think of where to go next.

"Okay. You don't want to be a pilot. What do you want to do?"

She looked up at the fowl of the year chicken tacked prostrate inside its oak frame. She seemed to be feeling him out. "I'm majoring in biophysics and minoring in environmental engineering. I have this idea. I want to be an astronaut. I want to live on a space station."

"You want to work for NASA?"

"In time. It's all part of the plan. The thing is, I want to be the first woman on Mars."

"The first woman on Mars."

"That's right. Can you imagine it? The first woman on Mars. I've got it all worked out. I want to live in the first Mars biohabitat. I want to nurture the first plant life. I want to foster the first bacteria. And I want to have a baby. The first Mars baby."

"The first Mars baby."

She nodded, flicked her bitsy eyebrows. "Pretty good, isn't it? It's a lot of work, but think of the press. Think of the career possibilities. A few years in space—not uninteresting stuff—and then I'll go full-term on Mars, have the baby. I'll be famous forever. I'll be the Chuck Yeager of the twenty-first century."

"Is your mother aware of this?"

"My mother." She sighed. Paula Snowe's mother was Senator Janet Snowe of Wyoming, a college friend of General Long, and this particular fact had driven Waller to consider in careful detail how he would break the news about Cadet Snowe's expulsion to his boss. That was another reason he'd invited her to his office and why he was taking such liberal time with her now.

"Actually," she continued, "it was her idea."

Waller momentarily imagined his wife, Lauren, coming up with that kind of harebrained plan for the girls and silently, for the millionth time, thanked the sweet Lord he had married her.

"So to get back to the issue at hand, I'd like to ask you something now. If by some minute possibility you were to stay here, not be expelled, would you cheat again if the opportunity arose?" he asked.

She studied the model of the F-117. "Do you want the truth, sir? Really? The straight truth?"

Waller nodded almost invisibly. Since when did you have to give permission to speak the truth?

"I might, sir, yes," she said, finally, "to win."

"You would cheat in an institution whose foundation depends on integrity?"

"I might, to survive. That's what the F-117 is all about, isn't it? Evading, surviving until you hit your goal?"

Now he looked at the Stealth, the *wobblin' goblin*, its four elevons on the trailing edge of the wings, the dark aluminum surface designed to absorb radar waves and appear invisible in the night sky. Technology and character—she'd mixed her metaphors. A common mistake, but a hard one to fix.

"And since you're being honest, tell me why you would cheat when, since you're clearly bright, you must understand that by refusing to learn the foundations, by simply taking what you call your due, you place in danger those very principles upon which the military owes its existence. You would disregard all who walked before you, who created the highly complex system called the military. You would hurl it back into barbarism."

"I'm sorry, sir. I don't think I follow you."

"I'm saying that the opportunities that the military provides, the groundbreaking stuff you talk about, is not a natural right. It's not something owed to you. You have to earn it."

"But I *have* earned it. I mean, I am earning it. I made a mistake, it's true. I had no idea it would be taken so seriously, and believe me, I won't do it again. I won't say that I'm entitled to a commission any more than anyone else, except that I'm motivated. I'm smart. I can help the military. I have talent. I'm confident. Everybody here has some of that, but how many people here have all that together, in one package? The military *needs* people like me."

Waller turned toward the window so he could carefully consider her argument. He knew there was a good counterargument but he couldn't seem to bring it to mind. The small flight of cadets was still on the Terrazzo, one upper-class cadet strolling among them. Now the question that had prodded his conscience earlier broke into the realm of thought.

"What are they doing out there?" he asked.

"That's the Hogs, my squadron," Snowe said.

"Who's leading them?"

"Bregs," she said.

"Who's Bregs?"

"He's the training officer. Since we're being frank, sir, I'll tell you, he's crazy."

Her ankles were weary. Her knees stung. Before them, the spearheads of the chapel lay exposed to the thickening gray sky. *One eternal wing of cadets. Once ever, and always in our memory. How proudly we hail and one nation under God.*

Keep quiet, and give them the flesh.

She squeezed her buttocks, enjoying the numb sensation of frozen skin against polyester. She'd gotten the idea of doing butt exercises in formation. Curl and release. *Ten, nine, eight.* Did Billy Claymore, standing behind her, notice her squeezing her ass muscles? What did he think of *her* neck?

Thine is the kingdom and the power. Before her, the chapel rose, a monolith of the future. This was theology without mercy, liturgy without fat. Only a god weary of ambivalence could live here, crouched righteously at the foot of the Rocky Mountains, delivering his immutable dogma.

She was almost delirious with the cold. The tip of her nose had gone numb, its ruby crest flaring vaguely before her eyes. Only now had the other members of the wing begun to join them, shuffling into ranks. She could go on standing forever. That's what the academy taught you, that you could endure the intolerable. If she died here, it would be a peaceful death. What did they say? The cold made you sleepy. It made you want to sleep, and under the cover of sleep you could travel anywhere. Be still, she thought, and give them the flesh.

This, too, she would keep to herself. This little secret of survival she would keep in the limbic part of the brain, where words are forbidden. Give them the flesh, and stay inside, one inch below the surface, where they can't touch you.

She was thinking this when Bregs stepped into her line of view.

He was short and gleaming, Napoleonic. His full, pale lips were curled down, almost sensually, in disdain.

"Did you visit the beauty shop yesterday?"

She stood at rigid attention, her back arched fiercely back, as if recoiling in pain. He leaned over to inspect the line of her hair, straight as the earth's horizon and clipped indecorously at the base of her neck. Brook smelled the soap on his skin and something like starch coming off his jacket. "Did you hear me, miss?" he asked softly.

"Yes, sir."

"Then why didn't you answer?"

"N-no, sir," she said, stuttering. A wave of self-loathing washed over her. All her resolve to confront him with some subtle repartee had vanished. He looked directly at her, his face square and pale, his lips pursed in a frown. Denied the privilege of returning his gaze, she stared at Cherry's head. He would tease her later. Or not, since he'd been the one to lose a glove.

"Falling behind again. When will you ever catch up?"

In another life, Brook might have looked down at Bregs, or beyond him. But that didn't matter now. Where she came from, *what* she came from made no difference. That was the blessing and the curse of this place. Bregs was the training officer. He had to be obeyed.

"You'll walk tours for disregarding my order. It was a courtesy, really. I shouldn't have had to ask you at all."

Brook stared at Cherry's head, waiting for it to end.

But he continued to gaze at her. What could it be? A streak of dirt on her face? Blush? No, she'd given up wearing makeup. Perhaps a hair had dislodged and lay promiscuously across her collar.

"Is it too much for you to handle, miss?"

"What, sir?"

"Everything. The marching. The tours. Academics. Don't you want to just go to a nice private college with the rest of your girl-friends?"

"No, sir. I'd rather march tours."

"Good. I'll assign extra ones for you."

I'd like that, sir, she wanted to say. She'd be the hit of the squadron in their late-night review of the day. The notoriety was worth a few extra tours, but she couldn't bring herself to say it.

She shifted her eyes to meet his, buried deep in the shadow of the wheel cap, dark and shiny, like a snake's eyes, like a predator's. On the left side of his nose, a whitehead protruded from the porous skin of his nostril. She wondered if he was still a virgin. The thought almost made her laugh.

"What are you looking at?" he said. His voice was flat and hard. "Answer me."

"A pimple, sir," she said before she could catch the words.

"A *what?*"

It was too late. A ripple of snorts erupted around her. Bregs looked incredulous. "What did you say?"

"Nothing, sir."

"Do you have any idea—" His nose twitched almost imperceptibly, as though he was resisting the urge to touch the side of it, to see for himself. "You'll be marching on the Terrazzo for the next week. You hear me, miss?"

"Yes, sir."

"You know something? I've watched you. I've watched you a long time. And I'll tell you something. You don't belong here. You don't. Go ahead and look at me. You know it, don't you?"

She looked at him hard. She said nothing, because he was close to the truth and she was not sure whether he knew it. *Patience is a lion*. That's what her father had told her. And here, in moments of doubt, she thought of him sitting in the darkness of his small study saying those words. And it helped, because in formation, the body had to stand just so, but the mind could go anywhere.

"What's the matter, miss? Cat gotcha tongue?"

"No, sir."

He leaned over, whispered to her, "You are unworthy. *Girlie*."

And then he was gone, on to the next victim, to pull out his heart by the cords or maybe to give a curt nod of approval and move on. There was a vague sort of buzzing where Bregs's voice had been. A dull ache throbbed from the center of her shoulder blades.

The other squadrons had begun forming for the lunchtime parade. Falling into ranks on either side of Spirit Hill, they mirrored each other, standing wordlessly on either side of the green, like ancient, opposing armies waiting for the order to attack.

In and out she breathed, not wanting to hear it. Too much like prey, it sounded, under the soft and sure chorus of footsteps.

He had dismissed her and turned back to the window. On the Terrazzo, the cadets were moving now, a snake uncoiling itself, unwinding and lengthening toward the ramp that led to Mitchell Hall. A pretty sight they made, four thousand footsteps in unison. They were perfect this way, turning their crisp corners and marching out to the commands issued by the upperclassmen, the chapel behind them jutting toward the mountains and the mountains lifting into the sky. He couldn't hear the commands, but he could see the cadets' mouths opening, their chests tightening as they shouted. Buttoned in their blue coats, they were identical except for the one squadron oddly devoid of gloves. He loved them with a fierce pride and a heart that was clear and golden and knew no uncertainty.

He was considering Paula Snowe's words, her compelling if stubborn confidence, when the counterargument struck him with such force, such brilliant simplicity, that he sat back in his chair and laughed.

Just then, his deputy, Colonel Silas Metz, who oversaw dormitory regulations, sexual harassment issues, and other pieces of cadet affairs, stuck his head in the doorway.

"Sir, General Holly's on the phone for you."

Lieutenant General "Bud" Holly was the commander of the Eighth Air Force, the former boss and mentor of Waller, and Waller wanted to speak to him very badly. There was his promotion and return to the fighter world to discuss. But a king salmon–size catch of wisdom had just leaped into his lap and he needed a moment to savor it. It was a truth that shot Paula Snowe's logic to pieces, a truth he could repeat in the next commandant's call, a truth so deep and profound it brought a mist to his weary, pilot-sad eyes. He had to voice it, write it down, before it slipped back into the cold depths of oblivion.

"Tell him I'll call him right back."

Metz's thin face and eyes were as pale as new corn. He stared wide-eyed at Waller. He had been brought up in the kind of Air Force that never refused, at any cost, the request of a senior officer.

"Sir, I think he wants to talk now."

He had been on the brink of voicing it. It would be his maxim, the single bit of brilliant clarity for which he would be known. It would surface in the pages of some respectable history book, his name in italics below. Perhaps even in his memoir. Perhaps, indeed, he would write a memoir. The outline, his life history, flashed instantly before him. This one epigram could serve as the theme. The making of his life. People would quote it. With that one phrase, he might not have to utter another intelligent word for the rest of his life. A world of fresh possibilities cracked open before him. There was no need to despair, after all.

"I'll call him right back."

Waller dug for a pen, jiggled the mouse on his computer, trying frantically to hold on to the sentence that, like a fish, thrashed and wiggled in his inexperienced hands. The words were still there, jumbled like a kind of anagram. Purity justice clear vision simplicity. He stared at Metz, trying to reconstruct the right order. But Metz,

whose skin looked like pickled pear and whose jaw had gone somewhat slack waiting for a response, was the wrong kind of muse.

"Close the door, would you?"

And then he turned toward the window to clear his sights. Metz
dutifully retreated, but as though swept along with an ebbing tide,
the beautiful words slithered away and were gone.

Chapter Two

Before dawn, before any part of the building was awake, she pulled herself out of sleep, her body still wallowing in the warmth of bed, her mind lolling in its own enchantments. Brook had marvelous dreams. Had the trainers guessed at the brilliance, the sheer color of these dreams, they would have tried to muffle them. Brook woke most mornings in the wake of lavender mists, the pixels of some magnificent mirage splattering around her. The dreams had an accustomed urgency. She was running, maddeningly fast or slowly, or driving or sometimes flying, straining her eyes, legs, engine to get to whatever she had missed, whatever evaded her. That part was mundane; what clung to her was the imagery. She woke reminiscing in the feel of sun-warmed stone ledges, brilliant blue pools, the soothing voice of some long-hoped-for friend.

Brook had never slept in her bed. She slept on top of it, coiled in a sleeping bag, dressed in her sweats and a running bra to save precious minutes in the morning. She swung to sitting, planted her feet on the cold tile. Her roommate, Lex Rolstein, was breathing heavily on the other side of the room. The silence felt like the silence of prayer, so many hopeful thoughts inside a building bare enough that the wind sometimes echoed in the walls. You didn't exactly wake in a place like this. The body came out of hiding, resumed its fears and obligations.

She rolled up her sleeping bag and stowed it in the closet, pulling out her running shoes in the same bending movement and sitting back on the floor to lace them and strap on the watch. She pulled the wool cap over her head and stood, the muscles in her thighs awake now. Her shoes sounded like a squeegee on the floor. At the doorway, she turned around to shut off her alarm clock so that it wouldn't wake Lex, and then she was out in the hallway where the silence was even more rare and precious. Within the hour, three thousand bodies would rise, lock away their dreams, and attack the day.

She spread her arms, owning the hallway, stealing that slice of territory from the upperclassmen who made a point of swaggering along the corridors in the daytime, flaunting the kind of indifference that came with ownership. Brook lived that year on the west side of Sijan Hall, shoved up so close to the mountains that in the daytime, she could watch the tufts of snow tumbling through the pines. The pines were heroically tall and their branches bowed deeply under the snow. When the snow fell away, it left crystalline clouds in its wake and the branches soared upward like the wings of a great bird. She had never seen trees this tall or mountains and a sky so large and pure that they left you feeling stripped bare under the elements. Even in formation, locked in tandem with her classmates, she could feel the power of the mountain weather, its uncompromising reality, and she wanted to be up in it, tumbling through the sky, and the thought made all the hours on the ground bearable.

She walked down the middle of the corridor, swinging her arms and hopping a little on her toes. It felt rebellious. Jogging down the stairs, she pushed open the fire door and stepped into the darkness. The cold slapped her. Stung her teeth. Overhead, stars shattered the cold blue shell of sky. She couldn't see the mountains, just the line of blackness where the stars disappeared. She buried her chin in the scratchy blue wool of the scarf and set off. The sidewalk veered around to the parking lot, but she ran straight, charging through the snow and straight up the hill to the road.

Her feet made a crunching sound on the ice. A halo of snow had crept in under her running socks. She hurtled a bank and was on the pavement, pushing back the cold and the ache in her ankles. The air burned in her lungs. She was breathing hard, already, a little giddy in the high altitude. She liked the lightness of the mountain air, couldn't imagine running again in the thick, milky air at sea level.

She was warming up now, her breath evening out, her feet pounding steadily on the ice. Cadets were supposed to run in the afternoon. There was a safety regulation put out about running in the dark. There were safety regulations about everything, as though their own bodies couldn't be trusted, or were being saved for a greater purpose. She didn't care. There was too much traffic out here in the afternoons, cadets one after another running the back loop by Stanley Canyon and then back down by the hospital and the stadium and around to the dorms. It was worth the risk of getting caught. A sort of freedom lingered in the predawn darkness, an array of possibilities that existed only before the day had yet to take hold and establish its regimens.

Her calves began to ache. The hill fell away under her feet, a giant wave she rode with the motion of her stride. She owned it now, not just a slice of darkness on this patch of road, but the whole base, the whole world. The sweat rolled off her hairline, breaking the freeze barrier on her forehead, but she kept running. Her lungs hurt, burning like a coal fire to fuel the engine of her legs.

She was reaching the peak where the road curved around and dropped back toward the campus, but she wanted to keep climbing. There was a metal gate to the left barring the entrance to Stanley Canyon. The path wasn't plowed, and Stanley Canyon was off-limits to smacks, anyway, but she'd run out of hill and she wanted to keep going. Her lungs felt scorched, but she wanted to run up through the canyon to the saddle and along the ridge all the way to Cathedral Rock.

Her father had said that gravity was the weakest force in the universe. This from a Boston-bred lawyer who'd never spent a full day out of the office. How could he possibly know? And yet, the words hit her now. Gravity was indeed the least of her worries.

Girlie. Jesus. Was that the best Bregs could do?

"Sir, permission to enter," she hollered at no one in particular. Dawn was beginning to emerge and the houses clustered below in the valley were taking shape. She ducked under the gate and waded knee deep in the snow, making giant, exaggerated steps, punching through the crust of ice. The sweat began to cool on her face. She shivered. The light rising behind her painted a pinkish-blue sheen on the snow. She climbed a bare chunk of granite boulder sticking out of the hillside and listened. The silence out here was much different from in the dorms. It wasn't the silence of holding in, of hoarding one more private minute. It was the silence of letting go.

The air was clean and smelled of pine. In the late winter chill, it felt austere, puritan, as though stripped of unnecessary elements. Brook sensed the tremor of something powerful, the way the air sometimes feels thin and calm before a storm blows. Next to the trail lay the frozen bed of a stream, and beyond the stream was a steep rock face, and on a chink of rock stood a round-horned Rocky Mountain sheep, gazing across the canyon at her.

"Mornin'," she called. "I've got to pee. Don't tell, okay?"

He woke, surprised to see the light rising and Lauren already out of bed. Morning's dull routine played out on the haphazard contents of their room. Their furniture, small and mismatched, made the room seem cluttered and oversized at the same time. The last commandant's wife had painted the walls peach and left the vacant pockmarks of old pictures. The single bit of ornamentation came from Lauren's porcelain dolls, perched on her bureau, that stared at him, judging him with their blue eyes.

In the night, the dream hadn't come.

He knew it because his body wasn't tense and exhausted, though a slight nausea churned in his stomach. This was how he'd begun to measure his nights, whether the dream came or whether it stayed away, hopping like some raven at the willowy fringes of sleep. He blinked at the room, a kind of victory, light over darkness. When had night become such an enemy of peace?

The evening before, he'd returned from the office weary, a tenderness nipping at his gut. He'd cut the sputtering engine in the MG and made his way around the recycling barrels and through the shadowy clutter of the laundry room. Lauren, her back turned, frying hamburgers at the stove, said, "I bought you a book."

He dropped his flight cap and keys on the bar and picked it up. As usual, a biography. Franklin Pierce, fourteenth American president. No doubt someone long misquoted, long misunderstood. This seemed to be a pattern in the books Lauren brought home, but whether it was Lauren's doing or simply a common formula behind biographies, he couldn't tell. He scanned the back cover. *The "dark horse" victor of the fourteenth American presidency has long been blamed for igniting the first sparks of the Civil War.*

"I see you got yourself in the paper again with the cheating scandal," Lauren said.

"How did I sound this week? Like last time? What did you call it before?"

"Draconian."

"Yes, draconian. Was it like that?"

"Pretty much."

"I don't think she likes me much, Betty Wise. I think she wants to make me look bad."

"That's probably it," she said.

Waller placed the book on the counter next to his flight cap.

"Where are the girls?"

"Valerie's out with Keith. Toni's downstairs on the rowing machine."

The commandant's house sat on four acres of grass and ancient trees, a Spanish-style mansion that might have been elegant save for the clutter. Combs, barrettes, elastics, belts, bows, pins covered the house. The two girls lived like cats, curling up amid their teenage debris: magazines, schoolbooks, electronics, their rooms a hodgepodge of clothes and compact discs, posters of soft-focus puppies and the black-and-white movie stars of his own era. They left a trail of adolescent gobbledygook throughout the house that Lauren occasionally swept into piles but that he did not dare touch, having more than once been accused of throwing out some precious item.

Waller sighed forcefully, feeling the slight letdown of an evening at home. Driving home with the air leaking through the rusty floor of the convertible MG, he'd felt an anticipation of something, a slight sense of warmth and elation. The nightly illusion. Part of this was the MG's fault. It wasn't a car in any practical sense. Small and loud, prone to fits, churlish in both hot and cold weather, it spit fumes and demanded attention. His colleagues thought it was some desperate attempt to regain his youth. Let them think. He'd bought it from a captain transferring back to the flying world and had it towed up from base, coaxing it into inspection standards in his spare time. Called "tiger lily yellow," the color resembled acid bile. No woman in her right mind would come near it. That wasn't the point. When he drove it down Academy Boulevard with the icy wind streaming through its pores, the mountains to his right settling under a twilight sky, he felt uncommonly happy. A childish hopefulness.

When he turned into the housing area with its rows of boxy houses, a kind of gravity kicked in, as though home and office were two polar spheres tossing him back and forth. Coasting along the driveway, passing under the great willow trees, he felt lifted by a momentary surge of lightness. Then, turning, the lights of the MG shone on the recycling tubs at the back of the garage. It was something about all those crushed, gleaming cans of Diet Coke and Coors Light spilling out of the tubs that depressed him. Stacked beside them, cardboard cases of new, shiny cans that Lauren bought at the commissary waited to be pulled into the cycle. He cut the engine and the MG barked and sputtered to a stop.

Upstairs, he walked past the girls' bathroom, a mystical, frightening place, strewn with cosmetics and hair rollers, curling irons, tiny drip-drying bras, and ducked into the bedroom, changing into denims and a flannel shirt. Back downstairs, Lauren was setting the table.

Waller took a Coors Light from the refrigerator and sat on a stool. It was true—the cans in the garage were for him, also. He knew that and yet they bothered him, their futility and constant pressure. Toni, the boyish, big-boned, thirteen-year-old, emerged red faced from the basement, then plopped with feigned exhaustion onto her father's shoulder.

"Did you cross the Atlantic down there?"

"No, Dad," she said. Her eyes were light, not yet clouded with advanced adolescence like her older sister's. She punched playfully at his ribs.

"Just the Bering Strait."

"Yeah."

They sat on one side of the oak table and ate quietly, none of them much inclined to describe the day's small agonies. Waller asked about school, received shrugs, ambiguous monosyllables. He had a vague idea of what his daughters did during the day. The school was an echoing monolith off a highway bypass from whose doors poured creatures of Toni's and Valerie's relative size but got up like carnival performers or street people, pierced and studded with small ornaments, brazen with chemically contaminated hair. They frightened Waller. Waiting once in the Cherokee to pick up his daughters, he'd watched them wander off in thuggish clusters. When his daughters appeared, rosy and chattering, adequately dressed, hair the color and smell of dried oak leaves, he'd felt a wave of relief and deep gratitude. Gratitude to God and to Lauren, who'd watched out where he'd been remiss.

Now Toni had decided she wanted to become a Marine. She'd announced it some weeks ago while they were watching a documentary on Navy SEALs.

"Why the Marines?" he'd asked. "Why not the Air Force?"

"I like the motto," she said. "*Semper Fidelis.* Nobody else has a motto."

Since then, she'd stopped eating Mounds bars, had begun a training program on Waller's old rowing machine, and had asked for a set of free weights. She was putting on muscle, eating meat and salads.

Now, at the dinner table, she asked for a second helping of chicken, peeling the skin off and pushing it to the side.

"There's an open house next month at the prep school," Waller said. He meant the preparatory school at the Air Force Academy. "Would you like to go?"

"Sure," Toni said. "But I really want to go to Parris Island. When can we go there?"

"I don't know. There's no rush."

"You're not going to talk me out of it, Dad. I'll go see the prep school, but don't think that's going to change my mind."

"Okay, okay. Just thought you might want to look at all your options."

She looked at Lauren and rolled her eyes. Lauren smiled at her—she was taking this well, which meant she thought Toni would grow out of it. Waller took his cues from her.

"So," Waller said, "you must have heard about the guy who sat down in a crowded bar and announced he was going to tell a Marine joke." Toni shook her head. "The guy next to him says, 'Let me tell you, I'm six feet tall, two hundred and fifty pounds, and I'm a Marine, and the guy next to me is six feet tall, two hundred and fifty pounds, and he's a Marine, and the guy next to him is the same. Now, you still want to tell that joke?' 'Nah,' the guy says, 'I don't want to have to explain it three times.'"

Toni smiled and turned back to her chicken.

After dinner, Lauren started the dishwasher and switched on the television. Toni retreated to the phone. Waller poured a bourbon over crushed ice and picked up the book. *In this new biography, Pierce is shown for his real, uncensored self, a heroic man who took the presidency just months after the death of his child, a man not afraid to stand up to the biases of his time, to make bold decisions despite his narrow victory.*

He fell asleep in the chair and woke long after midnight, switched off the television, and made his way up to the bathroom to urinate. Shedding his clothes, he folded himself into the bed and thought about Franklin Pierce, fourteenth American president, a man he'd never heard of, working through bits of loathing and doubt in his conscience to extend the country westward into Arizona while the country swirled into civil war. He didn't know whether Pierce suffered doubt and loathing, but he gave him those qualities.

He didn't think about flying. He held a talisman against the dream, bartering for a peaceable sleep. He drifted off imagining Colorado full of dust and gold, trains and horseback thieves, the stuff of childhood games. He didn't ask for majestic things, great truths. He wanted simple things: a clean conscience, a good night's sleep, to wake without stiffness and pain.

And the dream didn't come. He slept. In the morning, his mind felt clear. Then, rising in the bare light of the windows, he felt a jolt of pain in his side. Fell back with a defeated laugh. Figures. Probably a muscle acting up after his caper a few days ago in the gym. Lifting free weights, he'd gotten the idea he could still bench two hundred and forty pounds. He only wanted one clean press, but spitting and swearing, he couldn't get the bar more than a few inches off his chest. What had he been thinking? Now a pain in his side, swift and sharp, like a kick in the ass.

Lauren was already in the kitchen, starting the coffee, warming the oatmeal in the microwave. He lay back, gathering his strength. He had to get moving. The bed rode high between four clawed posts. It reminded him of an Arabian horse—their one elaborate purchase, made when the girls were still young enough to curl up between them in the early mornings. They'd bought it to rectify a mistake he'd made once on a trip to Las Vegas. His one transgression, which he'd vowed to keep secret and had ultimately confessed. It had caused so much pain—not the transgression itself, which seemed to him unavoidable, a necessary evil—but his confessing it. Was it noble or cowardly? He still couldn't decide.

Late, he thought. *Must go.* But a memory surged up inside him. Despite him. He'd been a young captain flying in an exercise at Nellis Air Force Base. They'd gone to the officer's club, as was the custom on Friday nights. She'd come in with the other women, wearing a black dress that glittered. She drank Jeremiah Weed with them. He'd flown well that week. They'd told him he'd be promoted to flight lead, quite an honor for a young captain. He felt good. No—better than good—invincible. Maybe she sensed it. All those pilots in the bar, and she'd gone for him. Maybe that's why he took her back to his room.

He reached down now, flirting with a treacherous memory. Her hair was twisted in a kind of chignon and coming loose, loping over his stomach, the glitter on her cheeks rubbing off on his hips, in his pubic hair, her nipples popping out of the satin-lined bodice of her dress and bobbing in his hands, along the tops of his thighs. She'd done the thing Lauren wouldn't do, and then she sat up gleaming, her lipstick gone and her lips pale as old cream, and she had worked him in her hands until he was ready again, and this time he rolled her over and worked the taffeta ruffles over her hips and took her like that, with her knees jouncing in the air and the dress folded back like a tutu over her hips. It didn't take long, her hair undone now and coiled around her neck, the breasts propped over the lip of the dress. Ragged, perfect, her arms entwined in the bedposts, willfully or perhaps he'd held them that way. He'd soiled her dress, pulled out prudishly at the last moment and she laughed at him. He bristled with the memory, the sweet infusion of desire and shame. God, she could still do it for him.

Sighed deeply, let his hand drop, the pain gone from his side.

An awkward mix: sexy and invincible, guilty and sick. He'd flown home the next day with stiffness lingering in his balls. Her smell seemed, even after the shower, where he'd scrubbed her phone number off the back of his hand, to linger on his skin.

At home—they were living in Alamogordo, New Mexico, then, in a stucco house whose corners sprouted scorpion hatchlings—Lauren had sensed something. After minor resistance, he confessed.

But she wanted details.

Only fellatio, he lied, resenting her a little for having to give up even that. He'd not kept the woman's number, but he'd wanted to hold on to that secret, the woman's hair twisted over her head and falling loose over his stomach, the glitter on her cheeks.

Only fellatio, Lauren said. She stood up, straightening things around the room, disappearing finally to make a dinner that neither of them would eat.

It had bothered him to give that secret away. He sat stubbornly on the old bed in the old room not yet ready to beg for forgiveness. Some trace of resentment lingered. Why? If he had not been ready to ask for forgiveness, why had he told her at all?

He succumbed, eventually. He pleaded, wooed. Delivered little gifts. They had their portrait taken, hanging an oversize print in the foyer. They bought the new bed, consecrated it, pronouncing a new start. The resentment receded, then flared at sudden moments, brought on by the smell of musky perfume, the swish of a rustling dress. Or by nothing at all, only a vague desire, the bloodlust of a hunter.

He stood now on the pale Berber carpet, walked through the dressing area into the bathroom, and showered in the fiberglass stall, cursing the soft handles of flesh that had begun to gather at his waist. There were twin sinks in the bathroom, Lauren's covered with an array of bottles and jars, his with an electric razor and a toothbrush, stained with paste and mashed to a prickly moss. He spat into the lime-stained basin and shaved, favoring his right side. Then, in the bedroom, he zipped himself into a flight suit, allowed on "warrior day" Fridays. The lip of the fitted sheet had peeled back, exposing a corner of the mattress. He felt a vague surge of shame. He had confessed, though only partially, because he'd thought it was the honorable thing to do.

Downstairs, he followed the smell of evaporating coffee. The television was on, tuned to *Good Morning America*, and Lauren sat in front of it with a mug of coffee, folding laundry. The guest on the show had lost a son fighting with the Army in Iraq and then decided to knit an afghan with the names of all the dead service members in it. The woman was holding up the afghan. The names of the service members were in blue or red and the background was white. The afghan was already twenty-seven yards long.

Valerie, Waller's older daughter, sat at the kitchen table filling out a mail-order form for vitamins. The remnants of someone's oatmeal lay hardening in a bowl by the sink. Waller poured the last of the lukewarm coffee into his mug.

"Hi, Dad," Valerie said. She stood up with the folded order form and pecked him softly on the cheek.

"Want some breakfast?" he asked. He was loading a plate with cold bacon and eggs.

She scrunched up her nose. "I don't eat pig flesh."

"Oh, right, I forgot."

Valerie took supplements called photochemicals and mushroom immune enhancers, elements he distrusted the same way he'd distrusted them in the 1960s. She'd tried to get him to try them—his "aura" bothered her, she said—but he'd told her, only partially joking, that he was afraid of testing positive on one of the occasional no-notice urine inspections.

In the driveway, two chirpy quarter notes sang out of Valerie's boyfriend's mother's VW, battered with chafed bumper stickers that read *Free Tibet* and *What's Worth Dying For Is Not Worth Killing For.* Valerie was frantically shuffling through the drawer under the kitchen phone.

"Where are the stamps? I can't find anything in this place," she said.

"They're under the coupon envelope," her mother called from the couch.

Valerie seized her bounty, called, "Bye!" and ran out the door.

Waller went to the door and watched Valerie get into the car. Keith waved to him, and he waved back. He liked Keith, even though his mother was a hippie who drove a VW and worked at a bead store in Monument. It wasn't her politics that bothered him. He didn't give a damn what she thought. Waller expected no thanks. It was enough simply to do his duty. The only thing that troubled him with the loose-end politics on either side—either loud-mouthed side—was the moralistic yammer such crap was peddled with. Worse, the self-serving stench of so many elected politicians, especially those who turned up in all their self-importance at the Academy and had to be heard out. No way to duck them. All he really wanted to do was fly airplanes, and fly them well.

Lauren sat in jersey pajamas on the couch. The television show was taking a break, though the television was not.

"Morning," he said, kissing the bed-mussed clump of short curls on her head. He touched her gingerly with his fingers, an act of atonement. She smelled of lavender and skin cream.

"Isn't that something about the afghan?" she asked. "How can they do those things?"

"They have to do something."

"They don't have to go on *Good Morning America*."

"Toni up yet?" he asked, going in search of his coffee.

"She's not going to school today."

"Why not?"

"It's her birthday. She wants to go shopping."

"She can't shop after school?" he asked, but she ignored him. He found his mug on the breakfast bar where Valerie's purple day planner, with the picture of her and Keith clasping each other on some picnic table, sat at his elbow. He fought the temptation to open it and turned instead to watch Lauren. She held her thin, white arms in front of her, shaking a towel and folding it by thirds, her eyes fixed on the television.

"You're coming home for the party, right?" she asked. "You remember?"

"What time is it?"

"Four o'clock."

"I'll be here."

"With the cake. Don't forget the cake. Pick it up at the commissary."

"Okay."

"I'll call you."

"You don't have to."

"Sure, I don't."

In the garage, he shoehorned himself into the MG, where he

stashed gloves and a wool cap in the glove compartment on winter days. Once inside, the cockpit felt like a well-tailored suit. He drove through the officers' residential area, the engine louder than a T-37, past the BMWs, the midsized wagons, the SUVs tucked against the eaves of their wire-fenced studio homes. He hugged the stick snugly in one gloved palm, the wheel in the other. It was an intimate cockpit, like that of a sailplane.

He drove through the housing area and up to the main part of base, night shedding off the sky. The pale moon, a lone coyote, hovered in the east. Above the ridgeline, a long, flat cloud spread thinly in the high air. He watched it, knowing and feeling what the air would be doing to that cloud and wanting to be up in it, rising in the great wake lift that was invisible but that he could see.

He felt, more than usual, a kind of malevolent force radiating from his office. The Paula Snowe issue remained. He'd have to meet with General Long again, no getting around that. And then Paula Snowe would have to be dismissed. There was no other possibility. What wearied him was the effort it would take to get to that point. There was the personal connection—the political connection—between Long and Snowe's mother that would weigh things down. It angered him—he had no interest in complications.

The sky was clear except for that single long, thin cloud at the tip of Pikes Peak. Waller stared at it. From that one cloud, Waller could tell that the wind was strong at that altitude and that air above and below the cloud was stable enough so that particles of air were being whipped over the cloud and then sucked downward into the valley where they would rise again, and that if Waller were to take a glider into that air, he might soar to altitudes of twenty-five thousand using nothing but wind.

He hadn't been up in a glider in weeks. The temptation was overwhelming. So overwhelming that he told himself Paula Snowe could wait. She had nothing good coming to her, and she could wait a little longer before finding out. It was unfortunate. She had plenty of the right qualities—composure, a certain quickness, but she had learned how to get around discipline. That was the kiss of death. If they figured out how to skirt the rules, you couldn't scare them. And he knew the makings of the best officers began with fear. Fear, privation, and want. Napoleon said that was what made good soldiers, that courage came second. *I made all my generals of mud*, he said, and Waller liked that, because most of the generals he knew were still mud.

He turned right, off Academy Boulevard and down the road to the hangar.

The parking lot was almost empty. It was that point in the morning before the gliders cranked up and after the Wings of Blue, the parachute team, had already been up and floated down. Ben Railey, who ran the glider program, had parked his truck by the hangar door next to the cement barrier that read NO PARKING. TOW AREA. When Waller punched in the code and walked into the front office, the lights were on, and Rails was on the flight computer looking at the weather. Without looking back, he said, "I knew as soon as I saw that cloud, you'd be showing up."

"You're going to get your car towed," Waller said.

"You got wave riding up to thirty thousand by the looks of it." He turned now, his shoulders stooped with too much time in small plane cockpits. "I put that sign up myself to keep the cadets out of my space."

Rails was thin and small. His face was rough and grayish-brown from sun and hangar food, and his jeans were streaked with grease. He stood up and rubbed his nose roughly on the cuff of his shirt, and then he said, "Which one do you want to take?"

"What makes you think I came here to fly?"

"I didn't figure you came for breakfast. You want the Ximango or should I tow you up in the Kestrel?"

"Well, if you're offering."

He nodded. "I figured it. I'll get ready if you want to call for clearance. I'd shoot high if I were you."

"Thirty?"

"That'll do." Rails yanked open the metal door to the hangar and let it close behind him. He was a good pilot, both on the tow and in the glider. He'd flown A-4s in the dead years between Korea and Vietnam. Somehow he had missed both wars, and Waller felt bad for him. Sometimes after flying, Railey would pop some beers from the mini fridge under his desk, and they would sit in the lumpy chairs in the back office trading flying stories, and Waller was careful to only tell stories about flying in peacetime.

Waller called air traffic control for the clearance, and the controller was cheerful, as though the lenticular cloud had put him in a good mood, too. Waller, after getting the information, thanked him and told him to have a great morning, which meant: Take care of me, watch over me while I'm out having a great morning. He hung up the phone, and the whole thought of Paula Snowe was gone from him now. She was some unfortunate thing that had happened a long time ago to somebody else. If he thought about her at all, in passing, it was that she would be gone soon, and she would miss all this without ever knowing it.

Waller went into the hangar, still cool from the night air, and walked across the cement floor. His boots echoed off the aluminum walls. The airplanes, high-wing Cessnas, were packed in together so that he had to weave between the wingtips. He put his fingers on them as he went. Rails had finished the walk-around and was towing the Skylane out of its berth and toward the fuel pump.

Waller trotted over to clear the wingtips, and then he went to the glider, already waiting on the ramp, and checked the body and then moved the stick, forward and back, right to left, a kind of genuflection, checking the rudder and ailerons but also going through a sacred act, one he revered as much as the flying itself. There were spots of discolor on the airfoils from bits of debris on the runway, but he overlooked these, running his fingers along the leading edge of the wing, tracing the nose, the sleek fuselage.

He never spoke during the walk-around. It was a sort of bread breaking with the craft before going airborne, laying out the laws of peace. The craft was a partner in this. There was no hierarchy. This was the way he saw it; the sailplane had equal voice with him in the air. They worked together, and often he would talk to it, not to soothe, as with an animal, but to suggest or speculate. In this way, he felt he learned as much from the craft as it learned from him.

By the time they got the glider pushed over to the strip and hooked up to the Skylane, and Waller was strapped in with the canopy fastened and waiting for a radio check from Rails, the sun had cleared the hills on the east side of the valley. Bits of tender, pink cloud had begun to moss over the ridgeline. High above, the lenticular cloud still hung, woven as tightly as a moth's cocoon, suspended inside a fierce, invisible wind.

Waller set the flaps to zero and leveled the trim. Rails finished the ground checks and called the tower for permission to take off. When the tower gave clearance, Rails pushed up the throttles, and almost instantly, the sailplane behind him was airborne. Waller kept it steady over the ground while Rails gained speed and lifted, at last, into the air, pulling the Kestrel along. Waller flew a clean line. Rails banked left, toward the ridge, and Waller nudged the stick to stay in his wake. They circled in a spiraling climb through a thousand feet above the ground, then fifteen hundred. Waller shifted into high formation, so attuned to Rails's moves that the rope between them seemed almost extraneous. Rails felt none of the tugs and jinks he felt with the students. They were two old pilots rehearsing a maneuver they knew by heart.

When Rails pulled through eleven thousand feet above sea level, Waller was still on the towline. "Heads up. We're going to hit the rotor now," Rails called.

In a blink, the air exploded into an invisible froth of motion, the towplane sliding from one side of the canopy to the other. Waller tried to keep the towplane in sight—that was all he could do. There was no staying behind in any orderly way. He flew the glider by letting it bounce against the swirls and pockets of air. It was like roller skating on marbles. He held on, knowing it would end, knowing he had only to keep the towplane in view, keep the towplane in view—

And then they were through it, and the air was as calm as a morning lake.

"Still got your head on straight?" Rails called.

"Get ready. Okay. Now." Waller pulled the release and the rope fell away. He broke right at the same time Rails broke left.

"Have a good one," Rails said, and then the noise of the Skylane faded off and Waller was left alone in the quiet air.

The clock started, a meter against carelessness. The air is a complicated place, full of pockets and pitfalls, convection and condensation, most of it invisible. A sailplane makes alliances with the air. The pilot sends out his wings like envoys, dipping and shuddering, negotiating lift. The trick with a wave was to avoid flying through it. To sit on top of it, like a surfer, and let the wave ride under you, carry you upward. The air pitched past, the sound as smooth as falling water. The wind whispered against the canopy. The valley fell under him and the first lip of the Rocky Mountains puckered up and the sun rose up behind him, frosting the peaks, stirring the air from sleep.

His hands and feet worked in unison, pushing and giving, bargaining with the wind. Small changes in the fingers and the soles of the feet, making peace between the ailerons and rudder. Make peace. Make peace. The sailplane knew that already, so he kept the words to himself, to stop from surging ahead.

A faint warning. A reminder.

She hoisted up her sweatpants, regarded the little melting pocket left in the snow. The sky was light now. Above her, a glider drifted through the air. It gleamed like a dragonfly in the sun.

Early for gliders, she thought. They came out in flocks in the afternoons, thermaling under the big, puffy cumulus clouds that gathered in midmorning or floating on a cushion of air along the ridgeline. Smacks weren't allowed to soar. They had to live out their year on the ground, and the gliders became a dream of liberation. Even the word *soar* had the mystical quality of deliverance. Brook believed it. She longed to feel herself lift into the air, cut the cable, and drift into the silent, inevitable physics of flight.

Closing her eyes, she spread her arms out, letting the breeze run under her. Imagined herself lifting up over the canyon, over the base and the city and the mountains and up, higher, in circles, the way the hawks did it, rising in the thermals with their wings dipping and catching the modulation in the breeze.

Opened her eyes and blinked. The trees swayed around her, homage to the dream of flight. The glider drifted silently above her, its belly pink in the rising sun.

Reveille hadn't sounded, or it was too far away. She settled back on the rock so that she could look straight up. She would catch hell for this, probably. The stone chilled her. She spread her arms along the cold stone, willed the sky to lift her.

"Fly," she whispered. "Fly, fly, fly."

And why should he warn himself? What had he to fear?

He swept upward, now, as if through some godly doing, rising in the wake lift. The earth fell under him and disappeared into bland shadows. He'd reached the lenticular cloud and vaulted himself off it, soaring up into the power of a fierce, steady wind. He kept his eyes fixed on a single mountain top west of Pikes Peak. It was like surfing an invisible ocean. The whole world rode under him.

The air whispered outside. The earth curved under him. It was immense. He felt couched inside something powerful. A sense of joy flooded his body, sprang into the crown of his head and his toes. The sky was his playing field. He arced the glider until he was upside down, nosed it over until he saw the horizon and then moved the stick to the left. Who else knew this kind of freedom?

In a glider, the sky was one's fuel. Soaring was flying in the purest sense, with nothing more than wings and a rudder, skill and intuition. It was a kind of physical eloquence, a stripping down of the elements to the absolutely essential. Wings, rudder, wind. To say you were happy in a sailplane, that you enjoyed it, was to cage the experience inside a petty collection of words. You could not be happy or sad or any other thing that could be weighed in language. And he believed that words were heavy, serious things. His desk had been stockpiled with them, yet they failed in the face of experience. To ride a perfect wave, *this* perfect wave, to keep himself in one position, buoyed by the racing wind, was something no one would ever see. To balance on the thin blue line between stillness and chaos was a skill he owned. It was like a kind of atonement.

———

In the canyon, her back fixed against the rock, bolted to the earth spinning through space like a pedestal under which the glider performed its magic, she watched. She *absorbed*.

———

Something popped. Not jolted—as in, he didn't *feel* it, he didn't feel any imminent danger. But it popped. All at once, his senses contracted, focused into that single sound.

The glider responded, and he pushed it until he was wings level, and then he straightened the stick again. Another pop. Waller blinked, listened. Moved left. Pop. Straightened. Pop. It felt as though something had been caught in the aileron, but that was impossible up here. What could it be? He moved the stick again. Pop. Straightened. Pop.

His hands tingled, his shoulders tensed a little too much. He knew—that is, his *mind* knew that nothing drastic had gone wrong, that the problem, whatever it was, could be managed. The glider could be landed. But his body knew a different truth, that all accidents start small, the first step to oblivion was always an innocent blunder. *Oh, shit.* Stop it. Circle down. You have time. He talked to himself, talked to the craft. There's all the time in the world.

But his body said, *no, no—*

This was it. This was the dream.

His fingers clasping a stick and trigger. Seven Navy SEALs crouching in the rocks below him. The smell of cordite in the air. He was no longer in a glider but in the A-10 fighter, a rough-and-tumble tank killer, a kind of hornet swatting the heads of an enemy army, and he had loved this flying job—his first—and he had thought there was no end.

His A-10 squadron was deployed to a place they called SISA—somewhere in South America—which everyone knew was Panama though they would deny it, shrug it off. They lived in bungalows, where the air smelled like warm, rotting fruit and the soft, brown bodies of the women came cheaply, along with *ceviche* and rum.

One mission: he was flying cover over seven Navy SEALs trapped in ambush by the mountain guerrillas. He did not know why the SEALs were there or whose guerrillas had trapped them or what the guerrillas wanted or what kind of weapons they had. He only knew he had to take out enough guerrillas so that the SEALs could get out from behind the outcropping of rock and get to their rendezvous point. The guerrillas were hiding in the brush dotting the hillside. Easy kills.

The SEALs were talking over an FM radio, directing the A-10s toward the rocks where the guerrillas were hiding. Waller breathed hard. He flew toward the hillside, green and rugged and steep, and he watched for the last moment he could pull up and out of the canyon. He had the trigger squeezed all the way down, as though by squeezing it more he could release more bullets, and then he peeled off while his flight lead came forward. This way, they kept a constant stream of bullets on the rocks hiding the guerrillas after that first pass, which he had botched.

The guerrillas couldn't move without being shot at by either Waller or his wingman or the SEALs, and Waller was sure they would kill enough of them so that the others would flee and the SEALs could get out. He pushed the sickness out of his stomach from the first botched pass, suppressed a wild urge to pray. His trigger had stuck the first time, when all the guerrillas were out in the open. Now, when he turned toward the hillside, he looked for movement in the bushes to shoot at, or he shot randomly, strafing the clusters of greenery before turning cold to climb again. He could feel the firing of the gun in his feet.

Then his flight lead called low on fuel. It surprised him. He checked his own fuel, and it was also low, and the SEALs were still trapped under the rock outcropping and this was the first time he began to feel afraid.

This was where the dream and the past began to bleed together. He shot at the guerrillas hiding in the bushes and each time he missed. Every time he turned hot and began to fire, there were more guerrillas, and the SEALs were now only shadows between the rocks. They called to him on the radio, but their calls were garbled. He couldn't understand where the guerrillas were and he began to fire randomly into the nakedness of the hillside.

By now, they had only enough fuel to get back to the base. Waller sent his wingman back and went around one more time. One time to make up for that first pass, though of course there was no making up for it. The hillside was gray. It was too dark to make out the bodies and too light to see the flashes bursting from their weapons. Waller was flying on fumes, now, shooting the last of his ordnance.

In the end, he pulled away.

"Hold out," he called. "We'll send more."

"Thanks, Balls," one of the SEALS called. They were always so calm.

But when the next flight of A-10s arrived, the fight was over. The guerrillas had vanished. Two Blackhawks went in the next morning to pick up the bodies.

Thanks, Balls.

He hadn't stopped flying. A death, a failure, couldn't keep him from that. He'd always wanted to be a great soldier. A great *air* soldier. Why was there no equivalent to "soldier" in the Air Force, anyway? Because of the otherworldly speed of a fighter aircraft, its prophylactic sense of safety? Did they think the seclusion of a cockpit offered the gift of impunity?

It did not.

Slowly, he worked the glider into final approach, his mind focused, the dream not so far behind, billowing on the great wave.

On the ground, he tried the aileron with his hands, poked under it, found nothing. He went to find Rails.

"How'd it go?" Rails looked up from the *Gazette*.

"Great until the left aileron gave me some trouble."

"What's wrong with it?" Rails frowned, coming around the counter.

"I don't know. It was working fine and then it seemed to stick, so I brought it down, and now it seems to be fine again. All the same, better have it looked at."

"Let me go take a look. Do me a favor and write it up."

Waller did the paperwork and went out. There was always paperwork with flying, too much paperwork and usually it came to no use.

Finished, he threw Rails a casual salute and drove down into base. In the cadet area, he parked and walked up through the entrance to his office. He was still tingling with the feeling of flight. The conference room down the corridor from his office was lit, and there were voices inside. Curious, he popped his head in, but what attracted his attention was not the three majors sitting inside, but something out the window, a bit of white rustling from the roof of the library. The majors stood when he walked into the room. He ignored them. He walked to the window. Fastened to the library roof was a bed sheet painted with four black, bold letters.

Waller stared at it. It was a kind of message, but what did it mean?

Chapter Three

When the glider turned toward the runway, Brook jogged back to the road and ran hard down the hill. She slipped back into Sijan Hall, face burning, and quietly trotted up the stairs and made her way down the side of the hallway like a sewer rat.

The showers were running and there was the sweet, damp smell of soap and voices behind the doors, but the only person in view was Mac Cherry, who stood at the end of the hallway calling the minutes to morning formation. She winked secretly at him.

"Hey," Lex said when Brook ducked into the room. The overhead lights washed out the room in a flat, sterile light. "Where you been?"

Brook coughed, her lungs burning from the frozen air. "I saw a glider," was all she could manage.

Lex had already returned from the women's room wearing her ankle-length gray issue bathrobe crossed snugly at the neck, and she was half in her uniform, fastening one end of her shirt garters at the hem of her blue blouse and the other end on the cuff of her black socks. Shirt garters were bands of thick black elastic with clips on either end, and there was no way to look cool wearing them, but they kept your shirt tucked neatly inside your trousers all day without the rumpling folds that attracted demerits.

"Tell Bregs that," she said.

Lex was from Baton Rouge and had skin the color of eggplant. She had a reedy upper body and wide, saddle-flattened hips that were certainly the mark of some genetic curse. She flowed and then flattened like the Mississippi delta. Their uniforms had been cut for the slim, straight bodies of men, and hers had to be tailored extensively. On her desk sat a silver-framed picture of herself in a communion gown, smiling at the side of a minister. The robes gleamed against their skin. Her uncle, she had explained early on. He had died of typhus soon after her communion.

The phlegm was building a bypass across Brook's throat. She offered a muted cough. "I need a shower." Her voice cracked. "Call to minutes is, what—"

At the end of the hallway, Cherry shouted, "Twelve minutes to morning meal formation! Uniform of the day is: blues! topcoat! wheel cap! scarf! gloves! Menu is: scrambled eggs! bacon! oatmeal! orange juice! Twelve minutes to morning meal formation!"

"Go on," Lex said. "I'll do your bed for you. You go over knowledge yet?"

"No time." Her voice was both hoarse and whiny. She stripped down, tossing her clothes into the laundry bag, grabbed her robe from the closet hook, toilet kit from the shelf, closed the door, then opened it again to get her flip-flops. So many loose ends, she thought—all these details are what eat up the day.

"Whatcha got for an article?" Lex asked.

"I don't know. Shit. I don't know." Her skin was still burning from the cold air.

"Here, quick, flip through this," Lex said. She tossed a copy of the *Colorado Springs Gazette* on Brook's bed. *Thirty-six die in car bomb. British Intelligence "ignored" WMD doubts.* Every morning, the smacks had to be prepared to recite a current article from the press. These were not the kinds of stories that could be quoted at the academy, yet it was becoming increasingly difficult to find military stories that could be quoted.

Intelligence chiefs dismissed warnings from their own staff that seri-

*ous doubts had arisen concerning Iraq's chemical and biological weap-
ons capabilities, a former intelligence official told the Hutton inquiry
today.* It was a waste of time reading this—it didn't have the right
tone—but Brook couldn't pull her eyes away. *His testimony comes
as the House of Commons is preparing to debate Hutton findings in the
death of weapons specialist Dr. David Kelly.*

She skimmed the article. It was impossible to grasp its importance. Was this the piece that would prove that the Iraq war was
based on false intelligence, or was it another puff piece? Who was Dr.
David Kelly, and was his death entwined in some deep conspiracy?
Impossible to know. There was no time to absorb all the information
about the war, and she was left with a tremor of fear, a general state
of uncertainty. She couldn't have said how she felt about the war,
and it was perhaps a good thing that nobody ever asked her.

"Ten minutes to morning meal formation—," Cherry shouted.

"Shit." Brook trotted toward the door as Lex knelt down, prayer
style, to pull the sheets taut under her mattress. Even if you didn't
sleep in the bed, it loosened during the night like (as Cadet First-
Class Ragley, their flight commander, had pointed out to them on
more than one occasion) a pretty girl's face with age. Lex worked
quickly, reciting the summary of her own article about the President
visiting a C-5 guard unit in California. The summary had four sen-
tences that were good and long and used dependent clauses and one
quote, and Brook envied her.

In the hallway, a few other cadets dressed in robes and flip-flops,
towels and toiletries tucked under their arms, were making their
morning commute to and from the showers. Passing the men's room,
she heard the sound of running water. One of the firsties was singing
a drinking song. The hallway smelled of soap and dampness.

Three other smacks were standing at attention against the wall
near the CQ desk, where Cherry stood calling out the minutes.
A two-degree was grilling them on knowledge from the *Contrails*
booklet they all had to carry with them. The smacks were reciting
quietly. "*'Without a word, this uniform also whispers of freezing troops,
injured bodies, and Americans left in foreign fields. It documents every*

serviceman's courage, who by accepting this uniform, promises the one gift he truly has to give …'"

They said the words slowly, like a prayer or a chant, where each syllable was rationed an equal stress and significance.

The three-degree, Charlie Basil, corrected them softly. "Like this … *'the one gift he truly has to give: his life. I wear my uniform for the heritage of sacrifice …'"*

The three smacks resumed. *"'I wear my uniform …'"*

Brook shivered, hurrying past, hoping not to be stopped and braced against the wall herself with so little time to spare, and ducked into the relative safety of the women's showers.

All the stalls were empty and wet. She chose the furthest one, pulling the curtain closed behind her. Her eyes stung with early morning fatigue. A faint menstrual nausea swelled in her stomach. She slid out of her robe. There, naked, her body cooling in the chill of the drafty air, she stepped under the water and leaned back against the wall, eyes closed, letting the warm spray run over her. The tile was cold. She turned around and put her palms against it, letting the water warm her back. She'd forgotten her washcloth. She tried the squirt soap, but this was the shower with the broken dispenser. She squeezed a dollop of someone's forgotten shampoo into her palm and ran it over her body. She could hear the echoes of the men talking loudly in the bathroom on the other side of the wall. Someone came into the bathroom and turned on the water in the sink.

"Five minutes," the voice said.

It was Val Burns, the girl on the rugby team who had elbowed her during a scrum the previous day. Brook closed her eyes under the water. She wasn't ready for the Terrazzo. Not yet. In one more minute, she would go. Sixty seconds for her, just her body and the warm water in the seclusion of the shower.

Brook had taken up rugby as a sort of deprecatory challenge. It was the most savage sport she could think of. A gymnast in the early grades, she had strength and a certain mark of grace. She'd been better on the uneven bars and the floor, so-so on the beam. She'd tried hard to conquer on the vault because it had been her mother's event, but the vault eluded her. In the ninth grade, she earned a trophy for "most improved," but then, to her horror, her body exploded in a freakish display of breasts and hips. She grew four inches. She fell from third place to seventh, tossing it in by the end of her junior year. She studied women's magazines with their slimming tips. They said to keep your shoulders up and back—it was supposed to make you appear slimmer, but it always seemed to Brook a gesture that took up even more space, made her appear larger. She developed a slight hunch. At the academy, she resigned herself to rugby, a fitting mockery, but then, surprisingly, she'd grown to like it. She liked the messiness of the game, and she was quick.

"Hey, you coming?" Val called.

"Uh-huh."

"What?"

"I'm coming."

In the room, she dressed in blue pants and blouse, running her fingers over each agonizing button, fastening the shirt garters, grabbing the cap from the top shelf of the closet. What was she missing? Body check, she thought, patting herself. Socks. Shoes. Belt. The *Contrails* handbook. Okay.

"Quick, quick," Lex said, then to herself, like a kind of prayer, "President George W. Bush spoke in California today..."

Brook had concocted a private vow never to quote the President, in subtle protest to what her father called his vulgar dogma. Her father told her that statesmen should be eloquent and unpretentious, and this one was neither. No one at the academy seemed to have noticed. The supremacy of certain things, like God and the Republican Party, were simply taken for granted. One was Right, or one was UltraRight. There were no other options.

Outside, every smack in the wing had lined up on the Terrazzo. Shadows of faces converged. She couldn't make them out, but she didn't have to. She knew where to stand. She knew by feel who should be in her circumference. The morning's breeze rustled the Air Garden honey locust trees into a tepid percussion.

She did a little jig with her knees to keep the blood flowing.

They were all filing out, forming. This was Recognition, the last day of Hell Week. Afterward, they could wear the Corfam shoes that shined without constant polishing, and they would no longer have to run the strips on the Terrazzo, but could walk like regular people, and could wear their prop and wings on their caps to show everyone that they were no longer smacks.

"Look up there," someone said. They turned their heads. There, hanging suspended by ropes from the roof of the library, was a sign, black letters painted on a white sheet—a vague sort of summons that, by its very brazenness, alarmed Brook more than any Hell Week hazing.

WWJD

The second sign this month. Last week, there had been leaflets praising the New Testament in the dining hall. The work of the Cadets for Christian Fellowship—CCF—or the Christ Brigade, as they were known among the nonconformed. To the staff, they were dependable cadets with consistent grades, outstanding military etiquette, and unblemished morals. They didn't smoke or drink. They didn't get arrested for driving under the influence or starting bar fights or sodomizing minors or selling pornography, as some of the cadets in recent years had. They didn't drag the Air Force Academy through the press with scandalous stories. They wore their hair shorn and their uniforms neat. They seemed to have an innate understanding of duty and sacrifice. They met on Friday nights in the chapel, and their meetings were attended by the occasional officer, or even the vice commandant. Their only fault seemed to be a compulsion to express their views rather elaborately around the cadet area. The CCF saw their efforts as a kind of public service, a way of helping their fellow cadets. They whistled their faith cheerfully. The few Muslim and Jewish cadets and the adamantly unaffiliated were welcomed into the light or could simply look the other way and wait for hell to come and collect them.

Brook had never seen such proselytizing. Her family had been quietly Catholic, redeeming their patchy faith with other sheepish

Cape Cod families twice a year, at Christmas and Easter. Brook's father had said it was like reading the first and last chapters of a novel. The heart understood the rest.

But it seemed to Brook that at the academy, the heart had been turned inside out, the contents emptied and inventoried. Found wanting.

Bregs pointed up at the sign, waving slightly in the breeze. "Do you see that?" he said, hands clasped behind his back as he walked among them like some welcome guru. "God is everywhere. You can't hide from Him."

Brook knew the CCF was a kind of mafia. The members were tight. They controlled things. They had influence with certain staff. You were either with them or you left them alone and hoped they did the same to you.

Bregs walked over to Cherry, leaned close to his face.

"Do you believe in God, Cadet Cherry?"

"Yes, sir."

"Do you believe in the almighty power of Jesus Christ?"

"No, sir."

"Why not?"

"Because I'm Jewish."

"You're *Jewish*?"

"Yes, sir."

"Does your father know that?" Cherry's father was a two-star general in the Army. He didn't answer Bregs's question, and Brook awarded him silent points for bravery.

"Get down on your face."

That was the order to do push-ups. Cherry bent down and began punching them out. He was small and he could do them quickly. Bregs left him there.

"Anyone else not believe in Jesus Christ?" He walked slowly around the squadron of smacks, the final twenty-one who would be recognized that night and stood in silent, unanimous thanks that they would never have to suffer Bregs's humiliations again.

"What about you, pretty boy? Do you believe in God?"

It was Billy. She could hear Bregs behind her.

"Yes, sir," he said.

"Jesus is your savior?"

"Yes, sir, He's the man. The blessed King. Footprints in the sand. I don't go anywhere without him."

"Are you mocking the Almighty God?"

"No, sir."

"I hope not."

Bully, Brook thought. She had known bullies. Bullies with freckles. Bullies with thickening guts. Frog squeezers. Drowners of kittens. In grade school, they ruled the hallways and the cafeteria. They'd passed by her or swept her up in their random terror, stealing her hat, pulling her hair, leaving her queasy and shaking. The first one had been Chevas Billard, not long after her mother had abandoned them. Brook remembered him with the freshness of a first lover. He had lunged at her, splattering red paint on her dress, in kindergarten. She'd hated him as she hated Bregs now, with powerless rage.

Cherry was panting. Bregs walked over and loomed above him. Cherry stopped in the upright position and took a deep breath, then he bent down and tried to squeeze one more push-up out of his quivering arms. Bregs put his foot on Cherry's back and pushed him down. Cherry lay flat on the ground under Bregs's foot.

"It gets a lot worse in hell," Bregs said.

Cherry breathed heavily. The rest of them stood perfectly still, as though that were all there was left in the world to do. Finally, Bregs lifted his foot from Cherry's back. Cherry stood, brushed off his uniform, and resumed his place.

Brook watched his shoulders rise and fall. Why did he put up with it—why did *she*, instead of turning abruptly out of formation and walking at a regular, human pace up to her room to gather her clothes in a laundry sack and walk to Arnold Hall and call a taxi? She wondered it all the while they marched to breakfast. She wondered it, dumbstruck, with fury mounting. She wondered it with such ferocity that she thought any moment her body might betray her, give up its rigid roboto walk and turn against the current, move through the tight-knit squadron of cadets like a disoriented fish.

Shouting something disruptive like *Get out of my way! I'm moving, here!* She'd swat at them like flies. She'd go to Arnie's and order a cheeseburger and one of their thick, toxic shakes, and she would say *Fuck you!* to any upperclassman who wandered near.

But her body did not revolt, and she was still wondering why as she and the other smacks served the upperclassmen their meals at breakfast. Bags Ragley, at the head of the table, took orange juice to an inch below the rims with a single ice cube. Dillan Bregs took half orange juice, half pineapple juice, no ice. Brook filled the cups and sat quietly at the table, waiting until each of the upperclassmen was served, before she and the other smacks could feed like hyenas on whatever was left over. The servers rolled carts through the aisles, handing out trays of oatmeal and bacon and platters of buttered toast. It was food that could only be eaten quickly, slurped down with cups of watery orange juice and milk. It was a great source of pride to the academy that they could feed the entire cadet wing in twenty minutes or less.

At Ragley's starboard, two seats down from Dillan Bregs and directly opposite Billy Claymore, Brook perched stiffly on the front two inches of her seat, lifting forkfuls of eggs and hash browns to her mouth at right angles, chewing no more than three times, wondering why she was doing it.

"What's your article today, Cadet Searcy?" Bregs leaned over to ask her.

Lex was farther down the table, listening, but there was nothing she could do to help. Brook had read only one article this morning. She put her fork down and began.

"Sir, as reported on page one of the *Colorado Springs Gazette*, the British House of Commons is investigating suspicions into erroneous intelligence reports concerning weapons of mass destruction in Iraq."

All the upperclassmen at the table, except Ragley, stopped chewing and stared at her. She wanted to stop, to make something up, but there was nowhere else to go. She continued, "A former intelligence officer told the Hutton inquiry that members of MI6 ignored and in some cases distorted intelligence reports that suggested a limited biological and chemical weapons capability in Iraq."

"And do you believe that, Miss Searcy?" Bregs asked.

"Do I believe what, sir?"

"That there are no WMDs in Iraq. That the story was fabricated to give us an excuse to go to war with Iraq."

"I do not know, sir."

"Well, what do you think? Do you think our government would do something like that? Do you think our government would send hundreds of thousands of soldiers to Iraq based on a lie?"

"I do not know, sir."

"You don't *know*?"

Even the smacks had stopped eating and were slewing their eyeballs in her direction, trying to catch a glimpse of the situation and warn her off her current path. Directly across, Billy pummeled her with widened eyes. The only person who took no interest was Ragley, who had been slouching in his chair, constructing an ingenious fountain out of bowls and plates.

"You better start knowing, girlie, if you want to stay here another day," Bregs said.

Brook wanted to tell him that that was precisely what she was considering.

Ragley lifted the pitcher of orange juice and emptied it over the topmost bowl. The juice cascaded down the ledges of plates and flooded into a widening pool on the table. Bregs eyed the spectacle with disgust and turned his attention back to Brook.

"We're talking serious aptitude probation here. We're talking months of sitting in your room writing essays about why you deserve to be a cadet at the United States Air Force Academy."

Brook considered her options. The temptation was overwhelming. So overwhelming it was suddenly laughable. She might simply stand up. Bregs might utterly disappear as an influence on her life. She tingled with the possibility. But still, she didn't move. It was enough, for now, just to think about it.

"Sir, permission to summarize my article," Billy offered.

"Permission denied."

"Go ahead, Billy," Ragley said. Rags nourished an idle hatred for Bregs by doing whatever convenient thing he could to thwart him. Also, he looked forward to Billy's reports, which were usually obscene and disgusting. He had once quoted an article in *Penthouse*, which had earned him seventeen tours on the Terrazzo, one for each spire on the chapel.

"Sir, as reported on page forty-seven of this month's *National Geographic*, juvenile wild elephants prepare for adulthood by stomping through vegetation, tossing their heads, and charging at pretend foes. They run with a loose, floppy gait and raised tails. Males spar with their trunks to test their strength. In the past, female elephants simply waited for them, but the newer breeds of cosmopolitan female elephants have lost interest in male bravado and have discovered they can use their own trunks for autoerotica."

"Bravo," Ragley said.

Bregs's face had turned Yosemite Sam red. He stared hotly at Billy.

"To be honest, sir," Billy continued, "I made that last part up. I don't actually know what female elephants do."

"They come to the academy," came a voice from down the table. Someone made a high-pitched hum, but the upperclassmen let the comment pass.

Bregs began to sulk in his Wheatena. The smacks resumed eating in silence. Billy's report seemed to take the wind out of the morning inquisition. The smacks wily enough to secure seats at the dead end of the table squared their meals in unimpeded bliss.

Brook always forgot to muscle into those coveted seats. The usual smacks had established their places there: Mac Cherry; George Brimmer; Lex Rolstein; Sal Osferos, their Mexican exchange student. The smacks were not allowed to speak unless spoken to. They mushed warily on soft foods: eggs and grits at breakfast, stew and succotash at lunch. They might have been left in peace if a disturbance hadn't erupted on the far end of the dining hall.

One of the smacks, a Kentucky boy, had made it known that he could imitate turkey calls. He'd been instructed to weave through the tables, chased by another smack, evidently pulled at random for this task, who had to hold out his hand and pretend to shoot the turkey every few seconds. Every time he yelled, "Bang!" the first smack had to make a noise that sounded like *bloogebloogebloogeblooge*.

When the spectacle began, the upperclassmen watched the show, cheering for fowl and hunter, but the smacks had to sit in solemn composure, chewing thrice and swallowing.

"Bang!"

"*Bloogebloogebloogeblooge!*"

Brook stared across at the eyes of Billy Claymore. They were blue, light as air, with flecks of green around the iris. Billy stared back at her with equal composure.

"Bang!"

"*Bloogebloogebloogeblooge!*"

Billy's eyes flared momentarily. "*Nice shiner,*" he mouthed. Brook had a purplish welt under her eye from a collision in rugby practice the previous day. She almost cracked, but she clung on despite him. She struggled for a sobering thought. She pictured him on the soccer field, running, dodging, quick on his toes. Not so different from rugby, really. Feet instead of hands. Either way, you had to be quick.

"Bang!"

"*Bloogebloogebloogeblooge!*"

Brook had quickness in her genes, a talent for running. When Brook was four, her mother had walked out of the house and never come back. Brook kept a picture hidden under the smiling socks in her drawer—a foolish gesture, she told herself, that might be uncovered during any room inspection. She'd resolved more than once to move it. The picture was of her mother at a gymnastics competition in the late seventies, in Montreal, right around the time the world had woken up to Nadia Comaneci. Her mother had the Nadia look, small and thin, with a ponytail. She was posing on a thick mat, the horse behind her, in the awkward stance gymnasts took after dismounting, chest thrust out and arms stretching overhead. She had evidently just completed a vault. On the back of the photo, which was gray and stained, were simply the words "Tsukahara 9.75." A world-class vault at the time. Brook wondered if she'd really pulled it off.

As a young girl in Cape Cod, Brook had outclimbed and outdared her older twin brothers. They'd stood back tightly, distrusting her courage. They'd suspected it came from their mother. Unlike Brook, the twins remembered their mother's face, her long arms, saw her reflected in Brook. Her father set the boys on their luxurious path through Harvard and expected Brook to follow. But she had a fatal flaw. In high school, she failed at debate. A stutter caught her tongue at crucial moments. The audience—a cast of potential embedded bullies—bewitched her.

Her father lowered his sights to corporate law. If he knew what happened to their mother, he never let on. Her brothers, twin, content, incurious academics, sprinted through private schools on their way to law study. They would take the bar next year and join their father's practice in Weymouth. *Searcy and Searcy, Barr.* One might have thought, living in their comfortable eighteenth-century home above a cranberry bog, that life was perfect, and not that a woman had disappeared, apparently of her own will. That certain questions needn't be asked. It had been easy for the brothers to let go. Brook had to get out. She had to see for herself.

Which, of course, answered the question of why she was here. Or rather, it answered the question of why she had come. Why she stayed, why she did not adopt some other, less sadistic goal, she couldn't say. Only that this choice seemed so otherworldly, so ripe with the promise of setting her free from the past. *Anything can happen there*, one recruiter had said.

Tsukahara 9.75

Well, Brook had goals, too.

When the hall filled with applause—the turkey shoot had ended—Brook and Billy blinked at each other as if to congratulate themselves on what the academy would call their upright military bearing. Then she shifted her eyes back to the nothingness just beyond the line of his right shoulder and waited to be dismissed.

Chapter Four

The oak and frosted-glass paneled doors to Group Command could be eyed and dreaded from the center stairwell, thirty-four steps and a squared corner from the Terrazzo entrance of Fairchild Hall. Hundreds of cadets, hopeful, woeful, resigned, indignant, had crept toward those opaque doors, etched at the top corners with a pair of diffident-looking lions (the result of a low-bidding contractor), concealing a patch of ominous geography—the commandant's lair. The hallway seemed artificially long, like a Michelangelo stairway. It stretched a hundred feet but seemed, as in childhood nightmares, to span a distance much longer. The cadets called it the blue mile, though the carpet was pinto bean brown and changed every few years, depending on wear.

Through the stately doors, which had drawn silently to a close upon the heels of such visiting statesmen as Senator Strom Thurmond and Senator Barry Goldwater, Captain Kord and Mrs. Purvel presided over the daily struggle for peace and order. Kord managed General Waller's schedule and papers. Mrs. Purvel took messages and set appointments for General Waller and his deputy, Colonel Metz, and she spent a fair amount of time on the phone with her daughter, a young, blond divorcée whose picture reminded Kord dangerously of Pamela Anderson. The daughter, Nicki, worked at TJ Maxx and had just called her mother to discuss in maddening detail the recently delivered stock.

"Does it have a flouncy bodice?" Mrs. Purvel asked. "Why is everything ribbons this year? I just want a nice white blouse. Or maybe a blue one with polka dots. I had one like that in the sixties, and I adored it, but then your father spilled Pepto-Bismol on it one New Year's Eve."

Kord sat fitfully, trying to block out her nasally voice, trying to carry his mind somewhere, anywhere, away from here.

"Yes, I know I've told you that before. And I don't like mock turtlenecks. They make my neck itch. What color is it?"

Sometimes Kord looked at the picture of Nicki, filling out that pale blue sweatshirt while she smiled into the sun, and imagined driving down to TJ Maxx, taking her into the dressing rooms, and nailing her over and over for each of the interminable conversations he'd had to endure.

The oak door opened. Footsteps approached. It was Kord's most vulnerable moment. He listened for clues about the encroacher—tentative footsteps (a student, therefore irrelevant), the swish of stockings (female, open to charm); confident and rushed (most of the self-obsessed staff). He'd trained himself not to glance up when the door opened—it gave too much away. Waller was an eagle-eyed prig whose imposing moral authority got on everyone's nerves, and he had an innate sense for when Kord had been screwing off.

"What's on for the morning?" boomed Waller. Kord resisted the urge to flinch, trained his body to move only at the eyes, lifting toward the general.

"I thought you were out today, sir."

"What made you think that?"

"It's on your calendar. Your daughter's birthday, sir."

"That's later. I've got to see General Long." Waller gestured to Mrs. Purvel. She smiled broadly, waving message slips at him with the phone cocked between ear and shoulder.

"Hold on," she told her daughter, and then cupping the mouth-piece, said, "Civil engineering called. They said there's a sign hanging off the library roof."

"No kidding."

"Again?" Kord asked.

"You didn't see it?"

"I parked up the hill today." Kord knew at once he'd made a mistake. There was no way to fix it.

"Late, eh?"

"I hit the gym early, sir."

"Sure you did. When's CE going to get it down?"

"They're working on it," Mrs. Purvel said over the mouthpiece, and Kord wondered briefly how she got away with it, when he was accountable for every minute.

"Metz in yet?" Waller glanced into Metz's darkened office, the desk as clean and bare as an altar.

"Haven't seen him. Would you like some coffee, sir?"

"If you're going, fine."

There were 143 e-mails in Waller's inbox, another 175 in junk. He grouped them together by sender and then deleted, in satisfy-ing blocks, every cheerful and conscientious public notice from the health, welfare, and recreation division, from a certain secretary who felt compelled to notify the wing of every pizza party and farewell lunch; and from his zealous security officer, a brutish and insolent Neanderthal who was not an officer at all but a civilian thug whom Waller would fire if he had the patience to figure out the paperwork. The rest had to be fingered through individually and deleted by sub-ject heading.

The military online early brief headline read "Explosion Kills Six in Falluja." He paused over that one, absorbing the number. He didn't know Falluja well enough to picture it, to relive it now with the freshly dead. He knew Kuwait and the northern Saudi Arabian city of Dhahran, and he'd flown over Baghdad and other parts of Iraq, but he'd never set foot in that country. His war—the Gulf War—had happened over ten years ago, and already his experience was dated. He offered a brief, wordless prayer, and deleted the message.

The fluorescent light flickered over his desk, cast ghost shadows on the screen. Kord ought to have noticed the light and had the bulb changed, but Kord was not the kind of XO to notice faulty lightbulbs, and Waller refused to point it out to him. Pointing out such things to Kord would only introduce him to an awareness of detail he'd either forgotten or failed to achieve during his own training. It would improve his officership. Waller had no desire to make Kord a better officer. He wanted to make Kord's experience at the academy as miserable and unenlightening as possible so that Kord would put in his papers for separation.

In fact, Kord yearned to get back to flying F-16 fighters, which he'd been lured away from with the assurance that a staff position would increase his chances for promotion. It was clear to him now that the only thing that would increase his chances for promotion was to get back in the cockpit as soon as possible and qualify for instructor pilot. He had a vague but very sincere intention of getting revenge on the flight commander who'd persuaded him to come to the academy. He made it a point to be the worst XO he could be without getting fired so that General Waller would return him to the F-16s as quickly as possible. For a week, he'd noticed the light flickering over Waller's desk, and with growing amusement and pride, he'd failed to offer to replace it.

After deleting the extraneous messages, Waller had twenty-six e-mails left: comments on the new Parent's Weekend slide show at the visitor's center, a request to purchase artwork for the new hallway in Fairchild, some issue—buried deep in a bantering conversation that he finally gave up on—about the junior-officer shifts for snow removal.

And one e-mail from someone called upstandingcadet@hotmail. com, which read:

Dear Sir:

When honor is compromised, the integrity of the whole institution is put at risk. It is your job, and dare I say your calling, to ensure that honor is given its highest mark.

Sincerely,
A concerned cadet

"...if you have faith as small as a mustard seed, you can say to this mountain, 'Move from here to there' and it will move." —Matthew, 17:20

P.S. WWJD

Another WWJD. What did it mean? Who had sent it? He read it again. The words were true enough, but they were phrased as an accusation. The added passage seemed to chide, as biblical quotes often did. It irked him that he didn't understand the message itself and couldn't read anything into it. He had no idea who'd sent it or why. The person—the coward—had not come to his office directly, had not expressed his concerns in specific, manageable detail. This angered him. A pointless message, meant to confuse rather than clarify.

Unless it was a well-known acronym. As a cadet, he had known all the slang acronyms on academy grounds, but as the commandant, he admitted to himself that he might not be as clued in as he thought he was. On a whim, he opened his web browser to Google and typed in "WWJD." He came up with:

What Would Jesus Do? (sometimes abbreviated to WWJD) became a motto for thousands of Christians in the 1990s....

Also:

WWJD...jewelry, CDs, books, sportswear, customizable...secure online ordering WWJD...

Walk With Jesus Daily. 365 days of private meditations...order now...

Kord appeared, his face blank as an elevator door. "Sir, General Long is ready for you," he said.

Waller frowned and stood slowly. The words circled in his mind. He looked up, and his mind swung in a new direction. What *would* Jesus do? Honor had been compromised—it was being compromised all around him. Look at his executive officer, whose indifferent face met everyone who came through the doors of Group Command, who represented him—Waller—with his passive and pathetic deflection of duty. How many times had Waller sent him back with spelling errors on the officer performance reports? Kord was part of that silent mass, that mediocre body of officer corps that drifted along the outer edges of responsibility. It was lucky the enlisted ranks could still be counted on. Without them, the Air Force would have fallen apart.

"You all right, sir?" Kord still hung distractingly in the doorway. Had he, Waller, actually just criticized Kord for missing spelling errors on OPRs? Was that all he could muster in silent defense of honor? Was this what he'd come to? He made himself a silent promise to leave staff duty and get back to a flying unit as quickly as possible.

"Listen," he grunted, gathering his pen and legal pad, and waving his hand upward as he brushed by Kord. "Fix this goddamn light."

Outside, the cadets going back and forth between classes divided before him, passing him in a widening arc, like fish avoiding a barracuda. They saluted smartly and moved along, talking noiselessly, their jackets zipped against the chill. Faces that warded against ridicule, against attention of any kind. Tightened jaws and a resilient curl to the lips. Which one of them wrote the e-mail, and why? There was no emotion in their eyes, no joy, panic, fear, whimsy, hope, but Waller could sense a slight apprehension. He'd felt it, too, as a cadet: a constant, low-level dread of attracting attention, of being called up short to answer for some unforeseen offense.

He'd forgotten his gloves. He clenched his hands to warm them. His knee ached with its accustomed throbbing. Old age was not one big defeating blow. It was a series of small ones.

General Long's office sat in Fairchild Hall, across the Terrazzo from Waller's. This gave the leadership a two-sided glimpse of activities on the Terrazzo, like opposing royalty on a chessboard. He had to walk through all manner of weather for their meetings, but one happy result was that they avoided accidental run-ins. Their meetings were scheduled, their biweekly golf games staged with a collection of rotating senior staff. He preferred it this way. He didn't like her.

He'd wanted to like her. He'd tried. He'd not known many female officers, certainly no commanders. It hadn't bothered him to be working under her, and he'd been relieved to discover this about himself, that he was fair-minded and impartial after all. She'd come through the ranks as an engineer, working in weapons development, and had spent large chunks of her career at the Pentagon. Smart and critical, she'd worked hard, burning through three marriages on her way to becoming the first female three-star general in the Air Force. This ought to have earned his respect and even a bracing admiration. The only thing wrong with her was that she had never been a pilot.

And yet, on warrior days, she wore a flight suit rather than the battle dress uniform worn by ground officers. It needled him. She wore it without the wings she had not earned. She wore it snug, with the tabs cinched tight over her narrow wrists and waist, either not knowing or not caring that pilots wore their bags floppy and shapeless, the tabs loose and the cuffs folded once under the sleeves. She wore it with the knife pocket still sewn on the inside left thigh because she'd never had it ripped off during a drunken night at the officers' club. She might not even know the knife pocket was useless when you strapped on a G suit. If, as a young officer, she had ever walked into an officers' club in a flight suit cinched tight with the knife pocket intact and no wings on her chest, the pilots would have left her alone. They would have known that if they went for the knife pocket, she would have screamed murder.

At any rate, she wore the flight suit on warrior days. At cadet functions and conferences, she took the head seat, and Waller—her "wingman'" as she called him—sat at her right hand. She had, on occasion, drawn him into long conversations about leadership and the Air Force. She spoke with authority. Indeed, at times she seemed to think she knew more than he did.

He hurried along through the Air Garden, by the dwarf honey locusts with their buds closed tightly against the chill. The garden had been installed in the years after he graduated, one tree planted for every graduate who'd died in the Vietnam War. He'd been a cadet in the last years of that war, when the country was licking its wounds. It had been up to the cadets, with their fresh energy and their disdain for the madness of the sixties, to restore the vigor of the academy. They had done it. He'd felt then a kind of purity, a monkishness about the Air Force, to which only certain men were called, and fewer among them could handle it. So the garden was a tribute to him, too.

From the Air Garden, he cut forty-five degrees toward the northeast quadrant. There, on the enclosing wall, was the cadet's oath in burnished steel over the Terrazzo: I WILL NOT LIE, CHEAT, OR STEAL, NOR TOLERATE THOSE AMONG US WHO DO. As a cadet, he had stared at those words, honored them, hated them, believed in them.

But it hadn't gone the way he'd imagined. Pilots no longer controlled the Air Force. It had been a question of honor for man to triumph over space and time. Once, the sky had needed conquering and the pilots had done it, but now the sky was no longer a mystery. The pilots had learned the secrets and the engineers had stolen them. Now, the sky was nothing more than a medium for electronic waves, bursts of light and energy, missiles and unmanned drones controlled from thousands of miles away. How they worked, he hardly understood.

He felt a flatness, as though the old heroes couldn't talk to him.

The engineers wanted victory, but they disdained the sky, preferring the machine. They lusted for technology, but they took it for granted, like the spontaneous fruit of some paradisiacal tree. *He*—and other pilots—had invented doctrine. *He* had taught the engineers what an airplane could do. But then the engineers had taken over—how had they done it?—the engineers and the psychological operations creeps like Colonel Coyle. Together, they had squeezed the art out of fighting wars and turned it into a science.

Someone was hailing him. The head chaplain had descended the stairs across the quad and was hurrying forward.

"General," he said, "I've been looking for you."

"Hello, Chaplain," he called, waving. "I haven't got time right now. I'm off to see the superintendent."

"I'll walk with you, if you don't mind." The chaplain caught up with him, exhilarated. "How are you today, sir?"

"I'm well, thanks. You?"

"It's a marvelous day. Spring is coming." The chaplain, a black man not many years younger than Waller, had the trim body of a runner.

"I suppose."

"I guess you noticed that sign hanging from the library this morning?"

"Hard to miss."

"I thought so, sir. You know my study group, the Cadets for Christian Fellowship. They're very disciplined. They do Bible study groups and community service. But over the last year, there's been a kind of rift within the group. There's a more—I don't want to use the word, radical—a more zealous group that has broken off and begun its own study sessions."

"A splinter group."

"They have, shall we say, more stubborn beliefs. They feel it's their obligation to spread the word."

"And they're doing it, evidently."

"I think I can put the reins on them if you'll give me a little time. I'd like to bring them around the Christian way."

"And not, say, the military way."

The chaplain smiled appreciatively. "I fear that confronting them will only make them more adamant. They haven't done any real harm. Let me try to work with them a little. Let me show them that God works just as well in a quiet voice."

"All right, Chaplain. But please do it quickly. I don't want any more signs or crosses. One of them sent me an e-mail this morning."

"I will, sir. Thank you." He turned and walked back toward the stairs that led to the chapel. Waller had met his family on certain occasions, a lovely wife and four children, happy and polite. They had a kind of wholeness that Waller desired without wanting to work for it. That is, the sacrifice for such wholeness—working reasonable hours, abandoning his run for a second star, giving up his nightly retreats into his biographies (perhaps his only vice, if it *was* a vice)—was not one he was willing to make. He would always provide for his family. That was his promise. But he had ambitions, too.

Waller attacked the stairs and toughened himself for the next battle. He strode past Long's office and into the conference room reserved for high-level gatherings. Her office contained a round mahogany table, suitable for small meetings, but she used it only for special visits from the chief of staff or certain politicians. Otherwise, it sat in a corner, decorated with a vase of fresh flowers, like an ornament.

In the conference room, at one end of an enormous oval table, sitting under a lithograph of an F-4G Wild Weasel, Colonel Metz, wearing starched BDUs that flopped at the arms, leaned over a crumbling doughnut. Waller gave him a passing glance. There was a pitcher of lukewarm water on the table next to a stack of plastic cups. Waller filled one of the cups, gulped it down, filled it again.

"Good morning, sir," Metz said.

Waller sat across from him and grunted in reply. He hadn't expected to see his deputy here and wondered why Long had invited him. Metz was busy contending with the doughnut, trying to get bits of it into his mouth while keeping the rest contained in a pile on a party napkin.

"There are more in the snack room."

Waller looked flatly at him.

"I was in early. I didn't get breakfast."

"You saw the sign, then?"

"Hmm. They went a little too far, didn't they?"

"Who?"

Just then, Susan Long walked into the room, wearing her snug flight suit and smiling broadly. She carried a thermos of ice water. Waller had never seen her drink coffee or eat junk food or have more than two glasses of chardonnay at the occasional Friday-night officers' call. He knew she drank chardonnay, because he'd ordered it for her on several occasions—a beer and a chardonnay—as though he were ordering for a date.

"Sorry I'm late, fellas." The two men made a show of rising before Long waved them down. "Whatcha got for me?"

She was a southern woman, small and artificially blond. She kept herself in shape with Pilates. She had a habit of pressing her lips together while she listened to people. She sometimes grimaced, too, as though trying to get something out of her teeth. She did that now, waiting for either of them to speak.

"Well," Waller said. "I looked into the cheating scandal. I got to the bottom of it, I think. I found the ringleader. There was only one, as far as I know."

"Good. Who is it?"

"Paula Snowe."

Long took in a breath, sat in momentary stillness, and then nodded slowly. Waller admired her composure. He enjoyed it.

"I met with her. We talked for a long while about the incident. She seems utterly unremorseful, even a little proud."

"I see."

"I recommend we expel her and put the others on probation."

"I see."

"She was the ringleader. That was who you asked me to find."

Long nodded, to herself really, and lifted her fingers off the table where she'd been resting them, as a sign for Waller to be silent.

"I foresee a problem," she said slowly.

"Ma'am?" Waller asked.

She opened her mouth, closed it again, considered her words.

"I don't want to sound—what's the word—involved." She paused here, tightened her lips. Waller harnessed a grin, delivered a look of respectable interest. She was, he thought, going to mete this one out carefully. "My concern for the academy supersedes all others. But it is sometimes the most obvious and direct route that, in the end, causes us the greatest amount of trouble. Do you follow?"

Waller said nothing, only notched up two insolent brows. Long looked at her nails—newly manicured, squared at the tips, and painted fire-engine red—and let them fall on the table with a sound like the chamber emptying on a .22-caliber gun. Did she paint them herself, Waller wondered, or did she go somewhere? And why that color? It didn't suit her hands, which were bony and flecked with age spots. Was it a sort of defiance, an insistence on flaunting her femininity? Or a sign of power? It was surely not for her own pleasure. Susan Long did nothing purely for pleasure.

Metz was glaring at him, imploring him silently to see reason. Even a general officer ought to know his place in rank—this was what Metz would be thinking. Only a pilot would be so crass.

"Let's look at it this way," Long said. "We're promoting a Culture of Transformation." She used the phrase "Culture of Transformation" because General Beddle, the chief of staff of the Air Force (CSAF), had used it with her. He had used it twice last spring during a conversation over a mug of oily black coffee while they sat in his Pentagon office with the tall, sunlit windows overlooking a park. He had paused when he said it to her, and she paused now when she said it to Waller.

She was considering her words carefully because she knew more than Waller about how to run an institution like the Air Force Academy, but she needed Waller to be on her side. The problem was that she could see his side of it. Probably the girl *was* guilty. Of course he would want to throw her out. But he'd not been with Long in the Pentagon office of the CSAF during the height of the rape scandal when *that* general had asked her to use a gentle hand on the corps of the Air Force Academy. Beddle had been inclined to think she was the right person to lead the academy through a Culture of Transformation, and she had been inclined to believe him. The fact that

Senator Jan Snowe had telephoned the secretary's office earlier that week to suggest that General Long might be the right choice for the superintendent's position did not come up during the conversation. Long knew the position was a stepping stone to a fourth star. She also knew that no other woman had ever earned four stars in any branch of the military. There was a great deal in the conversation with the CSAF that was not spoken but was understood.

"Listen, John, you've worked hard on this. I know it. I'm only asking you to—what's the word—prioritize."

"I'm trying to prioritize, ma'am. The honor code is my number one priority."

Long nodded that she understood, appreciated. A man would have given Waller his marching orders and dismissed him. But Long prided herself on her patience, her air of deference. She would rather coax an allegiance than be heavy-handed. It gained you more in the long run. She wasn't impeded by ego, a constant need to prove herself. Waller was a fighter pilot who, like all fighter pilots, flattered himself for being dispassionate and fair. But like the others, he clung to a certain order, a certain conviction that even reason could not uproot. Which was: Men made better pilots, and better pilots made better leaders. It was an old belief, and full of myth. Long had known hordes of these pilots, worked and battled with them, been marginalized by them, and eventually passed them on the promotions list. Waller was no threat to her.

"Mine, too, John," she said. "But I come at it from a different angle. I'm trying to create a culture."

"A Culture of Transformation," he echoed. It pleased him that she couldn't bring herself to call him Balls.

"That's right. It's a whole movement. It's a revolution in military education. The CoT will change the way people think. It undercuts the usual assumptions. No more sexual politics. No more minority-majority propaganda. It's so simple, it's brilliant. Sil did up a great PowerPoint presentation."

She motioned toward Metz, who nodded vigorously. Long

paused, twisting on her widow finger the ruby ring that had been a gift from her third husband.

"The point is that Paula Snowe is a perfect candidate, a perfect case study for CoT. We can help her. We can *transform* her. And she, in turn, can help transform us. Do you see?"

Waller did not see, but he held back from saying so. Metz watched the interplay but said nothing. He was learning a great deal from General Long.

"It's not a smooth transition," she added. "It takes work and compromise."

"With all due respect, ma'am, this has nothing to do with transformation or sexual politics or whatever you want to call it. She cheated on a test. She violated the honor code."

"But why did she cheat, John? Tell me that. Why did she cheat? What forces at work under the surface led her to compromise the values she believed in?"

He realized then that this was one battle he was going to lose. They could talk about the end of sexual politics, but once they mentioned forces under the surface, implying certain injustices that a certain minority of the Air Force had for too long believed had been dealt them, and once you started making statements either directly or indirectly to a member—especially a senior-ranking member—of that minority, you were headed into hell's wide jaws.

"Believe me, John, Paula Snowe's no charity case. When it's her time to go, I'll be the first to say it. I'll be the first one to send Paula Snowe packing."

He ought to have known the moment he walked in and saw Metz. Metz was there to be a witness to something, this visionary stand of hers, so that he could repeat it to the press one day, probably, or to some biographer. Maybe she was going to put it in *her* memoir.

"What would you like me to do now?" he asked.

"Good question," she said. "We still have to do something, don't we?"

"Why don't you talk to Colonel Coyle?" Metz suggested. "I'll bet he's got some ideas."

"Good idea, Sil," Long said. "Coyle will think up something clever."

Waller wanted to say that he'd already talked to Coyle. He'd done it before Long and Metz had gotten involved, and now they were back to the same plan he'd concocted in the first place.

The meeting ended shortly afterward. Metz stopped Long in the doorway to ask about Lieutenant General Holly, who had been planning to visit for some time. Bud Holly had been Waller's supervisor and friend at the Fighting Fifty-third in Alamogordo, and normally, hearing his name from his deputy would have caused him to stop and listen. It wasn't that Waller was possessive of Bud—he was a three-star general and bound to have other connections here. Waller would call Bud later himself. He yearned to discuss his future possibilities, but he was in no mood to linger with Long and Metz at that moment and, without excusing himself, walked out in a funk.

He pushed through the fire door, stewing over Long's touchy-feely, let's-all-be-nice approach to Snowe's clear violation of the honor code, which he saw as a grave transgression from his responsibility as commandant, which was to teach the cadets how to fight a war. How was he supposed to train professional airmen if the rules were negotiable?

The sign above the library had been removed, and the noon meal parade was forming on the Terrazzo. It revived him a little. The squadrons assembled in their neat blue rows. The staff officers, captains and majors, watched intently from the sidelines. They saluted him as he approached.

"Afternoon, sir."

"How's the wing today?"

"It's a fine Air Force day."

Waller smiled. This was spoken by a Marine officer, Major Wein of the Thirty-second "Warthogs." He wore crisp BDUs that were folded neatly over his biceps. He was a helicopter-pilot exchange from Parris Island. Waller liked him a great deal.

They spoke for a moment. The squadrons were being graded today, and the marks would count toward off-base privileges. They were in fine form, waiting for the adjutant's call. Four thousand cadets stood in grids on the Terrazzo. Waller breathed in the cool air. All was quiet and still. When the colors went by, he stood at attention with the rest of them, watching the tight line of cadets move slowly and carefully past. They held the flagpoles in their white-gloved fists. The American flag ruffled in the breeze. Its crisp, bright colors sang glory against the dull blue lines of their service coats. The eye could not help but forgive old wounds, extol unfought victories. Waller watched it pass. It gave hope and fortitude, like the beat of a heart.

Following the colors came the squadrons in a row. They stepped forward and moved down along the corps, sparking the inevitable chain, a match being struck and slowly coming alight.

Yet how sweet the sound along the marching street of drum and fife, and I forget the wet eyes of widows, and the whole dark butchery without a soul.

It had always been the same, since the first great armies of Rome.

They marched along but then, dismissed some twenty steps from the chow hall, dissolved into a formless mob waiting to squeeze through the doors into the dining room.

Waller always felt a slight disappointment at this moment, as though the whole parade had been a ruse and not, as he saw it, a tribute to the great soldiers of history. A group of soldiers could be summed up instantly by their marching skills. It was the most fundamental discipline, from which everything else sprang. Its lessons on teamwork and order and attention to detail were not so much learned as absorbed. They took root in the body first, before flowering in the mind.

Or they never took root at all.

Chapter Five

Brook still had no answer to her question by the time classes were over and she was walking briskly down the hallway of Sijan Hall, her shoulder skimming the white wall, to borrow a can of Kiwi polish from Cherry and Billy. She'd been so lulled into the urgency of every moment's spurious demands that she was beginning to wonder whether she had some kind of passivity complex and would spend the rest of her life being cannon-shot between one tragicomic humiliation and the next.

"That eye is just a beaut," Billy said in the doorway. He hinged the door at ninety degrees and stepped back to let Brook enter.

Inside, Mac Cherry sat cross-legged on the nylon carpet in camouflage pants and a black T-shirt, scrubbing the side of a boot with a bristle brush. The room smelled of wax and floor polish and brass cleaner. Billy had run cold water from the sink into the tin cover, and he dipped fresh cotton balls into that and rubbed it in tiny circles across the wax. Billy had fantastic boots. The toes and heels were so glossy that he could view with narcissistic clarity the reflection of his blond hair and solid cheekbones. Brook settled in next to him. Their splayed legs made a pattern of browns and greens under the fluorescent light. Brook swiped a cotton ball across the tin of wax and rubbed a tornado of glossy circles across her boot.

"Glorious week I'm having," Cherry said without looking up. "Must have polished my boots seventeen times. Done two thousand push-ups. Made my bed twice a day—a bed I don't sleep in, mind you. Scraped smeared toothpaste off the window with a razor. Frozen toothpaste feels like chalk—I didn't know that until yesterday. Cornered Ragley's pet ferret in the men's room. Foul bastard bit me on the thumb. And lost my frigging glove."

"You should keep two sets," Billy said. He stood and leaned toward the mirror over the sink, running a dry razor over his jaw.

"You'd probably steal 'em like you stole my first pair."

"Why would I do that?"

"'Cause you're a lying rat."

"A sniveling rat," Brook corrected.

"That, too."

"At least I'm not a Jew," Billy said. "Jesus Christ."

"You can say that," Cherry said.

Brook preferred it here. Back in her room, Lex was humming quietly, intent on her own small accomplishments.

"You heard about Paula Snowe?" she asked, to break into things.

"Hmm," Cherry said. "Another lying cow."

"Don't call me a cow," Billy said to the mirror.

Cherry soaked a cotton ball in the water and rubbed it against the heel of his boot. His mouth hung open slightly, his tongue resting on his lip. There was a sweet smell on his skin that hung under the scent of the boot polish.

"They're not going to throw her out," Brook said.

"Oh, stop the press. What a surprise," Billy said.

"But it was an honor violation," Brook said. "Why wouldn't they throw her out?"

"Oh, Brook, you're so sweet and innocent," Billy said. "So much like the Madonna herself."

"That's nice of you," Brook said. "Do you think you could write that in a note to Bregs?"

"He might try to crown you," Cherry said.

"Ignorant Jew," Billy said. He turned each cheek to the mirror

81

one last time and then sprawled between them on the floor.

"Which Madonna are we talking about?" Cherry said. "I thought Madonna *was* Jewish."

He kept polishing. Two bones stuck out of his shoulders, showing through his shirt, where muscles should have been. He had a pointy face and sickly white skin. The name Cherry so ill-suited him that the cadets called him that out of irony. Or they called him "the virgin," which everyone suspected he was.

Brook could smell the chalky soap and shaving foam on Billy's skin. She could smell everything: the wax, the stale odor of too many bodies in one place, old sweat and dust mixed with the pungent sting of ammonia and brass polish.

"Why did you put up with it this morning?" Brook asked Cherry. It felt both good and scary to have her question out in the open. "Why do we all put up with it?"

Cherry suddenly stopped polishing and turned to Brook. "Don't worry about Bregs. Don't waste your time."

"He's a fanatic," Brook said.

"He's a goat. He's the apotheosis of all that is common and crude. He's a collection of prejudices and slogans and other mind clutter."

"Mind clutter," Billy said. "This whole place is mind clutter."

"Do you know why he's so stupid?" Cherry asked. "Because he never thinks of doubting himself."

Cherry wanted to be a pilot more than anything else in the world. They were all going to be pilots if they got their way, except for a particular few who were disqualified for medical reasons and had to settle on futures in engineering or medicine or law. But Cherry wanted it with everything he had. They knew how badly he wanted it because he never talked about it. He endured everything, even his father, and didn't talk about it. As a captain, Cherry's father had fallen in love with a French girl named Marshe. Marshe was Jewish. She had married him on the condition that all of their children, who turned out to be Mac, were raised Jewish, and this had not seemed like an unreasonable condition at the time. Cherry loved his mother and respected his father, knowing that love and respect were different things. They reciprocated in kind, and he endured that, too, without talking about it.

"Imagine fucking Bregs in pilot training," Billy said.

"Who said anything about *fucking* Bregs?" Cherry asked.

"He'll never make it outside this place," Billy said. Brook wasn't so sure. She saw him down the road, at future assignments, as Brook's flight commander, the officer in charge, calling her *girlie*.

"Someday, he'll wander into a live fire zone and wind up as somebody's frag," Billy said. "Mine, I hope."

"I admire your cold-bloodedness, Claymore," Cherry said.

"You should work at it," Billy said.

"Listen," Cherry said, leaning over to Brook so that she had to look up and look into his eyes, which were bright hazel, like an overcast sky. "Bregs is not your problem. You are. Be true to yourself. Focus on that. Be true to *yourself*."

"Don't start that shit, Cherry. There's a secret to this place. Learn that, and you're golden. It's all you need to know."

"I can't wait for this," Cherry said.

"Keep your uniform clean, keep your hair cut, look the officers in the eye when they talk to you. Do that, and you can get away with anything." Billy was toying with his boots. He never seemed to polish them.

"How do you get your boots so shiny?" Brook asked.

"Karma," Cherry said.

"You've got too much wax," Billy said. "Here, rub some of it off."

He handed her a rag and Brook began to rub the wax off her boots. "I've heard you can light a match over your boots to make them glossy," Cherry said.

"Care to try?" Billy said.

"Sure. Hand me your boots."

Brook went to the sink and threw out the cotton balls and the water, and then she dried the tin cover with a paper towel. Muffled voices arose from each end of the hallway. Marty Pride, another smack, passed by, hugging the opposite wall, his mouth fit and his eyes masked with resolve. He was a strange one, had never set in with the other smacks. In return, they had sniffed weakness, looking the other way when the upperclassmen abused him. Brook felt a momentary elation just being inside a room. The hallway meant trouble. A smack might be braced up and grilled on Knowledge or be made to suffer any number of humiliations. She was no safer inside a room. An upperclassman could invade at any time. But they all took refuge in numbers. Smacks kept in tight packs, like dogs.

Brook stood at the sink scrubbing her hands.

One, two, three, four, five.

Once I caught a fish alive.

Six, seven, eight, nine, ten.

Then I let it go again.

Why did you let it go?

Because it bit my fucking finger so.

Which fucking finger did it bite?

This middle finger on my right.

By this time in the day, she could not keep the jodies from jitterbugging through her head. They hopped and swirled around her with their iambic doggedness, try as she might to sweep them out.

Mind clutter. At least it kept the questions at bay.

Late afternoon, they all found themselves in athletic gear, braced against the cement wall of the squadron corridor. Bregs stood at the top of the column like a missionary among savages, commanding them to pray. Brook had no choice but to lower her eyes. She was tired, with the kind of tiredness that will submit to anything. Seven months in training, and now one final ceremony and they would be Recognized. There was a vaguely sweet sound to it, as though all the abuse, all the drilling and shouting of three-fourths of a year could be suddenly erased.

"'Yea, though I pass through the valley of the shadow of death—'"

Brook tried to focus. It seemed important in these last official moments of smackdom to submit. Why not? She had come this far. Why not pray for strength, for humility? The tile floor had been overwaxed and gleamed dully in the industrial light. Sets of black boots lined her peripheral vision in both directions, varying in depth of shine. Billy's gleamed with the luster of gunmetal. Bregs murmured on. The pronouncements, the aphorisms, never ceased. She had learned to memorize them quickly, recite them with convincing vigor. And here was her reward.

Rec.og.ni.tion: an acceptance as true or valid; acknowledgment.

After the prayer, upperclassmen prowled the hallway, not just Bregs, but all of them, sniffing at their uniforms, snarling orders. Brook was ordered by a two-degree to march up and down the hallway bellowing the Air Force song. She set off as though it was a perfectly natural request, singing out loud, peering into the rooms as she marched along. In one room, an upperclassman was teaching Sal Oseferos how to play a game he called Mexican jukebox. The upperclassman dropped a quarter in the closet, and Sal, locked inside, had to sing *La Cucaracha*. She passed two cadets reciting the Gettysburg address. Others were in grueling poses like "sitting" with one's back against the wall, "standing" in push-up position until one's arms trembled. Val Burns was trying to balance a lacrosse stick on her chin. Brook thought: crazy is relative.

The hallway rang out with historical speeches, military hymns, rote answers to essential questions.

How many spires are on the academy chapel?

Seventeen, sir!

None of it made sense. None of it had to.

They bumped and collided, ran crab races in the corridors, sang and shouted, working themselves into a hysterical entropy. The body reduced to an exhausting series of commands. High-knee sprints down the corridor. Every floor of the dorm churned out an ocean of noise, a frat party on steroids. Brook gave herself over to it, let herself be an object of random will.

Hollering: *Off we go, into the wild blue yonder, riding high into the sun. Here they come, zooming to meet our thunder. At 'em boys, give her the gun!*

Why was she doing this?

Rec.og.ni.tion.

From lithographs on the wall, the faces of famous fighter pilots smiled down at her.

The smacks changed clothes six times in forty minutes, bursting into their rooms and clawing through their closets in an avalanche of polyester, dressing and appearing half buttoned in the hallway, appeasing their superiors, only to be told to change clothes again. The body endured. That was the point. They were intent on breaking you down. Breaking you down and building you up again. Would she feel it, the point of collapse, or would the transition simply take her, she thought, the way faith takes the gullible?

Ragley's pet ferret had gotten loose and scampered under her legs and down the hall. Its name was Dodger, and it had belonged to another first-class cadet before being handed down to Ragley. It was the squadron's triumphal mascot, having survived countless no-notice inspections and one long weekend locked in Major Wein's office with a bag of pellet food. It was every smack's responsibility to make sure the ferret was fed and exercised. Brook watched it disappear into the men's room. Later, she thought, someone would find it cowering in the corner of a toilet stall and return it to the cardboard box in Ragley's closet.

In an alcove by the CQ desk, Bregs had Mac Cherry braced against the wall with his legs bent, as though sitting in an invisible chair. Bregs held a thick stack of books, placing one upon another on Cherry's thighs. He was ordering Cherry to do something, shouting in his ear, but Cherry stared straight ahead, his back rigid against the wall, chin jutted out and nostrils flaring like an anxious horse. Bregs took another book and placed it on Cherry's legs. He twitched, steadied himself. Brook edged closer to them, turned her head to hear what Bregs was yelling, but she caught only pieces of it. Cherry trembled under the weight of the books, lips wet with bubbling spit, eyes hot with some primal emotion.

Above him hung a lithograph of Captain Lance Sijan, for whom Sijan Hall had been named. An F-4 pilot in Vietnam, he'd been shot down, his legs broken on a steep fortified hillside in North Vietnam, hiding without food or water for 42 days—she'd memorized how many days, would remember it for the rest of her life—and eventually, he was captured, or his story might have been lost. Some fellow pilots had caught up with him in a POW camp. He was beaten to a bloody bone for refusing to answer the interrogators' questions, and once for flipping the North Vietnamese guards the finger. Soon after, he died of pneumonia in the cold, fetid water of his cell.

Which fucking finger did it bite?

This middle finger on my right.

There were hundreds of hero stories, but this one had stuck with her.

She was still watching Cherry, watching for the moment he would collapse from the weight of the books, when Bregs saw her. He turned away from Cherry without another word and ordered her to report to her room. She followed him and stood at attention by her bed, as was the procedure.

Bregs opened her drawers and began to fling her folded T-shirts on the floor. She could only watch him and calculate the time it would take to reorganize her room.

He tore her room apart. She was getting used to it by now. The first intrusion hurts, but after a while, they blend together in one seamless, comic disaster. Bregs was meticulous. She could say that. All her socks unraveled, strewn on the floor. T-shirts, blouses, pants. It was amazing how much stuff one had, even in a place as hermetic as this.

"Tell me about the dawn of flight," he commanded.

"Sir, although history records man's dreams of flight in myth and legend from ancient times, two French brothers, Joseph and Etienne de Montgolfier—" he pulled her blouses off the hangers, kicked her shoes across the floor. "—launched the first modern hot air balloon—"

All of it strewn on the floor. Sock garters, nylons. He left the bras and panties fastidiously untouched—this, she thought, was the irony of the academy, that such an assault on one's room might carry the air of propriety. Hats, jackets, shoes. The human body was so dependent on the mere trifle of elements. All of it down. All this undoing of what's done. He seemed gleeful. What could she do but watch?

Let him go. Let him go on and on. Once the initial trespass is made, the rest is only procedure.

He was tossing socks over his shoulder like something in a comedy skit, and then he paused, lifting something from the drawer. Then he lifted the picture of her mother from the drawer and examined it.

"Ah," he said. "What's this?"

A picture, she wanted to say. But she stood, watching the tedious process of reason unfold inside his cramped and inadequate brain. She knew she should be angry, or scared, but she was too tired for that. Her nerves had gone numb. Why not? was all she thought. Why shouldn't Bregs be the one to find the picture of her mother?

"I don't know, sir."

And now she'd told a lie. A little lie, but what did that matter in a place like this? A lie was a lie, and she'd told one. Maybe this was the end, after all. She felt fate steeling itself around her, but she was too tired to be afraid.

"You don't know? You sure?"

She'd have told another lie, but she couldn't think of one.

"Awful strange," he said. "Having a photo in your socks and not knowing who it is."

She hardly ever looked at the photo, but she kept it with her like a sort of dark icon, reminding her that she lived in the shadow of some past offense, some blunder she'd committed as a toddler that had sent her mother out of their lives. It made no sense, no one had ever agreed, but her heart knew it to be true. It was so crucial at the academy to be normal, to be unshakably sane, and yet here it was, in her past, this glimmer of madness.

And now Bregs, the exemplar of madness, held the picture in his fingers. It was nothing personal. Brook knew that. Just a random strafing of a cadet's life. Something like pain rose in her chest, but she ignored it.

"Go on," she said. "Take it."

"It's that kind of arrogance," he said, with a softness cultivated for moments like this. "That kind of arrogance that leads me to—" He shrugged, flicked the corner of the picture against his knuckles. It didn't much matter what he said next. What mattered was the stage he'd created, the anticipation. Whatever followed would lead from that moment, whatever he selected out of thin air, she would remember.

But as he began to speak, Paula Snowe appeared in the doorway, having just returned from her second, and more satisfying, discussion with the commandant. She paused, took in the destruction. The hallway had been chaos, the new cadets in their final hour of hazing. It was idiotic. A bestial hazing ritual that served those in control more than the cadets it was supposed to serve.

"What is this, your little mock interrogation?" she sneered at Bregs.

"Haven't they thrown you out yet?" He turned and faced her, his face reddening again in its spectacular, unabashed way.

"You're a fucking idiot. I can't believe no one's figured that out." She was a petite girl, a pretty girl, her hair bobbing pertly in a ponytail. The words didn't seem to fit. Brook tried to put the picture together. Cute but fierce. A kind of Odyssean paradox.

"Get out of here," he shouted. She gave him one quick, disgusted laugh and walked past him into the room.

"Why do you let this idiot treat you this way?" she said to Brook.

"What choice do I have?"

"He's a moron. He has a power complex. He's afraid someone will learn his little secret."

Brook stood at attention, but the pose seemed ridiculous now. She ought to do something. Should she come to parade rest? Sit on her bed? There was no guide in the *Contrails* handbook for this. It was extraordinary how the mind so eagerly relinquished control of the self to a list of categorical options.

"Don't you get it?" Paula asked. "You better get smart, quick."

Paula had turned to glare again at Bregs. She noticed the photo he was holding.

"Give it back," she said.

"What?"

"*What*," Paula mocked. "The fucking picture. Give it back to her."

"What's it to you?"

"Do it now," Paula said. Brook envied her nerve. To her surprise, Bregs cast the picture down. He'd meant to throw it on the floor, but it caught the air, floated harmlessly to the corner of Lex's bed. He stared at Paula the whole time.

Paula turned to Brook. "You better learn the game, honey. You better learn how to hide."

Then she bullied Bregs out of the room. Lex, who had walked in during the confrontation with a substance that looked like cough syrup oozing down the left side of her face, took the picture from the desk and handed it to Brook. Brook fingered the curled edges, tried to straighten them.

"What was that all about?" Lex asked.

"I wish I knew."

In a ruthless, final binge, the smacks were ordered to gather outside with the firsties. When they'd assembled, they all set off trotting across the Terrazzo to Cathedral Rock. The traditional run, smacks and firsties, while the middle classes waited behind. The sign on the library had been taken down by now, but nobody noticed. Nobody cared. Nobody remembered how Cherry had been humiliated on the Terrazzo only hours ago. Brook buried her chin in the scratchy brown lip of her zip-up undershirt. Her boots felt heavy. They ran up the stairs by the chapel. The sidewalk veered around to Arnold Hall. Already they were huffing, grunting. She hopped the curve, and they were on the road, pushing back the cold and the raw ache in their ankles. The air burned their lungs like menthol, thin and brittle. At least she was out of the dorms, away from the smell of close living. The air out here was pure. She inhaled again. Pure. Her breath began to even out. Her vision narrowed in a way that didn't alarm her. It was simply ridding her of excess. She needed only to see the long road in front of her, the next mile, and then the next.

The clap of boot steps reverberated on the road. Patches of lingering snow glowed like white rabbits in the dusk.

"*Hut two,*" someone yelled. "Come on."

A two-mile run, uphill. Time began to spread out. Brook listened to the boot steps, let the rhythm dispel pain and exhaustion. Her calves complained. She forced them to be quiet. Pushed the road under her like a giant wave.

Someone sang out:

> *Ma, Ma, Ma, Ma, look at me.*
>
> *What the Air Force done to me.*
>
> *A RUMP titty RUMP titty RUMP titty RUMP*
>
> *Took away my Michelob,*
>
> *Got me drinkin' H_2O*
>
> *A RUMP titty RUMP titty RUMP titty RUMP*
>
> *Took away my old blue jeans*
>
> *Got me wearin' nasty greens*
>
> *A RUMP titty RUMP titty RUMP titty RUMP*

Let the left leg take over. Let it rule the body.

A RUMP titty RUMP titty RUMP titty RUMP.

Right leg now. Let the left leg take the unstress. Brook's ears rang faintly. Exhaustion settled in strange places, the eye sockets, the throat. She'd forgotten to change her Tampax. A dampness collected between her legs. She'd have to scrub her panties in the sink tonight.

They ran, forgetting there was any other thing in life. Their feet forgot it was possible to stop. They forgot their pasts, their futures, pain, hunger, color, joy, fear, and thought only of running. When they reached Cathedral Rock, they turned and ran back.

When they returned, their rooms had been cleaned. Everything had been folded and replaced in its proper drawer, their blues laid out neatly on their beds, the forbidden Corfams placed on the floor. The smacks stared in exhausted wonder. They were ordered to report to the hallway for inspection. The smacks dressed, glowing with secret hope, and assembled quietly.

"No corrections!"

Words they had dreamed of. The sheer thrill of a satisfactory mark.

The firsties went around and handed out the prop and wings. Ven Gladstone, whom everyone called Seven, was walking down the line delivering handshakes and passing out the pins. Brook waited her turn. Though it was not Ven but Paula Snowe who presented her with the pin.

"I'll take care of you," she said. "Don't worry. I don't bite."

They mingled in the hallway, patting each other on the back as though it had all been an elaborate game. Even Bregs shook Brook's hand. She shook his back dumbly, as though it had all been an amusing prank.

Above, the words on the corridor wall said:

> INTEGRITY FIRST.
> SERVICE BEFORE SELF.
> EXCELLENCE IN ALL WE DO.

The next evening, after the air officer commanding, Major Wein, had left for the spring break, several new upperclassmen from the Thirty-second Squadron "Hogs" broke into his office, rubber-cemented his wheel cap and extra shoes to the closet shelf, and left a two-pound bass on the radiator.

Chapter Six

Spring break. An added warmth in the air. Brook left the receding chill of Colorado and went home to the house on the cranberry bog. New England was soggy and brown, weary from winter.

The house smelled of old, brittle plaster that made Brook think instantly of plaster of paris and rubber cement, construction paper and blunt-tipped scissors, the cumbersome building tools of elementary school. She followed her father into the darkened hallway where he lit a yellow lamp by the stairs.

"There."

She stood with a single regulation black duffel slung over her shoulder. She'd refused to surrender it to her father at the airport and he'd shrugged, sinking his hands into his pockets, confounding, she supposed, all his ideas about women who travel. He'd walked on her left, which was all wrong, and she'd had to resist the urge to scuttle around to the other side of him so that he could walk in the senior position. Now she stood in the doorway, forcing back the disagreeable and senseless image of papier-mâché and other childhood artifacts.

"Care for a beer?"

"I would," she said, a little surprised. "Where's Max?"

Her father flipped a trail of switches on his way to the kitchen and disappeared into a tunnel of light.

"Probably sleeping by the radiator," he called. "A couple of times a day, he perks his ears up and yelps. I think he's dreaming of squirrels."

"Is he totally blind?"

"Depends on what you mean by totally."

"Ah, the lawyer speaks."

She dropped her bag by the stairs and crept slowly through a broad doorway into the darkened library, trusting that the sofa and high-backed chairs and lamp tables were still fixed as she remembered. A wall clock her mother had brought from Montreal decades ago clucked away, metering out the uncanny silence of her father's life.

"Max," she called softly, clicking her tongue.

"The vet says he sees light. And he migrates along with the sunny spots on the floor. But he still bumps into chairs and walls. So is he blind? I suppose so. And yet, if that's the case, it can't be said that to be blind means that one cannot see."

She reached Max, gently thumping his tail on the floor, and crouched beside him. "I see you haven't lost your enchantment with contradictions. Perhaps he just senses the warmth."

"You see, Brook?" He stood in the doorway, edging the light on with his elbow while holding two glasses of beer. "You should have been a lawyer."

"I couldn't," she says. "I've recently learned that I'm not a good liar."

She stood and ran her fingers over her favorite sections of the library. All the books on New England had torn, subdued covers, like seaside cottages, as though they'd personally weathered the seasons and lived to tell about it.

"So how are you liking it?" He handed her a glass and stood by her, straightening the book spines on an upper shelf idly with his thumb.

"Liking it?" She laughed. "Nobody likes it."

"Nobody?"

"Only a few."

"Not you, though."

"No." And then, "It gets better."

"So you're going to stay."

"Did you think I wouldn't?"

"I didn't know. I still don't."

"No, Counselor, I guess you don't."

She raised her glass to him. The beer tasted good.

"Sit," he said, moving toward the brown sofa in the center of the room. "Sit with me."

Her brothers hadn't yet arrived. This she had expected. What she had not expected was that, upstairs, her bed would be turned down, the fresh linens tucked delicately back, three towels lain at the foot of the down comforter. It was a touching display of her father's loneliness. She unzipped her bag on the floor of her bedroom. The room was cold, sitting at the north corner of the house. It reflected, she thought, her mother's idea of what a young girl's room ought to look like. Red-and-white-gingham curtains laced the two windows on the north and east walls. White wallpaper with small delicate outlines of something that might be a little girl in a frock or might be a squirrel climbing a tree. The bed was tucked into a corner nook of the room, surrounded by white bookshelves and scattered with an assortment of striped and checkered pillows. There was a rocking chair in another corner with cushions of a similar design. A cold, beautiful room.

Brook lay down in the bed her mother had conceived, and it occurred to her for the first time that the room had not been designed for her—Brook—at all, but for her mother. Perhaps it was the kind of room her mother would have liked to live in. It was not, after all, the kind of room suited for a child of three. There were too many delicate objects, too many hazardous shelves. Had Brook been sleeping here when her mother left? She couldn't remember, and it was not something she could ever possibly ask. Fathers drink and are commonly absent, but mothers never leave—this was the lesson she understood early on from girls who dragged their mothers to every occasion, who consulted them on issues of dress and behavior, even as they raised their eyes and feigned impatience. Dates, proms, shopping trips. It mildly irritated Brook, all the flurry of belonging and acceptance. Because that's all it was, really. A social contract between members of the same apprehensive tribe.

Brook wanted none of it. Her life was cool and quiet. Her brothers were the most sentimental of the family. They'd taken it the hardest when she announced she was going to the Air Force Academy. They'd been frightened and appalled at first, but then they'd simmered down to mere chiding. Her father had gone out and bought her sturdy luggage. What would her mother have done, fussed or crooned, bragged or begged her not to go? Either way, it would have been a nuisance. Femininity was just one big, synthetic hassle, physically draining, hazardous to the ozone. Her mother had gone off into the world. Belin was her name, an odd kind of name. Brook had never known anyone else to have it.

She wanted to tell her mother, to assure her, that she, in fact, had made it. She'd been recognized. *Rec.og.nized.* The words tumbled through her head. She had made it and could afford to toss a salute to her mother from those depths. Heights. She was getting sleepy. Could wave to her from that distance, alone and in the peace of knowing—

Knowing. No. Of course she couldn't. Knowing her mother had left them and gone on to other things. Brook would want to know, of course, why she had left, and that was a question that could never be satisfactorily answered.

Instead, she fell asleep in her mother's bed, armed against her dreams.

In the morning, she woke to the voices of her brothers, boisterous and giddy in the kitchen.

"Hiya," she said downstairs, standing in her paisley pajamas.

"You sleep this late at the academy?" Phil asked. "Coffee?"

"If you insist." She hugged him and turned to Chad.

"You feel solid," he said.

"You feel soft."

"We brought bagels from Cambridge." Phil rattled the bag and held up a container of cinnamon cream cheese, her favorite. A vase of tulips, her favorite flowers, sat on the table. A gift from Phil, certainly, who would have bought them on a whim, with the bagels. He wouldn't mention them before she did, and in order to spare him the anticipation, she kissed him on the cheek and said, "You old sweetie."

"Oh, stop it," he said, grinning. She released him and accepted the coffee he held for her.

"How do you know they weren't my idea?" Chad asked.

"Because you're a thoughtless cad."

"Phil is just as thoughtless as I am. He just hides it better."

"If I were a girl," Brook said. "I'd marry him."

"Well," Chad said, "it's a good thing you're not."

The afternoon crept in. The brothers had brought a roast, which they stuffed and broiled, and good cabernet, which they opened and drank. Brook had changed into jeans and a gray T-shirt that read "Air Force." It was not a shirt she would ordinarily have worn, but she needed to establish herself.

"This will be a disappointment compared to what you're used to," Phil said, chopping pine nuts and sage.

"It's true," she said. "I could barely swallow the eggs this morning. They weren't even powdered."

Over dinner, they talked about the faculty at Harvard Law and about the club in Cambridge with no name on the door that only admitted the most prestigious students, and Brook knew without asking that it was the kind of club that admitted only men. It was a merry night. Her father's face was rosy with wine. It was one of the rare nights they'd spent together without the sense of something missing.

In the morning, the boys left for class. They folded themselves like jolly, oversize clowns into their father's ancient BMW, while Brook and her father stood at the door and watched. Her father chuckled twice, as though enjoying a private joke, and turned away. Brook followed him into the house where, even with the faint, melodious farewells still trailing away, the silence came out of hiding and resumed its watch over the house.

Her father still worked at his office in town during the day, but home in the evenings, he cooked a meal of soup and bread and ate it in front of *The NewsHour with Jim Lehrer*, folding the bread and dipping it into the soup. When the news was over, he turned off the television and sat in the library with a book on his lap. Brook sat with him, feeling she'd stirred a restlessness into the solid quiet forced upon the household by sheer neurosis.

Why had her father never remarried? She wanted to ask him.

A few nights later, she went out with an old high school friend, Emily Montaigne, who seemed annoyed that the war was still going on.

"Why are we still there, anyway? Why don't they just send everyone home?"

They went to a bar called the Dubliner, where Emily used a fake ID and knew the bouncer, so she could get Brook in. Emily smoked a cigarette at the bar, waving the smoke out of her face. College boys came to talk to them, and Emily introduced Brook and said she was a student at the Air Force Academy. In the midwest or south, this might have impressed them, but here it seemed to imply that there was something wrong with her.

"Wow," they said, nodding, and then they turned back to Emily.

On a small stage near the window, a man in blue jeans was setting up to play his guitar. A line began to form outside the door.

Brook had never been in a real bar. She sat at the counter feeling out the stool, the waxy wood, and when the bartender looked at her, she hastily ordered a beer from the tap. It felt good to sit at a bar in her civilian clothes. The boys were her age and some of them looked good, but the good-looking ones didn't look at her. They looked at Emily, who had long, very curly blond hair that looked beautiful any way she wore it. Brook had light blue eyes that sang out in the daylight, matched the blue of her uniform, though she didn't know it because no one at the academy had ever commented on her eyes, but here in the dim light of the bar, her eyes were unlined and her lips were untinted, and next to the other girls, she looked rather plain.

Emily was talking with two guys now. One of them was a hockey player. Brook couldn't hear much of what they were saying because the one who wasn't a hockey player had jockeyed around so that he could stand next to Emily, leaving Brook the back of his shoulder. Brook had wanted to go out to talk to Emily, and Emily had wanted that, too, but now that they were here, Emily was caught up in the flurry of the place. Later, she'd apologize and say she hated the fact that any guy could take her attention away in a bar, but that's how it was. Brook had forgotten that this was what it was like to go out with Emily.

The man sitting next to Brook looked a little older and was dressed better than the students. He talked to the woman bartender and then took two small plastic hippopotamuses out of his sport coat and put them on the bar. The other bartender, whose name was Mike, reached over and put one of the hippos on the man's martini glass so that its snout was in the gin, and they all had a laugh about that.

"I love hippos," he told Brook. "They're the strongest animals in Africa. Did you know that? You can download their calls from the Internet."

"Why would you do that?"

The man shrugged. "You've got to love something. I love them so much I've got a whole shop dedicated to them, everything hippos."

"Are they stronger than elephants?"

"They run over elephants."

"What about rhinos?"

"They eat rhinos for lunch."

"But those horns."

"Those horns are nothing to a hippo."

The woman who sat next to the man with the hippos was not a college student either and had probably never been one. She was trying to talk on a cell phone, leaning down over the bar with her face buried in her hair. When she straightened up and put the phone down, she told the woman bartender she wasn't going to talk on the phone anymore that night, but the bartenders were busy and the man with the hippos wouldn't look at her. Her bag was on the bar, leaning against the wall where the bathrooms were, and she put the phone on top of it, so that it was away from her but she could still see it.

"Hey, Mike," the hippo man said to the bartender. "I'm in the *Globe* today, section three, front page."

"Oh, yeah?" Mike looked sufficiently interested while his hands worked behind the bar.

"They quoted me for a story. I got two paragraphs."

"Did you bring it with you?" Mike asked.

"I've got it in the car." He turned to Brook. "I'm a political consultant. A guy at the *Globe* knows me."

"I thought you had a hippo shop."

He laughed. "She thought I had a hippo shop," he said to Mike, but Mike was taking an order from the waitress. Brook slid off the stool and went to the bathroom, which was hot and crowded. When she returned, there was a fresh glass of beer with a hippo in it at her seat.

"Very nice," she said.

"I wish I did have a hippo shop," he said. "But who would come in?"

The man onstage was singing Irish songs. Most of them were dirty, and everyone cheered at the end of the verses. Brook tried to remember the words so that she could sing them to Mac and Billy. The beer made her feel warm. She missed them, Mac and Billy. It occurred to her that *they* were her friends now. She leaned two coasters against each other and made a tent of them. She knew how to make a tent out of parachute silk, how to pull the fabric taut so that the rain beaded across it instead of seeping through, how to wrap the cord around a tree in a double half hitch that you could pull down in a hurry if you had to.

Emily poked her in the ribs, laughing.

"Brook's a soldier babe at the academy, did you know that?"

They nodded—they knew—and the nonhockey player said, "My brother applied to Annapolis."

"He didn't make it?" It was impossible to speak in a normal tone of voice and be heard. She felt herself pushing the words out from her diaphragm, the way you shouted commands on the drill pad.

"Nah. He's at Zoo Mass."

"We call the academy the Zoo, too."

"Yeah? Why's that?"

"I don't know. Everybody's always watching us."

"Is it as bad as they say out there? All those rapes?"

"It's the same as it is at any college, maybe safer. The press made it sound worse than it was."

"But weren't you scared to go?"

"No," she lied. She'd been terrified. But she'd gone because it surprised everyone she knew, especially as they'd watched the rape scandal playing out on the news, and because it was every bit as impressive as scoring a 9.75 on a Tsukahara in 1977.

They drifted into the politics of war. This was something that happened. When people—civilians, she found herself calling them—found out she was an academy cadet, they wanted to talk about the war and tell her what a mistake it all was. And maybe it was. Maybe it was all wrong. But she was on the other side of things, now, and the war was *real*. That's what they couldn't understand. It was like saying rain was wrong.

"I mean," the hockey player said, "war is bad, right?"

She agreed that it was.

"Why don't they ever learn?"

She shrugged.

"Well," he said, moving around so that he could rest his arm on the bar behind her. "What do you do out there for fun?"

"We march around and shoot things."

"Yeah? I bet you look nice dressed up like a soldier."

He was taking an interest in her now because it was clear he'd lost to the hockey player whatever chance he'd had with Emily. Brook turned to look at the hippo guy, but his seat was empty and the hippos were gone. Her beer was still on the bar. It looked naked without the hippo. The woman with the cell phone was gone, too, and a guy in a rugby shirt was sitting on the stool making out with a girl.

"Emily, I want to go," she said firmly in her friend's ear.

"What?"

"I want to go."

"Great. These guys want to take us back to their frat house," Emily said. Her face was flushed and she was smiling.

"Oh, you're kidding," Brook said, but her words vanished in the short space between them.

"Okay?" Emily nodded brightly.

Brook shook her head and then let herself be dragged emphatically to the ladies' room.

"Is there something wrong? I know the one you're talking to is kind of a dork, but it will be okay. We'll just hang around for a while."

"I don't think so, Emily." Brook felt herself sounding slightly prudish, but she wasn't going to waste part of her vacation fighting off a guy she would never see again.

"You really don't want to go?" Emily was getting annoyed with her. Whatever she saw in the hockey player was something she didn't want to miss.

"You go," Brook said. "I drove, so I'll just go home by myself."

"That won't work."

"Why not?"

"I can't leave by myself with two guys."

Brook thought about it. "Okay. We'll go together in my car, but then when we get there, I'll say I have a headache and I have to leave."

Emily frowned. This was not the scenario she'd hoped for. "You've got to loosen up, Brook. This isn't the military. I thought we were going to come out and have some fun."

Brook nodded. She wanted to have fun and she was having trouble expressing why all this did not seem fun to her. A year ago, it would have seemed fun. Now it just seemed like debauchery. Brook had nothing against debauchery, but it was better with an element of risk. No one here seemed to have anything to lose. No life-altering blunders, no mortal mistakes. Limitless debauchery, debauchery as an end in itself, seemed pointless and dull. That's what she wanted to tell Emily, but she didn't know how.

The frat house was very dark, with a big open space on the ground floor that was, Brook guessed, where they held parties. Upstairs, there was a television room and two or three other frat boys, lounging in chairs and drinking beer, who didn't look up when the four of them walked in. They were watching the news about something that had exploded in Baghdad.

"Let's sit back here," the hockey player said. They sat on two couches in the back of the room. Emily and the hockey player began almost at once to make out. Brook crossed her legs and turned to the other guy, whose name was Fred.

"I should be going," she said.

"Why?" Emily asked, breaking off so abruptly that they all turned to her. The hockey player's mouth was red with lipstick, and Brook started to laugh. She wished Cherry was there. He would have seen what she saw and been able to put it into words.

"This is a lot of fun," she said, "but I have to be going. It was nice meeting you." She rose, and the two guys looked at her without moving. Evidently they'd never seen a girl walk out on them before. She was putting on her coat when Emily began to whisper something to them. It was something about Brook, she could tell from the flatness of her voice, and the hockey player began to nod, sizing Brook up with a new kind of understanding. Brook walked toward the door.

"I'll call you tomorrow," Emily called brightly.

"Don't bother," Brook said. She was angry that she'd wasted her leave time. There was more whispering and Emily began to giggle. She was probably drunk, but Brook couldn't forgive her.

"Say hello to the baby-killers," Fred called.

Brook tried to think of something to say in return, but nothing came. She went down the stairs and got in her car. It was not yet midnight when she pulled into the driveway, and the light in her father's library was still lit; when she went inside, she saw he had fallen asleep in his reading chair with a book on his lap.

She sat across from him and thought about all the questions she wanted to ask. She wanted to ask him why he lived this way. Why had he never let a woman come into his life who would lift the book off his lap and guide him gently to his bed? Why had he never voiced longing, or complained, or questioned what had happened? Whatever had happened. She sat watching him. The clock ticked on the dark wall. Max's tail thumped nearby. Her father woke up and looked at her.

"So, no second thoughts?" he asked.

She wondered if he had been reading her mind.

"I learned that from you."

He smiled. "I'm afraid you're going to waste yourself out there."

He might have meant out there at the academy or out there in the military, or even out there in general, where he could not watch over her.

"The boys are close by. I can't always be here."

He nodded, forced a tight smile.

"I'm sorry," she said. "I didn't mean it that way."

She knew from long experience that she could not resent him. He'd raised them well, and lovingly, and he'd done nothing wrong. The guilt was not with him. It lived with her. Men could leave; that was fine, expected. But women were not supposed to leave, especially if they were needed, and yet her mother had done it, and now she was doing it, too.

———————————

Lex was already back when Brook arrived, pushing through the door with a bag hoisted over her shoulder. Lex was lying on the bed trying to balance a tennis ball on her knees. She looked up when Brook came in.

"You're back early," Brook said.

"So are you."

She shrugged and went to the closet. "Might as well get a jump on things."

"That's what I thought, too."

Brook worked in silence for a few minutes, unrolling the socks and rolling them in the proper shape and doing the same with her other clothes. She'd not expected to see Lex right away.

"Did you have a good leave?"

"Grand."

There ought to have been more to say about it, but already the time at home seemed to be slipping into history. She longed to get back on schedule. At least getting back into training would give them something to talk about.

"You ready for classes?"

"I guess." Lex had not moved from the bed, and she kept rolling the tennis ball along the seam between her knees.

"Why did you come back early?"

"I don't know. Nobody likes the war."

Lex had seen her old friends from high school and they'd talked mainly about how much they could drink now and told stories about all the places and under what circumstances they'd built up their drinking ability. They'd felt sorry for Lex missing all that.

"Don't they know we got Saddam?" Brook asked.

"Sure they know. They wanted to know why we didn't get bin Laden."

Saddam Hussein had been captured some months before in a cellar in Tikrit. He'd surrendered. The news of it was running thin, but they kept subsisting on its thin gruel of victory. Bin Laden had started the war, but he had not been caught. He'd disappeared, and he kept taunting the West with videotapes about how inept and cruel America was. He was like a house parrot that wouldn't shut up.

"Well."

Lex stood up from the bed and went to her closet. All her clothes were folded inside, with all the toiletry bottles scrubbed clean and at least halfway full. Evidently, she'd been here for some time.

"I'm going to take a shower."

"Listen, Lex, fuck them."

"Yeah, I know. The thing is, *that* was my home. At least I thought it was. Now I don't know. Is this my home? God help me if it is."

Lex took her towel and toilet bag and left the room. Brook sat on the bed. The sun had sunk behind the mountains, but she did not move to turn on the light. At home, her father would be making his soup, or he would have rinsed the bowl and be sitting in his reading chair. The boys would be in Cambridge doing the things they did. Somewhere bin Laden was in a cave, making speeches, carving plans in the dirt. Somewhere her mother was living her life. She had vaulted high over them and disappeared like a magic fish. People could do that. People could vanish. Bin Laden had done it. Lance Sijan, the Vietnam War hero, had done it, too. It seemed to be an important lesson, though Brook could not say exactly why.

PART II
Gliding

Chapter Seven

I n June, the graduating class marched in a sparkling ceremony
beneath the hot, crowded bleachers. They were dressed in white
pants and blue dress jackets with yellow sashes looped at the waist,
launching their wheel caps into the sky and departing the scene before the caps had even touched the ground. A mournful silence took
over, remained a day or two, and then the new class reported in.

Buses arrived from the airport, depositing hordes of sloppy,
mongrel-looking teenagers, dressed pitifully in jeans and T-shirts, at
the base of the Terrazzo ramp.

They stepped down from the buses, huddling momentarily near
the relative safety, the familiar world, of the doorways.

"Move out! Move out!"

Five upperclassmen stood in a vague semicircle around forty
white boot prints painted in rows on the sidewalk, and started
herding the appointees forward like shelties corralling sheep. The
appointees ran in clusters toward the boot prints and then spread
out to inhabit them. The prints, cartoonishly sized to accommodate
even the most cloddish pair of shoes, were turned out at precisely
forty-five degrees, and the new cadets looked down, adjusting their
feet.

"Heels together!" shouted Cadet Sherman Foster, who two

years before had himself stood trembling in the white footsteps, wadding up a tissue against an ill-timed bloody nose.

"If the person in front of you is *taller* than you, tap him or her on the shoulder and change places." *Tap, tap, tap.*

"If the person to your left is *shorter* than you, tap shoulders and change places." *Tap, tap, tap.*

"When you are addressed," Foster shouted, "there are only seven acceptable responses!"

Brook, Billy, and Cherry stood by the ramp, watching. Four of the new smacks were already doing push-ups on the pavement. The others stood with chests butting out, elbows cocked, shoulders hiked up their necks, resembling rockets about to blast off. One or two would inevitably lock his knees for too long and collapse on the pavement. Some two-degrees and firsties walked among them, correcting posture, challenging, berating.

Brook shivered. She remembered the cold well of dread pooling in her stomach during those first few days, the bile that crept into her throat, a tremor that clutched her chest, made it hard to breathe, hard to answer the barrage of incomprehensible questions. She felt the muscle memory of fear. How long ago had that been? Only a year? It felt like a lifetime, and yet, she still had a lifetime ahead.

Cherry savored a mint, clicking it between his teeth.

"Got another?" Brook asked.

Billy whistled softly. "It's good, isn't it? Being on the other side?"

They'd been playing racquetball at the gym and were on their way to the falconry, where Cherry was learning to train the birds, and they'd stopped to watch the first moments of cadet initiation. Brook felt the sweat drying in the roots of her hair. She had stood in the white footprints, like all of them, trying to stop her body from fleeing, her mind from deciding she'd made a terrible mistake. She'd been afraid they would use her sex against her, and they had, but only in the same way they used something against everybody.

She reached up now, fingering the prop and wings on her cap.

"No, sir!"

"Yes, sir!"

"No excuse, ma'am!"

The new smacks treated everyone equally, with trust and fear. Within minutes, they had formed a rookie squadron, learned to square corners and follow orders, speaking only when spoken to. Up they marched, as commanded, through the portal announcing the academy's safe and inoffensive motto: INTEGRITY FIRST. SERVICE BEFORE SELF. EXCELLENCE IN ALL WE DO. had replaced the old motto. Within hours, they would be shorn and uniformed, their belongings locked away, their rooms assembled, their every moment occupied. Within days, they would be able to recite from memory the code of conduct, the Air Force mission statement, the core competencies, the Air Force song, all four verses of "The Star-Spangled Banner," the oath of allegiance, their chain of command, and various quotes on airpower doctrine pronounced by generals who had in almost every case been court-martialed or fired at the height of their careers, though this particular paradox was overlooked.

Brook watched them go. "Poor fuckers," she said.

"Come on," Cherry said. "Let's go feed the birds."

They walked up the ramp and along the opposite side of the Terrazzo from where the smacks were being marched from one in-processing station to another, and then up the stairs and by the athletic fields lying clipped and quiet under the morning sun.

Brook had moved further from Lex, closer to Billy and Cherry. A prickly energy ran between them that intrigued her. It was like a marriage of convenience that had grown appreciative, conciliatory. Billy had come from a family of salesmen. His father and uncle co-owned the Claymore Car Depot in Tucson. After Billy drunkenly crashed a car into an overpass his high school junior year, his father worked the charges down to reckless driving and set up a series of trusts that would come into being only after Billy graduated from the military academy of his choice. Billy decided it might be fun to fly airplanes. Cherry's father was an Army general who wore a bronze star on his uniform and had lived seventeen years praying and urging his son toward West Point. But Cherry hated camping, hunting, backpacking, and dark, confined spaces. General Cherry's first spark of hope appeared soon after Cherry's eleventh birthday, when he saw the Thunderbirds perform at a local air base and spent the rest of his teenage years joy-sticking through every flight simulator on the market.

Across from the soccer fields, one of the early groups of smacks, dressed in athletic gear, was undergoing some kind of drill. Two cadets were stretching out an orange parachute panel and several others were watching from one side. Two upperclassmen from Brook's squadron, Seven Gladstone and Paula Snowe, were teaching. They were showing the new cadets how to properly fold an American flag by making a thin, tight panel and then having one cadet fold the panel triangle over triangle while the other one held the panel taut.

Brook, Billy, and Cherry stopped to watch because it was Paula doing the teaching, and there was always the temptation to stop and watch Paula and wait for the bombs to explode behind her.

She was standing next to the cadet doing the folding. Her voice was like a tissue on the breeze, but they could see that she was showing him how to fold perfect right triangles by smoothing the wrinkles in the fabric and then stepping forward, chewing the flag into lesser polygons until the cadet doing the folding stood face-to-face with the cadet holding the outer edge.

"Petite" was the first word Brook would have used to describe Paula, a particularly malicious word in Brook's dictionary, partly because it was something she would never be. Handsome. Healthy. Broad shouldered. Quick. But never petite. In her high school, the petite girls like Emily made the rules, set the standards. They had sanctioned impossible fashions—those that flattered their straight, bitsy bodies and made Brook look like an elephant in tights. A tender wound for young Brook, but one that toughened with age—she would watch these kinds of girls grow up to brown their puckering skin under the Bahamian sun, refusing to bear children so their willow-thin bodies might wither with vapid endurance. Later in life, Brook would pity them as the trophy wives of her pilot friends. But here at the academy, the perky boldness of anyone in a size-two, A-cup bra flustered and bewildered her.

The other smacks stood in a tight cluster, following Paula's lesson, except for one, a tall, thin boy who had turned his head away and was gazing at a tree. Seven and Paula were so intent on the lesson that they didn't notice him.

"Watch this," Billy said. He strode forward toward the group. "What are you looking at?" he demanded from the boy.

The cadet snapped into an immutable pose, chin jutting out, elbows cocked back like stabilizing wings. The others, startled and unsure of what to do, snapped to attention also. Seven and Paula looked up from their lesson.

"No excuse, sir!"

"Answer the question."

"I'm sorry, sir. I've never seen trees this big, sir." The cadet stared into the air over Billy's head. Billy turned his gaze to the giant ponderosa pine near the road that the cadet had been gazing at.

"Oh, no? Well, come on, let's go take a better look."

Billy strolled over to the tree and the cadet followed in rigid, roboto-walk steps.

"What the fuck is he doing?" Brook whispered to Cherry.

"Who knows," Cherry said.

As they approached the pine, Billy said, "Closer. A little closer."

The cadet inched up so that he was within breathing distance of the bark.

"Nice, isn't it?"

"Yes, sir."

"Big."

"Yes, sir."

"The bark has a particular smell. Did you notice it?"

"No, sir."

"Give it a whiff."

The cadet put his nose tentatively up to the tree. Paula had left the group and was strolling toward Billy.

"Closer," Billy said. "Get your nose up in there. Take a big sniff."

The cadet did as he was told.

"What does it smell like?"

"Vanilla, sir."

"Vanilla, eh? Not butterscotch? Are you sure?"

"Yes, sir."

"Sometimes that happens, depending on the season. Sometimes it's vanilla. Sometimes it's butterscotch."

Billy was leaning against the tree with his ankles crossed as if they were having a casual conversation. The cadet stood at attention, his nose confronting the thick, meandering rivulets in the bark.

"Why don't you taste it, see if it tastes like vanilla."

"Why don't *you* taste it?" Paula said, behind him. "Or maybe we could get on with our training here, if that's okay with you."

Billy looked sharply at her, then pushed himself away from the tree.

"He wasn't paying attention," Billy said. "He was gazing."

"If you're looking for extra duties, I'll try to find some for you." She turned to the new cadet. "Go back to your flight," she told him. The new cadet hustled back into place with the other doolies.

Paula and Billy walked away from the group, toward Brook and Cherry.

"If I need your help, I'll ask for it," Paula said. "Is that clear?"

"Yes, it's clear."

"I don't want to see that hazing crap from you again. Didn't you learn anything from Recognition?"

They were standing near Brook and Cherry now, though Paula was looking directly at Billy and hadn't noticed either of them.

"Didn't you?" she asked.

Billy had gone red and the corners of his lips were twitching.

"It was my fault," Brook said. "I dared him to go over there."

Paula turned her head now and regarded Brook.

"I don't buy that," she said. "Just get out of here. You've got a long way to go, still." This last part was directed at Billy, and then she spun around and walked back to the new cadets where Seven had taken over the lesson.

Brook, Billy, and Cherry started up the road again, and when they moved out of earshot, Billy said, "Little bitch."

"You were out of line, dude," Cherry said. "She was right about that."

"She didn't have to dress me down in front of the new cadets. That was embarrassing."

"You asked for it. What were you thinking?"

"I was just having a little fun. It would have been funny if she hadn't walked over."

"It was only moderately funny," Cherry said. "Trust me on that."

"Look, it was just a joke," he said. He was trying to shrug it off.

"It's something Bregs would have done," Brook said.

"That's not fair," Billy said.

They walked up a dirt road to the small blue building in the trees that was the falconry. The front room was small and messy and smelled like stale blood. Tony, the firstie who ran the falcon program, was in the back room inspecting the cages. Cherry called to him and then went to the refrigerator and took a package of butcher's paper off the rack. He carried it to the sink and unwrapped the cold, blood-clotted bodies of seven quail chicks. A desk was pushed up against the wall, and Billy sat in the swivel chair next to it and pulled three darts with bent wings off a broken dartboard on the corner of the desk. He began to throw darts at a topographical chart on the wall.

"I don't know why you took this job," Brook said.

"It's important," Cherry said, gutting and beheading the chicks at the sink. "The care and feeding of our mascot. Besides, it gets me out of parades."

"Mac Cherry, unsung hero," Billy said. Brook sat on the desk and watched the fan, clotted with dust, send ripples of air through an untacked corner of the topographical chart.

"Who needs heroes?" Cherry said. "Frankly, I'm tired of them."

"What does that mean?" Brook said. "Billy, I'm not sure you should be throwing darts at that chart."

"Why not?" Billy asked. "It's already got holes in it."

"Those were push pins," Cherry said without looking up. "From when the falcons got away and they had to track them along the ridge."

"Can't blame them, can you?" Brook asked. "Wanting to get away."

"Because heroes aren't heroes anymore," Cherry said. "They only represent heroism."

"So what's wrong with that?" Billy asked. "What's wrong with standing for something?"

"Because that's all you are. Billy Claymore, war ace, at the ATM machine. Billy Claymore, war ace, ordering the veal parmesan. Who needs it?"

"You'd get chicks. You'd get out of speeding tickets."

"You'd suffocate. You'd be known as a small fragment of your actual self."

Cherry's small frame was moving gently with the motion of the knife.

"Actually," Brook said, "there are no more aces."

"That's true," Billy said. "We've shot down everything that flies. But there are still heroes. Look at Torrance Shane. Shot down and rescued in the Afghanistan war and *whammo*, he's a hero."

"Torrance Shane. Thank you. You drop the argument on my doorstep." Cherry had a way of going off, suddenly and theatrically, on topics that moved him. "And what about the guys who rescued him. Aren't they heroes? I mean, they *didn't* get shot down."

Tony came out of the back room with the falcon, a gray-and-white show bird named Freedom, harnessed to his stiff leather glove. The bird was not wearing blinders, and Tony cupped his hands over its eyes while he walked so the bird would not get anxious and try to fly.

"Hi, Cherry. I thought maybe you weren't coming."

"We got caught up."

The gyr falcon had crisp gray speckles dotting each of its wings. It regarded the room, shuffling nervously along the glove, and jerked its head toward Billy, who had lurched forward suddenly to stroke its breast, and pecked at him. Billy drew his hand back sharply. "Fuck," he said.

"It's okay, baby," Tony said, calmly stroking the falcon. "These guys are predators. You have to move slowly." Tony was from Brooklyn. He had a way of sounding soft-spoken and tough at the same time.

"Can I pet him?" Brook asked.

"Sure. Do it like this."

She reached forward and stroked the bird with the back of her finger. The feathers were even softer than they looked. Tony was possessive of the bird, proud of it. He seemed to enjoy the attention as much as the falcon.

Billy turned away and threw another dart at the wall.

"Please don't do that," Tony said.

Cherry brought one of the quail chicks over. Tony showed him how to hold the quail in his fist so that the bird didn't see it too early and get excited.

"You have to be quick," he said. The bird had sensed the quail and began to flutter its wings in excitement. Tony held the quail in his other glove and the falcon went for it at once, tearing off bits of flesh and feather with its beak. "He'll eat the whole thing, bone and all."

The bird swallowed, turning its sharp eyes on every corner of the room, though it seemed to have forgotten Tony. Cherry went back to the sink and continued gutting the chicks. Billy watched the bird from his seat by the desk, but he didn't stand up and try to touch it again.

"Let's get him fed, and we'll take the peregrine out to the fields," Tony said.

"Does he ever get to fly?" Brook asked.

"Freedom?" Tony said. "No. He's the mascot. He's just for show."

When the falcon was done feeding, Tony took it into the back room where the cages were. Cherry had finished gutting the chicks. He rewrapped them in the butcher's paper and put them in the refrigerator, all except for one, which he carried over, closed in his fist, for the peregrine.

"Freedom's our mascot," Cherry said, rolling his eyes. "Our *mascot*, and he's not allowed to fly. Do you see what I *mean*?"

When Tony came out of the back room with Mustang, the small brown peregrine falcon, on his glove, Cherry took the kite with the lure off the desk and they set off down the hill toward the soccer fields. It was breezy, and Tony kept looking at the sky.

"Why don't you let Freedom fly?" Brook asked.

"He's not trained for it. He's a show bird. This girl is built to hunt." He held his arm up incrementally and Mustang, whose leg was strapped to the glove and whose eyes were covered with minia-ture leather blinders, did a little hop.

"I wonder if he misses it," Brook said.

"That's a dumb thing to say," Billy said.

"What do you mean?" she asked.

"Nobody else worries about how the bird feels."

"He gets a free meal every day," Tony said. "A clean cage. Lots of attention. He has everything he needs."

When they got to the field, they stood on the edge of a short slope that angled down to the playing fields. Tony regarded the sky once again. The wind seemed to be gaining strength.

"Cherry, you raise the kite," he said. "Then, I'll take the blinders off. You get it steady, and we'll make sure she gets a good, hard look at it before I set her free."

The kite rose easily in the wind. The lure, a brown bag the size of a mouse, dangled off the bottom. The idea was that once released, the falcon would fly up and attack the lure, and Cherry would lower the kite down, and that was the signal to the falcon that she would get her reward.

"Okay, here we go."

Tony untied the strap and the blinders and pushed the falcon off his glove. It took off, a small, dark dart over the broad lawns of the soccer fields, turned and flapped wildly into the wind, not lifting—the wind was too strong—and angled off, gliding with the breeze to the opposite side of the field, where it flared its wings and perched on the white rim of the goal.

"Little bitch," Tony said.

"What's wrong?" Brook asked.

"She ate yesterday. She doesn't want it enough."

Cherry held the kite steady, but the falcon seemed content to sit on the goal and watch them.

"She's playing with us," Tony said.

"She's having fun," Brook said. She was enjoying the falcon's stubbornness. "Or maybe that's a dumb thing to say."

Billy didn't answer, but walked off down the slope toward Cherry.

"What's wrong with him?" Tony asked.

"Paula Snowe gave him a what-for."

"Oh, Paula. That girl's a piece of work."

"You don't like her?"

"I've got nothing against her. She's a stick of dynamite in a ponytail."

"What does that mean?" Brook asked. It sounded condescending, but at this stage in her academy career, she had trouble telling the difference between insult and genuine observation.

The bird had pushed off the goal and now flew upwind across the field, landing on the grass by the roadway.

"Oh, no," Tony said.

"What?"

"I've got a bad feeling about this."

Brook looked down at Cherry. He was staring up at the kite, trying to fly it high and steady and somehow entice the falcon to attack it. The falcon lifted off the grass and flew toward them. The wind carried her forward. Brook waited for the bird to swoop down on the lure, that simultaneous moment of release and captivity when the falcon entered into a kind of wild, visceral tryst with man. They all waited for it. The falcon flapped across the field, small and determined, heading straight for the lure. It was easy work for her. She pitched up, and all eyes watched for the talons to sweep out and clutch their prize. But, instead, the falcon grazed the lure, flirting with it. She banked, her small wings flapping furiously in the wind. The tips of her feathers glinted in the sunlight. It was like a dance now, the lure drifting and the falcon beating a kind of flamenco in the air. The bird drove forward, lunging at the lure and grasping it in her talons. Brook's heart lightly skipped. It was supposed to be over. Cherry would lower the kite and Tony would feed the bird. But the moment Cherry tugged on the kite, the falcon let it go. She circled around, once, as though to say good-bye, and then flew off toward the ridge, disappearing almost at once in the shadows. They stood watching the place she had been, trying to capture the fading pixels of her wings in the dusty light.

She had been right here. That's what they all were thinking, as if remembering her talons on the lure might bring her back.

"What do we do now?" Billy said. Cherry was gazing off toward the ridgeline, absently holding the kite string. He'd almost forgotten about the lure in his hands. He'd been watching the bird closely, how it seemed to know instinctively where to find the rising and sinking pockets of air.

"Damn," Tony said, peering into the distance. "What we do now is go get her."

Chapter Eight

Sunday morning. The house, silent with sleep, submerged in darkness. Waller woke from the dream, the harness straps still pulling at his shoulders, the tightness of the oxygen mask like tape over his mouth. He'd been flying through the canyon, the SEALs crouched in the rocks under him. The face was impossibly steep—he couldn't see the top of it—with a narrow black gash between the sheer walls leading into the mountain. He was pulling up after his first pass.

Always it began here.

The canyon seemed to loom over him at an impossible angle. Below him, the shadows of a hundred men were scrambling along the hillside. It was here that the terror set in. He had made a mistake.

That was the part of the dream that didn't need reliving, the moment on the first pass when he squeezed the trigger but the trigger, still locked in safety position, didn't move. He had to pull up out of the canyon before he could check it, but already his mind was flying forward—*please tell me the safety isn't locked*—and backward—*please tell me I released the safety on the inbound.*

He hadn't released the safety. In whatever cruel trick fate had played on him, he'd *thought* he released it, or he'd *tried* to release it, but here was the safety, locked forward in mutinous obstinacy, and now he lifted the switch up and flipped it back on the hinge. Such a small motion, and he did it with elaborate care. *Live—don't live*: How could fate hang upon such a miniature pendulum? His heart was pounding but he didn't allow the pounding to go down into his fingers. He needed steady hands. Already he'd made a mistake.

On the first pass, the guerrillas hadn't expected them, and they'd been partially exposed to the sky, but by the second pass, they had taken cover in the shrubbery and rocks and he couldn't find them. It was so imperative to find them now after the first botched pass and he couldn't, he couldn't—

The dream ended. It ended, yet never ended.

Waller rose from the bed. He went to the bathroom, relieved himself, washed his face in the sink. A thorn of pain struck his side as he bent over. He ignored it, and then as he rose it struck again. He winced, cursed, straightened despite it.

They had flayed him in the debriefing. Once they landed, he had gone with his flight lead into the small briefing room where the director of operations and the chief of training were waiting for him, and he had sat at the table and watched while the flight lead had laid out point by careful point what had gone wrong on the first pass. His flight lead had been Captain Bud Holly. Bud had not been trying to make him feel bad, or feel good. He'd been trying to make him a better pilot. Waller had known that, and he'd sat in the debriefing room taking it, rolling a pen back and forth on the desk, remembering that first horrible moment when he squeezed the trigger and nothing happened.

Waller lifted his arm to try to stretch the pain out of his side, but it pulled back, refused to move. Let it go, he told himself. He meant the dream or the pain in his side or both, as though he might sever them, as though they might fly off into the darkness.

Bud had let him have it in the debriefing, and Waller had gone back to his room alone and not to the bar with the other pilots. The important thing was to get some rest and go up again the next day. He would have to work harder to regain their trust. He would have to prove himself all over again. He was taking it badly, as they knew he would. As they wanted him to. They didn't care about his pride, or his career. They only wanted to make him a better pilot. And Waller had become a better pilot, or at least a better detail man. A believer in checklists, fastidious and reliable. A first-rate flight lead. No doubt that's how he'd wound up as Commandant at the Air Force Academy.

Now, he walked to the window and looked outside. The sky was still dark. He fingered his side. The pain had been growing worse over the last few months. It came in the mornings and sometimes in the afternoons. He would lean back at his desk or stand after a meeting and the pain would envelop him and then just as quickly be gone, leaving behind the numb sensation of a surprise attack. Lauren had urged him to see a doctor, but he wouldn't go. Something muscular, he told her, aging pains.

He had too much to think about without the pains, without the memories of a mistake, whose damage had long since passed, holding him back. For instance, Bud Holly was coming out for a visit in August. Ever since Paula Snowe had been allowed to stay at the academy and suffer whatever punishment had been given to the students of the behavioral sciences department, Waller had felt an acute sense that his work at the Air Force Academy was less than spectacular. Perhaps he had made a mistake, here, too, in letting her stay. Not fighting hard enough to have her dismissed.

He had made too many mistakes.

Now Bud was coming, and what would Waller have to show for his tenure? They'd brought him in after the overpublicized rape scandal had sent the academy reeling. They wanted strong leadership. They'd pulled him out of a fighter wing and put him here. At first he'd resisted—no pilot ever wanted to leave the fighters— and then he'd embraced it. They wanted leadership—okay, he'd give it to them. And now he had one cheating scandal under his belt. What else? An increasingly militant Christian group called the CCF—Cadets for Christian Fellowship. At least he'd put them in their place. At least he'd done one thing right, though it would probably never be acknowledged. That was the trouble with good work—if you did your job well, nobody ever found out about it. In April, he'd banned all proselytizing on academy grounds after the CCF constructed an eight-foot cross outside the dining hall on Easter Sunday. The evangelical chaplains had been upset with him, but what could he do? What choice did he have? The academy was a military training school, not a religious one. Waller's heart reserved a place for God, but it was, ultimately, the heart of a soldier. That one had been a no-brainer.

Take the cross down, he'd commanded, and put a lock on the CCF. There. He'd made a decision and acted on it. Was it so hard?

Two months of relative peace, and now the new class was here. This was, in fact, their first day of training. He might go down to the Terrazzo this morning and meet them for their first five A.M. run. Surprise them, bring a talisman of goodwill. They were up before the sun, performing forced calisthenics, tired and overwhelmed by thoughts of the hellish summer ahead, but things weren't as bad as they seemed. Their general would be among them. The idea cheered him.

Waller changed into sweats and tied his running shoes. Never mind the pain. This would be good for him. Youth was like a garden and age was a weed that slipped in incrementally, so that if you weren't careful, it would take over. That's how Waller thought of the pain, a kind of weed slipping into his otherwise youthful body—look in the mirror, the remnants of a washboard stomach, the barely puckering love handles at his side—all this at fifty-two! The only way to get rid of the pain was to work it out. He made his way out quickly, Lauren and the girls still fast asleep.

On the Terrazzo, the new cadets were lined up in rows doing their stretches—toe touches, side twists, squat thrusts—and shouting out the numbers—*One! Two! Three!*—in the crisp silence of the dawn. He came upon them through the relative darkness while the upperclassmen in charge of the training stood facing the new cadets, precisely the way they had faced him thirty years ago.

"Group, *'ten hut!*"

Someone had caught sight of him and called the rest to attention. It pleased him. That was the way it was supposed to happen.

"Carry on!" he yelled. His voice echoed against the sides of the buildings, the way other voices had echoed before his. The cadets went on with their stretches. He stood at their flanks, watching. This was how the great militaries of the world were formed. This was how it began. Five A.M. on a summer morning, the body weary and rebellious, facing two miles of high-altitude hills. Somewhere among these ranks, now belting out the order for jumping jacks, was a future general. A general who would outlast him, fighting in wars he would never see. He was brimming with nostalgia. He couldn't help it. Early-morning formations brought it out in him.

Stepping closer, he noticed now that the rows were not perfectly straight. Here and there, a cadet stood a shoulder's breadth forward or back, giving the lines a jagged look. He waited to see if the upperclassmen would notice. At the end of one row, a lanky boy whose gym shorts hung on his skinny legs was pulling alternating knees up to his chest.

"Your shoe's untied," Waller said.

"Thank you, sir." He bent over to tie it.

"You should double-knot them."

"Yes, sir."

A few rows ahead, he noticed one cadet with his shirt hem pulled out flopping and over his shorts. There were four or five upperclassmen facing the rows, yelling out the drill commands. None of them moved to straighten the rows, to check for sloppy uniforms and untied shoes.

Waller walked toward the front of the rows, where the trainers stood at intervals.

"Good morning, sir," one of them, a female, said. He had not looked closely at her before, but now, when she spoke, he recognized her at once as Paula Snowe. A sourness rose in his mouth. She wore her hair clipped back in a ponytail and her uniform, at least, looked neat and orderly.

"Call them to attention," he said.

"Group, *'ten hut!*"

There was utter silence on the Terrazzo. Waller walked slowly, with painful deliberation, along the front of the ranks while they all stood at attention waiting for him to speak or at least put them at ease. He did neither. Technical instructors, the fierce enlisted-corps trainers, wore taps on their shoes so that, at times like this, the cadets could stand listening to the clink of metal on cement that was like a slow drum beat preluding some imminent ass chewing. It was an effective technique. But Waller wore only running shoes that padded silently across the stone. To compensate, he stopped and waited for a long, ponderous moment before he began to speak.

"Ladies and gentlemen. It must by now be painfully obvious to you that you are not at an ordinary college, but at a military training institution. If you came here expecting a little glory, a little Colorado fun, a free education, you're about to discover your miserable mistake. Nothing here comes for free."

He shot a glance at Paula Snowe, standing at attention with her ponytail bobbing just above the collar of her gym shirt.

"If you want the best, most comprehensive education in the country, if you want to fly the airplanes you see overhead every day, if you want to walk in the ranks of America's best warriors, you must earn it. You *will* earn it."

He was walking again. He was addressing the group, but as he walked along, he glared at the trainers leading the group.

"If you decide to take a shortcut, to cheat, even just a little bit, and you think you are getting away with something, think again. If you believe you can pretend to embrace discipline and honor, and that I won't notice, think again. I notice everything. I notice things you haven't even thought of."

He had turned and circled back to the lead trainer, standing at the front of the group, and now Waller addressed him directly.

"Isn't that right, Cadet?"

"Yes, sir!"

"Attention to detail."

"Yes, sir!"

"That's all I have. Now let's get ready to run!"

The lead trainer took over again.

Waller walked away from the ranks and stood once again off to the side. The lead trainer was shouting at them to fall in. His voice was sharper now. They were like children. Waller loved them, but it was his job to keep them in line.

They set out along the road above the chapel. A few of the new cadets fell out right away. These, he knew, would be the first ones to quit Beast—basic cadet training, the six weeks of military training that prepared the new cadets for doolie year. They would drop out through the summer and the squadrons would thin, and the survivors would begin their first and most difficult year.

Around him, the cadets were panting heavily in the dim light. The altitude did it. They could come prepared, in the best shape, but their bodies wouldn't be ready for the thinness of the air. There were so many surprises waiting for them. This was only one. It was best that they couldn't see that now. You had to show them slowly, gradually, all the things that would happen to them, or else they would quit.

A prickly pain gathered in his side. Goddamn cramp, he thought. He wouldn't let himself believe it was anything more. He stretched his arm up. The pain resisted, coiled under his rib cage. He fought it.

He would always fight.

As a boy, he had fought his father's conviction that the military was a sound choice for some, meaning *for some*, as for somebody without his distinctions. His father had appreciated the military the way people appreciated federal bank insurance and town sewage. It made life easier, made all those patriotic aphorisms easier to bear. He had argued with Waller and then, in a series of spiteful moves, cut Waller's inheritance. That was all right. That made the decision easier. Waller's brother, now an investment broker in Charleston, had taken the money. Waller didn't begrudge it to him.

That had been so many years ago, before Waller had joined the family of the military. He'd been longer, now, in this family, along with Lauren and the girls, than with his first one. He hardly spoke to his brother. He hadn't, despite himself, been able to repress a certain satisfaction some years ago when his brother had divorced, had remarried a thin, perpetually tanned woman and started traveling on Citizen of the World tours.

Citizen of the world, indeed.

Whenever Waller flew into foreign countries, a part of his mind always worked out how he might launch an air attack on whatever airport or air base—Frankfurt, Corsica, Ismir, Bahrain, whatever—they were coming into. He hid imaginary missiles and artillery to defend against his attack, and he thought of ways to circumvent the defenses and what weapons—cluster bombs or laser-guided munitions—to drop. He always landed in those countries with a sense of already knowing it, emerging from the jet with the faint air of a conquering hero.

"Good morning, sir." Paula Snowe had moved in beside him.

"Good morning, Paula."

"Thanks for that speech, sir. It was wonderful."

He tried to even out his breath to release the growing pain. Someone in the ranks behind them coughed and threw up.

"Why did you think so?"

"It reminds us of how important it is to stay vigilant. I have, by the way, sir, ever since our talk in your office."

"I'm glad to hear it."

The breathing made things worse. The pain was like the claw of a pitchfork thrusting against his side. He could visualize it, an actual pitchfork, brown with dirt and rust, piercing his abdomen with every breath. On any other run, he would have fallen back to a walk.

"And Colonel Coyle made things pretty tough on us, but he was right. I saw that in the end."

End of what? Waller wanted to ask, but the pain was radiating into his ribs and groin. What had Coyle done with them? He wanted to know, but some apprehension, some squeamishness, kept him from finding out.

"Anyway, thank you, sir."

Paula Snowe moved off. Waller was sweating now. The cadets seemed to be slipping past him. He picked up his pace and a wave of nausea ran through him. He pressed forward. He would not stop. They were circling around and back toward the cadet area. Only the hard-core cadets were left, the ones who had prepared. He would not let them down.

Trembling, with waves of heat and cold flashing through him, he made it back to the Terrazzo with the lead group. He wiped his face on his sleeve. Some of the trainers gave him a courteous smile. He could tell they thought he was too old to run with them. That wasn't it, he wanted to say. Something was wrong with his body, some kind of pain had taken over his side and he *still* ran with them. That's what he wanted to say. That's what you have to do, keep going *in spite of* yourself. That was the lesson the best of them would learn.

He was in desperate need of a bathroom.

His office was on the other side of the Terrazzo, but up one flight of stairs and more private, at this hour, than the cadet dorms, was the chapel. He waved to the lead trainer and padded off. The trainers watched him limp away.

I'm not a hypocrite, he wanted to yell back, *I'm in fucking agony.*

At the chapel, he clutched the rail on the way up the stairs, but the doors were locked. Too early for services. He turned; he would have to walk across to his office after all. For a single, wild moment, he considered finding a nearby bush, or some dark corner along the foundation, but abandoned it immediately. The Terrazzo was clearing out, the cadets marching back toward the dorms, getting ready for inspections and drills.

It is a mistake to think that the average man loves freedom. Freedom is a difficult thing. It is easier to remain in slavery.

This quote came to him now, suddenly, surprisingly. It was the voice from a biography Lauren had brought him last week, *The Teachings of Nikolay Berdyayev*. Berdyayev, a Russian, had written during the First World War. It was good, thoughtful work, and Waller had read this particular passage several times. He agreed with it, but it made him frown to recall it now, watching his own cadets march toward a day of difficult training that was surely *not* slavery, was surely something they chose of their own free will.

"Good morning, General."

It took him a moment to recognize, walking up the stairs below him, his deputy, Sil Metz, dressed in civilian clothes, and half a step behind him, his wife, Sarah, dressed in a gray skirt.

"Hello, Sil, Sarah. Where are the girls?"

It pleased Waller that he remembered Sil's wife's name and the fact that they had three teenage girls, even though he'd not seen them or spoken to them for months—a fact that was, Waller realized, highly unusual among senior military staff. Normally, the senior staff at any military base would have frequent social engagements—dinners, golf or bowling outings—and he'd neglected to cultivate any sort of social relationship with Metz.

"They're at Bible camp." Metz smiled thinly at him. Perhaps he felt slighted, Waller thought. Waller had put a wrap on the CCF earlier in the year and Metz had not said a word to him. Of course, Metz had been active in the CCF. Waller had known that. He must feel slighted, belonging to a social group that Waller had shut down. Waller would make a point of inviting the Metz family to dinner one night.

It was true that he and Metz had little in common. Metz had just returned from a week of leave at some kind of spiritual retreat that Waller wasn't much interested in hearing about. In fact, the retreat had been a national rally in Daytona Beach with the Faith Force Multiplier–sponsored FAITH Institute. Metz had been invited by the leading pastor to be the keynote speaker at a four-thousand-strong conference titled Prepare for Battle: Arming for Spiritual Warfare. Metz had been honored, wearing his pressed Class-A blues and speaking about the duty of the American soldier to take back the nation in the name of God—but this was hardly the kind of information he'd pass along to his half-pagan supervisor, the commandant, who would only lecture him (needlessly, Metz was well aware of the rules he was breaking) on the strict regulations against any military officer condoning a religious organization. Metz could not reconcile military service in any capacity other than in the name of Jesus Christ, but this was one of the many secrets Metz carried in the service of God.

Metz was carrying a paperback under his arm. *The Warrior Leader.* It sported a picture of a soldier in helmet and camouflage. Waller was about to ask him about it. A curious text for Sunday worship. But Metz spoke first.

"Pardon my asking, but what are you doing here, sir?"

Waller briefly considered lying, saying that he'd come for chapel services, but the lie was absurd because Waller never came for chapel services and, anyway, it was far too early for any service.

"Actually, I was looking for a bathroom."

Metz sniffed and fumbled with the keys. "Let me show you."

Waller followed Metz down a hallway to the men's room. Waller shut himself inside, relieved himself, washed his face and hands in the small white sink. His work was over. He would go home and have breakfast with the girls. Maybe they would go for a drive. Where would they want to go? To the mall, probably. All right, he would take them to the mall. He would buy them some more things to scatter around the house. He went out into the now empty hallway. All the rooms were dark. He blinked his eyes and peered into the dimness. There was the movement of a figure outside one of the rooms. It was Sarah Metz. He walked toward her in the narrow corridor, his fingers trailing along the wall. Why was she standing in the dark? She was looking at him. He could tell that much. When he reached her, she put a finger to her lips and turned her head into the doorway. Waller peered over her shoulder. There was Metz, folded on his knees on the office floor, mouthing a prayer before a small cross mounted on the desk.

Waller watched him for a moment. Metz's eyes were shut, his head bowed in earnest appeal. It was a dramatic change from the Metz he had just seen standing in the early light of the chapel stairs. He looked back at Sarah. Her face was plain and severe, even in the dim light, and offered a sympathetic smile. He shook his head to show that he didn't understand. Sarah leaned forward and whispered in his ear.

"He's praying for you."

Her breath smelled like old hay. Waller pulled back. A wave of unease rose up in him. What did she mean? Praying for what, exactly—the slight lapse of foresight, of careful planning, he'd displayed these last months, the needling of his own unfortunate past, the pain that whinnied in his side?

Ridiculous. Embarrassing. He might pull Metz up by the elbow and ask him to stop acting so dramatic. There was no rule for this, dealing with a deputy who folded himself, unprompted, on the floor and began to pray. For a superior. He thought of waiting until Metz was finished and then upbraiding him, but that didn't seem appropriate either. They were in the basement of a chapel, after all. Maybe the prayer was well-intentioned. Maybe he prayed for everyone. Maybe this was a casual gesture. Waller stood for a moment in the dark hallway, the quiet flooding his ears. Sarah stood at a respectable distance. Perhaps she expected Waller to join him. Instead, he turned on his heels and walked quickly out of the chapel.

The light struck him. He squinted at the Terrazzo, alive with activity now, the squadrons assembling for early-morning drill. He was making his way down the stairs when something wavering over the ridgeline caught his attention. He shaded his eyes to look. A kite, red and blue, hovering over Stanley Canyon. It had a black lure dangling from it. A bad omen that spoke to Waller. A falcon had been lost. He cursed to himself. Despite the pain, he would walk up the canyon to find out what was going on.

He made his way up the road to the path, trying not to remember the whispered words, Sarah's fingers on his arm, her woody-smelling clothes, Metz's small figure folded on the floor and his horrible concentration. Only the dead warranted that kind of attention. And he was not dead. Far from it.

He's praying for you.

It sent a chill through his body. He imagined Metz standing, brushing the dust from his knees. Would he look at Sarah? Make some pronouncement on Waller's fate? He could hardly chastise his deputy for praying for him, but there was something wrong with how it had been done, there in the dark office, as though some need had spontaneously leaped up.

He didn't need praying for. Perhaps Metz was the one who needed the praying, perhaps his austere wife, but not Waller. Now that he was out in the sunshine, breathing the fresh air, the whole idea seemed absurd. Metz was a vain man. A vain, self-righteous man. How else could it be explained?

Waller made his way slowly up the ridge. There was no breeze and the air smelled of warm, sweet pine. The pain pulled at his side, but he ignored it. He was not, had never been, a victim of anything. He did not need sympathy. One step he took, and then another, and then another. Nothing was too difficult at a slow, steady cadence. His whole life had been managed that way.

He saw three cadets across a gully of scrub pine. They were talking. He couldn't hear their voices, but he began to make his way toward them. The coarse bark and the thick needles scratched his legs as he picked his way along. It was only a short distance, and then he would have to scale a small boulder and he would be there. He was not a vain man. A vain man wouldn't walk through a giant pincushion to ask about a lost bird. A vain man wouldn't have carried on the way he did after a cluster of SEALs had died *on his watch* on a mountainside not terribly different from this one.

His foot was stuck. He reached down to pry it out from under one of the underlying branches. When he looked up, he saw that the cadets had spotted him.

"Hello, Tony!" he called. He squinted up toward them. They waved casually. One of them was Tony Mastings, the head of the falconry, though he didn't recognize the other two. None of them seemed to recognize him.

"Got a falcon AWOL?" he called.

One of them said something he couldn't understand. He made his way through the last of the pine—his calves were in shreds now—and hoisted himself over the boulder. He reached them with dirt and sweat plastered to his face and shirt. They looked at him blankly for a moment, and then Tony said, "Sir! I'm sorry! Yes, sir, we've lost one!"

He nodded. He was working to even his breath. The female cadet held her hand over her eyes and squinted at him. Her legs and arms were also covered with scratches.

"How long ago?"

"Yesterday afternoon, sir. Somebody sighted her. She came up over there this morning." Tony was pointing at a piece of rock, high above them, that jutted out of the mountain.

Waller looked at the rock as if it might tell him something, as though any second, the falcon might fly up over the slab of granite and go for the lure. As though something might come back to life.

"What's your plan?" he asked. But he was not really listening. He was imagining what it would be like to have such merciless cover, a few scrubby trees and bits of rock, to have to depend upon a fighting force from the air and have that force fail you. Utterly fail you.

Tony Mastings was pointing up higher on the ridge. He was describing their plan. They would zigzag up the ridge. They'd cover one section by nightfall and begin again tomorrow. They would do everything they could. He nodded emphatically and the two other cadets nodded behind him.

Waller was barely listening. He was in a foreign country. When did hope finally give out? Was it when the light fell? When the ammunition ran out? What was the last thing the last man ever said?

Thanks, Balls.

Their final radio transmission, recorded on some tape that had long since been destroyed.

He was not vain. He told himself this. He was not vain, and yet why cling to such a memory—why define himself by it, as though such an enduring wound was somehow proof of his greatness? He was a practical man. All his life, he'd been practical. And so he had risen. Yet he'd clung to this memory even after he'd witnessed other deaths, other tragedies.

Perhaps because he'd always believed *he* would be the one to die in battle. It made for a good epitaph. God—perhaps he *was* vain. He'd wanted to be understood as someone who would happily die in a wash of sparks over some foreign country, if dying would lead to the win.

If dying would lead to the win.

And what if it didn't? What if you simply died on a hillside because some fool forgot to arm his gun?

Maybe he did need praying for, after all.

Tony had stopped talking. The cadets were waiting for him to speak. "And then?" he said. "That's the plan?"

"That's it, sir. You see, things don't look good when they get away for this long. They have no way of knowing how to get back."

"No homing device?"

"No, sir, they're not like pigeons. They're not trained for that."

"I see." He was looking out over the ridge as though there were something to see. There was so much he didn't know about the flying world, about himself, even now. Tony glanced up, hoping to spot what Waller was looking for, and then turned back toward the commandant, trying to draw his attention downward again, away from the empty sky.

Cherry stepped forward. "It was my fault, sir."

Waller looked closely at him for the first time. He was a small kid with pale skin that had gone blotchy in the heat. He didn't look like a boy who would make a good pilot, but Waller admired the fact that he'd come forward. It showed a little fortitude.

"How so?" he asked.

"I shook the kite at the last moment. I think I startled her."

In a perfect world, he would know every single cadet. He would teach them himself, teach them to avoid the mistakes he'd made and show them the shortcuts he'd discovered and send them all into promising futures. He'd had the vague notion of doing that when he accepted the post. But, of course, that was impossible. He could know only so many of them, and those were usually the troublemakers. He had to trust the system to teach the rest.

He nodded. "Well, let's get her back."

"Yes, sir," Cherry said. "We'll try."

"What are the chances?"

"To be honest, sir, they're not good," Tony said. "I hate to say this. We'll try like hell to get her back. We really will. But the chances are not good. In fact, they're pretty bad. The chances are that she's gone."

Chapter Nine

T he falcon never came back.

By midweek, Brook was only halfheartedly offering to go along on the hunts. There were papers and tests calling for her attention. Cherry never asked her to go, but he and Tony went out every day for two weeks. Billy went along most of the time. He didn't mind sending out the kite, waiting, reeling it in. He called it sky fishing. It was a kind of sport. Anyway, he enjoyed hiking in the mountains. The only thing he minded was Tony, who cursed the bird at every step. It was Tony's head, of course. His head on a platter before the commandant, who'd had the good fortune to catch them up on the ridge on Sunday. Pea-brained bird. Half-wit animal. Tony was graduating in May and couldn't wait to get out of this place. Tired of being responsible for things utterly beyond his control.

Cherry went along silently. He didn't tell Tony and Billy it was his fault because he thought they already knew. He had been the one holding the kite. He'd frightened the falcon off. He'd been watching the bird so closely, watching her dip and flare in the wind, perhaps he'd jerked the kite at the wrong moment and spooked her. He'd scared her away. He knew it in his bones.

So he went along, day after day, with the fading hope that she might return.

Brook didn't know this, or she might have gone out again. She told herself later that whatever tests or papers had stolen her attention could have waited—*would* have waited, if she'd known how much finding the falcon meant to Cherry.

But after a few weeks, they learned how to glide, and the gliding so overshadowed everything, it was only much later that Brook remembered the look on Cherry's face, cold, withdrawn, anytime someone joked about the missing falcon.

It was falcon love, they said. *Or coyote bait.*

He turned away from the teasing, pretended not to care, or maybe he didn't. They'd begun glider training, starting in the classroom and then venturing outside, to the gliders, where they walked around them admiring the low, sleek lines of the wings while the instructor, Ben Railey, talked to them about how to keep the wings from banking too steeply, from funneling into the ground, and how to calculate their descent angle, and a thousand other things that seemed to Brook impossible to grasp until she could get up in the air herself and *feel* it. The falcon was gone, now. They were sprouting their own wings.

It was the best summer of her life—later, she would remember it that way. Their first nip of freedom after the long doolie year, the warm, sweet days of running, training, learning to glide, the evenings loaded with idle time. Though she could never remember those lofty, weightless days without also calling to mind the white breast of a sunlit falcon and the gleam of a glider's wings before disappearing into the shadow of a mountain that ran counterweight to the newness of soaring in the near silence of a wind's breath.

In August, they each took two flights side by side with an instructor in the motorized Ximango and then a number of rides in the Kestrel, which had to be towed, a two-seater where the instructor sat in back and the student sat in front, seeming, aside from the nagging voice behind, to be the only pilot in the world.

"Can you believe they're paying us to do this?" Billy asked one morning while they sat on the grass next to the runway. He leaned back against the rim of an aluminum chair, eyes closed, tilting his face to the sun. Only ten o'clock in the morning and already heating up. The sky was that enormous shade of blue so peculiar to the West. The fields surrounding the academy were beginning to cook. The air above them stirred, rose. Near the ridge, some late-morning cumulus clouds had begun to build, enormous ivory castles against a sheet of perfect blue. They were also pulling the air higher. Air rising and sinking in invisible patterns. And above the clouds and the peaks, something called rotor that sometimes churned in a watery froth of gust and wind shear and couldn't be seen but could only be guessed at, and that you entered only in order to climb into the wild, smooth mountain wave that rose above everything. Brook tried to map it out, tried to memorize the sky before going up into it, even knowing that once she was in it, the sky and the clouds would look entirely different.

The cadets went up five at a time. The towplanes shuttled back and forth, pulling one glider into the sky and then turning back toward the field and landing, taxiing across the grass to hitch up the next glider lined up and waiting on the narrow strip of runway running parallel to the main runway.

Billy went up in the first group. They rose and circulated through the thermal like a kind of heavenly mobile. Brook, scheduled for the third group, waiting her turn, sitting in the metal fold-out chairs by the hangar and watching the gliders launch one after the other.

A clunky, high-winged Schweitzer was parked off to the side, as if abandoned. Billy's wave of Kestrels rose and spiraled into a sort of airborne waltz. They funneled upward into a widening arc. It all seemed orchestrated, symphonic. So predictable that by the time they landed, and Billy returned, red faced and grinning with accomplishment, she could predict where each glider would go and how it would rise and fall. It was almost boring to watch.

"Awesome air today," Billy said. He fell into the lawn chair next to her. The chairs themselves were such luxurious items, so incongruous at the academy, that the cadets lounged in them like depraved children.

"Like you're an expert now," Brook said, but he ignored her.

"*This* is what I'm talking about," he said. "*This* is the Air Force."

It was hot sitting in the sun, and Brook felt a growing apprehension about the ride. So much was at stake. If they failed glider training, they would never become Air Force pilots.

"We shouldn't have to do inspections anymore," he said. "We should be past all that. This is what we should be doing."

"Go tell the commandant."

"I'm serious. What can we learn that we haven't learned already? A year of making beds, polishing floors and door handles and boots and everything else that shines. We've got it. Roger. Attention to detail. Let's move on."

He was excited after the flight. One sailplane after another rose up, breaking in the same spot, driving into the well-laid-out map of sky charted by the ones before.

"Maybe they want to keep us humble."

"Humble, fuck. Flying isn't about being humble."

The previous night, Paula Snowe had knocked on the door of Cherry and Billy's room and pulled from her bag a bottle of Bacardi 151. Brook had been inside, scrolling through the songs on Billy's iPod.

"A token of peace," she said, handing it to Billy.

"For what?"

"For the tree thing. Don't tell me you forgot?"

"I had," Billy said. "I forgot all about it."

"Sure you did."

Cherry said, "Well, hand over the bottle and you guys can work it out."

He and Tony had stopped looking for the falcon, but he didn't talk about it, and Brook and Billy didn't go with him to the falconry anymore.

"I just wanted to stop by, that's all," Paula said. She was moving toward the door.

"Stay for a while," Cherry said.

"That's okay. I'll take you guys out sometime, though, if you'd like. I'll show you a bar I know."

"What are we supposed to do with this?" Billy asked, holding up the bottle. Cadets weren't allowed to keep alcohol in the dorms, and bottles were almost impossible to hide.

"I'll show you a little magic," Paula said.

She told Cherry to empty the drawer under his bed, and then she climbed into it and told them to shut the drawer. There was the sound of the bottle sliding along wood and then she asked him to open the drawer again.

"Voilà," she said, holding her hands up. "All gone. Anytime you want it, just climb into the drawer and reach under the headboard."

"We want it now," Billy said.

They had drunk a third of it after Paula left, enough to feel tipsy. Billy had reached across Brook once for the outstretched bottle and accidentally touched her breast.

"Sorry," he said.

Brook was prudish enough to blush. "Not like you didn't mean it."

"If I mean it, you'll know it," he said, but he was blushing, too.

He was sitting in the chair next to her, now, watching the gliders. Cherry had gone up in the second wave. She glanced at Billy. He had a beautiful body, an athlete's body. He would be a catch for any girl, and yet she'd hardly ever looked at him. She was sure it was mutual. They saw too much of each other to really see each other.

"Third wave up!" someone called.

Summoned, she bolted out of the chair, forgetting the heat. She took Billy's water bottle and gulped from it, handed it back to him. She looked around for her instructor and trotted off toward him. She was trembling slightly with excitement, ready to push or pull, do whatever was needed to get the glider set up.

"Stand there a minute," her instructor, Ben Railey, said. He wore a fishing cap with a shallow brim wilting over his face. He was somewhere in middle age, though all the instructor pilots looked older than they really were. He jostled the right wing of the T-10 until it was lined up the way he wanted it.

"Okay. Hop in."

Brook let herself down in the front seat and strapped in. Railey got into the backseat and they pulled the hatches shut and locked them. Each seat had a stick and rudders and a basic instrument panel.

"You ever water-ski?" he asked.

"Sure. I did a pretty good slalom." She tried to sound casual, to keep her voice from shaking.

"Good. Staying behind the tow is a little like that. You don't want to cut inside on the turns because you'll put too much slack on the rope and jerk us around. The tow pilots don't like it either. If you go too wide on the turns, we'll end up whipping around and then, again, we'll have too much slack. Stay right behind him but anticipate. I'm going to show you."

"Okay."

"Keep your feet on the rudders as we go and watch what I do with the stick. When we're up, I'll hand it to you."

"Okay."

As soon as the towplane picked up a little speed, the glider lifted off the runway. It was like floating on a cushion of air just over the ground. He was trying to keep the wings level until the towplane could get airborne. It seemed to Brook that they were skipping along the ground. She could feel through the balls of her feet that he wasn't using any rudder this low and she tried to remember that. She tried to burn the memory into her feet. *Stable rudder, low*. It was like waterskiing, as he'd said. The first part, rising out of the water, was always the trickiest.

When they lifted off, the towplane rose into a spiraling racetrack while they gained height. She knew why all the instructors wore fishing hats. The heat came barreling through the canopy, a clear bubble that opened up on the world. There was no escape from the sun.

"Okay, you ready?" he asked. The air behind the tow was rough. It surprised her.

"Sure. I'm ready. I've got the stick." She *was* ready. She had checked the fear. It folded up inside her. She was ready to learn.

"Okay," he said. "Keep her steady."

He let go. Almost immediately, the glider began to waver back and forth. The seamless, honeyed flow was gone. She clenched the stick, tried to wrestle the glider back in line.

"Relax your shoulders. You're not driving a tank."

She loosened her grip, but her fingers tightened as soon as she took her mind off them. She stared at the plane in front of her, but it seemed like a darting rabbit. Horrified, she thought she was failing. It felt like a horse she had once ridden in high school, one that was beyond her level and that she'd taken only to impress a boy. She'd held a tight rein, but the horse had bent his head in determination and ridden her instead. That's what the glider felt like, as though it was riding her. The only good part of that memory was that the boy, Zachary, was still back in Cape Cod, long gone and irrelevant.

"Lay off the stick," he said. "Easy rudder. Little movements."

Get control, she told herself. *Breathe*. It was okay to be afraid. She knew that. The trick was not to let on.

I'm a good pilot, she told herself. *I'm a competent pilot*. It seemed to work. It calmed her. The glider began to smooth out behind the towplane.

"Good," Ben said. Brook didn't let herself be pleased. She kept working. She was supposed to move up slightly higher than the towplane, in a place called high tow, but when she tried to nudge the nose higher, she began to porpoise and rock.

"Don't overcorrect. You're all over the slipstream. See, look, I'll take it."

She let go of the stick and the glider smoothed out at once.

"Once you get out of the turbulence, see how it calms down? See? That's all you have to do."

But when he gave it back to her, it began to rock and dance again. The plane towing them seemed to be caught in some kind of choppy air.

"Why is the towplane all over the sky?" she asked.

"It's you. You're all over the sky."

She could not have said, then, where they were or where they were going or where the airfield was. Nothing at all was synchronized. She knew there were other sailplanes in the air. She saw two of them, but it occurred to her that there might be others, right under or over her. They might be anywhere. They might come out of anywhere and go anywhere and she would have to watch out all the time to see that they weren't flying into her. This thought went flitting by while she kept trying to steady the sailplane behind the tow. She glanced down at the altimeter. They were only at eight thousand feet and had another thousand to go. It felt as if they'd been in the air for an hour.

"When you get good," he said, "you'll be able to box the tow-plane's prop wash. That means you can draw a square behind the tow, going from one corner to another. See?" He took the stick again and demonstrated. The glider responded promptly. "Just nudge. A little here and there. Not too much stick and rudder. You see? Too much and you end up in trouble. You work yourself into an oscillation and you might even break the rope. But you're not going to do that."

"How do you know?"

"Because I'm your instructor. I won't let you."

They came off the tow at seven thousand feet. As soon as the tow turned away, the air grew quiet. The sound was like that of a strong wind outside a house. Railey turned right and gave her the stick.

"Trim up," he said. "We'll do a clearing turn."

A kind of majesty took over now. There was no struggle to stay in an unnatural flow with the towplane. Everything seemed open, their place in the air, the mountains to their left and the airfield behind them; the broad, magnificent view of everything, and the wind singing outside the cockpit.

"Amazing," she said.

"What's our altitude?" he asked. "Are we climbing or descending?"

She studied the dials. It took her a moment to read them. "We're at 8900 feet. We're sinking."

"Now, what's the wind? Which way are we drifting?"

She had no idea.

"Mark your turn," he said. "Always mark your turn."

They rolled out a little to the west of where they began, closer to the mountains. They would naturally drift toward the mountains, he told her. Almost always. You had to be careful. The glider was fiberglass and the mountains were mountains.

They began the sequence of air work. She tried her first Dutch rolls, banking on a single point on the horizon, working the stick and rudder to keep the wings from sliding on the surface of the air. Here you had to be heavy on the rudder. She tried to keep the wings from sliding forward as she turned. She tried turns on a point and kept rolling out west of the mark, and they had to move back east so she could try it again. The way to tell a good turn was by watching a piece of yarn tied to the pitot tube. If the yarn was coming straight back at you, it meant the airflow was coming over the nose parallel to the axis of the glider, and you were making a perfect turn. It was delightfully simple, but the yarn flopped and swayed, and she could not make it do what she wanted it to do.

"Let go. Let go," he told her. She thought, for a moment, that he meant the stick, that she should let go of the stick, but then it occurred to her that he meant something else. She'd been holding her breath, taking gulps of it and then squeezing it inside her ribs. She let the breath go. She took one even breath and let that one go, too.

"Good," he said. "That's better. You see? In a glider, you have to feel it."

After the air drills, he guided them into the thermal, a large pocket of air swirling clockwise under a great cumulus cloud.

"In the thermal, you're in turns all the time, so you have to get good at them," he said. "You need to know the edge of your stall."

She felt a little bumping and jostling in the thermal, as if they were riding on tennis balls. When she looked at the variometer, she was surprised to see that they were climbing. It seemed like a kind of magic, that you could rise in invisible air—that somehow you could *predict* that. She was busy watching the instruments, busy marking the outlays and slant of the thermal, but the magic of it enchanted her. You could climb, motorless, through invisible air.

The cumulus cloud loomed over them, swallowed the sun as they rose. The other gliders were in the air and she'd caught glimpses of them, but she would not have been able to say where they were going or whether they might collide, and she wondered how Rails seemed always to know.

He showed her how to pitch out of the thermal using the correct angle of bank and how to judge the lineup with the runway.

"It comes fast when you're descending," he told her.

"Is it over?" Brook asked.

"We've been up for an hour."

The air had grown rough since they'd left the thermal. Brook held the stick firmly and entered the base leg as she'd been trained to do in the Ximango and circled around to line up with the runway. Rails was right that the ground came very fast in a glider.

"That was so wonderful," she said when they were on the ground and had unlatched the canopy and climbed out. "Thank you so much."

Rails shook her outstretched hand, amused.

"You can always try for the cross-country team. Or the acrobatics team."

"Do you think I'll make it?" She was flushed and excited.

"It's worth a shot." He nodded at her. He was enjoying her enthusiasm.

She trotted back to the aluminum chair. Billy had gone—she looked for him and saw that he was going up again. She waved. He was right—why should they do all that marching when they could do *this* with their days?

Cherry walked up with a soda and sat next to her.

"How'd you like it?" he asked.

"It's incredible."

"You looked good."

"You could see me?"

"Of course."

Cherry popped the soda and took a swig. He looked at the thunderclouds along the ridgeline and said, "The clouds are building."

"I guess they are."

"There's a storm coming."

"We always get rain in the afternoon."

"Not like this. Look up there."

He pointed north, toward Denver, where a dark bulwark of clouds was bearing down on them.

"I didn't even see that."

"They say that's when the soaring is best."

"When it's raining?" She smiled at him. She thought he was joking.

"I mean wave soaring. Way up above the mountains. That's what they say, anyway."

"Who?"

"Rails."

"He didn't tell me."

Cherry said nothing. Instead, he studied the long, lean cloud running along the east side of the ridge. The storm would be on them in less than an hour. He knew the instructors would have to bring the gliders down soon, which was a shame because the soaring above Pikes Peak was probably spectacular. And very dangerous. With only three rides under his belt, Cherry was beginning to understand what the sky could do.

"That's a lenticular," he said, pointing at the cloud. "That's how you know there's wave soaring. I bet you can get up to twenty-five thousand feet right now."

Brook turned to him. "How do you know that?"

He shrugged at her. To him it was obvious, though he didn't have the words, yet, to explain it.

The gliders were coming in now, and the instructors on the ground were using ropes to tow them into the hangars.

"We should go help them," Cherry said. "We're going to get hammered soon."

As they stood, Ben Railey came toward them and gave Cherry a friendly push on the shoulder so that Cherry stumbled back a step and then smiled. Brook smiled also.

Rails said to her, "This kid's ready to solo."

"Are you kidding?"

"He was born for this."

Brook felt a pang of envy. Rails had not said the same thing about her. They all walked toward the hangar, where the other instructors were pulling the gliders in one by one. Rails and Cherry were talking and Brook was wondering what he had done in the air that she hadn't done. He was her friend, but it bothered her that he'd set himself apart so quickly. They were hurrying along now, Rails and Cherry talking like colleagues. The clouds had overtaken the sun, and there was the sudden look of a patina on everything, the hangar and the cars and the aluminum chairs and the flight suits of all the glider pilots, and the feel of a quick-coming storm.

Chapter Ten

In August, Lieutenant General Bud Holly stepped down from his C-12, fit, shorn, hoisting his golf clubs over his shoulder. A colonel scuttled after him carrying the baggage. A swollen, orange sun melted into the mountains. Holly strode over to Waller and ratcheted his hand, swallowed Waller's in a wrenching grip. Clasped his shoulder as they stood, two aging, war-weary generals half a world away from the battlefield, Phobos and Deimos greeting on the Olympian flank.

"Great to see you, Balls! Great to see you!"

It was Friday afternoon. Bud had timed his visit for the Air Force Academy end-of-season golf tournament. Waller had a car waiting to escort him to the distinguished visitors quarters, where he had ice chilling and a bottle of Chivas at the ready.

"It's such a pleasure, Bud," Waller said, emotion welling in the wrinkles of his eyes.

The general's suite was patterned in thick, floral brocade and had lacquered Bombay Company–style furniture. The on-call protocol officer, Major Spitl, had put yellow daffodils in a vase in the dining nook. The general tossed his flight cap on the coffee table and looked around for an iced washcloth to use to pat down his face. Bud had been afflicted with bouts of eczema and had grown accustomed to this and other particularities (crisp cotton sheets on the bed, oatmeal soap in the bathroom) that had been outlined in numerous e-mails by the general's protocol office, and yet somewhere, the message had gone afoul. There was no little metal tray with a chilled washcloth at hand. His thin, sprightly executive officer, Colonel Hussit, noticed the oversight and sprang at once into the kitchen to fetch his boss an iced towelette.

"The by-products of staff duty," Bud said, as Waller watched him, alarmed equally by Bud's dependence on such obsessive pampering and by his own staff's oversight. "You understand, I never used to need these things."

Face blotched and sweating, he waved the towelette to the side. His XO lunged forward to extract it. Waller smiled nervously. He'd never known his mentor to need anything more after a flight than a cold beer.

"Are you tired, Bud? Would you rather I send a car in the morning?"

"None of that!" He waved at the floral couch facing the TV cabinet. "Sit down. Sit down. Have a drink."

Waller sat and had a healthy scotch on ice handed to him. Bud clutched his glass in a battle-weathered claw, sighed heavily, and said, "Hell of a war we've got."

As commander of the Eighth Air Force, Bud had equipped, trained, and sent hundreds of pilots to the war, a war that unnerved him because no matter how many pilots he sent to it, they couldn't seem to win. It was not a pilot's war. It was a street fighter's war, and Bud could do nothing more than offer up pilots to bomb the few remaining places that were left to bomb. He felt that if it had been a pilot's war, a war of standing armies and airplanes, they would have won it by now.

"We didn't ask for it," Waller said.

"I suppose not. But we have to finish it. Somebody does. Maybe they do." Bud jerked his head toward the cadet area.

Waller swallowed his scotch. It wasn't pleasant to think about his cadets inheriting a war his generation had begun—or, at the very least, a war they had not been able to end. "Well," he said. "I'm glad you could spare the time."

"None of that." Bud stretched his arm over the top of the sofa, looked out the window at a cluster of milkweed, and said, "So tell me, what's your take on Susan Long?"

There was a moment of disappointment, the slightest pang, like a pail falling to the depths of a well within Waller's chest. He'd flattered himself that Bud's only reason for the trip had been to counsel him and discuss his career. Naive of him. Selfish. There was, within the military, a certain sense of familial love. A brotherly bond. Waller had known it many times with both superiors (though none as deeply as Bud) and lower-ranking officers. And yet, sometimes, the strings pulled back. Sometimes the give-and-take was just so—a bargain between two bargaining parties. Quid pro quo. Bud needed him. He ought to be pleased.

"I think she's in the race for a fourth star."

Bud sniffed, sat back discontentedly. Of course, he was in the race, too. Why hadn't Waller seen this? Why hadn't he known right along that Susan Long and Bud were both in the running for a fourth star?

"I figured it," Bud said. Somewhere overhead, an air system faintly hummed. "She has it written all over her. Sucking up to the CSAF. She's at the Pentagon, what, about every other week?"

"You noticed that?"

"It's my job to notice."

Waller wanted to suggest to his mentor that his job was to support the war in Iraq, but he kept that to himself.

"But surely," he said, "your résumé beats hers. You're supporting the war. You're the commander of a numbered Air Force. A combat pilot. She's just the superintendent of the academy. She has a background in engineering. I doubt she's ever seen the inside of a cockpit."

"You don't see it, Balls." Bud gave a small laugh, the kind Waller had seen him toss at people he didn't respect. Again, he felt a sinking feeling. "I admire that about you. You have the warrior spirit, the kind I'm always hammering into my troops. You have it. You always did. I knew it a long time ago, way back in Alamogordo."

"I owe some of that to you."

"No, you don't. I helped you out a little, but you had it in you from the start. I saw it after that time—where was it—Panama, that time the SEALs took it up the ass. A lesser pilot would have quit. Nowadays, a screw-up like that, and a lesser pilot would sign a big, fat book contract and go out on a lecture circuit and bleed his heart out. You wouldn't do that. You got right back in the cockpit the next day and flew a solid mission. We were all watching you. You did it. You never said a word about those SEALs. You were a true pro."

Waller didn't know what to say. A compliment, surely, and not something meant to jab or hurt. Bud had no idea—

"But enough of that. The point is, Balls, that Susan Long's a woman. I'm sorry to say it, but facts are facts. She's no combat veteran, but she's got a good track record and a list of contacts a mile long. Nobody I talk to wants to put a woman up for a fourth star, but they think they have to. They think it's time. They think it will make Congress happy. You know what will make Congress happy? Ending this goddamn war, but since that doesn't seem likely, we'll put a woman up for a fourth star and look like we're getting somewhere."

"Are you sure that's the thinking in Washington?"

"Maybe. Don't get me wrong. I've got nothing against women in uniform. They're here to stay. I know that. But when you take someone who's not up to the position and promote her based on sex, well, that's just wrong. It's wrong for everybody. We all know it. Susan ought to see that herself. An *engineer*, for God's sake. She's not even a pilot. Not even a *transport* pilot."

"We're broadening. You've said this yourself. The Air Force wants a composite force. A force of specialists. Think of the Culture of Transformation. It's not just about the pilots anymore."

"Transformation, my ass," Bud said. "The only thing Susan Long's going to transform is the number of stars on her epaulets. She's made a career out of confusing the war zone. The engineers were supposed to streamline the process, but what happened? These days, you need a computer to take a shit. One half of the computer doesn't talk to the other half and you've got to go find an engineer every time you touch something. That's no way to fight a war. We're transforming ourselves into a force of pussies."

"I couldn't agree more, Bud."

Bud emptied his scotch and set the glass on the table. The glass was swept away and refilled.

"I knew you would. Now, how are we going to turn this around?"

"I'm doing everything I can. That's why I'm here."

"And you're doing the right thing. When these kids graduate, maybe we've got half a chance. But what I mean is, what are we going to do *right now*?"

We. A promising pronoun. God help him, Waller sensed complicity. Their problems were, really, one and the same. Promotion. If they could get Bud promoted, Waller would surely be in line for a second star.

"Susan hasn't exactly been a champion of the warrior," Waller said.

"Exactly my point!" He reached forward and knuckled Waller on the leg. "She's been groomed for this. She's a political stand-in."

"She doesn't understand what makes a fighter."

"Right."

"How could she? She's never been one herself." As a kind of heavenly reward, a second scotch floated into Waller's waving hand. "Frankly, Bud, I'm looking forward to getting back to the flying world."

"That's a given." Bud waved off invisible insects in the air. "The thing is what to do about Susan."

"I'm eager to fly again."

"The fighter world needs you."

"I need it, too."

"There's got to be some way to get to Susan, shoot down this ridiculous Culture of Transformation."

"But it was the CSAF's idea."

"Not if it goes to shit, it wasn't."

"She's pretty smart," Waller said.

"She's no fighter pilot."

The two generals sat on the brocade couch until late in the evening, discussing matters eminent to the future health and security of the United States Air Force. Bud stood once to make his way to the bathroom, and on returning, relieved Colonel Hussit of the scotch bottle, filling their glasses himself and then leaving it on the table within easy reach of both of them. Colonel Hussit resisted the urge to put a coaster under it, preferring to face the irritation of the academy's protocol office over that of his boss, and he retired to a corner of the dimly lit kitchen, where he began to attack the day's e-mail. Some hours later, as Waller stood up to leave, he had trouble locating his car keys, which were in his pocket. At any rate, his car was still at the runway, from where he'd ridden in the protocol sedan with his dear old mentor. But Hussit emerged from the shadows, retrieved Waller's fallen keys from the floor, and once the old general had been dispatched to the rear section of the DV quarters, offered to drive the young general home.

Inching his way into consciousness the next morning, Waller tried to recall whether he'd said anything absurd, boastful, or otherwise ridiculous to Bud the previous night. He had called him a "brilliant strategist," a "memorable pilot," and, he thought, wincing, "the greatest friend of my life." He had reminisced about certain flying missions back in the Fighting Fifty-third, testing the elasticity of certain truths and, at least in one instance, giving Bud credit for a spectacular mission he, himself, had flown.

It was quite possible that Bud, who had nodded at each story with his yellowing eyes that crowned with Chablis-colored tears during that one particular story about Panama Waller had found himself retelling, didn't remember anything.

Waller hoped so. He pushed up from the bed, struggled to a sitting position, and felt another searing pain in his side. Always the pain. Some ravenous bird clawing and tearing at his gut. He dressed and shaved, favoring his right side, and made his way downstairs.

"Are you all right?" Valerie asked. "You look pale."

"Late night. Would you mind pouring me some coffee?"

Waller eased himself onto a bar stool. He just needed a good belt of coffee and a moment to breathe.

Lauren came in from the patio looking flushed and motherly.

"Beautiful morning," she said. "Are you going out to play golf?"

Waller wanted to answer her, but he'd taken the one good belt of coffee and it had fired up the revolution in his side. The pain radiated outward in a blinding circuitry of raw nerves. It had ambushed him. He took a deep breath, tried to speak calmly.

"Are you all right?" She came to him, her hands like the petals of flowers on his arms.

"Have—to—get—to—the—golf—tourna—ment."

Lauren nodded sympathetically. In their twenty-two years of marriage, she had watched her husband claw his way toward many seemingly pointless goals. She'd decided early on that the need to prove oneself loudly was a male issue, and not one to be given too much consideration. "There, there," she said, "I'll find your shoes."

The tournament began precisely at nine. Next to the first fairway, the canvas golf flags twitched in the shifting breeze. Golf had been mandatory at the academy. It still was—the sport of generals, and therefore the sport of everyone else. Waller had adopted golf the way he had adopted crud tournaments and Jeremiah Weed mash whiskey and Friday-afternoon officers' calls, with a shameless gratitude that, in exchange, they'd let him be a fighter pilot. He'd even grown to like it.

In the clubhouse, the lemon-ringed ice tea and the onion dip sat on a long table under a tinted vase of bulbous flowers crinkling at the edges. The floor had been swept, the tables set. Three Polynesian servers sat chatting with the bartender. Two officers stood near the window drinking iced tea. One of them was Colonel Coyle. Waller nodded at him, and he nodded back. They hadn't spoken since the cheating scandal. True to his word, Coyle had handled it. Waller hadn't heard another word. But what had he done? Waller hesitated, considered approaching Coyle, but at that moment a great wave of nausea came over him. He strode across the parquet floor into the men's room, secured the stall latch, and threw up in the bowl.

When he came out of the bathroom, Coyle was outside talking to Bud.

"You know each other?" Waller asked.

"From Desert Storm," Bud said, beaming. Waller wondered where he got the stamina. From the cotton sheets? The oatmeal soap?

"This guy did some impressive stuff over there," Bud said.

Waller nodded. "He's doing some impressive stuff here." He longed to ask Colonel Coyle about the cheating ring, how he had handled it, but it was bad form to mention problems in front of senior officers. Coyle stared at him with what looked like a suffused grin, daring him to ask. Waller fingered the clubs in his bag, twirled the head on his six iron.

"We try to give the cadets a little taste of what they're going to see out there in the real Air Force," Coyle said.

"See from whom, the enemy?" Waller asked.

"From everyone."

"That's it," Bud said.

Generals Long, Holly, and Waller had been matched in the first group along with Colonel Metz. That General Long's and General Holly's executive officers, both of whom had been fingered for appointments to brigadier general and technically outranked Metz, had not been paired in the lead group suggested a kind of randomness to the groupings that Metz had hoped would seem apparent when he'd spent an evening in his office meticulously constructing them.

Waller shifted the clubs nervously in his bag. His XO, Captain Kord, had offered to caddie for him rather than play in a later group with other company-grade officers, an offer Waller wanted to accept since he did not think it would be possible for him to carry his own clubs given the pain searing his abdomen. He only wished there was a way that Kord could swing for him, too. But none of the other generals had brought their XOs along as caddies, so Waller reluctantly sent Kord back to tee off with the other company-grade officers.

Susan Long, as the local ranking officer and tournament host, invited Bud to take the first tee. He positioned himself at the blue—pro—tee and shot a solid 220-yard drive. Waller smiled. He and Bud had played many golf tournaments in Alamogordo. He'd been paired with Bud, Long with Metz. The four of them had put up twenty dollars a hole. Watching the perfect first drive, Waller felt a momentary sense of peace. The peace of the righteous. He believed all would end well.

Next, Waller bulked up behind the ball, pummeled it into a high, arcing slice. A wincing pain shot through his body. Suppressing a grunt, he looked for the ball but saw instead an enormous Roman candle explode, launching a cascade of brilliant stars over the fairway.

"You all right, Balls?" Bud asked.

"Where'd it go?"

"Into the trees."

Waller suppressed a limp as he made his way back to his bag, unclasped the top of a plastic water bottle, and leaned on his club. The sweat had begun a patchwork across his chest and back. It was only the first hole. He would have to pull himself together.

"A day like this sure beats sitting in the office," Bud said, squinting at the fairway. He hadn't noticed anything seriously wrong with Waller. This was encouraging. Maybe if he could get his drive under control, he could pull it off.

Metz positioned himself at the tee. Waller had never asked him about the prayer session and Metz had acted as though it had never happened. Perhaps it hadn't. Perhaps it was all in Waller's imagination, or perhaps Waller had misunderstood Sarah's words. *He's praying for you.* Unlikely words for the man in pale blue shorts and plaid shirt now flexing his knees. A large vein meandered along his solid calf—he stair-stepped in the gym every day at lunchtime—diving into the folds of his socks. He combed his dangerously thin hair away from his face, revealing a tanned, glossy scalp, which was at the moment masked by a white visor. Metz was an exceptional player. His

putting was superb, a fact that Waller attributed to the two staff tours
he had served at the Pentagon. He launched the ball in a magnificent
arc that bounced once, twice, and rolled into perfect position for a
birdie on the first hole.

Bud whistled. "Beauty. You know how to pick 'em, Susan."

Long smiled graciously, almost flirting, and carried her ball to
the foremost tee. She squared up, danced from foot to foot, her thin,
tanned legs flexing under her Bermuda shorts, and paired driver to
ball once, twice, finally lifting the club and dropping her shoulder
to swing. She cracked the ball up into a high, graceful arc along the
fairway. The three men standing back at their own tee offered muted
applause.

"Nice shot, ma'am," Metz said.

"We could have made it ten dollars a hole," Susan said.

"Not on your life," Bud said. He was studying her. He watched
her move, listened to her talk with the lust of a hunter. Waller wondered if Susan was aware of it.

At Alamogordo, the golf course had been in a constant state of
flux, greening up as the groundwater, toxic with heavy metals and
buried rocket fuel, retreated, and then drying into a putty brown
crisp as the mountain rains ran off into the Tularosa Basin. They'd
looked forward to loading their golf clubs in the travel pods of their
jets and playing on temporary duty in Las Vegas and Florida. They'd
ridden golf carts around and kept beer in the back, and the joy of
those afternoons, when his muscles were tired and sore after days of
flying and the sun felt good on his back, were some of the fondest
memories of Waller's life.

It had been a way to relieve stress, but that had been taken away
from him. When he played golf now, it was always with senior officers battling for promotion or contractors competing for fat deals.
He decided he hated golf.

At the fourth hole, Bud was still watching Susan Long. He whispered to Waller, "She's smooth. She's impressive. We're going to have
to think about this."

"The game?" Waller asked.

"No," Bud hissed. "The bigger issue."

Waller watched Long crack a solid two-hundred-yard drive down the fairway. He'd soaked his shirt clean through, so it was solid blue again, several shades darker than when he'd begun. Soft bits of mulched aspen leaf clung to his socks. He'd managed to hit one par, though the others were bogies or worse. He was beginning to regret the day.

"Paula Snowe," he said in low tones.

"Who?" Bud asked.

Metz glanced over in their direction. He was torn between praising the superintendent and deciphering his immediate boss's conspiring undertones.

"Senator Snowe's daughter. She cheated on a test. Long overturned her dismissal as part of the Culture of Transformation."

Bud grunted, turned, and lifted his driver out of the bag. "Good," he said emphatically. He might have been talking to Waller or Long or all of them.

At the seventh hole, as they sighted, tracked, and moved toward their now dispersed balls in the tufted grass (Waller's had pattered into the reedy bank of a small frog pond), Bud, who could no longer confine himself to conspiratorial mumblings, asked brightly, "So, Susan, how's the Culture of Transformation coming along?"

"It's working wonderfully. Ask John."

Bud grunted, shot a glance at Waller's now mud-stained shoes. "But what's it accomplishing, Susan? How does it turn out better cadets? I've read all the mishmash on it, but I'm still not sure if I know what it even *is*."

"Sil put a wonderful PowerPoint presentation together for me. Why don't I have him fly out and brief it for you personally?"

Bud reached into his pocket for a handkerchief, dabbed his brow with it, and stuffed it back into his pants.

"I don't know if that would do any good, Susan. You see, how it was in the fighter squadrons was, you used empirical evidence. You measured things. How many bombs did we drop? Did they hit the targets? Yes or no. Were the targets destroyed or damaged? If damaged, how much? Was there collateral damage? That kind of thing. Simple questions. Answers even a fighter pilot could understand."

"Well, I appreciate your thoughts, Bud." She smiled at him. "I'd certainly like to hear more about them. In fact, I'll be meeting with the CSAF later next week and I'd be happy to carry your ideas to him personally."

Bud arched back a little and assessed the sky, where gentle cumulus puffballs trundled by.

"Next week, eh?"

"That's right."

Bud sniffed, cleared his throat. The Holly-Waller team was losing to the Long-Metz team by a considerable margin. Bud tried not to let that bother him. Waller was off to his right, at five o'clock, slouching by his clubs. His face had a wan, waxy look to it that Bud attributed to the late-night scotch. Bud had remembered Balls as a better drinker. Why wasn't he here backing him up like a good wingman?

"Nice shot, Sil," Long called, holding her hands up in cheery applause. Metz swung down with the grace and sureness of a hinged wooden bird dipping its beak in a cup of tinted water, plucked his ball out of the hole, and bounced upright, sailing the ball up into the air and catching it backhanded.

"Thank you, ma'am."

Their playing was clean and friendly. There was something too perfect about it. By the thirteenth hole, Bud had figured out how to deal with Susan Long.

"You run a hell of an institution, Susan. I want you to know that."

"That's kind of you."

"I'm very fond of this place. We all are. All the alumni. We've got a great attachment to the academy. Balls, here, too."

He looked back, but Waller was tugging his golf cart in a kind of stiff zombie trance. What had happened to Balls? The man couldn't even cart his own clubs.

"If you're alluding to the fact that I didn't attend the academy in the years before women were allowed—"

"The thing is, Susan," Bud interrupted, "when it comes down to it, a nice, friendly admonishment for violations to the honor code just doesn't cut it. There's no gray area in war. You live or die. You fight or surrender. We want kids who live and fight. The CSAF knows that. We're not interested in kids who can talk their way out of things, who can marginalize their own mistakes through self-analysis and some other mishmash. No, this Culture of Transformation thing will come and go. If I were you, I'd look for a bigger horse to ride."

By the fifteenth fairway, Waller could no longer follow through with his club. He was getting alternating hot and cold flashes. His hands were sweating and trembling so fiercely that he was afraid he might let go of the club itself and sail it off into a nearby bush.

Bud had been explaining to Susan Long the merits and importance of well-trained young officers steadily since the thirteenth hole, and now her game had finally begun to crumble. She sliced the ball into a nearby sand trap.

"Damn!" she said.

Bud had paused long enough for her to hit the ball and then, glancing sympathetically at the pit, continued midsentence, "...and when they finally get to us, they're looking for leadership. It's like they've never seen it before. We do our best, how can we not, but it's hard for them to have to unlearn some of the stuff that's been crammed into them by well-meaning, and I mean that sincerely" —and here he broke off his steadfast eye contact with Long to glance doggedly at Metz— "well-meaning staff officers who do their best to provide exceptional combat training but don't always have the best skills."

They ambled down the fairway, Bud chatting cheerfully to Susan, whose mouth was set in a grim, determined expression. Hardly pausing to breathe, Bud broke off for the green and shot a birdie to tie the score. It was up to Waller now. He'd managed to drop an impressive drive at the edge of the green, and even Bud paused in his monologue to watch for the moment when his team would surpass theirs. It was not about golf anymore. Perhaps it never had been. It had been about the tradition of the Air Force, the integrity of the fighter pilot.

It was a nice, easy shot. They'd make their money on this one. Both Susan and Bud had turned to watch. All eyes were on the ball. Waller bent his knees, relaxed his shoulders, eyed the line one more time. They were going to win, he and Bud. All through life, they had been a team. They had been like brothers. Bud had been more of a brother to Waller than his real brother had ever been. Waller felt a surge of gratitude. He'd been wrong that engineers were taking over. The Air Force loved its pilots, and the pilots would always rule. He took a breath and lifted his putter, not realizing he'd been using it to support his weight. Lifting the club was like kicking out one of the legs on a tripod. Another halo of stars burst overheard. A soothing warmth flowed through his body. Falling over, he passed out cold on the green.

After a moment of achingly blissful sleep, he came to in a series of cold-water splashes slapping his face. Bud and Susan were bending over him. Metz was dialing 911.

"I'm fine," he insisted, batting off the hands that tried to press him down. "Just a stomach bug."

But they would not let him sit up.

"Just take a rest there, son," Bud said, kneeling next to him. There was real concern in his face. Nobody had called him "son" in decades, perhaps not since his father had delivered his dying words to Waller one windswept morning in Greensboro. Tears welled up in his grateful eyes.

Susan tucked a towel tenderly under his head. He wanted to reach up and gently squeeze her hand.

Metz returned in a borrowed golf cart and they all packed their clubs into it and drove Waller back to the clubhouse, where an ambulance made its way safely and deliberately through the five-miles-per-hour-zone parking lot. Two jumpsuited EMTs disembarked and pulled a stretcher out of the back.

When they'd loaded Waller onto the stretcher and closed the

doors, Bud took his handkerchief out of his pants pocket and said, "Maybe you should think about providing the CSAF with some alternatives at your meeting next week, just to give him a few choices."

But Susan Long, who always took pains to be graceful and politic in all situations, had long since wearied of Bud's unceasing and cheap old school bullying. She turned to him, blushing faintly from the heat, and, with her beautiful high southern smile, said, "Well, Bud, it looks like your team's gone bust."

Chapter Eleven

T he best summer of her life.

She told herself this later. The images boiled down. A sun-drenched falcon skirting the lure, flapping into oblivion. The last rays of light on a pair of wings soaring along the ridge.

The week before fall term began, Billy turned nineteen. It was their last weekend of guaranteed off-base privileges before the squadron inspections started again with the new term. In a profound coincidence, an elderly aunt, the first wife of the founder of the Claymore Car Depot in Tuscon, died the following day, leaving Billy sixty thousand dollars that bypassed the labyrinthine circuitry of contingent trusts his father had set up to carrot-and-stick him through an Air Force career. To celebrate, they cashed in on Paula's promise to go out to a bar.

Billy wore loose khaki pants and an oxford-cloth shirt, unbut-toned and untucked, a crewneck T-shirt untucked beneath that. Cherry wore creased khaki pants and a collared jersey tucked into his cinched waist. He smelled of lemon and soap.

They stopped by Brook's room on the way out. She had fixed her hair and wore a flowing kind of tank top and jeans. Paula, wearing a short denim skirt and an aquamarine halter top, thin, silver earrings that spun on a miniature axis like a small, tangled pile of thread dangling from her ears, sat on the bed. Lex had already left with other friends for an early dinner at P.F. Changs.

"You almost look like girls," Billy said. In fact, they shocked him. They reminded him not of the cadets in their manly clothes whom he overlooked daily, but the girls back in Tuscon who walked around wearing jewelry and complicated layers of clothing with a confidence that put knots in his groin.

"Don't be fooled," Brook said. "I can drop you in a second."

They drove in a borrowed car—Ragley's red Mazda—through the gate and down I-25 to a state road that twisted through a canyon and into Manitou Springs. Brook had wanted to go north, to a college bar, but it was too risky, too many ways to be seen by an upperclassman who might know they were underage. Paula knew a local dive on Gun Club Road.

Inside, the bar was dark and subdued, the counter lined with the backs of formless men bent over their beers. Lamps hung over the two pool tables and cast a stale glow on the worn felt. A blue stream of neon ran under the liquor bottles behind the bar. There were two bartenders, a man and a woman, busy. A television flickered over their heads: news, another car bomb, seven dead in Basra. The four of them stood inside the doorway, trying to shake off the rigor of school.

"Who's drinking?" Paula asked.

Paula moved toward the tap and put her hand up while the others stood in a tight cluster behind her. The bar looked damp and sticky. At one of the pool tables, two women played badly, laughing about it, and a man gripping a longneck stood watching the game unravel.

"What are we having?" Paula called back. She ordered four drafts. The bartender shot them a look, summing them up, and turned away without answering. She took four plastic cups from the stack and filled them with beer and foam. She was singing along with the music—ZZ Top—bleating out of the jukebox. Set the beers on the bar and took Paula's outstretched cash without looking up.

"What a dive," Billy said.

"A little louder maybe," Cherry said.

"Where'd you find this place, Paula?"

"Recommended for local flavor and atmosphere. And the fact that they don't card."

"Well, cheers," Brook said. They tapped cups, careful not to spill.

"Let's sit back here," Paula said.

They squeezed into one of the booths on the far side of the pool tables. Brook set her beer down. It was watery and flat. Billy slid in next to her. Cherry jutted his neck out in time with the music. He looked like someone who'd just quit the monastery, or been released from intensive care. His near baldness looked either sickly or cultish. On the walls were black-and-white pictures of people who looked like old movie stars, standing with pool cues and beside pools and by old Italian cars. Billy leaned back, arms stretched over the sides of the booth, and watched the girls playing pool.

"Your shirt glows in the dark," Cherry told Paula. She looked down, smiling, gave a little jig. Cherry thought she looked vaguely like a hooker. Brook turned her cup in a semicircle. It left a trail of sweat on the table.

"Those girls aren't too bad looking," Billy said. He tapped his cup on the waxy wood, slung it back, and downed the contents.

"They're out of your league," Paula said.

"What makes you say that?"

"I can tell by looking at them. Go ahead, try."

A thin, long-haired waitress appeared at their table.

"Four beers," Billy said.

"Three beers and a vodka gimlet," Paula corrected.

"Two beers and two vodka gimlets," Brook said.

The waitress pulled a chair out and sat down at the table while she wrote the orders on the back of a beer coaster. Her hair fell over her pen.

"Crazy night," she said. "There's a poker tournament in town." Her hair was long and cut in layers, held back by a headband of crocheted yarn. It was the kind of hairstyle Brook could never have—impossible to pin up and keep the wisps from falling around the face and collar.

Cherry asked, "Did you make that headband yourself or was it a gift?"

The waitress touched it, flattered.

"He hasn't seen a girl in four months," Billy said. Brook blinked at him.

The girl smiled. "Well, I haven't seen a man in about that long." She stood up and went back to the bar, and Paula laughed, slapping her hands together in the air. "I haven't seen a man in about that long," she repeated. "Sweetheart, me, too."

Billy ignored her.

"She's beautiful," Cherry said, watching the waitress walk off.

"You need to masturbate more," Billy said.

"You do it enough for both of us."

The girl brought their drinks back and didn't charge them for Cherry's beer. Billy looked at her as if he'd been insulted.

Cherry shrugged at him. "What can I say? Girl needs glasses."

Billy wanted to play pool. The girls who had been playing were now bent over the jukebox with the man who'd been watching them. One of them had stuck a thumb in his back pocket. The man stood with one boot crossed over the other, leaning with his elbows on the glass, flipping through the songs. Billy racked, and then he broke, too. The crack of the balls hitting made one of the girls turn. They played eight ball because it was all they knew. Billy wasn't good, but Cherry was worse. The girl watching them smiled. There wasn't any doubt about who they were. They were academy boys.

The bar was getting crowded, and the waitress was running from the bar to the tables with a full tray. Brook went to the bar. The men sitting there watched her pass. She found a spot and hitched her foot on the dirty rail. This is freedom, she thought. Not so different from home, but here, in a strange, smoky place full of men who had worked more years than they'd been in school, she could be anybody, absolutely anybody, out for a Friday-night beer.

"How's things at the academy?" the man on the stool next to her asked. He was wearing a thin denim shirt with dirt crusted on the sleeves.

"How did you know?"

He laughed. His teeth were long and stained at the gums. "It's all over you."

"Whatcha need?" the bartender said. She was small and blond. She worked fast. Brook ordered two rum and cokes and two vodka gimlets. The woman turned away.

"You just down for some fun?" the man asked.

Brook smiled at him politely and dropped a crisp twenty on the bar. The woman swept it into the sea of commerce, brought back four soggy bills. Brook dropped one, and then another, on the bar, and carried the drinks across the room. Paula was watching the pool game.

Billy was leaning on his cue, studying the game, as though it had suddenly taken on serious proportions. Cherry missed a straight shot to the corner, leaving Billy a bank to the side pocket the long way down the rail. Billy glanced sideways at the girls by the jukebox and winked. He clutched the cue in his hand and walked around the survey angle like a circling hunter. Either shot would have shown that Billy had the touch. He missed. He looked at the girls, shrugged. Cherry shot and missed, too. It took three more songs for them to finish the game.

"Fucking dorks," Paula said.

"Do you play?" Brook asked.

"Not in a place like this."

One of the girls from the jukebox walked over to Brook and Paula. She wore old jeans and heavy boots.

"These guys with you?" she asked.

"Unfortunately," Paula said.

"You should make them take you to a nice place."

"It's not a date," Brook said. "We're just friends."

"Oh, right," the girl said. "It always starts that way."

"No. I mean, we're from the academy."

"Oh? I figured they were. You are, too?"

"Are you surprised?" Paula asked.

The girl shrugged. "I guess not. I don't know why I didn't think of it."

The girl took a cigarette out of a small black purse at her hip and tapped it on the back of her thumb.

"Got an extra?" Paula said. The girl nodded, offering the pack.

Brook had never seen a cadet smoke a cigarette. Paula pulled a cigarette out of the pack and took the lighter from the girl, then lit the cigarette, inhaling deeply.

"I didn't know you smoked," Brook said.

"Only in bars," Paula said.

The girl's name was Tina. She worked at a store that sold whirlpools and Jacuzzis. She was long out of high school. Brook could tell by the way she seemed a little bored, a little unimpressed with the bar they were all standing in. She called her friends over, Charlie and Sally. They all shook hands, and then Paula said, "What do you guys do down here for fun?"

"Fun," Tina said. "Jesus."

They were standing in a half circle against the table when Billy won the game. He passed Cherry a mock salute and swung around the table for introductions. Brook took a sip of her gimlet and twisted the cup in her hands.

"You ever play for cash?" Charlie asked Billy.

Billy shrugged, nodded tightly, the cue resting on his shoulder.

Charlie laughed. "I was just kidding, man. Rack 'em up."

"I got cash," Billy said. "You want to bet?"

"No, man. I don't want to kick your ass."

"What makes you say that?" Billy said. He was already racking up the balls. He felt good having beaten Cherry.

"Nothing. We can bet if you want to."

"Sure, let's bet," Billy said. They put down ten dollars. This time, the game went much faster and, to Brook's surprise, Billy won. Charlie racked again. The night seemed to be taking a turn, suddenly. A predatory energy came over the game. Billy was intent, circling the table. Brook noticed he was flexing his jaw. Charlie moved slowly, pondering the table, twisting the cube of chalk absently against his cue tip. He shot well and without any particular flourish, then stood slumped against a column while Billy spun the cue between his palms as if to warm it. Then Billy attacked the next shot. Missed. Charlie stepped forward, frowned as though considering a puzzle, and then shot four in a row to win the game. He shrugged at Billy with disinterest.

"Had enough whuppin' for a night, brother?" Cherry said. He had gone to the jukebox and fed more quarters into it and now was leaning back against the wall finishing his second rum and coke.

"Maybe just one more," Billy said.

"Is he your friend?" Tina asked Cherry.

"He's my roommate."

"You don't look like him."

"I know," Cherry said.

"I mean that in a good way."

Charlie won the third game, too, and Billy reached into his pocket for the money, but Charlie said, "Keep it down. They don't like that in here."

Billy nodded curtly and turned away. Brook had seen her brothers and their friends, who bet bottles of brandy on lacrosse games, compete; they never seemed ruffled when they lost because they never bet anything they couldn't afford to lose. She had thought Billy had been raised like them. He had the sheen of advantage, but there was a thinness to it. A kind of rawness. Her brothers had never been desperate for anything.

Sally was tugging at Charlie's back pocket. She whispered something in his ear.

"You guys want to come over? We've got a few beers at my house. Seeing as how our friends are getting along so well."

Cherry and Tina had moved off and were talking at one of the tables.

"How does he do it?" Billy asked. "Set him loose and he's like an animal."

"What do you say?" Charlie asked.

THE LAST BLUE MILE

"Sounds okay to me. Maybe things will liven up," Paula said.

"Let's go," Billy said. He was looking to recoup something, some particular loss that did not seem to be monetary.

"We've got to fly in the morning," Brook said. She felt like a prude, but she also felt the shaky wisdom of going to a stranger's house, the hint of bad judgment they were always being lectured against.

"Who's flying?" Paula asked.

"Me and Cherry. We're trying to get on the acrobatics team."

"Cherry doesn't seem worried," Paula said. "Come on, let's go out and live a little."

Charlie lived in the valley, in a stone-colored stucco house in a tightly cloned development. Gray forms trotted out of the headlights when they pulled onto the street: mule deer, common as dogs, grazing in the shadowed yards. His refrigerator was empty except for a twelve-pack of Miller, ripped open on one side, and a plastic lemon rolling in the doorway shelf. They had followed Charlie's flatbed, stopping at a gas station where Sally and Tina ran in for more beer and a gallon of sauvignon blanc, and now Charlie was sliding the bottles across the wire shelves. A cereal box had been left open on the counter and two bowls sat drying in a dish rack next to the stained sink.

Cherry and Tina settled at one end of the couch and Paula sprawled back on the arm of a ragged chair. She accepted a can of beer and swigged a good portion of it down.

"How about some music?" she asked. Billy flipped through a pile of cracked and scratchy CD cases. A small stereo sat on a TV stand in the corner. An unplugged television sat next to it on the floor.

"This is great. Look at this old stuff." Billy held up CDs of Warren Zevon and Pink Floyd. "Man, how old *are* you guys?"

Charlie either didn't hear Billy or ignored him. "I did some work at the academy once," he said.

"Oh yeah?" Billy asked. "What kind of work, Charlie?"

"Construction. You know that fountain by one of them halls, where you guys eat?"

"Mitchell Hall."

"We put that sucker in. Laid the pipes. Wired the lighting. All of it. Paid nice for it, too."

He pulled two chairs from the kitchen table and he and Sally sat down on them. Cherry and Tina were having their own quiet conversation. Billy sat on the floor by the stereo, where he could monitor it. He played Rush. Yes. Stuff their parents had listened to.

"Like to get back up there," Charlie said. "Government puts out a nice contract. You guys get paid, too, don't you? That must be nice, getting paid to go to school."

"We work for it," Brook said.

"Sure you do. The government pays fair, that's all I'm saying. But then, you guys are hooked after you graduate, right? You owe time?"

"Five years," Billy said. "Five years and your fucking soul." That was the mantra that every cadet had learned. He took a mouthful of beer to wash down the bitter words.

"*Five years and your fucking soul,*" Paula said in a deep voice. "Get over it, Billy. You act like you're the only person to ever get a shit deal."

"Maybe I should have gone to the academy," Charlie said.

"You're one to talk, Miss Privilege," Billy said. "What hasn't come down to you on a silver platter?"

"What's that supposed to mean?" Paula asked. "At least I don't act like I deserve more than other people."

"They wouldn't have had me, though," Charlie said. He looked at Sally and shrugged.

Sally put her hand on his arm and said, "Why do you say that? Don't talk like that."

"The hell you don't," Billy said. "Anybody else in your situation would have been thrown out of here after that cheating scandal."

"Anybody else wouldn't have had the balls to take that stupid folder, and then admit it. I never even denied it. How do you think they caught me?"

Cherry and Tina had begun to kiss. Cherry rubbed his thumb very gently over Tina's cheek. It surprised Brook. She had never seen him this way. If anything, Billy had seemed the one more outwardly sexual. But that was it. He was outwardly sexual. Cherry was something else altogether.

"Well, it don't make a difference now," Charlie said.

"All I'm saying is, don't talk like that," Sally said.

Charlie shrugged again and beat his thumbs against the back of the chair. "You guys ever been down in the tunnels?" he asked. He glanced at Cherry and Tina and said, "You know there's tunnels under the academy. You ever seen 'em?"

"What tunnels?" Brook said.

"There's all kinds of shit down there. Rooms with school desks. Stockpiled food. Miles and miles of tunnels. Some say they go all the way to Cheyenne Mountain."

"What are they doing there? How do you get in?" Brook asked.

"There's ways. I used to have a map somewhere around here."

"I've heard of them," Billy said. "I heard they're all closed up."

"They weren't a year ago," Charlie said. "That's where all the sewage pipes run. It's a little creepy. I've heard all kinds of crazy stuff. There's a replica of the Liberty Bell down there."

"You're shitting me," Billy said. He had put on some obscure, cracking, high-pitched recording of Neil Young, and Charlie was talking over it.

"I'm not. Copies of the Constitution and all the other important papers. Bill of Rights. Declaration of Independence. In case there was ever a nuke."

Cherry and Tina were still kissing. Paula said, "You guys want to go find a bedroom or something?"

Tina stood up and took Cherry's hand and walked outside. They could hear her laughter as they stepped off the porch. Charlie looked at the door closing and said, "They've even got a morgue."

"No shit," Billy said.

Charlie shrugged. "There's a sign, says, Morgue. Nobody inside, though. I guess they figured if they needed a bomb shelter, they might need a morgue, too."

Billy tipped his beer over, and then he reached out slowly and righted it again. He made no move to clean up the mess.

"Lot of weird stuff goes on up there," Charlie said. "The paper said there was some kind of religious stuff—cadets putting up crosses around the campus. What was all that about?"

"Oh, that," said Paula. "The Christ Brigade. They're harmless. A little wacko, but ultimately harmless. I grew up with one of their lead lemmings."

"Who?" Brook asked.

"Dillan Bregs, your pal."

Brook had almost forgotten that Paula had saved her from Bregs during the last day of Hell Week.

"You grew up with him?"

"Sort of. We're from the same state. Wyoming's not too big, you know. My mother nominated him for an appointment here."

"So you knew each other?"

"A little. I knew about him. For example, I knew that he was gay."

"Bregs is *gay?*" Billy asked.

Paula shrugged. "Who am I to say anything? I figured if he can make it through this place being gay, then maybe he deserves a commission."

"I can't fucking believe this," Billy said to the ceiling. "Why didn't I know this a year ago?"

Then Tina and Cherry were on the stairs and the door opened; the freshness of the cool night swept in, and the two of them entered, grinning mutely at the floor.

They sat back on the couch and Cherry let his head fall back lazily.

"It's too bright in here," he said. There was only the one dim lamp in the corner and the fluorescent light bleeding over from the kitchen.

"Mac, you know we've got to fly in the morning," Brook said.

"I thought about that, but you know, flying's only one thing."

"Are you okay, buddy?" Billy asked.

"I feel like dancing."

Tina curled into his side and gazed at the floor. He picked up Billy's beer and drank the rest of it. The effort seemed to exhaust him, and he let his arm flop on the couch.

"Cherry," Billy said. "You're not going to believe this. Dillan Bregs is gay."

"Yeah?" Cherry stroked Tina's head. "He doesn't know what he's missing."

"Can you believe it? Can you believe that son of a bitch?"

"It makes sense. All that repressed energy. Maybe he'd be happier if he dropped all the Christ Brigade stuff and focused on being gay."

"How can you say that, man?"

"Why not?" he asked. "I say live and let live."

They waited for him to go on, but Cherry seemed to have spent himself. He picked up a gum wrapper that had been ground into a seam in the sofa and examined it.

"Get over your homophobia, Billy," Paula said. "There's nothing wrong with being gay."

"It's fine, as long as you're not in the military."

"You probably think women don't belong, either," Paula said.

"That's not for me to say."

"What does that mean?"

"It just complicates things, that's all. War used to be simpler."

"How do you know?" Charlie asked. "Just out of curiosity, how do you know war used to be simpler?"

"I don't know. It's hard to explain." Billy held up his hands. "Men fighting men. Everyone had a gun. It's just more complicated these days."

"That's fucking brilliant," Paula said.

"At least I made it up myself."

Cherry said, "Man, when did we ever *live*?"

"I look at you guys," Charlie said, "and I can't believe I thought I couldn't get into the academy."

On the way home, the radio played "Radar Love" and Cherry sang under his breath.

"Wait!" He shot up suddenly from the backseat. "Stop!"

"What is it?" Billy said. They were driving north on the interstate.

"Stop! Pull over now!"

Billy put the signal on and pulled over onto the shoulder. Cherry scrambled out of the car.

"Open the trunk. Is there an old rag or something in here?"

"Cherry, what the fuck are you doing?" They had all climbed out. Cars shot by them on the interstate, buffeting them with mini windstorms.

"This is perfect. Come with me." Carrying a plastic tarp and a rope, he ran down the gravel shoulder.

"We better follow him," Brook said.

When they caught up with him, he was standing over a newly dead red fox on the side of the road.

"This is beautiful," he said. "It's not too mangled. Help me wrap it up."

"What do you want to do with it?" Brook asked. Cherry was laying the tarp out and nudging the fox onto it. Nobody moved to help him.

"Hold this." He pushed the rope into Brook's hands. "I need to get this baby in the trunk."

They closed the dead fox in the trunk, drove back to base, and smuggled the fox past the gate guards and into the cadet parking area.

"Now," Cherry said. "Let's find Bregs's car."

It took some searching, but they were able to find Bregs's drab beige Camry by its regulation-size "Jesus Saves" sticker on the rear window.

"Come on," Cherry said. "Watch this."

He pulled the fox out of the trunk and tied one end of the rope around its neck and the other around a sturdy hitch under the bumper. Then he kicked the fox far enough under the car that Bregs would not see it.

"Beautiful," Cherry said. "Beautiful."

In the morning, Brook felt like a heavy blanket had been pulled over her head. She rose and went to meet Cherry at the flight line.

"You're up first," he said. "You ready?"

"I hope I don't throw up."

It went better than she expected. She was gentler on the stick. Maybe she was just lagging, her reflexes slow, but it came off right. It was a good lesson. Her instructor was a former Hungarian soldier who'd defected after the revolution—a fact Brook knew, though she had only the vaguest notion of what it meant.

"Let the towplane pull you a *leetle*," he told her in a thick accent.

They were riding together. She felt good. She felt on.

"Good," he said. "Watch the bump. What's your altitude?"

"Twenty-eight," she said.

"You missed the call," he said.

"Sorry." She'd missed the call at twenty-five. She was supposed to call out to him every five hundred feet.

"That's okay. Keep going."

At three thousand, they broke. She drifted toward another glider, circling upward in a thermal over the valley. She entered behind and below him.

"Call his position," he said.

"Three o'clock high, crossing behind."

"That was too easy," he said. "But you're getting the hang of it. That's good."

Cherry went up in the next round. He was already flying solo. His instructor watched him from the ground. They all had monikers, the Hungarian defector, the Vietnam tar baby, the American virgin. Cherry's instructor was the American virgin. He was a good pilot, methodical, tame. Cherry preferred him to the Hungarian, who got angry when you missed critical steps.

"I don't need more emotion right then," he'd said. "That's the last thing I need."

Brook sat in a lawn chair by the hangar, watching Cherry come off the tow and bank right. He was heading toward the thermal over the parking lot in the western Springs. The Hungarian, whose name was Desi, was telling her about his defection.

"It was broad daylight," he said. "We ran across the fields."

He'd been in America for thirty years and his English was still hard to understand.

"Why did you go in daylight?" she asked.

"We knew a surveyor. An engineer who did work on the border. He knew the guards. I was in the Army, you see. I had a star on my helmet."

The story didn't make sense to her. They should have sneaked out at midnight, coming out of hiding in the trees, or found a place where they didn't have to come out of the trees at all. Surely the forests were thick between Hungary and Austria.

"You bribed them?"

"Yes, of course. I had my wife with me. We ran across a big field, from here to the ridge"—he motioned in real space, about a half mile—"and there was a sand pit where they could see your tracks. Deep sand."

Cherry banked right and went for the ridge. That was something new. They were supposed to master thermals before they went to the ridge. Perhaps he was that far ahead of the rest of them.

Desi had his head down, remembering.

"Did they shoot at you?"

"Of course they did. They shot at us and at once my wife fell."

"They hit her?"

"No, she got up, laughing."

Brook didn't understand the story at all. First they had run out into a field in broad daylight, and then they had not been hit, and his wife had thought it was funny.

"It was funny, you see. She fell just at the moment they took the shots."

"What did you do?"

"She got up and I dropped my overcoat. I dropped it in the sand."

"Sounds reasonable," I said.

"It had all the wealth I owned."

"Your money?"

"No. The west wouldn't take rubles. They were worthless. So our family gave us a gold amulet. I had it in my pocket. That's why they were shooting at us."

"They didn't want to hit you?"

"No, they didn't care about that. They could have mowed us down. They had rifles and it was broad daylight. They knew everyone kept their possessions in their coats, you see. They knew that. They shot at us to scare. So we'd drop them."

"Ah, I see now. So you went into Austria penniless."

"We went back. I had been a soldier. I spoke their language. I stood on the Austrian border with one of their guards and asked for my amulet back."

"What did they say?"

"They said, 'Come up in the guard shack and get it.'"

There were four sailplanes in the thermal and Cherry was now deep in the shadow of the ridge. The American virgin was talking into the radio.

"Look," Desi said. "What is he doing?"

"He's on the ridge," she said.

"Yes, I see that."

The glider had solid altitude. Brook thought he was keeping the altitude so that he could turn back east and try to land. Desi stood up.

"What are you going to do?" she asked him.

It was just then that the glider veered inward sharply, toward the ridge. It was possible he was going over it, or on top of it, to

181

bounce back in the rippling air. At any rate, he didn't climb. He flew inward, like a pin attracted to a great magnet. The glider flew into the mountain and disappeared. There was just a puff of smoke, or dirt, like spores bursting from a great mushroom, or a dud, smoky match struck and snuffed out on the unwavering slope of the hill.

Chapter Twelve

The pain in his side was like a kind of weasel. When he tried to locate it by twisting, it squirmed around, skimmed from his kidneys to his gallbladder, skated along his ribs, hopped across his balls, like two river rocks, and then leaped onto his pancreas and slid down his liver. If he could only catch it, he thought, he could throttle it. He lay alone on his king-size bed and pictured the writhing weasel of his pain limp and lifeless in his outstretched fist.

At the hospital, tests had been taken. He'd gone home to wait. The analysis would arrive soon, maybe today. He felt convinced that they would have to slice him open and that, once inside, they would find a small, wet weasel clawing at his organs. It would look up, with its beady black eyes, startled, and they would simply catch it and strangle it and throw it into a bucket. Waller would ask them beforehand to save the weasel so he could see it. He wanted to see how big it was.

Valerie had crept in and set a mug of odorless tea on the nightstand.

"It has yarrow flowers in it," she told him. He watched her with the wary lassitude of a wounded animal. She sat gingerly on the bed, tucked her hair behind her ears, and rubbed her palms to warm them. Then she let her hands rest in a hovering position over his abdomen. She seemed intent on something.

"What are you doing?"

"Practicing. Keith's mom is teaching me Reiki."

"Of course."

"Your energy is all over the place. I'm going to try to settle it."

The weasel seemed to have been alerted to the presence of the healing hands and was now cowering under his left kidney. If she could fix him, Waller thought he would never again doubt the existence of the mind-body psychobiological muck that arrived by the truckload addressed to "Val Waller or Current Resident."

"It's all about breath, Dad. You have to learn how to breathe."

"Do me a favor and run a hot bath, would you?" Which, to his surprise, she did, leaving him in privacy to somehow rise and make his way toward it. On the way, he stopped at the medicine cabinet and popped some not quite out-of-date Percocet from Lauren's bunion surgery last year. The bath helped for a few minutes, but then the water began to bite his skin. He returned, moist and quivering, to the bed, deciding it was okay to lie on the bed in the midafternoon as long as he didn't get into it. As long as he didn't get into the bed, he was still in control. He took alternating breaths. One deep, then one shallow. He was in control.

He tried to unclench his teeth. How long had it been since he'd swallowed the Percocet? He lifted his head incrementally to look over the lukewarm tea at the clock. Eleven minutes. He hoped that Lauren would come and check on him. He hoped she would bring him a scotch on ice.

When the phone rang, Lauren answered it in two rings and carried it up the stairs. Now, he thought, they were getting somewhere. He hoped for good news, followed by a nice fresh scotch.

But when she came into the room, she held only the phone, pressed tightly into her ear, and she was nodding gravely and not speaking into it. He watched her face, preparing himself. Whatever it was was bad.

She cupped the microphone.

"It's Sil," she said.

"Sil Metz?" Waller was intensely irritated. How could Metz have information about his diagnosis before he did. Had he called the hospital himself?

"What's he want?"

"Something terrible has happened at the base." She sat down on the bed. She looked like she might cry. "I don't want to tell you right now," she said. She still had the phone in her hand.

"Let Sil tell me."

She nodded as though that idea had not occurred to her. She handed him the phone.

"What's up, Sil?" he said.

"There's been an accident down here," Metz said. "A kid crashed a glider into the ridge."

"Jesus. How bad?"

"Bad. He didn't make it. The place is going crazy. I just wanted to let you know."

"I'm coming down."

"You don't have to. It's under control. I didn't mean it's crazy out of control. It's just that everyone's upset. Shocked. I figured you should know."

"I'm coming down." He didn't think about the pain, or how he would lift himself up and down to the car. He only thought of being there.

"I just need to know one thing," Metz said. "I assume you want to ground the fleet, right? I've got to tell them. The press will be down." His voice was tense but calm. Waller decided his deputy was thinking clearly.

"Ground the fleet. Definitely. Ground everything."

"Even the Cessnas?"

"Everything. Ground everything. I'll be down in ten minutes."

"You don't have to. I just wanted to check."

"I'll be right there."

Waller hung up the phone. Lauren had her hand on his leg. There were tears on her face.

"Oh, John," she said. He sat up as gingerly as he could and put his arms around her. He rocked her for a moment in his arms, pressed her hair to his lips. He had not asked the cadet's name, or whether the cadet had been male or female, and because of that he did not know who to visualize or how to construct his prayer, which he uttered wordlessly now, into the back of Lauren's auburn hair, mumbling over the pronouns and leaving a blank space for the cadet's name.

Chapter Thirteen

The four officers from the Accident Review Board who descended like quiet, unwelcome buzzards onto the scene discovered through independent laboratory results that Cherry's blood samples held traces of alcohol. Long before this was released in paragraph two of the executive summary and in section II(B)(1)c. and IV(F)(6)a. of the official accident report, word of it shot outward, both radically and randomly, like the fragments of a cluster bomb, through the cadet wing, the divisions of academics, athletics, and military training, and the Cadets for Christian Fellowship, coming finally to rest in the cool, impartial archives of the *Colorado Springs Gazette*:

> *After a shocking glider crash at the Air Force Academy earlier this week, traces of alcohol were discovered in the body of the cadet piloting the glider, officials at the academy said.*
>
> *"We're deeply concerned with this development," said the vice commandant, Colonel Silas Metz. "We're taking every possible precaution to ensure that this kind of tragedy never happens again."*
>
> *The cadet, MacArthur Cherry, 19, from Arlington, Virginia, died in the crash.*
>
> *"With God's help, we'll get through this," Colonel*

Metz continued. He said the investigation's findings would be part of an effort to revamp the academy's social environment after being rocked by a rape scandal two years ago. The effort, called the Culture of Transformation (CoT), will "teach our cadet corps how to integrate appropriately without relying on the usual excesses of their generation." CoT involves a three-stage plan called PAS: preparation, actualization, and self-implementation.

"Right now we're in preparation," Metz said. "But the idea is that the cadets will someday run the program themselves."

Commandant John Waller was undergoing gallbladder surgery after a sudden collapse and was not available for comment.

On Monday, despite the conviction that he ought to be in the office answering press calls, Waller had let Lauren and Metz convince him to go to the Air Base Wing General Surgery Clinic for an appointment with his primary care manager. His PCM, the mustached Nepalese flight doctor named Dr. Kwak, had nodded at the blood tests and then dutifully entered a consult into the clinic's cobalt-based computer system. Dr. Kwak handed Waller a blue sheet of paper and explained that once the consult was reviewed and approved, TriCare would have thirty days to contact him to schedule an initial appointment. Waller was still assessing the idea of waiting thirty days for an initial appointment, which in itself implied an indefinite period of time before any cutting was done, when he looked up to find that Dr. Kwak had left the room and a two-striper orderly had come in to clean up the ghost of his leftover debris. Waller scanned the blue sheet of paper, hoping for more encouraging information, but the paper said exactly what Dr. Kwak had just told him.

The orderly smiled pleasantly at him. "How are you, sir?"

"I'm fine. Is there any chance I could see a doctor?"

The orderly looked around. "Didn't you just see one, sir?"

"Not in the fullest sense."

The orderly nodded. "I think I understand, sir. Let me see what I can do."

He left the room at once, and Waller gave more silent thanks for the existence of a competent enlisted corps. Five minutes later, the orderly returned with a gray-haired man in a long white coat, a stethoscope around his neck.

"Are you a surgeon?" Waller asked.

"Yes, sir. What can I do for you?"

"You can cut this goddamn pain out of my gut."

The surgeon pecked at a filthy keyboard on the counter and studied a monochrome screen. "How about Friday?"

Waller called Captain Kord to have all his Friday appointments canceled and asked him to draft a letter of appreciation to an Airman First-Class Bullbecker of the Tenth Air Base Wing Medical Clinic for "uncanny resistance to bureaucratic inertia and solid common sense in the face of mind-blowing incompetence."

"Do you really want me to write that, sir?"

"No. Think of something appropriate." He hung up.

On Friday afternoon he lay on the operating table while the surgeon and the anesthesiologist talked about their college-age sons. Waller was curled in the fetal position beneath an umbrella of voices.

"What's wrong with kids these days?" the anesthesiologist said. His son was off with some Danish environmental group studying butterflies in Costa Rica.

"That's nothing," the surgeon said. "My son wants to go to Mongolia to spend a year in a monastery. All his friends are enrolled at the University of Denver. I keep asking him why he wants to go to Mongolia. Where *is* Mongolia, exactly?"

"Somewhere in China, I think."

Waller wanted to tell them they had it easy. Having teenage sons was nothing like having teenage daughters, one of whom spent forty-five minutes a day in the lotus position in the middle of the living room and one who wanted to join the Marines and do things that would have made even him flinch. He wanted to say that daughters were a divine curse, and he could not help but love them, but that love frightened him, frightened him terribly, because it was delicate and felt awkward in his hands, and he feared that if he handled it too tightly he would crush it, so he had taught himself to love his daughters from a distance, holding his breath, like a spectator watching a high-wire act with no safety net. Except that Lauren was the net. He hoped and trusted that she was the net, that she would be poised to catch them long before he noticed them wobble and fall.

"Take a deep breath," the anesthesiologist said, and Waller did. He was about to tell them everything, about his daughters and about Mac Cherry, whom he'd never known but was like a son, a son he'd failed, a son he would call back if he could, if he could reach out into the deep blue well of sky and draw him back. A part of him lifted into the sky, into the airiness that was smoother than any wave he'd ever flown—a son, a son, a son. He'd never had a son. He would never have one now. But he had, for a brief moment, known one and loved him, sent him into the blue—

The surgery was over. He woke up on a cot in the hallway with what felt like a small sheep draped over his legs. Somewhere, a room was being disinfected and readied, and a bed was being made. He spent the night in an uncomfortable, morphine-induced sleep. His dreams involved Toni hunkering down behind a rock while filthy, lecherous men shot at her from the cover of the caves, and Waller was trying to kill them, but somehow all his ammunition had been replaced with sawdust that fell helplessly from the 30-millimeter cannon on his airplane.

Thanks, Balls, came her voice over the radio.

He dreamed of Mac Cherry. They were looking for the lost bird.

She's gone, Cherry told him. But Waller could see the bird, high over them, circling in the sun. *Look up,* he said, but Cherry would not look up.

On Saturday morning, he tried to call Bud, but the DSN lines from the hospital were busy. He waited for Lauren to arrive and cart him home. He thought about the night's dreams, which had been ridiculous and had made him weep. What had he done? He had betrayed them. He had betrayed Lauren. Maybe he'd betrayed Mac Cherry, too.

When Lauren came and touched him with her sun-warm hands, he nearly wept again. She had brought clothes for him to change into—his Class-A blues, which he blinked at before he remembered that this morning was the memorial service for Mac Cherry. She laid the clothes over a chair and put her hands to his face, and he folded his hands over hers and held them firmly, like a rope that might pull him up from some perilous ground.

"Forgive me," he whispered.

"For what?" she asked.

He held her, squeezing his eyes to hold back the tears he was afraid would drown them both if he let them go. He had betrayed Lauren. He had gone to bed with another woman, but what was worse, so much worse, was that he had thought about her later, had brought her into their bed with his thoughts of lust and a hunger that was only vanity, was only a need to feed his own desire and ego. The ego of a fighter pilot. The vanity of his impenetrable heart. He'd held himself back from her. Lauren might not even know, but he hated himself for it.

"Forgive me," he cried. "Forgive me."

Chapter Fourteen

The memorial service was scheduled for ten o'clock on Saturday in order to accommodate the needs of Major General Patrick Cherry, who was flying in alone to attend the service before returning to Virginia for the official funeral at Arlington National Cemetery the following day. The upperclassmen in charge of military training planned to conduct Saturday-morning inspections as usual. They were debating the addition of a formal march to the mandatory chapel services for Cadet Cherry when discussions with certain officers who oversaw the military training program suggested such dedication to duty might be misconstrued by the public as somewhat overzealous. A ripple of disagreement arose within the staff—other officers argued that such dedication to duty was *precisely* the image that ought to be portrayed to the public. Dedication, restraint, order—these were the qualities of a functional military and ought to be displayed more, not *less* rigorously during moments of loss. The first group of officers counterargued that the cadets ought to have time to mourn the loss of a fellow cadet. The second group shot back that wars did not stop to allow time for mourning. A few humanities instructors wondered aloud what Mac Cherry might have wanted, and someone wrote an essay about it that was published in the cadet newspaper, *The Falconer*, the same day that Cherry's remains lay in the dark bay of a C-141 en route to Andrews Air Force Base.

Conflicting reports concerning duty hours, inspection time, and uniform of the day filtered hourly through the ranks to the general corps, so that most of the lowest-ranking cadets adopted a wait-and-see attitude. Official orders were muted, counteracted, and sometimes strengthened by a number of rumors generated in the whispery hallways, which sent the air into such a stir that Brook found herself riding above it in a sort of hemispheric calm.

"This is all such bullshit," Billy said on Thursday, when the waves of conflicting and superseding orders and rumors had reached their highest level of interference.

"What?" she asked, absently.

They were standing outside his room. Major Wein, the squadron air officer commanding, had gone to Billy's room the previous day with a captain and a staff sergeant to pack up all of Cherry's things and ship them back to Virginia. The bed that had been Cherry's was now a blue-and-white-pinstriped mattress. The desk was bare, and the corkboard over it was needled with the random eyes of metal pushpins. Billy was standing by the sink where his toilet bag was propped on the rim opposite two faint, glossy circles that were the outlines of Cherry's shaving cream and squirt soap. Brook resisted the urge to reach out and touch them. She had walked down the hall to talk to Billy, but now she couldn't bring herself to enter the room. Billy's bed was on the far end of the room, nearest the window, and she couldn't seem to walk through Cherry's half of the room to get to it.

"I wonder if the rum is still under there." She was looking at Cherry's headboard and remembering Paula tuck herself inside the drawer and show them how to hide the bottle. Brook couldn't remember if they'd finished the bottle or if Billy and Cherry had put it back under the headboard. "Are you getting a new roommate?"

"They asked me to change squadrons. They were pretty insistent."

"Are you going to?"

He shrugged. "I don't want to. I like all this space. Besides, we might all be kicked out before long."

Someone had checked the squadron logs on the night before the crash and discovered that Cherry had been out with Brook, Billy, and Paula. The three of them had been ordered immediately to the Office of Special Investigations to answer questions and write statements about where they had been and what they had done the previous night. They all told the truth because there wasn't enough time to coordinate a reasonable lie. They underwent blood and urine tests at the hospital. Traces of alcohol had been found, and now they were scheduled the following week for a disciplinary-action board. Lex had taken to spending all her free time in the library to distance herself from the controversy. Brook had no one to talk to. She had come down to talk to Billy, and now she couldn't walk into the room.

"You going to dinner?" he asked.

"I don't think so. No, definitely not."

The idea of pushing beyond this moment, of walking to Mitchell Hall with Billy and fingering over the trays of mushy food and sitting down to something so ordinary as dinner seemed impossible. Cherry wouldn't be there. Everywhere they went, Cherry wouldn't be.

"We don't have to go to Mitch's. We could go over to Arnie's. We could get a pizza."

Brook shook her head. What she wanted was for Billy to pull her into the room and close the door and put his arms around her, and she wanted to breathe in the skin on his chest and cry against him and have him whisper soothing things in her ear and stroke her hair, and maybe for him to kiss her, though she wouldn't think beyond that, just the skin and breath surrounding her, giving her a way to climb up out of all this icy deadness. She stood in the doorway staring at the corner of Cherry's mattress, breathing shallow breaths, as though stillness might invite him closer.

"What do you want to do, Brook?"

"I don't know. I thought I might come in."

He looked behind him, as if there might be some interesting thing he'd missed, and then he stepped back and opened his hand toward the chair next to Cherry's bare desk. She brushed by him, her eyes darting past the empty space between Cherry's bed and the closet. She couldn't bring herself to sit in his chair. She walked by it and sat on the edge of Billy's bed.

"It's so different now," she said.

He had gone out into the hallway to hinge the door at ninety degrees, as by regulation when two cadets of the opposite sex were in a room together, and now he came through the room and pulled his own chair out from his desk and sat in it.

"It is different," he said.

"I feel like it was our fault."

"It wasn't our fault."

"But if we hadn't gone out—"

"Don't think of it that way."

"How else can we think of it?"

"It was his choice. He knew what he was doing."

"If only we hadn't gone to Charlie's."

"It might not have made a difference."

"But what if it did?"

Her eyes were tearing now, and he reached over and put his hand on her leg.

"Cherry was such a good pilot," she said. "How could this happen?"

"He was just learning. He was brand new."

"He was good, and you know it."

"Yes, he was."

"I don't understand it."

"I don't either."

He had his other hand, the hand not on her leg, on the back of his chair with his chin resting on it, so that he had to look up slightly to see her eyes; she looked into the blueness of them and saw what she wanted to see.

"Don't you miss him being here?" she asked.

He nodded incrementally, his eyes never leaving hers.

"What will we do without him?"

Now he shrugged and withdrew his hand. He sat up in the chair. "We'll carry on. That's what he would want."

He stood up, and she thought it, whatever it was, was over. He went to the mirror over the sink and ran his hand through his hair.

She was trying to stand, trying to come up with the strength to leave. "Are you going over to Mitch's now?"

He turned to her. "Are you hungry?"

"No."

"Me neither."

"What are you going to do?"

He leaned against the sink and looked into it. He seemed to be debating something. Without looking up, he said, "I'll tell you, I was thinking about closing the door."

She nodded, though he wasn't looking at her. She stared at Cherry's bed. He suddenly seemed very far away.

"Why now?" she asked. Billy was still staring at the sink.

"Don't you want to?"

"I guess I do."

"We don't have to."

She said nothing, and he turned and looked out into the hallway, which was empty, and then unclasped the hinge at the top of the door and let it sweep shut, and then he walked over and sat next to her on the bed.

"We don't have to do anything," he said. "We could just lie down."

He touched her on the shoulder and then ran his fingers through her hair just the way she had wanted, and she closed her eyes and tried to still want it as much as she had when she stood at the door, and she tried not to think of it as a betrayal of Cherry.

"I feel guilty," she said.

"Don't."

"Have you wanted this all along?"

"All along, yes." In fact, it hadn't occurred to him until he saw her standing at the door, reluctant to leave, so that he couldn't go eat his dinner, and he'd been hungry, he was always hungry here, there was never enough to eat, but he had put that aside when he saw the way she stood in the doorway, and he kept it to himself now, along with the thought that he was hungry even now and would have to remember to walk over to Arnie's to get a sub before they closed.

He leaned over and kissed her, and a different kind of hunger took over, and he pulled her back onto the bed with a motion that was both natural and awkward, since he hadn't been with a girl since leaving Arizona, and until now he'd never thought of being with Brook, although now the idea seemed so obvious he began to believe he had planned it all along.

She held him a little too tightly. He thought she must be inexperienced the way she clamped onto him so that he had trouble moving his hands between them. Or maybe it was the grief, he thought, and he waited a little longer until she loosened up enough for him to get his hand up under her shirt. She felt maddeningly strong and soft, and he ran his fingers along her muscles and onto the soft hills of her breasts and back again.

She was wonderfully firm. He worked his fingers under the elastic of her shorts where the skin was a little moist with sweat but still soft, and he was beginning to think about the even moister region farther down, folded inside its cotton sheath, that he would find a way to tickle out of hiding, teasing his fingers along that delightful skin inside the hem of her athletic shorts—

"I think we should stop," she said, breathlessly.

"Why?" His mouth covered hers, tried to suppress any more words. He felt her stiffen now, her body bucking up in refusal, and he wanted to ease it open again like the soft leather of a saddle or a baseball glove that you only had to work long enough to make elastic.

"It's too soon. I'm not ready."

He knew the signs. He had been here before. You had to slow down, back up, give it a minute or two, or a day, or a week, and you would get what you wanted. The secret was to give the impression that you could wait indefinitely. And maybe you could. In a week or two, this might not seem so imperative.

He pulled her shirt down and patted her on the stomach. She lay on her back, looking up at him with something like regret and desire, and he thought he could wait a day or a week, or two, and he would still want it, and it would be worth the wait.

"You want to walk over to Arnie's now?" he asked.

She smiled and touched his cheek in a way that made him think for a moment that they would stay after all, but knowing better, he rose to a sitting position and looked at the clock. He had forty-five minutes before Arnie's closed, minus a five-minute walk. "What do you say? Should we go over to Arnie's?"

Something bothered her. It had not been the right time, and he had not refused, and that should have made her feel better, but instead it annoyed her. A moment before, she had been thinking about the closeness of him, his strength and the articulateness of his body, and how right it had felt—yes, the *rightness* of their bodies together, except that Cherry's bare bed lay three feet away and he wasn't yet cold in the ground, and that was what had made her stop, and he had done as she asked, and now he was sitting next to her talking about food.

"I think I'll stay," she said. She could not bear to sit across from him watching him stuff a sub into his mouth, which had so recently been on her face and neck—would he eat with the same enthusiasm?—and had so abruptly (at her request—she knew, she understood that—and yet so *abruptly*) risen into a neutral position.

"Well, do you want me to bring you back something?"

"No." She got up and walked out of the room without looking back.

———————————

SAMIs were canceled at the eleventh hour on Saturday morning, a relief to Brook since she hadn't bothered to clean her side of the room despite sharp looks from Lex. They wore service dress and wheel caps, picking the lint off each other's shoulders before meeting in the alcove outside Sijan Hall. It had been decided that they would not march, but they would walk together as squadrons, leaving the controlled area inside the metal gates and climbing the stairs to the chapel where various civilian bystanders stood watching them pass.

Brook walked up the steps with Billy. They were known to have been friends of the dead cadet, and the others let them pass with a kind of deference. So many parents and friends had sent flowers that they spilled out of the open doors and onto the outer steps. The anteroom and upper, Protestant area of the chapel were nauseatingly bright with them. Brook and Billy made their way into the pews. The chapel smelled of pine finish. Someone was playing the grand organ in the upper loft. The tall stained-glass windows beamed at them, flooding the room with an abstract, cheery geometry.

The chaplain was black. There was no particular reason that he shouldn't be black. It was just that Brook, coming from New England, had never seen a man of the cloth who was not old and graying, a bland and somewhat flinching look on his waxy face. Here, there was a black chaplain leading a mostly white congregation, a Christian chaplain leading a service for a Jewish cadet. A dead cadet. Brook's friend, the Jewish almost-pilot whose father had named him MacArthur. Whose father sat in the front row amid the senior Air Force officers, a green island in a sea of blue. The military embraced all things, smoothed them into unquestioning sameness. Why shouldn't the chaplain be black? Why shouldn't a cadet fly his glider into the side of a mountain? The military didn't judge. It took things in, accepted them, moved on.

"God is our refuge, and our strength."

The chaplain began in a low, generous voice. The microphone arced downward, like a dying tulip. The cadets sat stiffly, lining the shadowy rows of pews. What had been little more than a murmur of voices settled into an austere and uncomfortable silence. The air was warm. The cadets sat solemnly but without feeling much pity. Many of them blamed Cherry.

"Let us remember the story of David, who lost a son. David heard his servants whispering and asked them whether his child was dead. And they told him."

Brook tried to listen, but her attention drifted away. The stained glass glinted like heavy jewels. High above the spare stone altar, through the old, graying transoms, the clouds paraded across a procession of smoky panes. Brook watched them, God's little flying banners, dingy clouds passing over a dingy sky. Some of the phrases caught her attention.

"—gave everything to his life, but when death came, he let it go—"

Some of the cadets had begun to doze off. There was no coffin, only a wheel cap and his Corfam shoes to draw their eyes down, punctuate the chaplain's words. In the book cubby in front of Brook, a pamphlet had been curled between the New Testament and the hymnal. She pulled back the corner and read the words, "Deep Sea Scriptures."

She saw an open book, its weary, sun-bleached pages fluttering like sea grass in the cool blue water. She blinked. "Dead" was the word. She let the pamphlet slip away from her fingers.

Cherry's father's back and thick shoulders bobbed in the front row. He sat next to General Waller, emblazoned in brass. She might walk up to Mac's father after the service and shake hands. She wanted to know the part of Mac that was still living, would go on living back in Virginia, a place Brook might well never see. He was Mac's father, but he was also a two-star general. She couldn't exactly walk up to him and say hello.

He would be flanked by senior officers and their wives, and she would have to squeeze through them, their eyes falling on the nothingness of her cadet rank, as she explained that she had been Cherry's friend. He might misunderstand her. Or he might find it irrelevant. Perhaps Cherry's history at the academy had been too short for his father to appreciate it. Perhaps Cherry had never mentioned her in his e-mails. She knew they shared e-mails—she knew that about Cherry—but what did they talk about? How much did Mac share? In truth, she was chickenshit, she simply lacked the courage to walk up and introduce herself.

"Be quiet," Billy hissed. "Stop sobbing."

She wiped her face with the various parts of her hands and then placed them in an orderly way in her lap. The chaplain was reading from something.

"'—all the rivers run into the sea, and yet the sea is not full. To the place where the rivers flow, there they flow again—'"

There was no point, per se, in any one death. That was certainly true in war. It just happened. It swept down like a bird of prey and then escaped, leaving the sky blue and quiet. This was how you took the long view. This was how you soldiered on.

"Hush," Billy said. He touched her briefly on the leg, and the touch gave her an unwelcome thrill.

A rabbi stood, now, uttering something impressive sounding in Hebrew. Brook listened to his voice. It was a complicated sound, the way Judaism seemed to be a complicated religion. Cherry had never taken the authorized Friday allowance to attend temple. He had stayed in the squadron with everyone else, getting ready for SAMI. She tried to remember whether he had avoided certain foods at mealtimes and couldn't bring any to mind. She suspected he had not been a rigorous Jew, but then she might be wrong. She had known his shoe size, his height and weight, the shape and colorations of the back of his head, but she hadn't known things about him that seemed fundamental now.

After the rabbi sat down next to the chaplain, the vice commandant of cadets, Colonel Metz, stood up from the front pew and took the podium on the other side of the altar. His voice was high and unpleasant.

"Mac Cherry is someone we'll miss dearly. I hope we can remember him in our hearts and also remember the story in Luke of the man who was invited to the great supper but excused himself because he had to go and prove his oxen."

Some of the cadets who'd fallen asleep shifted now from the change in voice and straightened in the pews.

"All that we can do, as his friends, is embrace our Savior, Jesus Christ, and pray for the well-being of Mac Cherry's soul. He died preparing to meet the great enemy, the enemy who is Satan. But we must carry on. Our great institution is strong. We must overcome adversity. We must throw off the boobytrap of mortal sin, which threatens to ambush us at every turn."

"What's he talking about?" Brook whispered to Billy.

"We must not let doubt enter our minds," Metz continued. "We must not be swayed by moral relativism. We all make our own path to the Lord, but it is our responsibility as a fellowship of cadets to guide our brothers and sisters toward the *right* path. Because our enemy is so clearly a spiritual enemy. This is no Cold War. We may look back on those days as times of relative peace. But now, in this war, we are the righteous. We have divine moral compass."

Here Waller rose to a standing position, but the chaplain had bolted upright and grabbed his microphone.

"Thank you, Colonel Metz."

"Divine moral compass—"

"Thank you, sir. We're so pleased to have so many friends to help us mourn today. "

The pews were silent. The rabbi had sat bolt upright in his chair, watching Metz, and then the chaplain, with unfeigned distress. Waller, seeing that Metz had been deflected, turned his attention to Cherry's father, also sitting upright and staring at Metz as though he had not quite heard him correctly. Waller touched him on the shoulder.

"Are you all right, Pat?"

"Who *is* that guy?"

Metz began again: "Divine moral compass—"

"Thank you very much, Colonel." The chaplain had walked briskly past the altar to Metz's podium and was gently leading the vice commandant back to his seat.

"We'll be hosting a vigil—"

"Thank you for your words."

After the chaplain gave a final, moving prayer that nobody heard, the service ended and the congregation began to filter out into the sunlight, which produced the sensation of a hangover after the subdued lighting of the chapel. Brook and Billy shuffled with the crowd past the chrome-and-veneer tables in the anteroom. Brook caught sight of one of the brochures stacked neatly against the wall.

Consider your emotional tigers.

She imagined an ambush of Bengal cats lashing their thick, fur-lined paws at rage, contempt, loneliness. *Triggers* was what it said.

"What the hell was all that about?" she asked Billy.

"I don't know. I don't know fuck all that goes on around here."

Outside, a formation of Cessnas from the aeroclub motored across the athletic fields. The plane in the number-three slot lifted up and pulled back out of formation, and the remaining three, in missing-man formation, pattered overhead. The propellers gave off a pleasing hum. Some of the cadets on their way across the Terrazzo stopped to watch. The gap in the middle was like an empty tooth socket. Watching them, Brook began to cry, not noisily, but high up in the roof of her mouth, like a child.

"It's not supposed to happen like this," she said.

"It happens."

"Not like this. It doesn't happen like this."

The cadets began drifting away, toward the dorms, toward lunch. They had the afternoon off. Out on a rocky slope of the ridge, Brook imagined a few bits of metal still glinting in the sun.

"I'd like to climb up there," she said.

"You wouldn't see much. They've cleared most of it away."

"All the same, I'd like to go up."

She was hoping that Billy might offer to climb with her. But Tina, the girl from Charlie's house, had come out of the chapel and stopped to gaze at the airplanes. Her hair fell prettily over her shoulders. Billy trotted up the stairs and took her elbow. He led her back to Brook.

"I can't believe it," she said. "I just can't."

She wore a thin black dress with a flower sewn on the belt. A bit of tissue poked out from behind the flower, and she pulled it out and dabbed at her mascaraed eyes. "I probably don't belong here. I had to come, though."

Billy put his arm around her. Brook found herself resenting that.

"That must be his father," Tina said. She had turned to brush the hair from her eyes.

General Cherry was standing at the top of the stairs with General Waller and his wife and the chaplain. The chaplain seemed to be consoling him, or perhaps apologizing.

"I didn't know Mac very well," Tina said. "I think I loved him, though. I know that sounds crazy."

She was breaking down now, collapsing into tissue and hair. Brook looked up at the sky where the Cessnas were turning slowly toward the field. Tina didn't know Mac, she thought.

"It's okay," Billy said.

"I'm going back to the dorm," Brook said.

Billy nodded vaguely. "Come on," he said to Tina. "I'll take you home."

"So long," Brook said. She'd held visions of going back to the dorm with Billy, of breaking down there with him in teary passion. It never held up, what you hoped would happen. She would have to think of what to do now. Maybe she would hike up to the crash site. That would take the afternoon. She went back to her room and changed clothes—Lex had already escaped the service, had probably fled to the library—but she was suddenly tired. The idea of climbing alone through the thick, dry brush seemed miserable. She lay down on her bed and fell asleep.

She dreamed that Cherry was talking to her. "There's water under the trees," he said. "What do you mean?" she asked. "What trees?" She woke up longing to walk down the hall and tap on his door and say, "What was all that business about the water?"

The light was still high. She went out. She would hike to the crash site, after all. Why not be with him up there, now that the dorm was so empty, so mercilessly quiet? She found herself veering downhill, toward the hangar. Why not? She could go to the hangar, where Cherry had last been alive. She might talk to Ben Railey, Cherry's soaring instructor, about what had gone wrong. Maybe he would be in the mood to talk.

She walked across the airfield—it was quiet; everything had been grounded except for the one missing-man formation after the funeral—no more like a living airfield than the Hogs squadron hallway had been like a dorm. She couldn't decide whether it would be a better gesture to fly again as soon as possible, as much as possible, or never to fly again.

In the hangar, Railey was in the back room talking with someone. She could hear voices and tapped lightly on the door.

"Yeah."

Rails was sitting across from the commandant. General Waller was still wearing his Class-A uniform thick with ribbons over the chest, but the jacket was unbuttoned and he slouched awkwardly in the chair. Two cans of beer sat open on the desk. Brook backed away. "I'm sorry, sir."

"It's okay," Waller said. "Come in."

"I don't want to bother you."

"It's all right. Come in and talk. You were a friend of Cadet Cherry, weren't you?"

"Yes, sir."

"We met in Stanley Canyon one day, didn't we? You and Mac were looking for a falcon. What's your name?"

"Brook Searcy, sir."

"I'm very sorry about what happened."

She nodded. She had forgotten about the day in the canyon.

"You were out with him the night before." The Commandant had sharp eyes that met hers evenly, without shifting around the way most of the instructors' eyes did when they talked to her. His face looked pale and tired.

"Yes, sir."

"You should stop this now," Rails said. He had his feet crossed on the pulled-out drawer of his desk.

"You've already given a statement, haven't you?" Brook nodded. "Was it your opinion that he was drunk?"

"I mean, just call someone and have it put in writing," Rails said. He didn't look at Brook.

"No, sir."

"How much did he have to drink?"

"You are burning good evidence," Rails said.

"I'm not sure," she said. "He didn't seem drunk."

"Were you with him all night?"

"Except for a short time."

"What was happening in that short time?"

"We were in the living room talking and he was outside with a girl."

"With a cadet?"

"No, sir. A girl from downtown."

"Were they drinking?"

"I don't know, sir. He was pretty happy when he came back inside, but he wasn't gone all that long. I mean, it seemed like he had other things on his mind."

Waller nodded. The girl looked pale and frightened, but well enough in control. He wondered how this would affect her, this tragedy so early in her career. He at least had already been a fighter pilot by the time he witnessed his first death.

"Are you okay?" he asked.

"Yes, sir."

"It's a dumb question, isn't it? How could you be okay?"

Brook said nothing. She'd only seen the commandant up close the one time before, and otherwise from a distance, hurrying across the Terrazzo or on the stage in Arnold Hall, and now he was looking intently at her, not with the judgment she was so used to seeing in the faces of officers, but with what seemed like genuine concern.

"Are you going to keep flying?"

"The gliders are grounded, sir."

"I mean when they come back up. Are you going to fly again?"

"I hadn't thought about it, sir."

"You need to fly. I want you to promise me that you'll fly again. It's important to go back up."

"Yes, sir."

She thought that he must know she still had to go through a disciplinary board for having been out drinking the night before Cherry died, but it seemed unwise to bring that up now.

"You promise?"

"Yes, sir."

"All right, you can go."

Brook saluted and walked out of the office, closing the door. Behind her, the conversation resumed. A shadowy stillness hung in the hangar. All the airplanes seemed to be in mourning. She walked back across the airfield to the base. Would she fly again? Maybe. A chill ran over her. How could she ever fly without Cherry's breath behind her, and yet, what had he ever told her?

An image flashed: a pale wing shimmering in the sunlight, banking into a turn the wrong way, *into* the ridgeline. Had he seen the sunlight turn to shadow? Had he seen the tops of the trees and then the branches shiny with sap and then the reddish-brown floor of dead pine needles and the roots of the trees, and had he thought, *This is the last thing I will ever see?*

Over and over, she saw the wing banking low in the sunlight and the sunlight turning to shadow. She saw it as she imagined he had seen it, the way the purple dusk of the ridgeline must have washed over the wing and then with one swallow engulfed the glider. This one image that was so much clearer than any memory would stay with her for years, come to her in dreams, so that she would wake up with her hand clasped around an imaginary stick, pulling to the right to climb up out of the valley, as though the airplane could still be saved.

The Terrazzo was quiet. A few cadets walked here and there. The sun had started its long descent over the ridgeline. The chapel doors were closed and all the tourists and well-wishers had gone home. Everything was the same as always except for the flag, which flew at half-mast. The cadets on flag detail were standing around the pole with their white-gloved hands folded behind their backs. Brook hurried toward Sijan Hall, hoping to make the doors before the bugle sounded. If the bugle sounded while she was outside, she would have to stand at attention while the flag was lowered, hand over hand, to the bullhorned recording of "The Star Spangled Banner," and Brook was not ready to witness closure on this particular day.

Unseemly though it was, Brook picked up her pace to a trot. It was unbecoming to be caught evading the flag lowering, but she didn't care. She couldn't bear to stand at attention and watch the flag come down. It was too much to give.

"What's your rush?" one cadet called to her when she reached the Terrazzo. Brook ran faster. Someone would probably get her name, probably report her. She made it to Sijan just as the bugle began, and she closed the door behind her, catching her breath. Another cadet was standing inside the doors holding a packet of green pamphlets.

"Just made it." He smiled, handing her one.

She took it from him absently and started up the stairs. On the paper in her hand, there was a two-tone, shadow-heavy picture of Mac Cherry's official yearbook photograph with a caption underneath that read:

Where is Mac Cherry now??

Whoever sacrifices to any god, except Jesus alone,
shall be doomed.

CCF—guiding by Divine Moral Compass

Beneath the signature was an invitation to join in prayer for Cadet Cherry the following Friday. Brook read it. The commandant had suspended all evangelical activities inside the gated areas. The CCF was still allowed to meet in the chapel, but they weren't supposed to hand out pamphlets or other tangible evidence of their indefatigable faith, because it was considered an affront to other religious minorities. Brook had not realized there were religious minorities at the academy. She had not realized there were any minorities, herself included. So far had the academy gone in conditioning her own mind that she had truly believed the academy "would not tolerate injustices based on ethnic, religious, or gender differences," as they had stated along with the official sexual harassment policy in the opening pages of *Contrails*. In fact, the CCF itself had seemed to her a kind of religious minority that was being "tolerated" on the basis of its right to exist.

But appropriating Cherry into their cause went beyond tolerance. She stopped halfway up the stairs and turned around. The cadet was looking up at her, his eyes brown and wary, not unlike a fox. She glared at him, but for the millionth time, words escaped her. Lifting her hand up in the draft of the stairwell, she let the pamphlet drift down, gliding along the mild current of air to land with perfect, silent grace at his feet.

PART III

The Tunnels

Chapter Fifteen

The Cadets for Christian Fellowship vigil was attended by a quarter of the wing's four thousand cadets, as well as a number of instructors and administrative staff, and reporters from both the *Colorado Springs Gazette* and the *Denver Post*. Some of them stood through the speeches and prayers and candle lighting with the gentlest of intentions. Others went believing that through sheer vocalizing, they might coax Cherry's soul back onto a righteous path, and still others went to glory in the volume of their own voices. Some had agendas. Others had no agendas but sensed opportunity. A number of them were procrastinating over papers due the following week, as the semester had just begun, and some went purely for entertainment. But to a person, once inside the chapel with its night-blackened windows and rows of candles held aloft and swaying, they sang and listened to the impromptu speeches with an air of wistful mourning, as though they had known Mac Cherry all their lives.

Neither Brook nor Billy attended, but nor were they together. Brook was locked in her room, studying under lamplight. Billy was shooting baskets in the shadowy gym.

Billy held a Wilson NCAA Final Four Edition basketball in his hands, and Brook held a spiral-bound collection of essays from her Military Philosophy 201 class, folded to an essay by Nikolay Berdyayev called "Thoughts on the Nature of War." She read with her single pillow folded under her head, the text propped in her lap, a pint of ice cream—Twisted Monkey—with a cafeteria spoon sticking out of it propped next to her hip. She'd been gaining weight since the end of rugby season last spring. Well, the hell with them. She would gain weight.

> *At a glance, war is a clash of material masses, physical violence, killing, maiming, the working of monstrous mechanical weapons. It would seem that war is a submersion into matter and has no sort of relation to spirit.*

The mix of stimulant and depressant did colorful things to her brain and made it hard to focus. She needed to focus. There were large chunks of information to be memorized. Memorized and then forgotten.

> *One may desire to be fully clean and free of the guilt over the violence and the killing, and at the same time may want for oneself and one's family, one's native land, the peace and prosperity that comes at the price of killing. There is a redemption in the very act of accepting guilt in oneself. Therefore, the guilty are morally higher than the pure.*

She pried a spoonful from the carton of Twisted Monkey.

> *This selfsame guilt, at the basis of all culture, is also at the basis of war—*

Death was like a silent violin whose music came only when you didn't listen for it. This thought came to her suddenly. Death played on silent, invisible strings.

> *Each of us benefits from having the police—*

The accident report had not been released. Perhaps that was the problem, the lingering variable that kept everyone, cadets and staff alike, in a state of unrest. She thought that if the accident report might come out, might deliver some final, definitive reason for the crash, they could put it behind them. *She* could put it behind her. But until then, an indictment on Cherry's guilt or innocence could not be handed down. Had he made some fatal mistake, something that could be handed down to the rest of them as a lesson, or had he been victim to something beyond his control?

There was only one way for a pilot to know he would not die in an airplane: It was simply not to fly. If Cherry hadn't flown, he would probably be alive. His choice, and therefore he got what he had coming. This was what half the cadet wing thought. And yet, is it not an outrage that mechanics, or science, may fail us? (Science never fails us—that's what's taught to us by the scientists, but what do they know of putting all one's trust in a concoction of steel panels and bolts?) How was Cherry to know that this was the day he should refuse to fly? Such a pilot, who acted on impulse and superstition, was not worthy of flying. That was the thinking of the other half of the wing, the half who would argue that not flying meant not living.

This is to say that all pilots, whether they fly or not, must eventually die, though no one ever believes it will happen today. In many ways, they all wished the accident to be Cherry's fault, so that there would be a sound reason, and something to avoid, and not another chalk mark for ominous, wordless Fate. The cadets and the inexperienced staff believed the report would answer their questions. The CCF had practically staked their reputation on it. But to Brook, what seemed to hang in the balance was not the vindication of either side, but Cherry's soul, sitting in bureaucratic purgatory, and she longed to release it.

In formation, she now stared at the head and neck of one Richard Halburn, whom his friends called Hal, and whom Brook went out of her way not to know. It was conceivable that Richard Halburn was a very good cadet, but Brook didn't want to look at his head. She wanted to look at Cherry's head, with the translucent white flesh of a garden grub and ears percolating out from under his cap. Hal's head was peppered with rich, dark stubble that halted starkly before a pale neckline. An ugly mole poked out from under his collar. Hal had thick shoulders that dishonored Cherry's spindly frame. Brook resented him. He stood at attention, his back arched severely, as though a wedge had been driven under his spine, and he didn't seem to appreciate the fact that he was standing on hallowed ground.

They went on with their drills, their parades, their formations. In September, mandatory attendance at all academy football games began. An entire season of Saturday afternoons spent dressed in blues, shivering in the stands. Some of the cadets would tuck flasks of Jeremiah Weed, a kind of liquid branding iron, inside their uniforms of the day. Brook would take cautious nips of whatever passed within arm's length, the alcohol making her stomach turn, making the games seem doleful and long. Worse, they would be forced to sing the third stanza to the Air Force song—

> *Here's a toast to the host*
> *Of those who love the vastness of the sky,*
> *To a friend we send a message of his brother men who fly.*
> *We drink to those who gave their all of old,*
> *Then down we roar to score the rainbow's pot of gold—*

They would sing without a drop of irony, or worse, with sodden melodrama, dedicating the verse to their fallen brother. Brook couldn't stand it. Already, Cherry had become a symbol.

She longed for Billy to find her. They'd hardly spoken since the afternoon in his room. She had waited for him to come, but he had stayed away. It had never been complicated before, and now, suddenly, she was too shy to knock on his door. He looked at her every morning in formation, and then in the same place every afternoon. The academy staff, that contraption of policies and counter policies, had stepped up the afternoon parades to five per week—a token for the tourists who lined themselves more thickly than ever along the chapel wall now that a cadet had died. As they assembled, Billy looked at her with his uncanny blue eyes and a smile that might be lonely or complicit or guilty or all those things, and then he stood behind her and held thoughts she couldn't read. At meals, the upperclassmen grilled the new cadets and mocked the officers, in undertones, until their twenty minutes of mealtime ended and they were swept along in the current of the day. He had probably forgotten her.

Brook put the notebook down and went out to the bathroom. In the hallway, some firsties had just come in from the Terrazzo. They were drunk, swaying against each other. They looked like they might break into song. Brook watched them for a moment. They were happy drunks and they made her sick. They grinned vaguely in her direction. Clearly, they hadn't been at the vigil. They'd been downtown at a party, or up in Stanley Canyon, or down in the academy tunnels—a place full of rumor that sounded mysterious but was really, Brook suspected, the exaggerated concoction of so many bored cadets cooped up on campus for too long, better in the imagination than in the flesh, so she had never gone. Passing the firsties on the way to the bathroom, she gave them such a wide berth that her shoulder brushed the opposite wall. But they didn't even notice her.

In the bathroom, she decided to take a shower. She needed her towel. She would have to go back into the hallway and down to her room to get it. She waited, listened to the voices of the boys as they made their way along the corridor, jostling over some recent joke, but then she heard the latch of the fire door and more voices entering the hall. Was it curfew hour already? She stood at the sink, facing the mirror. Plain face, hair hanging limply over her ears, belly swelling after a half-pint of chocolate ice cream. The voices lingered in the hallway. She blinked at the mirror. *I'm hiding in the bathroom,* she thought. *This is not how I want to live.*

She pushed herself away from the counter and walked into the hallway. There was a cluster of them, five or six, swaggering in front of her. She would hold her ground. All she wanted to do was get past them and into her room. She walked straight down the hallway, cast a reproachful look in their direction.

"Whoa, Brook," one of them leered. "Looking sharp there, girl."

"It's amazing you can see straight in that condition," she said.

"Wha' was that?"

Brook closed herself in her room and fought the urge to lock it.

She would not give them the satisfaction of hearing the bolt latch. The staff had installed locks on the women's dorm rooms after the rape scandal, clustering all their rooms near the women's bathroom, like little hens, and it was a source of pride among the women that they never used their locks. Brook smiled to herself—she had held her ground, indeed.

There was no more reading of Berdyayev after that. No more theory for the night. She would not take a shower, after all, but would write her father a letter. She'd spoken to him only twice since her last brief trip, over the summer, to the house on the Cape. They didn't speak well on the phone. There was a halting quality to their conversations, too many pauses. But what they had discovered was that they could write letters.

Brook was surprised to learn that her father was an excellent letter writer. At home, he kept an old Remington manual typewriter in the corner of his study, using it so rarely that dust collected in little pockets on the keys. But this typewriter was what he used to write her letters, in blocky script all shoved together, single spaced so that she had to hold the letter close to read it. He X-ed out typos with such command that they indented the back of the bond paper. She loved the feel of these letters, the inky scent of them, and kept them together—there were four now—in her desk drawer. He told her stories about the neighborhood—Mrs. Cull's attempt to have rush-hour traffic banned from their road, little observations about the yard, the bog grasses that crept in constantly, threatening to overtake the lawn. She tried to make her letters just as observant, but it was hard. Her only topic was the academy, and she was too close to it to be able to see it clearly.

Dear Dad, she wrote on a piece of notepaper, *You'd be proud of me just now.*

There was a knock at the door. Billy. He'd come, finally. She tossed her notebook aside and swept off the bed. Her mind racing ahead, suddenly—it could not be curfew because Lex was not back from the library. Then what time was it? How much time did they have? What would he say to her? She threw open the door.

It was not Billy. It was Paula Snowe standing in the hallway, holding a tin of homemade brownies.

"I heard you out in the hallway."

"Did you hear what I said?" Brook smiled, trying to hide her disappointment.

"I laughed like hell. Can I come in?" she said.

"Come in. Come in."

"Have one of these. They're great. How are you holding up?"

"Did your mother make these?"

"My mother? No. Her cook."

Brook stepped aside, and Paula walked in, swept her eyes quickly along Lex's perfectly made bed, Brook's unkempt one.

"Does Lex spend all her time at the library?"

"I hardly see her."

"Probably just as well."

Paula flopped down on Brook's bed. "I'm so fucking disgusted," she said.

"Why?"

"Colonel Coyle. He's a pompous jerk."

"Who's Colonel Coyle?"

"You don't know him? He's head of the behavioral sciences division. He runs the BORG."

"I've never been in there."

"Believe me, you don't want to go."

"What did he do?" Brook eyed the brownies on her bed, next to Paula. Paula hadn't touched them since she'd walked in. She'd been staring off and on at a picture tacked over Lex's desk, a picture Brook had often tried to make out. It was a black-and-white snapshot of a fishing boat taken from too far away, probably from the shore, with two figures, one tall, one short, waving, the sun setting behind them.

"He told me that if I ever wanted the answers to the final exams, they were all in his desk, unlocked, filed by date and class number. He showed them to me. He gave me the pass code to the copier. He asked me if there was anything else I wanted to know."

"Was there?"

"I asked if he'd had surveillance cameras installed in his office. Do you know what he did? He laughed."

"So then you walk away. You never steal another test."

Paula leaned toward Brook now. "Don't you see? That's exactly what he *wants* me to do."

"I don't get it." She sat down near Paula, near the brownies.

"Brook," she said. "Oh, Brook, my dear. You have so much to learn. If I don't steal another test, he'll think he's *won*."

"Won what?"

"Won a mark against smart women."

"Are you kidding me?" Paula was so wrapped up in her argument now that she didn't notice Brook reach forward and take one of the brownies from the tin. Brook lifted it to her mouth. It was delicious, pungent with chocolate and studded with walnuts. She downed it in four heavenly bites.

"No, I'm not kidding. Don't you see? Don't you see how we're put in our place?"

"Sure," Brook said, engrossed in the surge of high-quality chocolate. "We're all put in our place. That's part of the point."

"But we're put in our place in a special way. Don't you see it?"

Brook sucked the chocolate residue off her thumb. "No," she said. "I don't see it at all."

"Jesus. Open your eyes. Look at how they pander to us. They don't appreciate our strengths and talents. They have no clue as to what we can do. They're just afraid we're going to sue them, or go to the press. They're scared shitless. To them, we're nothing but a big slippery scandal waiting to happen."

"I don't feel pandered to. Not in the least."

Paula leaned back sullenly. Brook watched her, worried she felt offended. Paula might leave, taking the brownies, and all future brownies, and what was far worse, some semblance of friendship, the first she'd felt since Cherry died.

"But if they are pandering to us," she said, "we'll never be truly equal."

220

Paula leaned forward again. "We'll never be equal *anyway*."

"Do you mean we *can't* be equal?"

"No. Of course we can. We can do everything they can do. But if we make a mistake, or if we do something in a different way than they would have, they'll say it's because they let women in the military. We could be absolutely perfect, but they would still preach that things would be better without us around. Do you see? We can fight them, but that's not the way to win. The way to win is to let them go on believing we're not as good as they are. What matters is that we're here. We have to use the tools we have to get where we want to go."

It sounded like a great argument. Brook sat on the bed wondering why it was such a great argument and whether it would hold up in a discussion with a male cadet. But then, of course, she was using the same standards of measurement that she'd been using all along—if a male cadet accepted it, then it was a good argument. What Paula was saying was just the opposite.

"Why haven't I thought of this before?"

"Because it's so simple. Because it's so obviously simple."

"Men use the tools *they* have to get what they want."

"That's right."

"Why shouldn't we?"

Paula gave her a look of overwhelming pride. "We need to get you a wardrobe," she said.

Under her Air Force–issue blue coverlet, Paula used linens from Frette. She wore Cosabella lingerie under her blues. Paula confided her secret pleasures and the flaws of her first lovers—one with a crooked penis, one who came prematurely—and Brook was flattered, intrigued. The academy had seemed so one-dimensional, so singularly focused. It had not occurred to her that a cadet could be other things—*female* things—underneath.

"Why are you telling me this?" Brook said.

"You need a friend. You need help. I never had a friend and God knows, I didn't go through what you did."

"But you're in as much trouble as I am."

"We're not in trouble. They're just going to give us a talking-to."
"How do you know?"
"Because I *know*."

———————

In the third week of September, Brook, Billy, and Paula were ordered to a disciplinary board hearing. Brook buttoned herself once again into her formal Class-A blues and walked the blue mile of the commandant's hallway, sitting in a dim alcove on a leatherette couch with Billy while Paula suffered the first round of questions. There was a lighted red sign over the doorway announcing a hearing in progress. Anxiety, like acidic bile, churned in her stomach, but it was a feeling she'd become so accustomed to, she hardly noticed it.

"Do you think they'll expel us?" Billy asked. He was sitting near her, slightly near her but far enough away that there was no chance of accidentally touching. If she reached out, she would need a reason.

"I doubt it."

"Why not?" He didn't look at her. He looked away, at something on the far wall. She looked there, too. The wall was painted robin's-egg blue. There were no discernible marks on it anywhere.

"That's what Paula says."

"Oh, Paula. She's nothing but trouble."

"This wasn't her fault." She ventured a glance at him, and he turned to look hotly at her.

He said, "Haven't you noticed that every time she's around, something goes wrong?"

"It doesn't seem to hurt her."

"No, exactly. It doesn't hurt *her*. What about everyone else?" He turned his head away again.

"But we were all out that night," she said. "We were all guilty."

"It was her idea."

"We didn't have to go." She was still looking at him, willing him to turn back to her.

"I still don't like being around her. You should stay away from her, too."

"I don't see how this is her fault."

"Maybe it's not. I just see a pattern. She's not part of the formula."

"What formula?"

"Keep your shoes shined, keep your uniform pressed, keep your attitude positive. Stay away from obvious trouble. That's all I'm saying."

"Well," she said. "I guess you'll go far."

Current copies of *Airman* magazine and *Air Force Times* were fanned on the coffee table in front of them. Brook picked up one of the magazines and flipped through it. There was a glossy picture of a soldier dressed in desert camouflage standing next to a tank on a dirt road leading through a field of rubble. She didn't know what kind of tank it was, and she knew that if she asked Billy, he would be able to tell her.

"Do you think we'll ever go?" she asked.

"Where?"

"To the war."

He shrugged. "If we ever get out of here."

"But do you think we will?"

"I don't know. I suppose."

"Don't you ever think about it?"

"Not really. I mean, you already accept it by being here. It's like how I never think about blinking."

"I think about it."

"You shouldn't."

"Why not?"

"You'll just spook yourself. How can you know what it's like before you get there?"

"You read the stories. You look at the pictures." She held up the magazine for him to see, and he leaned over and studied it.

"That's not what the war is like. That's just a split second in time. You have no idea what that guy is thinking."

"I bet he's thinking, Holy shit, I hope I don't get shot today."

"Maybe. Maybe he's thinking, How many rounds do I have in my

M16? Maybe he's thinking, Holy shit, I hope I finally get to shoot something today."

The shadow of the door widened, and Paula emerged, nodding at the figure on the other side of the doorway. Then she saluted again and turned smartly, walking past Billy and Brook with her face lifted, delivering the slightest wink toward them as she passed. Major Wein emerged and admitted Billy. Brook watched the door close. She heard footsteps approaching and turned to see Paula tiptoeing toward her.

"It's not bad," Paula whispered. She'd sneaked back down the hallway once the door closed. "It's not bad at all!"

"What'd you get?"

"I don't know yet. They're waiting until they talk to all of us. My guess is we'll get off scot-free." She grinned widely and squeezed Brook on the arm. "I'd better go. I'm not supposed to talk to you until this is all over. We'll be celebrating before long!"

Then she was gone.

Brook watched her after she left. She thought: This is nothing. After I get out of this, I'll still have to go to the war. She tried to picture herself flying a fighter jet, perhaps an F-22, strapping on the G-suit and sauntering out across a tarmac, blurry with heat, toward a jet with its canopy open and waiting for her. Harnessing in. Saluting the ground crew. (She'd seen it on TV. It always went the same way.) She would know what she was doing. That was the extraordinary part. She would be able to do things she could hardly imagine now. Would she feel, then, the same low-level nausea, the same churning in her stomach, or would it be much worse?

And here the God's-eye view of herself, with the turbines whining in the heat, told her that she would not worry, she would not fear. She would be too busy for that, or she would have surrendered herself to fate. The image she saw in the cockpit was a fierce, determined Brook, hardened by training. Wasn't the fighter pilot, after all, simply an extension of the machinery itself? The thinking cell at the center of a complex organism?

She might think of herself that way now. An extension of the machine. They might expel her or they might allow her to remain. Either way, she fit a role, the objective of which was to serve the Air Force. This was humility and discipline at its most fundamental. She had made an error and the error had caused a cadet to die. This idea went far beyond fate, or justice, or any other human quality. She might serve as an example, a rock over which they all hurled themselves, like in fast water, or she might be welcomed back into the current to become part of the force propelling itself forward. The Air Force was made up of people but, in the end, it was a system, and the system had to be served.

She picked up a copy of this week's *Air Force Times*. She felt better now, knowing her role had already been determined, knowing she had only to live through it and see the ending, whatever it was and already in place. The *Times*, with its full staff of reporters, had uncharacteristically printed a story from the Associated Press, and the story was titled "Religious Discrimination at the Academy."

> *A group called the Cadets for Christian Fellowship (CCF), with a vision "to see a spiritually transformed military, with ambassadors for Christ in uniform" has ignited a controversy over the recent death of an Air Force Academy cadet. Reportedly, some cadets have offended others by suggesting that the deceased cadet, MacArthur Cherry of Arlington, VA, is condemned to hell because he didn't embrace Christianity in his lifetime.*
>
> *"I'm afraid for his soul," said one CCF cadet who chose not to be identified.*
>
> *The academy has been accused of favoring evangelical Christianity and harassing those of other faiths. Complaints include professors urging cadets to convert to Christianity, Jews being harassed by other cadets, and campus leaders encouraging cadets to proselytize and spread their "born-again" Christian beliefs.*
>
> *"We're a training institution," Commandant John Waller said, denying the significance of the issue. "We're building officers to lead our troops into battle."*

> *But academy Vice Commandant Sil Metz said*
> *the group operates within the rules, as do other groups*
> *sanctioned by the chapel program. He said members*
> *do not evangelize while on duty but rather live a*
> *Christ-inspired life. "I prove my faith through my*
> *character, my integrity, my honesty. Our job is to share*
> *the gospel of Jesus."*

Brook was angry. To read about oneself in the news was like watching a bad home movie, where only some of the frames came through. Why did the CCF take over the press, just as they were trying to take over the cadet wing? The press had gotten it wrong, as usual. The CCF was a frightening institution—she was certain of this—but they were not what the academy was about.

Billy emerged. He looked tight-lipped as he walked past, and he didn't so much as glance in her direction. She watched him stride down the hall, but then Major Wein was waving her in.

She moved past him and reported, standing at attention before the board, a selection of upperclassmen from other squadrons and the one attending officer, Major Wein, who closed the door softly and took his place at the table. When he was comfortable, his papers arranged, he asked her to sit.

She complied, suddenly extraordinarily tired. It was difficult to keep her shoulders straight, to keep from crossing her ankles and sliding down in the chair. To stay focused. The room was warm. Did they do that intentionally, to make them sleepy? Her uniform felt tight in the thighs and shoulders. She had gained weight. They must have seen that instantly.

There was a shuffling of papers, a theatrical sniffling. She waited. Being before the board took on the feeling of having happened before. She had been here some previous time. She had been judged. And what had been the outcome?

Well, she would know soon enough. That was calming. She had defied her dreams by showing up on time and with her uniform on. What more could they expect? Probably considerably more. They didn't believe in dreams. They wouldn't appreciate what she'd overcome. She tried not to focus on that thought, coached herself to sound contrite, apologetic, submissive. She would have to convincingly ask for forgiveness.

"What positive contributions have you made to your squadron?" one of them, a buzz-haired, sharp two-degree, shot at her.

A rote question, but she had to answer. What was a positive contribution? Rising at five A.M. and running with the squadron? Cleaning her uniform just so, standing at attention, eating the bland, mandatory meals in the chow hall? These were things she had suffered daily, but they didn't seem exactly like contributions. These things were expected. She had done them without complaining, but that was expected, too.

"Well?"

"Sir?"

"What positive contributions? Tell me. Surely you can think of one or two."

I sleep on top of my bed. I salute properly. I march to meals. Sacrifices, all, but not exactly contributions. What was a contribution? Billy had once shined her boots for her—that was probably a contribution. During Beast the previous summer, Lex had sobbed in her bed over some incident—Brook could hardly remember what—and she had spent the night fighting sleep and talking to Lex, talking into the dark while Lex shifted and cried in the next bed, and the dreams had kept rolling in on her and then Lex would speak, and the dreams would scurry off like mice on a kitchen floor.

One of the trainers had called Lex a black bitch. She remembered now. Lex had stood trembling at attention, but she hadn't spoken out of line. She hadn't spoken at all until that night, sobbing in the bed.

"I don't know, sir. I try to be a good friend. I try to help."

"In what way? How have you helped?"

She had been trying to talk to Lex, but the dreams had kept slipping in, washing over her. They were allowed only a few hours of sleep. When the dreams finally overcame her, she slept deeply, unperturbed, and in the morning, Lex rose and put on her uniform, saying nothing about the night before, and Brook worried that she'd done something wrong.

"I helped search for the falcon."

"The falcon that went missing?"

"Yes, sir."

"And did you bring it back?"

"No, sir."

"And how was that a contribution?"

"I tried, sir."

In fact, she had not tried as hard as Cherry, or even as hard as Billy, and she thought that must be obvious to Major Wein and the other members of the disciplinary board, her peers, cadets one or two years older than herself, who now sat in judgment over her paltry showing of remorse.

"You haven't exactly been the strongest team player."

She wanted to ask how she had not been the strongest team player. What would a strong team player have done in her place? Were there things she hadn't considered? She hadn't been the weakest team player, either. She might have said that. Somewhere in the middle of the pack. Isn't that where they all strove to be?

"Let's talk about your history here," Major Wein said. He was thumbing through a thin sheaf of papers. "You had an issue with your training officer back in the spring. It's here in your folder. Cadet Bregs asked you for some information regarding a hidden photograph and it says here you refused to give it to him. What was that about?"

Here, now, the horrible wordlessness, her particular curse, crept in. She had forgotten about the incident. Bregs holding the photograph, flicking it in his fingers, waiting for an answer that she could not possibly give: *Who is she?* Lex had stumbled into the room with the purple sheen of Robitussin streaming down her face and over her uniform. Brook had thought for a moment that it was blood. *Who is she?* She couldn't answer it then any more than she could answer it now.

"I'm sorry, sir, I'm not quite sure what you're asking me."

"What?"

"Is this about what we did the night before Cherry's crash, or is it about something else? I just don't understand where we're going."

Major Wein frowned at her.

"We're trying to determine the quality of your character. We're trying to determine whether you deserve to stay at the Air Force Academy, whether you have the proper moral outlook of an officer in the United States Air Force. Does that answer your question?"

"Yes, sir." She was doing this all wrong.

"What matters is not where you were the night before Cadet Cherry's misfortune, or what you did or did not say to Cadet Bregs last spring during Recognition, but your behavior in all of these matters, because behavior is a reflection of attitude. Is that clear?"

"Yes, sir."

"Now, if you're ready, I'd like to continue. I'd like you to explain, in your own words, what happened between you and Cadet Bregs last spring regarding a photograph stored in an unauthorized place in your room."

"Sir, there was a photograph under my socks, and Cadet Bregs found it during a room inspection, and he asked me about it."

"And who was the photograph of?"

"My mother, sir."

"And why did you have a photograph of your mother hidden in your sock drawer?"

"I'm not sure, sir."

There was a silence, deep and concerned sounding. Major Wein frowned at his papers.

"I'm concerned about your attitude. I truly am." He looked like an honest person. He was probably a good officer, a good, well-intentioned squadron commander who might look through people and see the best for them. Or maybe he was genuinely concerned. Or maybe he had been taken in like some of the zombie officers who walked around spouting hollow dictums at them. She had no idea. She would never know. The fact was that Major Wein had a role to play, and so did she.

"We don't encourage sneakiness here. There's no room for that in a squadron where people must be able to depend on each other, and must be able to trust each other."

"Yes, sir."

"I'm going to have to think about this. I really am. My advice to you is to think deeply about your future here and what it means to you. My advice is that you think very seriously. I'll be in touch soon, once the board comes to a decision."

Brook saluted and walked out of the room, down the hallway, down the blue mile, down the stairwell and out onto the Terrazzo, shadowless in the crystal light. She wanted to cry out with rage. They had betrayed her.

Who?

They had. They had willfully misunderstood.

Who?

Them. All of them. She slung accusations in a blind, adolescent fury. Them. Them. Them.

Billy was right. She would keep her boots shined, her uniform neat. She would look officers in the eye. They had asked for much more, but in the end, that was all they really wanted.

They all came off with a 20/20/1. Twenty demerits, twenty tours, and a month of restriction for grossly poor judgment. Major Wein read the pronouncement to them in his office that night. Brook stood wedged in between Billy and Paula, trying to look grateful.

"Any questions?" he asked.

They had no questions.

"Brook, you'll stay behind a moment."

After Billy and Paula left, Wein delivered the final blow. Because of his concerns over her attitude, because she had not seemed terribly sorry at the disciplinary board—she had not even asked for forgiveness—

"Did they? Did they ask for forgiveness?" she interrupted.

"Of course."

What for? she wanted to ask. Not out of insolence. She wanted to know what she had done that could be forgiven.

"You see, Brook, this isn't all about you. This is about the cadet wing. This is about the future of the Air Force."

"Yes, sir."

Her month of restriction was to be handled like a probationary period, during which all her behavior would be documented. The board had been disturbed with certain of her comments, the whole photograph incident in particular, and they had come up with the probationary period as an opportunity for Brook to vindicate herself. To grow. If, at the end of a month, she'd proved her maturity, her willingness to take responsibility, then her normal status and full privileges would be reinstated. She was to use the month in contemplation and reflection, to consider her place in the squadron and the meaning of being a cadet in the United States Air Force.

Did she understand?

She did. She would be happy to sign the paperwork.

Major Wein offered her a clipboard. She read the chronology of signatures. The board's recommendation had been accepted by Major Wein and then by Vice Commandant Sil Metz, who handled all the lesser administrative issues, freeing the commandant and the superintendent to handle more serious affairs.

Chapter Sixteen

Dear ~~Lieutenant General Long~~, *Susan*

Let me express my most sincere condolences regarding the recent glider incident. Let me also commend you for dealing admirably with the situation. While the investigation remains open, it's my concern that the academy continue on its progress toward the Culture of Transformation. I'm certain this is your foremost objective. The media plays a central role in our nation's understanding of the Air Force Academy. I know you're doing your utmost to ensure that the media has first-rate, accurate information regarding the accident and the actions of the Cadets for Christian Fellowship, and that you will ensure our academy is represented in a fair and favorable light.

That the letter had arrived from General Beddle, on bond stationery and not via e-mail or telephone, revealed certain discouraging signs. She read it in silence, at the Louis XIV–style writing desk in the corner of her office. A lesser general would have read despair in the letter, but Susan Long read only opportunity and promise.

Next to the letter was the recent Associated Press story paperclipped to the CCF leaflet suggesting that Mac Cherry's soul was floating somewhere in limbo. She read neither opportunity nor promise here, but rather a kind of danger, a snare that might entrap her if she didn't maneuver carefully. In her earlier life, she had been an engineer, and she tended to view obstacles in three dimensions, with multiple ways of overcoming them. The three documents on her desk were connected. The trick was in discovering how.

Religion had been very simple in Pennsylvania. Every Sunday, her mother had wet and combed her hair (a memory that still pricked at her, all those tangles that had to be yanked out—she loathed the pain but loved the feel of the soft hair on her shoulders—a kind of atonement for the week's sins) and dressed her in a starched dress and clean white socks, and they had gone to sit in the stiff pews and sing flat-toned songs and nibble on cubes of hardened Wonder Bread and pass dolls' tumblers of grape juice, and then they had gone home and forgotten about church for another week. But religion was complicated now. What was sacred to one person offended another, and what was sacred could never be questioned or negotiated. Piety tended to quell discussion, and discussion was where she excelled. She must not be seen to take sides. That was the kiss of death. Yet she must do something, and do it quickly.

An Associated Press story was a seismic occurrence on Long's Richter scale. The *Gazette* could rant all they wanted, but the AP went over the wire. It might wind up anywhere, in one of the coastal *Times* or in the *Washington Post* or—and she suppressed a jolt of panic—on CNN. The academy had had quite enough of CNN.

Even during the rape scandal two years ago, which the current staff remembered in dark, medieval terms compared to the enlightened age of the Culture of Transformation, the academy had known it had answers to give. It had not known, however, exactly what the questions were, and so it had let the media figure them out. In a gesture of openness, the academy had agreed, during that particular waltz, to let the media lead. They had bared their breast, as it were, invited reporters into the cadet area and let them interview at large. The media had brought their view of the story to the public, and the academy had stood behind them, contrite, embarrassed, eager to make amends.

It had been the wrong approach. From her office in the Pentagon as senior deputy for acquisitions, Susan Long had watched the story cascade and had felt bad for the academy officials, who were sincere and hardworking, like John Waller, and ill equipped to handle the hard-tack two-bite morality of a media hungry for controversy. (Did they not remember Tailhook? Had they not learned from the Navy's mistakes?) Long saw instantly that the academy leaders would lose their jobs. It was the only way a revenge-hungry public could accept change. Long had found a reason to schedule a meeting with the chief of staff of the Air Force. Together, they had concocted the Culture of Transformation, a brilliantly packaged pitch trumpeting a world-class renovation of outmoded Air Force values. They had to be careful here—the generals who might back the Culture of Transformation were the same generals who had instilled those outmoded values—but after a ruthless campaign in D.C. and visits to four of the eight numbered Air Forces (Bud Holly had declined a visit), Long and Beddle, who lived for prettily packaged concepts like the CoT to champion, won enough support to drop hints in congressional circles that with the right leadership in place, big changes would be happening in the image department for the Air Force. So the academy leadership was rolled out, and Susan Long was promoted, and stood in line to be promoted again.

The official note from General Beddle was just a testy reminder of his patience, his dedication to their mutual desires. The question was how to appease him, how to keep the Christ Brigade satisfied while keeping Sil Metz out of the press, how to appear in the press as an academy that reflected solid American values, never mind that the values contradicted each other. How, in short, to get out of this muddle.

Beddle's voice in the letter was urging, faintly warning. The voice on the pamphlet was commanding and righteous. The CCF were a brazen lot. At first, they'd seemed to her so all-American, so charmingly anachronistic, such a perfect remedy to the rape scandal that she'd encouraged them. She'd kept Sil Metz on board and swept out the rest of the staff. He was going to be her token representative for the Culture of Transformation. The CCF was going to be her poster child. And then they'd brought out their own agenda, their proselytizing, their belief that their religion and the military were indelibly linked.

And yet, their agendas were not so different.

The Culture of Transformation meant eradicating excess and immorality from the academy. They'd come so far, already. There'd been no reports of rape all summer. Long and Waller had upped the penalties on drinking. And yet, those kids had been out drinking the night before the glider crash, and who had been among them but Paula Snowe? She was a menace, but what could be done? Best to forget her, get away from the academy as quickly as possible before Paula Snowe brought the whole place down. Unless the CCF beat her to it.

Long touched the pressure points over her eyes, pushed back a nascent headache. God was a *good* thing, wasn't He? God united them under a greater cause. What the CCF needed was a touch of humility—that's all—a touch of compassion, and they would make model cadets.

But where did one find compassion and humility?

She picked up the phone. Her soft-toned, meticulous executive officer answered immediately.

"Ma'am?"

"Get Waller in here."

Waller had shut down the CCF earlier in the year. So be it. Let him handle the crisis. He was a fighter pilot, after all, and fighter pilots worked well under pressure.

"CNN's on the phone!" bellowed Mrs. Purvel from her perch in the outer layer of the commandant's suite. Her voice drove him insane. Waller was bent over his computer, reading the Associated Press story, the fluorescent light fluttering overhead. That damn Kord hadn't had it fixed. Waller squinted at the words. By the tone of the article, he might have thought they were burning heretics at the stake outside his window. Jews, Muslims, and Buddhists all over the academy were complaining of religious intolerance. Where were they? Who were these cadets whose names and comments went straight from the anonymity of the Terrazzo to the Associated Press? Why had nobody told *him*?

"Tell them I'm not in," he yelled.

The side of his body had recovered. He had that to be thankful for. At least he could move around again without crumpling into a heap of pain. But now this—the fatal crash of one of his cadets had set off another insurgency inside the academy gates. Two years ago, it had been mere sexual harassment. A garden-variety college problem that the academy had bungled into mammoth proportions. But this seemed an altogether new category of conflict. Telling the boys to keep their pants zipped was one thing, but telling them where and how to pray, when one set of beliefs overlapped others—and with his deputy, the vice commandant, caught up in the fray—this seemed too much to handle. Had there been Jews and Muslims here when he was a cadet? He couldn't remember. Chapel had been mandatory, he remembered that. He remembered laboring through the services when he would have preferred to be sleeping or studying in his dorm, but he had tolerated them. They all had. Why was it so different now?

"Where is Sil Metz?" he shouted.

"He's not in the office."

"Find him."

He would like to have told the press that the academy had existed *for years* without religion, or rather where religion had existed as a staunch but vague backbone, a source of reliable support, but he knew that, like always, they would misquote him. He had tried trusting them, but over and over, they had been unkind. They listened to his words and purposefully misstated them. Or they quoted him accurately, but couched his comments in such one-sided commentary that he appeared as some sort of antiquated war fanatic. Now was not the time to trust the press.

"General Long just called," Kord said from the doorway. "She wants you over there ASAP."

"Damn," Waller said. "We've got the march of the old heroes at sunset, and I've got to get home first. I don't have time for this."

In a few hours, the cadets would be dressed in their uniforms, marching the two miles to the academy graveyard and back. If only the press could see this part of things, their pride in the past, which reflected their pride in the future. If only the media would take the time to notice.

"Do you want me to call her back?"

"No. No. Listen, I want to know something." He picked up the newspaper and then tossed it back on the desk. Long would have her own copy. "For months, I've asked you to change this light over my desk, and it never happens. Why is that?"

"It still isn't fixed? I didn't know, sir. I put in a work order at civil engineering. I'm amazed they haven't come."

"That's a load of shit, Alan. I'm not sending you back to the fighters. Not with that attitude. I'll send you down to public affairs for your next tour."

Kord swallowed, turned slightly pale. "But I'm not cut out for this, sir. I should be back in the cockpit."

"So should I. But you don't see me dragging my feet here, do you? *Do you?*"

"No, sir."

"I'm glad to hear it. You want to go back to the fighters? Be the best XO you can be."

"I'm afraid to do that, to be honest, sir."

"Afraid of what?"

"I'm afraid I'll be picked up as XO for General Long."

Waller shook his head and walked out. He walked quickly across the Terrazzo to General Long's office, passing the cadets absently as he went. When he arrived, breathless, Long was seated at her desk, each hand resting on two documents—one was the AP story and the other was a note typed on official bond stationery with four stars at the top, which meant that it could only have come from General Beddle.

"I know we haven't always seen eye to eye," she said. "But the

reputation of the academy is at stake here. We've got to work together."

Waller nodded, pulled a blue leather chair out from the conference table next to her desk, and sat down. "I know," he said.

"I think we should go to the press."

"Oh, not again," Waller groaned. "That never works. They'll turn
against us."

"They're not out to get us, John. They want heroes as much as
anyone else, but the smell of blood incenses them. They can't help it.
What we do is give them a good story. *We* deliver the message."

"Who's we?"

"You, actually."

Waller blinked, shot a look at the Terrazzo where the cadets,
spots of blue on a gray canvas, were moving between classes. "Why
not you?"

"Because you're the commandant of cadets. You're the face everyone sees."

"But you're the three-star, and you're a woman. That will look
better. They'll be kinder to you."

"Don't count on it. Besides, you're the old Air Force. You're
decorated. They'll respect you."

"I doubt that."

"Trust me. It's all in the message. I've got a great coach for you."

"Who?"

"Colonel Coyle."

"Then let him do it."

"No, it's got to come from you."

"And what am I supposed to say? I'm sorry we lost a cadet on my
watch? I'm sorry we've got an epidemic of religious fundamentalism
on base now and that my deputy won't shut up? Where is that little
bastard, anyway?"

"Sil's not the problem. We'll keep him out of the press, but we
need Sil. That's the thing you've never understood. People trust
him."

"He's my deputy and I don't trust him."

"But the CCF does, and they go way beyond the academy. This isn't just a rape scandal—though Lord knows, if we'd handled that properly, we wouldn't be getting so much heat right now. The CCF has support at every base, even at the Pentagon. That's what you have to understand. They're the new movement in the Air Force. Maybe they've been here all along, but they've grown, and this is their time."

"What do you mean, their time?"

Long drew in a breath, sucked her lips slightly inward. Was it possible he didn't see? "Look outside the academy gates. We have a war on terror. It's good versus evil, all over again. We did it with the Russians. We did it with the Germans. But this is so much *bigger*—we have an enemy we can't even see. We can't even name it. How much more mystical can you get? The CCF has been emboldened by the political reality of the world. The war against terror is their podium."

Long paused, considered her words. She picked up a pen and jotted them on a notepad. "The point is, we *need* them. They're going to carry us through the war."

"And then what?"

She shrugged. "Then they'll go back under a rock. It's not like they're going to take over the world."

Waller shook his head. "I want to go back to flying."

"You will, John. But you need to help me with this first."

"Okay," he said. "I'll do it. I hope it works."

At home, Lauren was sitting on the bed, pulling on stockings. Valerie's long hair was still wet, and Lauren had called to her to hurry up in drying it. Toni's was short, lopped off over the summer in her increasing passion to join the Marines.

Lauren looked beautiful. That was the first thing he noticed. Her hair had been set and dried, she wore a simple brown dress that reflected the color of her eyes, and she looked at him with impossible faith.

"Are we running late?" she asked.

"Not yet."

He wanted to sit next to her, stop her from inching the stockings up over her thighs. He wanted to touch her hand and tell her that they could stop rushing. They could stop moving and running from one thing to the next. It was clear to him now, after a religious scandal and a dead cadet, that no matter what happened with CNN, he would not be promoted to a second star.

It's all right, he wanted to tell her. We'll be just fine.

She looked at him with a smile that was perhaps hopeful or wistful, and he thought he read in it that she would be disappointed, just slightly, to learn that he wouldn't earn them one last promotion. It was going to hurt him to have to tell her, or perhaps she'd already guessed it, and that's why she was looking at him with such tenderness, as though trying to hide her disappointment.

In fact, she loved her husband, and to hear that he would not be promoted to major general would have pleased her more than any other single thing, knowing that they might settle down, that he might finally turn his attention if not exactly toward her then toward their common interests. For she believed they had common interests they had hardly begun to explore, and she looked forward to the time when they could send the girls to good schools and pull their attention inward, toward a peaceful commonality that would be settling to them both. But she merely smiled at him, knowing how much another promotion meant to him and knowing, too, that they would have to move again and start life at another base, or at the Pentagon, and the girls might have to graduate from another unfamiliar high school. And that she would do it, she would carry on and wait through all this, because she loved him.

"Toni got into a bit of trouble at school today," she said.

"Oh? What happened?"

"She punched a boy in the nose."

"Did she knock him out?"

Lauren suppressed a laugh. "It's not funny," she said.

On the nightstand, the phone rang.

"I got it!" Valerie yelled.

"Hurry up!" Lauren yelled, rising, smoothing her skirt. "We have to go!"

After a flurry of shoe hunting and coat and handbag gathering, they left the house and strapped themselves into the Cherokee.

"You can't go punching people in the nose," Waller told Toni, looking at her through the rearview mirror as he backed them out.

"He was a hockey player. It's not like he couldn't defend himself."

"You started a fight with a hockey player?"

"He started it."

"What did he do?"

"He called me a dyke."

Waller considered this. No father liked having his daughter called a dyke, no matter how true it might be.

"Well, he won't make that mistake again."

"Who was on the phone?" Lauren asked.

"Keith. Actually, Keith's mom."

"What did Keith's mom want?"

"Remember that yoga retreat I told you about? The one in October? I have to put down a deposit soon. Can I go? I really want to."

"And miss school?" Waller said.

"It's just two weeks."

"Two weeks of school? No way," Waller said. He shot a glance at Lauren to make sure she agreed with him, but she was staring straight ahead.

"But, Dad, I'll make it up. I promise."

"You and Keith's mom?"

"And Keith."

"And *Keith*? Why does Keith want to go on a yoga retreat? I can only think of one reason."

"His mother is going to be there."

"Believe me, that's not a selling point."

"Actually, I was thinking of letting her go," Lauren said.

"What?"

"She says she can make up the work. It's her responsibility. And Keith's mom will be there. It's not like anything will happen."

"We'll talk about it later."

"You always say that, Dad, and we never do."

"This is really not a good time."

"It never is."

"This is a particularly bad time."

"Well, maybe we can talk when we're dead."

"What does that mean?"

"It just means okay. It means I shouldn't have expected anything else."

"Listen," Waller said, to change the subject, "I'm thinking of going on CNN."

"Oh, dear," Lauren said.

"Do you think it's a bad idea?"

"I think it's a terrible idea."

"Why? Don't you think I can handle myself?"

"Of course you can handle yourself. CNN is another story."

"What do you mean? You think I'll be run over by CNN?"

"I think it's a risk."

"Dad, don't my issues matter to you?"

"Of course they do. We'll talk about it."

"I'll tell you," Lauren said, "the yoga thing is a better bet than CNN."

"No way. All those girls in leotards, and Keith there—in what, a leotard, I guess. How many guys are going to be there?"

"How should I know? I don't even care. I want to go for the yoga. I need to cleanse."

"You eat nothing but grapefruit and lettuce," Waller said. "You're the cleanest kid I know."

"It's not just your body, Dad. It's your mind. I feel *impure*."

"How else do I get the message out?" he asked, eyeing Lauren. She was smoothing her dress under the seat belt.

"What message?"

"The message. That we're a training institution, not an ideological"—here he waved his hand in the air to conjure up the next word—"camp."

"Oh, really?" Lauren said. "Then what are we all doing today?"

"The march for old heroes? This is about our connection with the past, not with some ideological"—and here, again, he paused for the right finish—"mind-set."

"Oh, please," Val said. "We're idealizing dead guys. We might as well be walking the stations of the cross."

"That's enough," Waller said. He turned back to Lauren. "What's gotten into you, anyway?"

"What do you mean?"

"You're so adamant. I've never seen you so—adamant."

"Why not?" she asked. "It's time. It's just time."

"Time for what?"

"It's time, John. All our lives, we've lived for something. We've lived for the next new thing. When is it going to be about us?"

"I personally don't want to glorify war," Val said. "I didn't even want to come to this."

"You should support your country," Toni said, who'd taken her headphones off now and was eyeing the B-52 on display near the north gate. "Whether you agree with it or not."

"It's always been about us," Waller said. "Don't you know that?"

"This is a *free* country," Val said. "The whole point is that I don't *have* to support it."

"That's just ignorance," Toni said.

"Please," Lauren said to Waller. "We'll talk later. This is not the time."

"What do you mean, this isn't the time? This is the perfect time."

"It's not ignorance," Val said. "I don't want to kill people. *That's* ignorance."

"It's absolutely the wrong time," Lauren said. "We're here. We have this *thing*."

They were pulling into the commandant's parking spot. Val and Toni looked out opposite windows. Lauren unharnessed herself and stepped out of the car.

As they were walking toward the Terrazzo, where the cadets had begun to form, Waller composed himself. Lauren was right, of course, it wasn't the time. Toni took his hand and said, quietly, "I don't want to kill people either, Dad."

Waller looked at her and put his arm over her shoulders. He loved his daughters, but Toni—how could he help but worship her?

"No good soldier does," he said.

His speech from a small podium propped before the assembled squadrons was about sacrifice. It was about offering one's life in myriad ways, giving up freedom and choice for the good of others, and concluded that the march for old heroes was therefore not merely a march for the dead.

From a squadron on the western flank, a cadet moved. One cadet in formation excused herself, moved out of formation, and walked away.

Chapter Seventeen

There's a party tonight. I want you to go.

The message from Paula popped up on the screen while Brook was typing an essay on integrity. She had fifty words to go.

I'm in enough trouble, she wrote back. **Believe me.**

As part of her probation, Brook had been required to write essays on such ambiguous topics as honor and duty. She could write them very well, and very quickly, and they seemed to satisfy Major Wein. She had written one paper about the loss of Freedom, their peregrine falcon, trying to replicate the feeling of the loss of the bird, and she was not quite able to do it. It was her most heartfelt essay, and it had dissatisfied Major Wein.

"That's the way with birds," he said. "They have no brains."

She took this without comment and moved on. It was important that in their weekly conferences she raise ponderous questions and seem thoughtful after his answers. Probation went very smoothly this way, but she was not quite out of it. She had a week to go.

Come anyway. You won't regret it. Torrance Shane is going to be there.

The war hero? How do you know? Brook shot back.

Who do you think you're talking to?

The party would happen downtown at one of the unauthorized apartments the firsties kept for such events. Everybody would be there. Secretly, Brook understood that everybody meant Billy. Billy would be there. Maybe they would finally talk.

Brook stood up from the computer and walked down to Paula's room.

"All right," she said "I'll go, but we have to be back before curfew."

"Good!" Paula said. "First, we're getting you some clothes."

Brook didn't sign out. She walked out with Paula. Paula swiped her proximity badge at the gate and then they were out in the parking lot, and all Brook had to do was get in the car and drive off base. It was that easy. She hadn't believed it could be that easy.

They went to a shopping mall, Brook's first whiff of freedom in weeks. She shuffled through the crowded walkways, slurping a smoothie, letting Paula guide her from one shop to the next.

"Try this on," Paula said, handing her flowery, frilly, *scanty* things she'd never imagined wearing, and then hurriedly, with a sense of mischief, she tried them on in the dressing room.

"Oh, it's perfect," Paula said.

"My shoulders are too big for this."

"You have breathtaking shoulders," the severe-looking attendant said, tugging a turquoise strap until it exposed the fringe of soft, white flesh at the breast line that had always been covered, even in summer, by a bikini top. "What are you celebrating?"

"It's a kind of coming out," Paula said.

The apartment they eventually found was filled with the buzz of cadets, mostly male and looking like precise replicas in their chinos and pale oxford-cloth shirts. Many of them glanced at Brook, and then at Paula, and then at Brook again, as they moved through the crowd. Brook tried to smile. Her face felt heavy with makeup, the work of a saleswoman who'd forced a barrage of creams and compacts upon her—things that were mysterious and beautiful and unspeakably expensive. She'd pulled out the credit card she kept for emergencies—this was a kind of emergency, wasn't it? A metamorphosis was always cause for alarm. She glanced around for Billy, but it was impossible to see through the crowd of cadets in the dim light.

"Hello," someone said.

She turned. A male cadet somewhat shorter than she was was smiling at her. It took her a moment to recognize him. It was Dillan Bregs.

"Hi." She smiled. For a moment, only a moment, she felt the familiar urge to snap to attention, to look beyond the line of his shoulder into an infinity she had pondered fruitlessly so many times. He was so short.

"I'm sorry about Cherry," he said.

"Are you?"

"I wouldn't wish that on anybody."

"But your fellowship—"

"I know. They're on the trail for salvation." He held up his fingers and waved them. Then he rolled his eyes. She couldn't believe she'd ever been frightened of him.

"So you're not with the CCF anymore?"

"Oh, I'm still with them. In a manner of speaking. They're still my brothers."

He wasn't holding a beer, and he wasn't likely to be going in search of a beer, and at the moment she badly wanted one. She smiled at him in a polite, dismissive way. She'd once thought of throwing her career away over him.

"And you?"

"And I what?"

"Are you still hanging around with that Billy Claymore guy?"

"Not too much."

"I never liked him. Do you know what I mean?"

"You never liked me, either."

"Sure I did."

"Could have fooled me."

He smiled. He seemed flattered. "Did you think I was that good?"

She'd parted her lips to answer when a hand fell heavily over her shoulder and a voice, familiar and warm, gushed into her ear.

"You're here," the voice said. She knew the voice. She had felt its tickle, its nearness.

"Hi, Billy."

All at once, Bregs was swept away, as on a receding tide. Billy filled her whole horizon.

"I thought you were still locked in jail."

"I am. In a manner of speaking."

"Well, here's to busting out."

With this, he cast a glance at her sweater, which had drifted in God knew what position at the bust line, but he seemed to be smiling, anyway. He held up a plastic cup of frothy beer.

"Where did you get that?"

"Come with me."

He led her away toward some corner of the room where a keg had been set up, and he pumped the tap and poured a cupful for her while she looked on. Paula had disappeared.

"Whose place is this, anyway?"

"Remember Ragley, our old flight commander?"

"Of course."

"It used to be his. Now it belongs to three guys from the Panthers."

"I wonder what happened to Rags."

"You didn't hear? He flunked out of pilot training and went over to the war as an intel officer. He's in Tikrit."

"Oh."

They wandered through the rooms. In one of them, Brook caught sight of Paula. She was playing cards at a coffee table. She'd taken off her sweater and was wearing only a bra, and some of the other players, who were all male, had taken off their shirts and socks, and one had taken off his pants and sat cross-legged on the floor in his boxers.

"You look really fantastic," Billy said.

"Thanks."

Across the room, two men were talking, two men who were clearly not cadets. One was Rails, the flight instructor. She recognized him by the sloppy clothes and haircut, the bad posture. The other she had seen on television and in the papers, and she had read enough about him and discussed him enough in classes to know him right away, even though he was tall and gangly, and his posture was also bad, and his haircut had grown beyond regulation. He was Torrance Shane, the fighter-pilot hero of the Afghan war.

"Ah, look," she said.

"I already met him," Billy said.

"What's he like? What's he doing here?"

"He's speaking at the leadership symposium on Monday. What can I say? He's a fucking hero."

"Cherry never thought so."

Billy took her hand and led her into another room, probably the bedroom, although there was no bed in it, just some sleeping bags and pillows piled in the corners, the dim light radiating from lamps propped in the corners. There was a circle of cadets, shouting. In the middle were two cadets, male and female, doing body shots. The female was Val Burns, the center from the rugby team. Brook didn't recognize the male. They joined the circle, watching.

The cadets were shouting something that sounded like, "Tusca! Tusca!"

The male cadet—Brook assigned him the name of Charlie, because he looked like a Charlie she had known at school—unbuttoned Val's shirt down the front and tipped her head back, holding her around the waist, a gesture out of a Klimt painting. She held a wedge of lime in her mouth. She tilted her neck back, graceful, docile, and he sucked the salt off her neck and poured the liquor over her breast. Such an old ritual, so gratifying. He caught some of the liquid in his mouth.

Another couple came forward. Where did they come from? The recesses of the party, hungry for exhibition.

"Tusca! Tusca!"

Brook was chanting it now, watching the quick liquor trickle over another breast—his and then hers, it hardly mattered who they were. She could taste the salt on their skin.

Then she felt herself thrust toward the center. Billy was gripping her waist.

"Is it okay?" he whispered.

She nodded, delirious with the momentum.

The lime was acrid in her mouth, the salt sprayed on her neck and then Billy's warm mouth over her—*Tusca! Tusca!*—her head tipped back and a cool, wet river between her breasts, again the sweet warmth of Billy's mouth. The lime snatched from her lips. Then it was her turn. She tasted the salt, and a saltiness that seemed a part of his skin, and a willingness behind it. She tasted the liquor, sweeter than the tequila she expected, and the curve of the breast muscle under it, and reached up on her toes to take the lime in her mouth.

The room swayed sweetly around her.

———————————

"Do you have a cigarette?" She was on a balcony somewhere, or a rooftop. Or Mars. She was addressing the question to Paula.

Paula nodded, dug in her handbag. She was wearing her sweater again. Brook wanted to ask her how much she had taken off, how the game had gone, but it seemed ages ago, and she feared Paula might not remember. She was standing with somebody outside Brook's narrowing field of vision, someone dark and tall.

"Thanks!" Brook shuffled a cigarette out of the pack as gracefully as she could manage and held it inexpertly to her mouth with one hand while she worked the lighter with the other.

"I didn't know you smoked," Billy said.

"Want one?"

Billy shrugged, shook his head. Brook momentarily regretted the smell. But she got the cigarette lit and pushed the lighter back into Paula's hand. She had no idea how to inhale, so she did it deeply, clogging her pink lungs. Exhaled in muted coughs, puffs of smoke bursting from her lips. But nobody was watching. Billy had gone to the bathroom, or for more drinks, or to the moon, and Paula had turned back into the pleasant melody of conversation.

There was some music thumping under them. Brook tried the cigarette again. She held the smoke in her mouth, inhaling nasally, trying to pull the smoke down by degrees, to make it more tolerable. It tasted good, like salted fish. She tried exhaling, smoother now, not exactly fluid but better. She wheezed softly.

The music was loose, liberating.

She wondered about the rhythm of smoking. A cigarette burned away quickly while you were smoking it (it took forever, of course, when it belonged to someone else). She kept taking small sucks, mingling the poison with oxygen. The clouds dispersed into the air. Her fingers smelled pleasant, like freshly burnt wood. There was no ashtray nearby. She extinguished it on the bottom of her sandal, held the soft, stubby butt in her fingers. This part was even better. The end of the cigarette. Something mutable and inert.

Billy came back with two cups of beer and stood next to her. She wondered what had happened to Charlie and Sally, their friends from town, and what had happened to Tina. Billy smiled at her, handed her the cup, which she gulped from to hide the aftertaste of the cigarette.

"You like the party?" he asked.

"It's nice." Billy's arm was firmly around her, had been all evening since the body shot. It both balanced her and threw things out of equilibrium. It made everything sharper and yet more elusive.

The hour of curfew was looming. Billy's body was firm against hers. Brook leaned in and used all her concentration to focus on Paula. "Paula, we have to go back."

Paula laughed euphorically. "Terry," she said, squeezing his shoulder. "We have to go."

"Well, then, let's go."

"Where should we go? What should we do?"

"We have to go back to base," Brook articulated carefully, hoisting herself over and around the words. Even drunk, she knew the consequences of being caught off base during probation.

"And do what?"

"Let's go to the tunnels." This was a new voice, the voice above Paula's shoulder. Brook aimed her concentration at it.

"The tunnels!"

"What tunnels?"

"*What* tunnels? The tunnels under the academy. I'll show you the Liberty Bell."

It was Torrance Shane. He stood a half head taller than Brook, which meant he was the average height of a fighter pilot, and he was thin and wore slacks and an oxford-cloth shirt. All of these things surprised Brook, though she could not have said why.

"Captain Shane?" Brook said.

"Howdy do," Terry said. "The name is Terry." He was grinning at her, his arm resting on Paula's shoulder. "You've never been down in the tunnels?"

So much had happened during the night, so much they would have to catch up on. She felt a genuine love for Paula. She wanted to grasp her by the hand, say something sisterly and proud. Paula seemed more composed. She was saying something flattering to Terry, who held his hand theatrically to his ear. "Oh, we're not gods. We're like gods, but I wouldn't go that far."

"I didn't say you were gods," Paula said, slapping his leg. "I said something different."

"You *didn't*? You *didn't*?" Terry was grinning at her with his chin down, like some hunting animal on the prowl. But Paula was laughing.

"Are you for real?" Brook asked. She swayed against Billy. He seemed to be propelling her.

Terry laughed. "Are you kidding? Who do you think I am?"

Outside, there was some discussion of how to handle the cars. It was decided, finally, that Terry would leave his car in the lot and pick it up the following day. He would ride with Paula. Brook would ride with Billy. They would stop, first, to pick up something to drink from the 7-Eleven across the street.

They rolled in just under the curfew and tucked the cars in dark slots in the parking area. Then they walked up to the gate and Paula swiped her proximity badge and they were on the Terrazzo. It was empty. It had rained earlier in the day and the cement was gleaming under the lampposts. There was a safeness, a regularity about being back on the Terrazzo. It made them feel bolder. They walked quietly through the wolfish mist.

"Where are we going?" Brook asked. She had forgotten.

"To the tunnels," Terry said.

Billy's arm was around her shoulder. They walked through the Air Garden. Brook stopped for a moment. The locust trees were in full bloom, and they rustled in the near darkness. They seemed to breathe. What had Cherry said about Torrance Shane?

Cherry.

He was still up on the hillside, in the midst of a turn. Billy touched her breasts from behind. She stood still, letting him spoil the moment.

"Come on," he whispered.

They crept down a ladder in the dark. The tunnels were cool. They smelled of dust and mold.

"I was down here once with one of the old staff colonels," Terry said. "There's all kinds of stuff, a morgue, classrooms."

"We heard about that," Billy said.

"Well, there used to be. Maybe they're gone now."

There were lanterns bolted every so often along the cement wall. They gave the place the feeling of someone having been there before. Billy squeezed her hand. She felt his breath on her neck.

"What about the Liberty Bell?" Paula asked.

"We'll get there."

They walked for some time. It was tiring. Brook's legs felt heavy. The smell, the closed-in dampness, nauseated her.

"Well, damn," Terry said.

"Damn what?" Paula said.

"I don't know where it is. It used to be here."

There was an empty doorway, the hinges wrenched from the wall, and a dark chamber that reeked of hell's own darkness. None of them would enter it.

"I guess it's gone," Terry said.

"Gone where?" Brook asked.

"Don't know. Maybe they took it somewhere else. "

They were hardly in a mood to be disappointed. Paula suggested, "Let's walk down a little farther, maybe you just forgot where it was."

They walked a little, and then Paula and Terry fell behind, laughing. Brook and Billy kept walking. Brook stumbled a bit, which seemed, in her state, more like a dance. She clung to Billy's side. They slowed and stood together, and then Billy took her hand and led her to a cold but suitable nest behind some water pipes. The air smelled grimy.

He put his arms around her. The muscles in his neck were strong and alive. He reached up under her shirt.

"I was thinking of Cherry," she said.

"Oh."

"He was right about Torrance Shane."

"He's Terry to us. I wish we had a blanket."

As it was, he had her sitting with her back against the damp, rusting edge of a large pipe. There was not quite enough space to lie all the way down, but he was pressing into her, working her downward, into the smell of mold and grime and rust. The edge of a bolt prodded her shoulder.

"Please," she said.

"Thatta girl."

"No. I mean please stop."

The darkness swam unpleasantly over her. It seemed they were not a few short steps to the ladder that could bring them to the surface, but miles and miles underground, lost in some forgotten mine.

"Don't worry," he said. "Take it easy." He was lying over her now, stroking her hair, his feet resting at odd angles because of some solid protuberance.

"How far down are we?"

"What do you mean?"

"From home. How far are we? Do you know where we are?"

"It's right up there. I'll take you there."

"Now?"

"In just a minute. You don't want to go now, do you?"

Her neck was cocked against the pipe, her back cold on the floor. It was not as uncomfortable as she thought it would be. What struck her was the quiet, the absolute anonymity of this dark little pocket, a place where no one would find her. Now that she knew they were not so far from the surface, she wished, indeed, she'd found it herself. It was not such a bad place to lie down and think.

"I don't want to, Billy."

"I thought so." He whispered this, breathing into her neck. He had loosened her bra, and his own shirt was unbuttoned and hanging down over her. Surely he'd done that, too. He was fumbling with her pants, the new ones she had bought with Paula, and for the first time it occurred to her that her outfit would be ruined from the dirt and rust.

"I mean I don't want to do this."

"Oh."

He had her pants unzipped and pulled down over her hips. She struggled under him, pushed her arms up against him and got the floor under her feet for leverage, but that brought her hips off the floor, and he slid her pants down over them and left her bare to the knees.

"This isn't right," she said. She was tired. His arms and shoulders seemed to be over her everywhere. And where were her hands? On him, everywhere on him, his back and shoulders and chest.

"It's okay," he said. "Don't feel bad." He hoisted his own pants down and rested the warm animal of his penis on her stomach. She could not bring herself to touch it, could not bring herself to push him away, to sit up and stop the madness.

"Is this your first time?" he asked.

"Yes," she lied. She'd been with one other boy, Zach, in a bed of hay in a horse stable that belonged to his parents.

"I'll be careful."

"I want to stop."

"No, you don't."

She might have slapped him. Why didn't she? He was positioning himself on her, tenderly, almost regretful, as though this might somehow soften the blow.

"I know you," he said. "Who knows you like I do?"

In truth, she couldn't think of anyone. Not Paula. Not her brothers or father. He was pressing himself on her, widening her with his fingers. Did he know her better than she did herself? Maybe. She'd come down here, after all. She'd followed him down. Why else had she come?

"Hush," he said, softly. "Don't cry."

He was in her now. She felt one quick slice of pain and then the pressure and then a nauseating sense of opening to him. She didn't move. There was nowhere to go. In another minute, he shuddered and was off her and she lay there with the coldness of the floor ground into her skin. The light on the ceiling was yellow, a trinity of light bulbs with one blown out. Ground glass and a silver rim. A porous, jaundiced ceiling. What did she feel? Numbness, disgust, a wish to be invisible, or at least to be gone, back in her bed, and morning coming, waking to realize none of this had happened, that she'd been smart and gone home after the party, showered, and was safe.

She sat up then, even though to sit up was to acknowledge that any of this had happened and that she'd been a part of it, and to look at him, his pants still crumpled around his ankles. She fastened her bra, found her pants and pulled them on.

"Are you okay?" he asked.

"I'm fine."

"Do you want to go back now?"

"Yes."

She would have liked to go back by herself, but she wasn't sure of the way. They ducked through an opening in the pipes and walked back down the hallway. There was no sign of Paula or Terry.

"Maybe they left," Billy said.

"Maybe."

They found the ladder and climbed it, pushing themselves through the manhole at the corner of Fairchild Hall and then walking quietly in the cool air back to the dorms. Brook didn't look at Billy or say good-bye. She turned the key in her door, closed and locked it behind her, and stood in the darkness. Lex snored softly. Brook dropped her clothes and climbed into bed, never mind the ritual at the sink, and drew the covers tight. Good night moon. Good night room. She would go to sleep in the silent darkness, away from the chaos, away from what seemed now a sinister desperation, or rather, a sinister loneliness that pushed other people out into the world and forced them to confront things. Tomorrow she would wake up. Tomorrow she would be, well—

She opened her eyes. She had forgotten her purse. Where had she left it, and could it wait until tomorrow? Probably not. All her identification, money, cell phone. She couldn't go snooping in the tunnels in broad daylight. She would have to go look. She dressed quickly and went out.

It was raining again, an unrelenting mist. She walked quickly across the Terrazzo, panic rising inside her. She'd had the purse in the car. That she was sure of. But then what? They had stopped in the Air Garden and then gone into the tunnels. She didn't want to go back there, and yet, not to go was to leave some trace remaining. All she wanted to do was wake up in the morning and forget what had happened. She had to find her purse.

Her hands were trembling now. She walked through the Air Garden, where she and Billy had stood, and she had been thinking about Cherry, and Billy had come behind her and touched her breast. There, on the bench, was her small black handbag, wet and gleaming. She picked it up.

She sat down and cried on the rain-soaked bench.

She could report it. But report what? That she'd been drinking at a party, had gone into the tunnels, had found a dark corner with

Billy, and then what? She could see exactly how it would go. Major Wein at his desk, the office they had all worked to rid of the smell of bass last year.

"I've been ..." What would she say? Abused. Assaulted. Fondled. Tricked. Not raped, no. Not exactly.

"Oh, you're one of those," Major Wein would say. "I'm surprised. I'd thought more of you."

It would start like this. Then it would grow formal. Procedural.

"So we'll go through the procedure here. Have you had a rape kit done?"

"No. It wasn't rape, exactly."

"Then what was it?"

"I don't know."

"You don't *know*?"

He would ask her what had happened, every detail. She'd gone to the Air Garden. She'd been thinking of Cherry. Billy had come up behind her and put his hands on her, and she had wavered and then told him no. Maybe there wasn't one point of transgression but a series of them, a slippery slope. It was bad enough to have done it, to have made a mistake, but then to be fingered for it—*Oh, you're one of those*—she gripped her handbag, thinking about the course of events ahead.

Wein would have a notepad on his lap. He would check the time.

"What's this for?"

"For the file," he'd say. "We'll have to start a file and gather facts. Then you can go to the hospital."

"I'm not sure ..." Brook knew her limitations. She saw herself closing up. She didn't want to accuse Billy. She only wanted to understand what had happened.

"Now, where were you?"

Off base, at a party, drinking. How could she tell him this when she was still on probation? There was an amnesty clause for girls who claimed they'd been raped, but Brook wasn't doing that. What *was* she doing?

She might report that she'd been a fool, and then a fool again to report it. No, she couldn't go to Major Wein. Maybe she could go to the counseling center in the morning. She would screw up her courage and go, or, more likely, she'd lose her nerve. No one wanted to be seen anywhere near the counseling center. No one wanted to give off a whiff of weakness. She could talk to Paula, but who knew what Paula would say or think?

In her purse, her cell phone was still dry. She called the only person she could think of.

"Hello? Brook? What's wrong? I can hardly hear you," her father said. The connection was poor. She was sitting in the wrong place, blocked by the monolithic expanse of Fairchild Hall. Always things in your way, weren't there? Unless you were up, flying. The commandant was right. Flying was the only way to go.

"I'm fine," she summarized. "It's nothing important."

"Are you sure? It's the middle of the night."

"I can't hear you," she said. "Nothing's wrong. I'm going to hang up now." And she did. She sat on the wet stone bench in the quiet vacuum of the rain.

Chapter Eighteen

A late September day, breezy and warm. Probation over, Brook was free from the threat of expulsion, but confined within the tight rhythm of class and drill. In the library, she waved to Lex, sitting alone at one end of a long table, and trotted quickly down the circular steps. Three-degree year was only mildly easier than doolie year. That had been a disappointment. The two-degrees and the enviable firsties had it made. And beyond them, the commissioned second lieutenants in their bright gold butter bars, walking to and from where—what important offices—she could only guess. They were like gods! Would she ever be among them?

Too far away to imagine. Whenever she cast her thoughts into such dark waters, she reeled them in again. The present was solid enough, but she didn't trust the future. Too much could happen. Too much could be taken away.

She was meeting Billy by the Air Garden. She'd gotten up the courage to ask for this, written it out on a piece of paper and slid it under his door. She'd not spoken to him since the night in the tunnels. She didn't know what she would say now, except that something had to be said. She couldn't hide forever, ducking between the dorm and the library, reporting to every formation at the last possible minute.

Outside, he was waiting for her, standing, impeccable in his blue jacket and slacks, his hair perfectly shorn and his black book bag slung over his perfect shoulder. Any woman would love him—it made Brook sick to realize this. She couldn't stand to look into his eyes.

"I thought you might come by before now," she said. "That's why I waited."

"I figured you didn't want to see me." He didn't look at her, either. They were like two people standing and waiting for a ride.

"You should have come anyway."

"Why?"

"That was the right thing to do."

"Is this why you wanted to meet? So you could tell me what I did wrong?"

"No, I thought you'd already figured that out."

"I *didn't* do anything wrong." He looked at her now, his eyes blue and fierce, and she realized she didn't know him at all.

"Is that what you think?"

"That's what I know." Around them, the cadets were walking, and they turned away, toward the wall of Fairchild Hall.

"I was drunk," she said.

"You want me to apologize because you were drunk? Sorry, missy, I didn't pump you full of booze."

"No, you had something else in mind."

He rocked slightly on his feet. He was staring at his shoes now, the shiny, black Corfam ones that didn't need polishing, the shoes they had worked so hard to earn. "So did you. And then you started feeling bad about it. And now, what, you're going to twist my balls up in your fist?"

"All I want is an apology. That's all."

They had edged into the Air Garden, but there were still cadets walking here and there, casting glances at them, and they worked to keep their voices down.

"All right. I'm sorry I screwed you."

His words slapped her. She stepped back and blinked, as though she'd been struck. "What happened to you, Billy?"

Billy shrugged, looking off toward the alcove under Fairchild Hall. "Nothing happened to me. I just don't want to talk about this. It was a mistake. You're right. It was a big mistake."

"What do you mean, you don't want to talk about it? Are you afraid I'm going to turn you in?"

Now he turned and faced her, leaning in so that he could say, quietly, "You turn me in and I'll deny everything. You were drunk and off base during probation. Everybody saw you. You report me and you'll bring us both down. Is that what you want?"

Brook stared at him, horrified. "I never said I was going to report you."

"But it's always there, isn't it? We have to live day and night with the threat that one of you girls will get pissed off and decide to take it out on us. How do you think that feels?"

"That's so unfair. I haven't threatened you with anything. You're the one who seems to be threatening me, as though all this were *my* fault."

"Oh, God forbid I accuse you of anything. Girls never take the fall for anything that happens around here."

"I don't believe this." Brook looked around her. It seemed that they were at two different academies, and they'd had two different experiences that had nothing to do with each other.

"Don't deny it. That's why you're so friendly with Paula. You girls can get away with anything."

"I haven't even talked to Paula since that night." It was true—she'd avoided Paula. She hadn't wanted to tell her what had happened. Instead, she'd taken Lex's lead, spending her free hours in a corner of the library. For the first time, she was beginning to complete her homework. She thought that was what it must feel like to go to an actual college, to complete one's reading assignments, to be prepared in class. Lex had had the right idea all along. Academics were the one thing you could actually control in this crazy place.

"That's only because she's spending all her time with Terry Shane. Can you get over that? If a *male* cadet was dating a *female* officer, that would be the end of both of them."

"So, good for Paula," Brook said. "But what does that have to do with me?"

"It just means you're too complicated. Cherry was smart. He stuck with civilian girls."

"Cherry would be disgusted if he could hear you now."

"Cherry *warned* me to stay away from you. Don't do it, he said. Damn if he wasn't right. That guy knew what he was talking about."

"Cherry was my friend, too."

"He was right. Everything he said was right."

"He called you a sniveling rat once. I guess he was right about that, too."

Before Billy could answer, Brook turned and walked across the Terrazzo as slowly and purposefully as she could manage, her mind not on the oncoming numbers of upperclassmen or on the new smacks hustling along the grid lines from one place to another, or on the two officers who now approached, absorbed in their own conversation. Brook walked right past them, her mind in another place altogether. Billy had been horrible, but then she had told him off. It surprised her, surprised them both. She'd seen the look on Billy's face the moment she turned away, a mixture of disbelief and admiration. The words had come—she hadn't stumbled over them, and she'd actually told him off.

"Excuse me there, Cadet?" The officers had stopped talking and turned to look at her.

"Yes, sir," she said, turning suddenly.

"Didn't you see us just walk by you?" one of them asked. They were both captains, midgrade officers who, to Brook's mind, possessed a frightening mix of power and inexperience.

"No excuse, sir. I'm very sorry." She stood at attention and snapped her most perfect salute, bringing the tips of her fingers to the outer tip of her eyebrow with such apparent force that her arm vibrated slightly, like the arm of a spring-loaded machine. It was a polished salute, and the officers seemed pleased by it. They nodded ever so slightly, and after a moment's pause—a kind of minor punishment for the crime of walking past them—they casually raised their arms to salute in return, releasing her from the pose.

"Stay on your toes, Cadet. Carry on."

Brook turned and headed once again across the Terrazzo. Where was she going? She wavered for a moment. Biology class. Normally, she'd be shaken after an encounter with officers, but there was too much else on her mind. She was ashamed of Billy and angry she'd ever cared for him. Not honorable, she thought. Billy is not honorable.

He was a good athlete, competent, well dressed, and he could perform all the things the academy required of him. But he was not honorable. She knew that much. But then, what the hell was honor? The academy had rammed honor down their throats for a year. It was like a threat. But all they'd really told her was that honor meant not cheating, not stealing, not lying, not tolerating. As though honor was in abstinence. As though to be honorable, you had only to be dead.

There had to be more to honor than avoiding mistakes. Already into her second year at the academy, and this was how far she'd come.

And how would she go about the next hour, the next day? She could keep her head down, hide herself inside the library, excel at her studies, but this suddenly didn't seem like enough. It was practical advice, but not satisfying. There was more to learn than what was in books. That was the point, wasn't it, of a military academy?

Cherry had been honorable.

This occurred to her, suddenly. How had he done it? She wished she'd paid more attention while he was alive. She wished she'd asked him about it. She wished she'd been closer to him, and she saw now that Billy had kept that from happening, not intentionally perhaps, but with his need to be in the center of things, and with his tendency to keep things casual and light. Now, Brook hated him more for having kept her from Cherry than for what had happened in the tunnels.

What had happened.

He hadn't raped her. Not exactly. But he had been dishonorable. That's what she should have told him. And what about her behavior? Had she been honorable? Was she being honorable now?

She would find a way to ask her father about it. She would write him a letter. She would ask him about honor, and she would do it in such a way that it wouldn't alarm him. She wouldn't tell him about the tunnels.

Be true to yourself. That's what Cherry had told her in his room last winter on the last day of Hell Week. It seemed like years ago, back in a more innocent time. What she regretted was that she hadn't bothered to ask him how.

She was almost at Fairchild, now, and she looked over toward the airfield, which was something she did instinctively whenever she thought about Cherry. There were gliders up, circling under the clouds. This surprised her. She'd thought the gliders were grounded. Evidently, they weren't anymore. It made sense. They had to start up again sometime. The grounding couldn't remain, as she'd imagined it, a kind of silent memorial to Cherry. But maybe it was a good sign. She'd flown three times, and she hadn't been as good as Cherry. Now she could work at it. She could throw herself into becoming a great pilot. Where else, at what other college, could she do such a thing?

She would keep flying. She would practice. She would join the acrobatic team. She'd do whatever it took to get accepted. She would pick up where Cherry had left off.

Chapter Nineteen

Waller sat at his desk, overlooking the Terrazzo, wondering how the interview could have gone as badly as it had. It could not have gone worse. He'd arrived in plenty of time at the Denver studio, and they'd handed him a jar of powder and asked him to "swab" himself, and he'd set about dusting his face into an ashen, flaky appearance, and then they had ushered him into the studio. He had never been interviewed on national television before, and he tried not to seem nervous. He was a fighter pilot, after all. He'd been through far worse than this. The important thing was to keep his composure, to look on camera the way a fighter pilot was supposed to look.

Two technicians were working in the surprisingly small, bright room. One was behind the camera and the other was typing on a computer. Waller sat on a hard stool, wearing his full Class-A uniform with the blue jacket and the rows of ribbons on his chest. The jacket was a little tight in the shoulders, and it itched and felt stifling under the lights. Now he understood what the powder was for, and he hoped he'd put enough of it on and that it had not drifted down like an avalanche of dandruff on his uniform.

"We're coming up in a few seconds," the man at the camera said. Waller nodded. In the few short seconds before going live—he had no idea what the questions would be, only that he would have to be ready for them—he abandoned all the confidence earned from the hundreds of hours he'd flown over war zones, the many times he'd acted quickly and bravely in the moment before disaster, the many colleagues who admired and looked up to him, and delved into a brief, titillating fantasy about his own fighter-pilot hero, the man who would never worry about powder on his face. He imagined he was John Wayne in *Flying Tigers*.

So when he came up live, facing an anonymous, million-strong audience of viewers, he had a slight, unnatural smirk to his lips and a squint that seemed to come not from the blinding sun at altitude, as he imagined, but from the harsh studio lights that made him look exposed and out of place.

A young woman came up, smiling, on the monitor. She was addressing not him, but the audience at large, introducing him with the canned biography that had been passed to them by the public affairs office. He nodded obligingly through all this, but then she said something that floored him.

Somehow, CNN had gotten hold of a copy of the investigation report from the glider crash, and she was telling the world this in such animated efficient words, that he could only watch in disbelief. There was no time to compose a response. No time to ask how they'd gotten it. Even he hadn't seen the report yet, and here CNN was getting ready to grill him on it, live, in front of the nation.

"Can you tell me precisely what caused the crash?" she asked.

"I haven't yet seen the report. I can't really comment—"

"It says here the pilot—the cadet, in this case—had been inexperienced and that there was, and I quote, 'possible physiological impairment due to the recent consumption of judgment-impairing substances.' Care to comment on that?"

She wielded the language of the report like a weapon she was not familiar with. Where was John Wayne now? Disappearing in a mirage of proud, hard-flying days that Waller yearned to have as his own history, his own present.

"I'm afraid I can't comment until I read the report." John Wayne blinked and turned away. Waller knew he sounded like a bureaucrat. He hated himself for it. Perhaps he'd always been one, so fastidious about checklists, so cautious about the steps in his own career. He'd always taken the responsible jobs—chief of evaluations, deputy of operations, squadron commander, desk jobs that led to advancement but that had taken him away from flying. Perhaps he'd not been the pilot he thought he was.

"It also says 'a hairline irregularity was discovered in the right aileron' of the airplane. Can you tell me what an aileron is?"

"It's a mechanism on the wing that helps turn the airplane."

"I see. So a hairline irregularity could mean there was something wrong with the glider before the cadet flew it."

He had flown in that glider, of course. He'd had a problem with the aileron, a popping noise that befuddled him. This he didn't tell her. Perhaps a better pilot would have known instinctively there was a serious problem. Perhaps a better pilot would not have simply filled out the maintenance forms and trusted the system to take over. And then, perhaps, Mac Cherry would be alive.

"It's impossible for me to comment until I read the report."

"Well, perhaps you could comment on how the cadet population has responded to the crash. Can you talk about the religious aspect of the incident?"

The goddamn CCF. He would see that Metz was fired for this. His mind was still grappling with what was, to him, the greater problem, the problem with the aileron. Why hadn't he known it? Why hadn't he made a point of flying that glider again to check it out for himself?

"I don't think the religious controversy is as serious as it's been shown in the press. We have a number of religious groups on the campus. They've always gotten along harmoniously."

John Wayne was gone now, utterly gone. Perhaps he'd never been with him at all.

"Well, it certainly *seems* serious. Cadet Cherry was Jewish, wasn't he?"

"Yes."

"And the majority of the cadet population is evangelical Christian?"

"The majority, no. A small minority. One small group became a little too vocal about their beliefs after the incident, but the academy is a broadly diverse place. We're not intolerant."

"But wasn't there some kind of vigil? Some kind of prayer over the fate of the cadet's soul?"

"The cadets have a wide variety of social outlets. It helps them deal with the intensity of military training. The vigil was a way for them to deal with their grief over a lost cadet." To his own horror, Waller now found himself defending the CCF. Had he lost his good sense? And yet, what could he do? He'd been broadsided with the crash report, forced to defend himself—that was it, they *wanted* him to sound defensive—and he couldn't publicly bad-mouth an academy institution, no matter how much he hated it.

"Didn't this same group build a cross outside the dining hall at Eastertime?"

"Well, yes. But it was quickly dismantled. The group was censured. We dealt with it."

"You dealt with it? What about the reports of harassment? What about the vigil for Mac Cherry's soul?"

Unfair, unfair. Whenever he tried to lead her away from the accident, away from the damn CCF, and toward his philosophy, which, to him, was the crux of the matter, his genuine intention of training professional airmen, she yanked him back to the present with yet another biting, impossible question. No, it had not gone well. It had been a mistake from the beginning.

Steaming with fury, he drove back to Colorado Springs, where the accident report, stamped FOR OFFICIAL USE ONLY (FOUO)— how had they gotten a copy?—sat waiting on his desk. He read it, sifting through the dense language that made him feel both ill and eerily sane at the same time. An accident report was, in a sense, a testimony to every other pilot that he himself had not crashed. One pilot had died and every other pilot had lived to read about it. In this sense, every crash was a kind of near miss for every other pilot. It could

have been Waller. As he read the report, a part of him removed Cadet Cherry's name and inserted his in its place. Waller knew that if
he ever came back as a dead soul to hover over the remnants of his
life, he would not linger over the funeral, as they sometimes did in
dreams, but over the accident report and the slouching shoulders of
the SOB reading it.

Well.

> On 28 August 200_ at sometime between 1328 and 1329
> Mountain Time, a TG-10B "Kestrel" sailplane S/N 85-77XX
> made a right aileron roll into a period of uncontrolled flight,
> leading to a Class-A mishap four miles west of Colorado Springs,
> CO, in Category E airspace.

The language was both starkly exact and impossibly vague. If only
they could pin down the seconds between 1328 and 1329, account
during each one of them for the exact wind conditions along the
ridge and the velocity and direction of the airplane and every single
thing Cherry had seen, heard, felt, sensed, and every thought he had
considered, then perhaps they would get somewhere. Perhaps they
would understand why a plane had crashed and a cadet was dead.

> The mishap TG-10B, call sign FALCON 21, assigned to the
> Ninety-fourth Flying Training Squadron, United States Air Force
> Academy, was on a student contract flying training mission. The
> student pilot (SP) sustained fatal injuries. The aircraft was de-
> stroyed after impacting the ground on an unpopulated mountain
> ridgeline, causing minimal damage to surrounding vegetation.
> There were no injuries to civilians on the ground.

There was always the urge to ask a dead pilot what he had been
thinking. Had he known there was trouble and was his head down
in the cockpit working on it, or was he dumbly soaring along and
sensed danger only at the end? If you could know the pilot's last
thoughts, then the riddle might be solved. This was, of course, the
idea behind the black boxes in multipilot aircraft. But there was
more to it than solving the riddle. There was a point when a pilot's
death went beyond the real and into the spiritual. He went up into

the sky and evaporated. In a way, Cherry was still alive. He was alive and Waller had known him all his life, knew him now better than he ever had, better than he had known anyone in his life, even better than Rails, who was probably the best friend Waller had. Cherry had passed Waller. He'd gone past him into that solid blue state of heaven. Heaven was blue, a cool, flat blue that stopped the imagination. The last blue mile.

> *The Accident Investigation Board president found two causes. First, the pilot of the TG-10B entered an unstable flight attitude too low to maintain adequate obstruction avoidance. Contributing factors were pilot's inexperience and possible physiological impairment due to the recent consumption of judgment-impairing substances. Second, a hairline irregularity was discovered in the right aileron of the TG-10B that may have hampered the pilot's ability to correct for the increasingly steep bank of his turn.*

Well, at least the CNN reporter had quoted it right. But what exactly was a hairline irregularity? A crack? A bulge?

It was quite clear to Waller now that he would not be earning a second star and would very probably not be returning to the fighter world in any capacity but would no doubt be put out to pasture in some career-terminating desk job in some moldy corner of the Pentagon.

It had happened to lesser people.

He studied all this with the calm, eerie rationality with which he had studied the accident report. One could not worry the facts out of being what they were. One dealt with them, taking certain calculated risks, and went on. He had taken a certain calculated risk when he'd gone back up in the A-10 the day after the SEALs had died on the ridge. He'd always believed it was because he needed to fly, but now he wasn't sure if it had been, in larger part, because he wanted to make the deputy of operations, Bud Holly, believe he was reliable enough to earn, in due time, promotion.

By all rights, according to his conscience, he shouldn't have flown that day. He should have sat down at his desk in the shabby room of the temporary officers' quarters and written a letter to his friend's widow. That's what had bothered him all these years. He'd betrayed himself.

Now, he looked up and saw the gliders flying out over the ridge. There was a lenticular cloud hanging there. It had been much too long since his last ride in the wake lift, and then he remembered again how, in that particular ride, he had taken the now defunct TG-10B S/N 85-7XX and had felt something popping in the aileron. The popping in the aileron had been documented and checked, cleared with the all-catching "CANNOT DUPLICATE" green light, and now the glider was defunct and the pilot who had flown it after him was dead.

There was nothing that could be drawn from this.

Maybe he should retire. Maybe, but the truth was that he didn't have the balls to retire yet. He loved the Air Force too much to leave it. It was too much a part of him. He was afraid to leave it, afraid of the darkness of the days that stretched out in the future, days whose structure wasn't clear, whose relationships weren't defined in any orderly way. He could fly airplanes, but he lacked the nerve to negotiate the ambiguities of civilian life. *Balls*. He hadn't lived up to his call sign.

They would have to put him out to pasture and then, reluctantly, he might unlatch himself from the military and go on to whatever came next. Until then, he would spend his free time in the hangar with Rails and fly the gliders more often until they decided the proper amount of time had passed before they could reassign him to whatever they chose as his terminal destination. He would also spend more time with Lauren and the girls. He would take the girls on trips, wherever they wanted to go. They would enjoy to the fullest extent possible their last—he was guessing—six months in Colorado. He saw all this very rationally, and with something like relief. The grief, the regret, was something he knew would come later.

Metz walked through the open door and stood as still as a cornstalk, waiting for Waller to look up.

"Did you get a chance to look at this?" Waller asked.

"Not yet. It's on my desk. We just got a call from General Long. The CSAF wants to call in and talk about this. His office is setting up a time later in the week."

Waller put his fingers over his eyes.

"Did General Beddle see the CNN piece?"

"He wanted to know why you didn't mention the Culture of Transformation."

"Is that all? Is that all he wanted to know?"

Metz shrugged. "You can ask him yourself on Thursday."

"What do you think about all this, Sil?"

"I think it's inevitable."

"What's inevitable?"

"The revolution."

"The *revolution*?"

"The Culture of Transformation is a revolution. It's a force multiplier. We aren't just training military officers. We have an influence over every aspect of their lives."

"CoT is a slogan. It will be forgotten in five years."

"But the steps we take, the changes, will be irrevocable."

"What changes?"

"Our ideological changes. Our greatest mission. We're fighting a war of spirit. Divine moral compass."

"I don't even know what you're talking about."

"The mission to fight evil."

"You're crazy." Waller was growing angry now. "You'd better put a lid on that. You put that into these kids' heads and you're going to get My Lai all over again."

"This isn't My Lai. This is good versus evil." Metz, too, was growing angry. "You think it's all about bravado. That's all you care about. All about fight and screw. Fight and screw. *Balls*. It's people like you who are becoming the minority."

"I've let this go on far too long," Waller said. "You're going to be in a heap of shit, Sil. You can't talk to these kids this way. We're trying to raise a military, not a religious mission. If you want to help, get off your holy perch and do something for the real cause."

"I *am* the military, John."

With that, he turned and walked out. Waller again stared at the report on his desk. He was fuming.

Who was the military? *He* was. He'd fought in war, killed in war. So had Bud. So had Coyle, for that matter. How did Metz come off thinking he was the military?

He would have to do something. How could he derail Metz? How had Metz gotten into a position that Balls had to derail him from? That was troubling enough. Had Susan Long put him up to it? Was she a closet theocrat?

Impossible. Susan Long thought only of herself. Then how had Metz become so sure of himself? No matter. Waller would squelch it. He would find a way to put Metz to pasture.

The phone rang. He ignored it. Kord walked into his office and, assuming it was another press call, Waller put his hand up to wave him away.

"It's Rails," Kord said. "He says you better get down to the hangar quick."

PART IV

The Last Blue Mile

Chapter Twenty

Soaring differs from gliding in one principle way. In gliding, one is a passenger on the air. The glider pilot is subject to the whims and quirks of a rising pocket of air under a heavy cloud, called the thermal, or a puff of wind that rides along a mountain ridge, called the ridge lift. Even a novice glider pilot can poke around and find rising air in these places. She will find enough lift to sustain her, to make her believe she can understand the air and get on top of it. Enough to make her euphoric later, a little cocky, trying to describe it—and she *will* try because the feel of it is so strong, though words will ultimately fail her because sailing through an invisible sea of air is not something that can be grounded in words.

Soaring, on the other hand, involves predicting the passages of air and weaving the glider through them. It's all well and good to sit upriver in a kayak and watch the water rushing over rocks and ledges, following the line of the most direct, least treacherous current, but a pilot can't do this with wind for the simple reason that wind is invisible.

How do you tell air from air?

You must learn a language that exists only between the mountains and clouds. You must look at a mountain like Pikes Peak, a single, isolated mountain poking out of a range of minor crests, and understand what the mountain does to the air around it. You must read the variometer. You must read the ground—are you riding on one point or are you riding through the wave and headed for a crash? You must read the clouds—are they opening or closing, are there little wispy clouds? A thousand things speak out to you about the precise picture of what the wind is doing, but only if you open your eyes to them.

This was what Rails told Brook while they stood outside the hangar with the breeze circling around them, twisting itself upward, like invisible smoke that doesn't dissipate but instead gains momentum, shifting and funneling into a secret passage through the troughs of the mountains and then pushing higher still, swirling into the silent, blue airways of a noiseless ocean.

"The air at those altitudes is a violent place," he said. "You have to work very hard. Gliding, the idea of gliding, is a complete misconception."

Brook nodded, impatient to fly. She wanted to qualify for the acrobatic team. Already, she was learning that to qualify for things, for the next level of flying or leadership, was the principle thing that mattered in the Air Force. But what she wanted most of all was to understand Cherry's passion. He had wanted to soar in a mountain wave, and without fully understanding why, she wanted to soar in one, too.

There was a long, thin lenticular cloud floating above Pikes Peak. Storm clouds to the north. The sky looked almost precisely the way it had looked after the first time she and Cherry and Billy had flown the Kestrels with their instructors sitting behind them, guiding them into the thermal like a flock of prescient birds. They had been sitting in lawn chairs, Cherry pointing something out to her that she'd never considered. Now, she was looking at the same kind of sky, talking to Rails about it. Cherry would be pleased.

"I want to fly that," she said. She pointed at the long cloud that seemed to swell but never to budge, even as the clouds from the north threatened to overrun it.

"You're not ready for that," he said. "You have to learn to read the wind."

"I can't very well learn standing here."

He ignored her. "Imagine a shoreline. The waves are coming in. Out in the ocean, they look big and smooth, easy to ride. That's where you want to be, but you have to get there first. You have to get past the waves that are breaking on the shore. The wind does the same thing when it comes over the mountains. It crashes down. It'll crush a glider. It'll kill you if you're not careful. You're not ready."

I'm ready, she thought.

"The way the wave crashes over the mountain is called the rotor. The only way to get to the wave is to go through the rotor, but it's nothing but trouble. It's easier to wrestle a bull to the ground with your bare hands."

He exaggerates, she thought. *He thinks too much of himself.*

"You ever done that?"

"What?"

"Wrestle a bull to the ground with your bare hands?"

Rails laughed. "I've flown in that," he said. "That's enough."

"So let's go up."

"No."

"You said you've done it."

"I can't. It's against the rules. Too risky."

"Okay. If I *was* going to fly it, how would I do it?"

"If you *were* going to fly it, which you might get away with if you get on the cross-country team, not the acrobatic team—I'm telling you this because you seem to be hell-bent on acrobatics, which is fun but something else altogether—if you get on the cross-country team, you might get a chance to fly something like this, if you're lucky, because you've got oxygen and GPS in the D models."

She waited for him to finish

"*How* do I do it, Rails?"

"How you would do it is to look downwind from the peak. To get good wave lift, you need a good strong westerly wind. That's why you see that nice thin cloud there. Don't try to circle in the lift or you'll get kicked out. A wave is like in the ocean. It's the same thing. If you want to ride the wave, you get on top of it, like a surfer."

They were both looking at the sky.

"Then again," he said, "waves are fickle. They change in a second. You learn something about how to fly a wave and in the next flight you can forget all about it."

"Why don't we just go, Rails? What's stopping us?"

"I'd like to. You can't ever tell for sure, but this is a good one. It just feels like it. Then again, I don't want to lose my job."

The sky around the cloud was still bright, a kind of contraction against the clouds bearing down from the north.

"I guess I'll just go up and fly the thermals, then."

"Weather's coming in quick," he said. "You don't have much time."

"I have enough time for one run."

He tapped his boot on the concrete. He was looking for something, an excuse.

"Report said we're clear until three."

He shrugged. He might sense something, and the sense might lead him to hesitate, but there was no arguing with the logic of a weather report.

"Well," he said. "It's hard to say."

Brook nodded, waiting. There was a kind of battle of wills here about who could seem the least interested. She looked at the sky. There was a thick chunk of cumulus cloud near the ridge, the same kind of cloud that choked up along the ridgeline almost every day. The sky around it was blue, and the long, thin cloud above hovered like a barracuda. She was learning to understand how the wind operated.

"Don't even think about it," he said.

"I'm not. I just want to go thermal in the practice area."

"That's what I wanted to hear."

"You going to tow me?"

"I'll tow you. Stay on the radio and come down when I say."

"All right."

The Cessna was already out and fueled. Rails only had to pre-flight it and take up the chocks, and they pulled the glider out of the hangar and got it set up. This took twenty minutes, and the storm clouds to the north hadn't moved discernibly.

"You might get lucky," Rails said. "You might get an hour."

She was preflighting the glider. He was hovering, distracting her. She walked around the glider, carefully checked the pins and the airfoils and the rudder, showing him that she knew what she was doing.

"Let me ask you something," she said. She didn't look at him. Instead, she moved the aileron on the left wing up and down, testing it.

"Go ahead."

"Did you really think Cherry was a gifted pilot?"

"I wouldn't worry too much about that."

She walked around, past the tail, to the right wing. She kept her eyes on the smooth, simple lines of the glider. He didn't answer her. Instead, he walked over to the Cessna and flipped the radio dial to the same channel as in the glider.

"Falcon forty-one, how do you copy?" came his voice, scratchy, over the radio.

"Loud and clear," she answered.

She said nothing else. When she was satisfied that the mechanics of the glider were functioning properly, she climbed into the cockpit and strapped herself in. Rails finished fiddling with the radio and came toward her, looking off to the side. She watched him come. He might look at her, give her a moment's credit for getting in a glider and going up on the ridge after watching Cherry die on it. He might recognize that in her.

"I guess you got it set up the way you want it?" he said, approaching.

"Yep."

They pushed the glider out into position and got it hooked up to the towplane.

"You want me to check your pins?"

"Okay," she said, strapping in. She moved the stick mechanically, left and right, forward and back.

"Good," he said. "All right."

By the time he had climbed into the Cessna and gotten the engine started, she had the canopy closed and latched over her. They each gave a thumbs-up—in a movie about flying, she thought, she would have flipped him the finger, a big *fuck you* because he was too chickenshit to talk about Cherry so soon after the crash, with her ready and waiting on the ramp, even though Cherry was still here with them. Rails was either too afraid or not smart enough to know what to say. Either way, in the movies, she would have flipped him the finger and they would laugh to themselves and be done with it. But the reality was too complicated, too fraught with the possibility of misunderstanding. She gave him a thumbs-up and waited for the tow.

Up they went. She flew the line as well as she could. She was better at it now. The rope didn't make her nervous. She tried to anticipate what the Cessna was doing and then she tried to do the same thing, knowing there was a delay in the time between the Cessna hitting a pocket of air and her hitting the same pocket but knowing, also, that the delay was built into the time it took for her mind to see what the Cessna was doing and the synapses to travel through her nervous system to her hand, which was resting tensely on the stick, and that those two delays counteracted each other. She knew this in her body, the way a toddler knows to put his hands out when he falls.

The lead plane climbed, and Brook moved into high position and climbed also. This was all very standard. She was complimenting herself on how standard it all was, how she could get herself up in a glider plane and get herself towed toward a nice, fat cumulus cloud, so that she could thermal up into it and down out of it as many times as she wanted, or until the weather came in.

At eleven thousand feet, she released the rope and turned sharply toward the thermal. It was a beautiful, big thermal, and she had no trouble finding it. But once she was inside, she began to eye the wave. How much would it take to jump from a thermal to a wave? She knew it could be done. She knew an experienced glider pilot could wrestle through it, but she knew she wasn't experienced, yet. Rails had told her as much. He was the expert, and he was trying to help her. To attempt the wave now would be to betray his trust in her, his mentorship. She was lucky to have him, lucky he'd agreed to help her.

But then again, the wave was here, right now. It couldn't be that hard. She might show him how good she really was. The sailplane seemed to be talking to her. It seemed to be willing to take her upward, up on a big, blue journey. It seemed to promise it would show her what Cherry knew, and that it would deliver her, afterward, to the safety of the ground.

She looked above her. She might make the leap. She might try her luck on the rotor, and if it was too hard, she could always turn back. That was the gift of altitude. There was always time to turn back.

"What's going on?" Waller asked.

"There's a cadet up in the wake lift without clearance. I can't get her on the radio."

"I'll be right down."

He slammed down the phone. What was wrong with these kids? Why couldn't he keep them from trying to kill themselves and their careers? He wanted to take each of them by the starched collars on their uniforms and shake them until they understood the world was not there to satisfy their every whim. Why couldn't they see that?

He sped down to the hangar, an ominous nausea rising in his gut. Rails was waiting outside, a pair of binoculars in his hands. The storm clouds were just off to the north, maybe twenty miles away, and the sun shone off them in an eerie light. The glider was facing away from the clouds—she wouldn't see them unless she knew to look—and pushing upward, past Pikes Peak, into the great wave flowing over the ridge.

"She doesn't see it," Rails said. "The weather's coming down hard. I shouldn't have let her go."

"Does she have oxygen?"

"She has it. I don't know if she knows how to use it."

"Does she know how to get down from the wave?"

"No."

"Who is it?"

"Brook Searcy."

Mac Cherry's friend. What was she trying to prove? "Jesus. Where's the Ximango? I'm going up."

"What are you going to do, lasso her? It's not like you can ride out in the prairie and bring her in like a renegade sheep."

"I'm going to fly with her. I'll get her to follow me down."

"You don't have much time."

It was partly instinct. The instinct was to get up in the air, that he could do something from there. He had been trained to understand that when there was trouble, he should get into an airplane. On the ground, you could do nothing, but if you were in the air, you were part of everything that was happening—it seemed to Waller that this way, at least you had a chance.

To jump from the thermal into the wave was no easy feat. She would have to get through the rotor first, that invisible chugging monster wind baffling off the crisp face of Pikes Peak. She worked the thermal, banking her wings to rise higher in the circling air. What if she were to tighten her turn, just a little, corkscrew her glider up to the top of the thermal, then what? Would she simply deflate, the thermal no longer propelling her upward? Or would she end up in another kind of world, above the clouds, where the rules were all different, whispered through a thin, blue chill?

Cherry was up there. If his spirit really did live in some middle ground, then so be it, he was up here on the blue highway that wove through the sleek lines of valleys and mountains, circling through the Rockies and the Sierras and up into Canada and back down along the continental ridge that led here, to this spot. Cherry had flown there. For the first time since she'd watched him disappear on the ridge, Brook was happy.

Don't bank too tightly, she thought, don't stall. When it seemed she couldn't climb any higher, she leaped—it was like a leap of faith, from that constant, trustworthy thermal into the naked air.

What now? She had the idea that Cherry would catch her, but there was nothing but a thin, whistling wind. She flexed her feet on the rudders, her fingers on the stick, and waited for whatever would come out to strike her next. She was still climbing, slowly, as though at the peak of a great arc, and soon, if she didn't find the rotor, she would begin to drift down, drift back into that other world that belonged to the cadets and the drill instructors marching here and there on the Terrazzo and the classrooms and Billy and Paula and even Rails, who would be standing on the ramp, worried about her now—though there was no need, she was in good hands—and she was not ready to go back. She tightened her breath, and waited.

When the first blast of rotor hit, it sounded as if she'd hit a rock wall. The bustling chunk of wind flipped her glider sharply toward the ridge, slamming her knees into the instrument panel. She cried out. A pain shot through her elbow—she must have struck the side of the canopy. But her fingers were still around the stick. She was still flying. Her glider was tossed back and forth on its invisible sea. The rotor wash struck her right side, then her left, then from above. Little wispy clouds, like torn cotton, churned around her. She was fighting a monster she couldn't see, both hands on the stick now swirling between her knees, trying to keep the horizon below her, though it rocked like the hull of a ship. Keep it below me, she thought. Nothing else matters.

She was climbing. Though the wind kicked her around, she was inching higher, fighting a fierce tide. It was nearly freezing in the cockpit, but she was sweating, and she didn't know she was sweating, and she didn't think that the air was getting thinner, and she didn't see the ice crystals begin to form at the corners of her canopy. She had no idea how long she'd been flying—minutes, she would have said, though in fact she'd been up almost an hour. These were all things she should have known, but all she had time to do was think about holding on through the next invisible collision. She kept working, keeping the peak in view, just below her. Yes, she was still climbing—the peak was *below* her.

And then, abruptly, she was through it. The storm released her. She waited, but nothing came at the glider. It was as though the storm had lost interest in her and let her go. Now, she was sitting on air so calm and quiet, it was like sitting in a canoe on the still surface of a lake at evening. The wind hardly whispered. It seemed to be holding its breath, bearing her gently upward on the rising wave. She was as small, as insignificant, as a dragonfly. She held the stick lightly in her tingling fingers. Tingling. She quickly pulled the oxygen mask over her head, took a deep breath. The tingling subsided. She was climbing quickly now, though she could hardly feel it. She had never felt anything so calm, had never seen the world spread so broadly under her, had never believed anyone could be so separate from the world, so aloft from it. It was godly here.

Hello, Mac.

The sweat on her face had begun to cool. She shivered. It was cold, so very, very cold. She wore only a thin shirt under her flight suit and no gloves. He fingertips were growing numb. She pinched them together. She would have to go down soon. It occurred to her now that she didn't quite know how to get down. If she rode out with the sinking air, she'd wind up on the other side of the ridge, where the jagged peaks would chew a glider to bits. How did she descend through rising air? She had just begun to consider this, to look behind her, when she saw the clouds. She'd forgotten about the weather, and now it was bearing down on the valley. Already, the campus was swallowed within the clouds and in a moment, she wouldn't be able to see the airfield. She would have to descend, but there was no rope to pull her down. Gravity seemed ambivalent up here. The air seemed to pull her into a broad, invisible current, to draw her out to the invisible regions of space. Already, everything under her was fading into a single, icy hue, swept clean and smooth. A desert of blue.

What if she stayed? Would she be wrenched apart, particle by particle, eaten by the hungry air? Her body felt thick with cold. It was madness to be out here. Perhaps she was crazy, after all. But she sensed it now: how to vanish. This was one way to escape, straight into the blue air. She could do it, too. Look at me now, Mother. If she flew high enough, the sky might dissect her, or swallow her whole.

He used the engine in the Ximango to work through the rotor. He fought it, motoring his way up to her. He could see that she'd worked through the rough air and was on the other side of it now, hovering like a kite in the wind. It was a beautiful sight, a glider riding in the wave. She was good. He had to admit that. He was surprised she'd made it through the rotor. He'd thought she wouldn't make it, would turn back, or worse, be driven into the ridge, but she'd fought her way through it, as he was now, crashing from one side of the canopy to the other. He'd gone through the rotor a hundred times. He knew to relax and let it take him, focus only on keeping the horizon as level as possible. He let it bounce him around. It was an irritation, nothing to be frightened of. He was only frightened for her. He was frightened of not getting to her before the wave swept her down into the mountains on the other side of the ridge.

Stay with me, he thought. He had the throttle maxed out, churning his way higher. He would not lose another cadet. He kept his eyes on her—she'd risen far above him, but as soon as he hit the wave, he could catch up. He suffered the rotor, cursing it, and then when he was through it, he debated keeping the engine on, but it was a little engine and had nothing to hold on to at this altitude. He switched it off and let the wings take over, guiding them into a perfect pitch for the wave. He rose. He began to climb toward her.

"Falcon forty-one," he called over the radio. "Falcon forty-one, this is Falcon forty-three, the Ximango behind you. I'm coming up on you. How do you copy?"

"Loud and clear," she said. "I can't see you, though. Can you see me?"

She was trembling now from the cold and from something else, some deep breath that seemed to whistle out from the invisible air. *I could die out here.*

"I have you at my twelve o'clock, about a thousand feet above. I want you to listen to me. Are you listening?"

"I'm not sure how to get down. Can you help me?"

She could hear the quick clutch of her voice on the radio. Panic. She tried to calm herself, to breathe. There was no Cherry up here, nothing but the bloodless cold. What had she expected?

"I want you to listen to me," said the voice. "The weather is coming under us, and we have to work quickly. I want you to do exactly what I say. Do you copy?"

"I copy."

"Bank to the left, ninety degrees, but take your time with it. Your glider won't turn very sharply up here."

"Okay."

"Start your turn now."

"Roger."

Her glider began a slow, wide turn back to the east. That was good, he thought. At least we're getting away from the mountains. We'll get over the valley first, out of the wave, and then we'll worry about the weather.

She knew there would be hell to pay for breaking the rules, for being so foolish that someone—she didn't know who, it hardly mattered—had to come up and get her and bring her down. There would be hell to pay. That was okay. She only wanted to get down, to land the glider and stand with her feet against the ground. Everything else could be dealt with.

Land. Land. Land. She willed the ground closer, but it seemed to tease, to veer away, like a grown-up in a pool with a child who hasn't quite learned to swim. *Please.* She prayed to the ground to come up and catch her, to bring her down safely and swiftly, as with giant arms.

The clouds were under them. They had rushed in like a tide and it seemed to her that they were stranded, cut off from the ground below. She couldn't see the valley or the mountains, couldn't be certain of where she was, except that the voice kept telling her what to do, and she followed it.

"Start a downward bank, now," he said, "and keep it at ten degrees. Try to follow me."

The Ximango had moved in front of her. He was guiding her down. She moved the stick forward enough so that she could tell only by reading the variometer that they were descending for sure. It seemed to take so long! The clouds were thick as soup under them, and she wondered how they would ever get through them, how she would keep her eyes on the Ximango when they entered the thick, white mass.

"I'm going to lead you through the foehn gap, but first, we're going to hit the rotor. Try to keep me somewhere in your windshield. Call out if you lose sight of me."

"All right."

Almost immediately, they hit the rotor. And again, as if they were riding a fierce current, the glider tossed here and there in the choppy wind. Her knees, already bruised from the upward run, slammed against the instrument panel. The pain made her weak, and the weariness traveled up her legs and made her hands tremble. She kept her eyes fixed on the Ximango in front of her as though it were the only thing in the world that could save her life.

"Do you still have me?" came the voice.

"I have you."

"Good. We're going through the foehn gap now. Do you see it in front of us? A small hole in the clouds? That's our only chance. Keep me close, but not too close. Once we get under that, we're home free. Are you ready?"

"I'm ready."

"Bank a little steeper now. Head for that hole."

The clouds came up and touched them, washing over them like ghosts. She watched the Ximango come up against the mouth of the clouds, like a great volcano, and then dip into it as though it had been swallowed whole. She couldn't see him now, just a small opening in the clouds and somewhere underneath, the dull reflection of land. It was trickier than she thought—when she pointed her nose down, the clouds came up on her quickly and the foehn gap seemed to shift and move, winking at her. She had gone through a layer of cloud, and now she was out of it again and could see the hole clearly. She aimed for it, and it came closer, closer, and she shot through it, and all at once the ground with all its bearings opened up below.

They were back in the practice area, which was as familiar as her own backyard. She could see the airfield and the mountains and the Ximango, a small white dot, in front of her, a little lower. He was setting up, entering the pattern. She came in behind him on the base leg. She was still trembling with the fear of what she had come through and the fear of what remained ahead, once they were safe on the ground, but she felt herself breathe, now, for the first time since the clouds had swept in. She was safe. She had flown a monster wave and now she was going to land.

"You go first," called the Ximango. "I'll circle around behind you."

She did as she was told, turning from the base leg into final and then dropping down as she had done before, landing smoothly on the runway and rolling gradually to a stop. She took off her headset and her oxygen and put them on the floor, and then she unlatched the canopy. The air outside felt different, so very tame. The clouds massed over them were another place, entirely, another world that was foreign and hostile—no, not hostile, merely indifferent—and so much more complicated than it looked from the ground.

The Ximango was coming down behind her. Rails was walking toward her, across the grass. She unstrapped herself and climbed shakily out of the glider. She wanted to be standing by the time he arrived.

"Are you all right?" he asked coldly. She'd lost his trust. She could see that. He wasn't going to give her any more help, not right now and probably ever. She nodded. She couldn't quite find her voice.

"You're in a whole shitload of trouble. I guess you know that. You just broke about twenty different regulations."

He wasn't looking at her. He was looking at the wings of the glider, searching for damage.

"I'm sorry," she said. "I don't know what I was thinking."

"Do you know who just brought you down?"

She shook her head.

"Here he comes. Take a look."

The commandant had taxied the Ximango toward the fuel pump near the hangar and climbed out. He was walking toward them across the grass.

Her heart dropped. Of all the people to save her, why had it been the commandant of cadets? Why was her luck so bad? Why had her luck always been so horribly bad?

"This is it," she whispered. Her Air Force career was over now. She'd be expelled and have to go back to the Cape, apply for prelaw at Harvard, or at Suffolk if Harvard wouldn't have her. And why would they after this? All her life, she had been behind her brothers, and now she'd fallen back even further. Fine, she'd go to Suffolk. There was nothing wrong with Suffolk. It's true, she'd become a mere echo of her brothers, a small voice inside what she could have been if—

If what? If her mother had stayed?

She saw all of this unfold as the commandant came forward. He came forward like the last man in an ancient army, in broad daylight across an empty field, without a moment of doubt.

If her mother had stayed, she would have been a gymnast, or a ballerina, or worked in advertising or a public relations firm, but she would not have come to the Air Force Academy. That was likely enough. She wouldn't be sitting here watching a one-man army walk toward her like the might of the world.

"For both of us, probably," Rails said. "I was stupid enough to let you go."

"I'm sorry," she said, but Rails had turned away and was getting ready to push the glider back to the hangar.

"I'll help you," she said.

"Forget it," he said, but he didn't stop her from lining up on the opposite wing.

It was her mother's fault, then. Her immediate problem. Her whole life up till now. Her mother could have made the difference.

When the commandant approached, he didn't look at her, either.

"Let's get this glider in the hangar before the rain starts," he said to Rails.

Waller and Rails began to work so smoothly together that Brook could hardly step aside quickly enough to get out of the way. She followed them, watching that the wingtips didn't come close to touching the sides of the hangar, though they hardly needed her to spot and ignored her when she said they were clear. When they got the glider where they wanted it, nested in a dark cove with the other gliders, Waller turned to Brook and said, "I think we'll go have a talk."

She followed him into Rails's office, and he flicked on the fluorescent light and shut the door.

"Have a seat," he said, his back to her.

She did as she was told. He sat down at Rails's desk, and now that the desk was between them, he looked at it for a moment and seemed to very tangibly consider it as though it had just appeared. He put his fingertips on the wood as if testing whether it might support his weight, and then he looked up at her and began to speak.

"When I was much younger," he said, "I thought I could do anything. That is, it never occurred to me that there was something I *couldn't* do, or something I couldn't will to happen if I wanted it badly enough. That is, I thought I was invincible."

She watched him with the docility of young people accustomed to receiving lectures.

"One day I learned that I was not invincible. I learned this very suddenly. I learned it in a way that, frankly, I would not have any person learn it, though it made me a better pilot. Ultimately, it wasn't worth the price. I only know that now. You see, good soldiers died because of something I did. Or rather, something I failed to do."

Now she began to listen. She leaned forward and had momentarily forgotten to breathe, so that when she finally did inhale, she could hear the air come through her nose and into her bronchial tubes and feel her lungs expand, as though needing to pursue the monotonous process of living even as this new information, this new evidence of the narrow margin of life, was unfolding. She sat as quietly as possible.

"I've lived with it a long time. It never quite goes away, though, as you can see, I did go on with my life. Some would suggest that I was quite successful. I'll level with you, though I'm not sure you'll understand, that it's never been enough. I've always wanted more. It's natural to want more. It's American. But I wanted it in another kind of way. I wanted it to justify the mistake I made a lot of years ago when some people underneath me died. The fact is that I can't bring them back, and I never thought I could, but I thought that at some point, their deaths would become worth the price. That probably sounds callous. I'm sure it does. But I thought that saving my career, making something of myself, would somehow repair the grave, probably criminal mistake I made so many years ago. I can tell you now that their deaths were not worth any price. There's nothing I can do for the cadets here, for you, for anyone, that is worth the deaths of those eleven people. There is absolutely nothing I can do. I realized that after your friend Mac died, but I couldn't express it until now, that is, until after I went up into the sky to get you."

He paused for a moment. Outside, the rain had begun. They could hear it pitter-patter on the aluminum roof.

"This is not the traditional tack to take. Typically, I would call you in here to have your hide, to dismiss you and make sure you don't ever do anything to hurt the other people in the Air Force. I would make sure your bags were packed tonight and you were escorted off the grounds in the morning. But the fact is, I can't keep you from hurting anyone. All I can do, ultimately, is relate my own experience and hope it's helpful in some way. All I can do is suggest, very strongly, that you don't follow my path. I'm not invincible, and neither are you."

"I believe you." The way she said it, it was almost a whisper.

"I don't think you do."

"I didn't go up there to kill myself."

"But you almost did."

"It was foolish, sir. I know that."

"Listen to me. Your friend is dead. You're not responsible for that. You're only responsible for what happens next."

"What killed him?"

"Flying killed him."

"Was it his fault?"

Waller had leaned forward across the desk with his hands clasped in front of him, and now he raised his thumbs in a kind of salute to fate. *I don't know*, is what he meant.

"I used to think I would write the book on leading officers," he said. "On flying. I was going to write a memoir. That was my idea not so long ago. But the fact is that I have very little to say."

They sat in silence for a minute, and then Waller continued, "This is it, really, and it's already been said. You have your life to lead. That is, in the last mile, there is only one life that you have led, and that's the only thing you have to judge. More people should understand that early on."

And then he stood up, and before she could spring to her feet, as was the custom in the presence of an officer, he had already reached the doorway and was out of it, and she had the good sense to wait until he'd left the building and couldn't turn around and change his mind.

In the main office, Rails was standing at the counter pretending to read a flying magazine and waiting for him.

"I need to log some instructor hours," Waller said.

"What are you talking about?" Rails tapped a pencil nervously on the counter. He'd been wondering about his own career, but now he looked at Waller as though he'd lost his mind.

"I'm sorry about the confusion, Rails. I know it's against policy, but I had forgotten to inform you beforehand that I would be taking a cadet up on a special training mission."

"Do you really want to do this? Tell me why you want to do this."

Waller looked like he might answer the question, but then he looked at the counter where Rails was now clenching the pencil between his fingers and said, "I know this stuff is supposed to be logged ahead of time. I forgot to do that. I'm sorry about it. If it's okay, I'd like to fill out the instructor forms now and give you the assurance that I won't be so careless in the future."

Rails nodded and looked out the window at the rain.

Chapter Twenty-one

Waller retired in the spring.

Kord organized a ceremony in the blue auditorium of Arnold Hall. There were two cowhide armchairs positioned on the stage, as if they had been lifted from the family room of a middle-class home and set down angled toward each other and toward the audience. Behind the chairs, three flags were suspended over three pedestals, one sporting the Air Force crest, one with the symbol of the Air Force Academy, and a blue flag with three white stars, indicating the rank of the attending senior officer. Normally, Susan Long would have been the one to retire a brigadier general under her command, but Bud Holly had flown out for the occasion, and now he sat in one of the armchairs, opposite Waller, the emblems sparkling on his uniform as he bowed his head and listened to the chaplain take his place at the podium and begin the convocation. An auditorium packed with cadets, company-grade officers, and field officers watched the ceremonial rambling with the wistful longing of Everest climbers who, injured or sick, with blackening urine and skin, have looked longingly toward the summit and had to turn back. There was a small table next to each chair and on each table was a small pitcher of water and an empty glass. When the chaplain finished his prayer, Waller reached over and poured a glass of water and lifted it to his lips. This resembled almost exactly every other retirement ceremony he had ever attended, with its strange mix of structure and informality intended to both recognize a lifetime of achievement and make the outgoing service member feel, for once in his career, happy and relaxed. And like every other ceremony, this one could not possibly do either.

Following the chaplain, it was Bud Holly's turn to speak. He rose and made his way to the podium, patting the chaplain on the shoulder as they met. Waller took in the crowd—cadets who had come on their free time to watch him retire, and in the front-most seats, his administrative staff, his deputy and executive officer, his secretary, and of course his former boss, and then, in their bright and elegant dresses, his wife and daughters. He smiled warmly at them, and Lauren smiled back.

Bud stood at the podium, sniffed and patted his face in a gesture that was more habit now than anything else, since his face sweated almost constantly and nothing could seem to stop it.

"I've known Balls for over twenty years," he began. "I knew him when he wasn't much older than all of you, when he was just learning his way around an A-10 cockpit, and he was young and eager to succeed, and even then I knew he had what it took, though I never would have guessed ..."

Waller listened, enjoying the words like a spectator. He hadn't looked forward to this. He'd fretted at the end, counted the devices on each ribbon—silver star, bronze star, air medal, others he sometimes got confused about because he hadn't really earned them or had earned them so long ago that he couldn't remember. He'd patted his uniform down, shaved carefully, approved the pretty dresses Lauren and the girls had chosen, and still he felt himself sweating like a bride—like a cadet—when he came through the doors of Arnold Hall. But it was better now. He liked this. He was an honorary judge at his own hanging.

A military retirement was, indeed, like a death. A life had been trained from him, not his life, exactly, but a life within him that had been honed, as a spike is honed from a block of wood. He knew he would not quite now be the man he had been. He would be just slightly less, just enough to notice a loosening in the trousers, a settling into the hem. Perhaps he would reinvent himself. Others had done it. They became hardware men, cooks, consultants. Airline pilots. He could fly for the airlines, or for cargoes, or commuters. He could shuffle back and forth across the continent. Drift toward some prosaic end.

He hoped he had saved one life.

He couldn't see her, though he suspected she was there, some-where, in the mass of faces. In fact, Brook was sitting in the middle of the center section, almost directly opposite Waller. Paula and Billy were in the audience, too, though she didn't sit with them, or know where they were sitting, or even wonder about it. Brook would learn throughout her career that friends in the Air Force came and went and came again, like on a kind of swirling amusement ride, and the friendships were always reliable and fun, light and nonbinding. There were always friends, old and new, at every base. She would run across Billy again in her career once or twice, and Paula as well, though more often, as the years went on, she would read about Paula in the aeronautical magazines after she left the Air Force and joined NASA. But she didn't think about them now. She wanted to hear Waller speak. She wanted to say good-bye.

"And how do we measure a life lived in pursuit of a singular goal, to defend democracy, to uphold the values of the United States, when that goal is something we need to achieve every single day of our lives?" Holly said. "John Waller never gave up. He did his best."

There wasn't a fair assessment, Waller thought. There can't be one, certainly not here, not now. How can you relive the complexity of a career in one hour without simplifying, without dousing every-thing with a sickly sweet coating of sugar? But he listened apprecia-tively. He felt loved.

When Bud was finished speaking, it was Waller's turn. He rose and stood at the podium. His last time. Everything had become a series of last times, a descent into the kind of nauseating nostalgia that the younger Waller abhorred. He didn't care. He looked out at them with pleasure, all those faces he had never met or met and would read about someday or would never hear of again. You served, you *did your best*, and then you stopped, and the Air Force marched on without you.

He began in the usual way, with humility.

"I'm thankful I've had the opportunity to serve our country. I loved the flying world. Maybe I should never have left it. Maybe it was a mistake, but if so, it was a mistake I embrace with a kind of gratitude. It must be hard to imagine that I might feel grateful for the extraordinary series of misfortunes that have unfolded since I accepted the role of commandant, and yet, aside from the death of Mac Cherry, I regret nothing, have done nothing I would not repeat. And so I do not repent. Perhaps these are the words of a misguided half-wit at the end of his tenure, or of a surly old fart. I don't know. I don't expect any of you to judge me here, today, but you might later. I wouldn't blame you."

There was a polite silence in the audience. Where did he expect to go from here? He looked around at the gathering, at Lauren, who looked up at him with an expression he couldn't readily interpret, and drove on.

"Indeed, when I accepted the position here, I'd hoped to instill in our—no, I have a tendency to get polemic at the worst moments—I wanted to change things, I wanted to bring a certain rawness back to cadet training. The old training wasn't perfect by a long shot, but at least it was real. And by real, I mean not drowned in theory. Not mired in abstraction and a touchy-feely fear of offending the wrong people. We didn't give a shit about that. What we wanted was officers."

There was a smattering of applause now.

"Officers who weren't afraid to lead in the face of indecision. Officers who weren't afraid to take risks. Those are the kinds of officers—even if imperfect, I'd want to serve under, and gentlemen—ladies—those are the kinds of officers I sought to mold. I thank you all for putting up with me for as long as you have. I'm proud of those of you I have known, and I regret having not met so many of you.

But it's your turn now. It's your turn to take over, and do with the Air Force what you will."

With that, he left the podium and walked back to his chair. There was an explosion of applause, but he didn't hear it. At the moment he settled into his seat, his former executive officer, Alan Kord, suddenly, in the stiff awkwardness of one who is out of practice, leaped to his feet and saluted.

The whole auditorium followed suit, each officer and cadet rising to his or her feet and saluting, and even Metz rising reluctantly and Bud Holly, saluting with a kind of swaggering grin, and Susan Long, who could not be persuaded to salute anyone beneath her rank, rose nonetheless and began to clap. Waller stood and gave his best, most respectful salute, one he hadn't practiced in years, and was surprised to find that he could still do it, could still make his arm quiver as he snapped his outstretched fingers to the tip of his temple.

"Thank you," he said in the stillness that followed. "Thank you so very much."

And then the applause began again, and Waller and Bud Holly were escorted off the stage.

Tears welled in Brook's eyes. She wanted to shake his hand after the ceremony, but there were so many people crowded around him that she changed her mind. Rather than lingering in the crowd, she went out into the sunshine and down the steps next to the chapel, across the Terrazzo and into the mail room. A new commandant had taken over—not Metz, as everyone (including him) had expected, but Colonel Coyle, who'd been promoted to brigadier general and would serve two years as commandant before going back to the world of psychological operations. General Long had been promoted, too, and she would be moving back to the Pentagon at the end of the school year. By next fall, the entire staff would have changed except for Metz, who would linger on as deputy, a tactical move by Colonel Coyle. Brook knew nothing of the workings inside the administrative offices, only that, like in the rest of the military, the staff came and went, and the Air Force went on under new leadership with new ideas and new agendas in an ever forward momentum of promotion and retirement. Coyle kept Metz as his deputy because he knew the art of deception far better than Waller ever had, and he invited Metz to backyard barbecues, allowing Metz to say grace. Coyle tinkered with CoT for another six months and let it die of disinterest after the CSAF retired and General Long discovered other mountains to conquer, and then he quietly went back to doing things the way they had done them in the years when he and Waller had been cadets. A year later, nobody remembered what CoT had stood for. The slogan they came to learn was Defined Moral Compass—DMC—a compromise between Coyle and Metz that went as far as the secretary of defense, who used it twice in official statements to the press.

The mail room was bright and empty.

There was a letter in Brook's mailbox. It was from her father. Her address had been typed in old courier style on the Remington, and she held it in her fingers, feeling its weight and substance, as she made her way back to her room. After she had closed herself inside and taken off her shoes and sat on her bed with the pillow behind her back, she opened the top of the envelope and unfolded the letter. This was one of her favorite moments, the highlight of her week, and she savored it.

> *My dearest Brook,*
>
> *Here we are at nine A.M. on April Fool's Day, which is a better day than most to consider folly. A few moments ago, there was a shriek of brakes, a tremendous crash, a silence, then the hee-haw, hee-haw of a police siren, and silence again. Someone evidently just made a mistake; always a foolish thing to do.*
>
> *There are people who believe it foolish to take a chance, to run a risk. I do not happen to be one of them. It seems to me that not being willing to accept the risk of living is the most foolish mistake of all, because none of us can escape the fact that to be born means that we will die.*
>
> *Birth and death are simply facts, and facts cannot be changed through worrying about them. It is nice to hope and*

pray, but to stake one's happiness on these things is to sacrifice to dreams and wishes the life one actually has. If one must rely on variables, it is better to consider the role that luck has played in ageless human experience.

Of all the gods who were ever imagined, Fortuna is my favorite. She was the ancient Roman god of luck, and the Romans built more temples to her than to any other god. They called her Bona Dea, meaning the good god. Fortuna issued no commandments and made no promises and ordained no rites. For these reasons, Bona Dea made more sense to the Italians than did the Christian one whom they more outwardly wor-shipped.

Lady Luck we call her. Don't push your luck. Don't ride it too long, for you are riding to a fall if you do. But more to the point, I suggest we follow the ancients' advice as to what to do when Fortuna appears: Grab her by the forelock, for she is bald behind!

How wise this is. Another way to think of it is to say: <u>never resist temptation, but embrace it immediately,</u> lest you lose what may be the only chance you'll ever have to improve your life.

There are things worth considering, such as happiness, beauty, and love, and perhaps even truth as well, and all these are just as much facts of life as all their opposites—though more difficult to describe.

I shall return to this matter presently, and indeed close my argument with it, offering final proof that the belief I hold comes straight out of the hard-learned facts of life. But first, let us revisit Dover Beach with Arnold, and see this world as so vast, so new, so various, so beautiful—

This particular letter went pages long, and it went on in a series of halts and spurts to describe those days so many years ago when her mother had left the family for good. The explanation was both painfully simple and impossibly complicated.

At the point when Brook was three, her mother began to feel trapped in a life where she couldn't breathe—those had been her words, which she had pelted him with tearfully for months before he had begun to listen to them. She wanted to go back to Canada, back to her family in Montreal. He asked her: Do you understand the consequences? She would not see her children grow up. She would not know them. Yes, she said, she accepted this. He had thought it was a terrible choice, not only for all of them, but also for her. He told her so. He loved her; he told her that also. Then he let her go, and she never came back.

He knew where her family lived, but he never wrote to them, and they never wrote to him. He spent years struggling with himself—had he let her go too easily? Should he have insisted she stay at least partially in their lives? Perhaps he had seemed too ambivalent and had pushed her away himself. He was a lawyer, after all, and used to seeing all the sides of an argument. But no, at length he decided that he had done the right thing. He had decided it, in fact, when Brook had been home on leave the previous spring. He saw that his children had grown up healthy and sound. It was only then that he allowed himself to believe that things had gone in the best possible way. He had been granted everything he had wished for.

He could not, he wrote, apologize for her mother's behavior because no apology would be adequate. Nor could he explain it, because in all the years that had gone by, he never understood why she had left. But he didn't have to understand it—she had gone; that was all.

He was sorry there couldn't be a better explanation. Sometimes in life there were no good explanations, and that was what he meant when he said that wishing for things would not make them so, but accepting the things that happened, <u>embracing life</u>—that was what mattered.

Brook read the letter six times and then dug out the picture of her mother that she had kept in her sock drawer. Her mother coming off the vault and landing the Tsukahara with a 9.75. She walked down the hallway. It was empty. It was often empty, so oddly free of the dangers she'd felt as a smack. She pushed through the doorway of the women's bathroom and stood momentarily in the howling silence. So her mother had left them. She had always known. Known and not known. And there it was. She dropped the picture in the trash barrel. It tunneled down, landed on a pile of crumpled towels from the roll dispenser. See, she thought, I can do it, too.

It was not final enough. She reached down and took the picture and picked it up. All that hope. Tsukahara 9.75. She had always wondered what it meant, and in the end, it didn't matter. Surely *she* had forgotten this moment long ago.

Brook tore the picture into little bits and flushed them down the toilet.

The pieces swirled around and a few bits popped back into the bowl with the new water. She flushed again. Flushed again. Flushed again. Flushed until all the pieces were gone into the pipes, down the Cold War–era circuitry of the academy and through the tunnels and out into the distant world.

Gone.

We spend far too much time worrying about the past, she thought. She walked into the hallway. It was empty—most of the cadets were at the reception for the commandant. She should be there, too. But she couldn't bring herself to go just now. She wanted to be in her room, alone. Nobody there would miss her. Certainly not Billy, who'd transferred to another squadron after all, and whom she saw occasionally on campus. But he went into the soccer season and then she went into rugby. Passing in the gym or on the Terrazzo, they smiled the smile of distant friends.

Which, after all, they were.

In her room, the door latched, Brook folded the letter carefully and put it where the picture had once lived, in a drawer, under her socks. Outside, a late-season storm had left the pine boughs droopy with snow. The sky was a perfect, glistening blue.

So vast, so new, so various, so beautiful—

How lucky she was to belong to the world, to be able to fly through it.

ACKNOWLEDGMENTS

I'm grateful for the assistance of the United States Air Force Academy staff in completing this novel, as well as the numerous cadets, past and present, who were so forthright with their experiences. I hope I've done them justice. I owe particular thanks to Lieutenant Colonel Lou Michels (retired) for always "being there," Colonel Bob Eskridge (retired), Colonel Deb Gray, Johnnie Whitaker, and John Van Winkle. I owe many thanks and hugs to my editor, Jill Schwartzman, along with Bill Goodman, Dan Conaway, Gail Hochman, Jeanette Perez, and Alison Callahan.

For so enthusiastically sharing their sailplane expertise, I thank Nancy Lincoln, Desi Harmond, Lew Neyland, and Rick Roelke.

Thanks, forever, to the "angels," Alix Strauss and River Jordan.

And to MGB for his wonderful insight.

The letter quoted in the final chapter was written largely by my deceased mentor, the writer and journalist John Keats.

And as always, I'm stunned by the inexhaustible patience and love of my husband, Bill, who served as early reader and confidant, and my children, who wait patiently for my work to be done.